# To Fight A

C000065750

By Ed

*Happy birthday, Jeff with best wishes*

*Ed Lane*

http://www.fast-print.net/bookshop

# TO FIGHT ANOTHER DAY
## Copyright © Ed Lane 2016

A catalogue record for this book is available from the British Library

ISBN 978-178456-369-1

First published 2016 by
FASTPRINT PUBLISHING
Peterborough, England.

# Full length Novels by Ed Lane:

*(All titles are available in all ebook formats from Amazon).*

## The 'Going Dark' Series

| | |
|---|---|
| A Circling of Vultures | **ASIN:** B005DHYG3C |
| Terrible Beauty | **ASIN:** B006ZDE2QE |
| The Lunatic Game | **ASIN:** B00ABL7L5K |
| A Circling of Hawks | **ASIN:** B00H7HDXJY |

The following are also available:

## The 'Fields of Fire' Trilogy

| | |
|---|---|
| Blood Debt | **ASIN:** B00KXJ62Y6 |
| Dragonfire | **ASIN:** B00Q1OPUX6 |
| Dust to Dust | **ASIN:** B00V45GOS2 |

Find Ed Lane on Facebook:
https://www.facebook.com/ed.lane.3

Visit his website for the latest news:
www.edtheauthor.wix.com/the-books-of-ed-lane

Email:
edtheauthor@gmail.com

To Fight Another Day

# Acknowledgements

Once again, I would like to thank my beta reader, Veronica Stonehouse, for suggesting improvements and finding and correcting my errors.


Spartan-Warrior is a non-profit organisation that helps sufferers combat Post Traumatic Stress Disorder (PTSD).
As they say, they are large enough to matter
but small enough to care.
You can check out their website at
**www.spartan-warrior.com**

I will be making a donation towards the charity from the proceeds of this book.

***The Legend of the Green Men.***
*England's symbol of resistance to*
*Norman oppression*

In the years immediately following the Norman invasion of 1066, in Lincolnshire, a dispossessed landowner named Hereward (later known as Hereward the Wake) put up an astounding display of bravery, holding out for years on the fen island of Ely with, as legend has it, an army of 'Green Men'.

Bands of men took to the woods, the marshes and the wastelands, with the tacit support of local populations, emerging to harass, harry and assassinate the Norman occupying forces.

**The 'legend' lives on.**

# Part 1
# Step Back

# 1

The sabre arced high, flashed in an angled sunbeam, smashed through a weak parry and edged an arm.

Green light. "Touché." The fencer raised his mask and grinned at his opponent. "Two hits."

The other swordsman took his helmet off and tucked it under his free arm. He gave a rueful grin. "You're good. Good enough to try out for the Great Britain Pentathlon team."

Chris Lennox, a tall, muscular, dark-haired twenty-four year old, gave a wry grin in return. "Not sure about that, Peter. I have my army career to think of and the Olympics are still three years away, a lot can happen in three years."

Peter Saunders laid his sabre on the judge's table and pulled off his gloves. "You're a shoe-in, Chris. You fence brilliantly, you shoot like Davy Crockett, you ride like a three day eventer, you swim like a dolphin and you run like the entire Taliban are on your tail."

"Maybe but the pentathlon uses foils, not sabres. I much prefer sabres, it's more my style."

"A minor detail. Will you think about it? There's a training camp coming up shortly and I'd like to put your name forward."

"Sorry, Peter. My leave is up tomorrow and I have to join my regiment. It's a new posting. My old C.O. was okay with me taking some time off but I have to make my mark with the new boss and that means putting in the hours."

"The army's usually pretty good at giving time to Olympic hopefuls. I could put in a word for you."

"No thanks. I've got to concentrate on my day job for now. Ask me again in a year or so."

"A lot can happen in a year, Chris."

Buried deep underground outside Zurich, hard up against the French border, the Large Hadron Collider the world's largest and most powerful particle collider, was being prepared for a test run. Several of the thousands of scientists and engineers involved with the work were making adjustments to the powerful super-conducting magnets. No one wanted a repeat of the Quench Incident where an electrical fault in September 2008 put several bending magnets off-line and led to a loss of nearly six tonnes of liquid helium, the magnets' cryogenic coolant, which was vented into the tunnel. The cost of repairs had been over sixteen million euros.

Dr Max Bruckner, the experiment head, leaned over the chief engineer's shoulder and fussed. "Is everything within calculated parameters?"

The engineer sighed. "Yes, Herr Doktor."

"You know how important this experiment is."

"Yes, Herr Doktor, I do."

"It is the first real attempt to create dark matter. The magnets must be in full working condition."

"I know. We would not want that to escape."

"Quite right, Johan. It would be disastrous. Who knows what might happen if it did."

"It's a moot point, Herr Doktor. It may only have a half life of a few milliseconds."

"No one knows, Johan. We are on the edge of a scientific unknown. A new frontier in man's knowledge of cosmological physics and what holds the universe together."

"Let's hope it's not the final frontier," Johan murmured to himself.

Bruckner did not hear the sotto voce comment. "Frankly I am much more concerned about the quintessence field accelerating the Lambda CDM model. That may be too much for the magnetic fields to control, even with the upgraded systems.

I must check and re-check the team's calculations before we run the experiment. We cannot afford to make any mistakes with this."

Lieutenant Chris Lennox was thrown into the thick of it as soon as he joined his new battalion of The Rifles, based in Bulford Camp on the edge of Salisbury Plain.

His platoon was equipped with the Foxhound Light Protected Patrol Vehicles, new to them, which meant Some retraining for the squaddies and the attached REME workshops. On top of that, they were due out on a major live field firing and urban warfare exercise in and around the deserted village of Imber.

Coming from Carlisle, just south of the Scottish border, Chris had no experience of the area and was intrigued by the huge Stone Age monument of Stonehenge, which he could see every time he passed on the A303. He had no time to explore as the training leading up to the field firing exercise was intense and time consuming. The edifice had got under his skin and it was an itch he was determined to scratch before too long. He pondered this as he checked his equipment for the next stage of the exercise due to start soon after first light.

He carried the same equipment as his men, a fully loaded Bergen back pack with his survival kit, a change of clothing, mess kit, personal role radio which clipped to his skeleton order harness and new Israeli designed Virtus body armour, heavy but still much lighter than the Osprey armour which had preceded it.

His side arm he kept with him together with four fully loaded magazines for the stubby 9mm bullets. The Glock 17 pistol magazines each held seventeen rounds but he loaded only sixteen rounds to avoid over-stressing the magazine springs.

His Kevlar Viking helmet and camouflaged smock were together in his locker. On his graduation from Sandhurst his father had given him twenty-two gold sovereigns, one for each year of his life. These he stitched into the hem of the jacket. He didn't know why he did this, just some odd idea that one day he may be stranded behind enemy lines and would need the money to buy his was back to safety. Gold was a safer bet than paper money in difficult times. His dad had also given him a Breitling wristwatch which he wore constantly. It kept good time and with its analogue dial could also double up as a compass in extremis.

He laid everything on his bed in order. A whistle, notebook, compass and map case was on his table ready for the briefing that was due later that evening. He ticked the items off in his mind. Proper planning and preparation …

Satisfied he pulled on his green beret and left for the barrack blocks where his men were billeted.

His platoon serjeant, Micky Norton, was an old hand. Not yet thirty-four, he had seen action in Afghanistan and knew his job inside out. He gave Chris a smart salute as he approached but coupled it with a wary smile. He still had not sussed out his new officer.

"Everything all right, Serjeant?"

"Yes, sir. Kosher. The section leaders are briefing the lads now. We don't want any cock-ups, do we?"

"Anything I should know about?"

"As I said, it's all kosher, sir. No problems. No one's on sick parade. All the kit's good, ammo returns are up to date. It's kosher."

"Okay, Serjeant, relax. I'm not here to hassle you. There's an O-group shortly and the boss is bound to ask."

"You can tell the major it's …"

"I know." Chris grinned. "It's kosher, I'll be sure to tell him that."

"There is one thing, sir. We'll be drawing weapons at 04.00. I'll keep your rifle with mine in the vehicle until you need it."

"Good, thanks. We'll be mounting up around 04.50. They reckon sunrise is at about 05.15 tomorrow so there'll be plenty of time."

"It's Imber again, sir. That's not too far. Fighting in a built up area. Word is the Gurkhas are the opposition. Going to be a tough day all round."

"One of the toughest," Chris agreed.

"Looks like there could be a storm or two brewing," Norton said and nodded to the sky darkening in the west."

"Summer storms. Most likely they will pass through without too much bother." Chris glanced at his Breitling. "Time to go. I'll brief the platoon at 20.00 hours. Then they'll need to get their heads down."

"Yes, sir." Norton threw him a salute and watched his back as he marched away. A section corporal wandered up beside him. "What did the Rupert want?"

"Just checkin' in."

"Hope he's better than the last one."

Norton grunted, his eyes still on Chris's retreating back. "Too early to say. He seems okay, not poking his nose in too much yet. Early days; but there is something about him I can't get a handle on. Time'll tell."

The machinery running the Hadron Collider was within expected parameters. The dial needles were all in the right places, the computer readouts satisfactory in all thirty-six participating countries. Dr Bruckner gave the nod to his engineers to increase the power on the collider. Separate streams of nuclear protons smashed together with increasing potency as it accelerated towards a maximum output of 6.5 Tera-electron Volts. The hundreds of electro magnets around the twenty-seven kilometre long tunnel were all at operating temperature, 1.9 Kelvins above absolute zero, and the giant Atlas recorder was already monitoring a flood of results.

Bruckner nodded again and crossed his fingers inside his pocket. This was now new territory as the combined output began to exceed 13TeVs. Then the lights flickered in such an infinitesimal period of time the human eye could not register it. Inside the tunnel, the feared quintessence field created by the undetected power fluctuation accelerated the proton streams to a combined 18TeVs as it also weakened the magnetic containment field. In that fraction of a millisecond, two colliding particles produced a particle of dark energy which streaked through the weakened containment field, ricocheted off the heavy side layer and was pulled at light speed towards an electromagnetic disturbance on the surface of the earth as a summer thunderstorm hit Stonehenge.

# 2

Chris had a plan. It wasn't a good one but it was all he had. They mounted up in the Foxhounds on time and rolled out of the camp onto the A3028. He radioed his driver. "Don't take the Larkhill Road, there's been a holdup there. Take the A345 south, turn west on the A303 and turn north on the A360."

His driver grunted an unrepeatable reply and turned the vehicle south as instructed.

Chris grinned to himself. His change of route would take his five-vehicle convoy past Stonehenge with enough time for him to stop, climb the chain-link fence and get in amongst the stones for a selfie with the famous monoliths he could send to his parents, both avid history buffs.

They turned onto the A360 and as the road dipped, Chris called his driver to stop.

Serjeant Norton gave him a quizzical look.

"I need to get out for a minute or two," Chris said.

Norton looked at his watch and grimaced. "Better be quick, sir, or we'll be late to the start line. The boss won't like that."

"Just a couple of minutes. I'll be back before you know it." Chris cracked the door in the Foxhound's side and dropped into the road. This early in the morning the traffic was sparse.

Norton ducked his head out of the door and peered around. "Better hurry, Mr Lennox, looks like a storm brewing just over there and the wind's blowing a southerly."

"Some rain never hurt anyone. It's a bit muggy, could do with freshening up."

Chris turned on his heel, loped across the tarmac and cleared the chain link fence around Stonehenge the way the army had trained him, easily and swiftly, even in body armour and carrying a Bergen. He strode across the gravel tourists' footpath onto forbidden ground right into the centre of the monolithic structure. He took out his smart phone and held it up. The sun was just rising in the east and he turned his face to it. Behind him, the dark forbidding thunderheads rolled in bringing drenching rain at the storm's leading edge.

High above the static charge built and flashed downward in sheet lightning capturing the tiny particle of dark matter as it lanced earthward. Chris raised the phone and smiled into it, the stones were eerily lit by the rim of the rising sun still visible through the rain beneath the covering of black cloud. It would be a stunning photograph. The lightning struck his raised arm and he knew no more.

"Dear god," Chris mouthed. He was supine on the ground. Every nerve in his body buzzed as if electricity coursed through each fibre. His head ached with the pounding of a blacksmith's hammer. He opened his eyes and could see nothing. Panic thrilled, more severe than the jangled nerves. He moved his arm; he could feel it which was a blessing. He put it to his head. The Viking helmet had ridden up with the chin guard across his eyes. He pushed it away and could see the ravaged sky but the storm had mostly passed. The helmet was split and he pulled it off, still too dazed to appreciate the massive force that could cleave Kevlar like peeling a Christmas satsuma.

He groaned and rolled into a recovery position. His nerve endings jangled even more and his muscles spasmed. He lay there until the sun peeked out from the trailing storm edge and bathed him with warm light. He pushed himself into a sitting position as the spasms eased, leaving him with the headache and now toothache in his lower jaw.

"What the hell happened?" he asked himself although he instinctively knew the answer as he looked at the dismal remains of his smart phone lying in pieces on the grass. His right arm was sore and he pulled up the sleeve of his combat jacket and recoiled at the fine tracery of blue lines, much like an intricate tattoo, which ran from the palm of his hand to his elbow and, for all he knew, to the shoulder. He hated tattoos.

Had he been out so long that the squaddies had played a joke on him? No that was inconceivable. It was still morning, it was the same storm, he was within the circle of the henge where the stones towered above him. There hadn't been time. The tracery must have been caused by the lightning strike following the rainwater trickling down his arm. He hoped it would soon fade.

He pushed himself to his knees and then, using a nearby stone as support, to his wobbly feet. A wave of nausea caused him to close his eyes and rest against the stone. Then he remembered why he was there, the waiting Foxhounds, the live firing exercise … and the time. He looked at the Breitling, it was still ticking. 05.20. The boss would be livid. He would get it in the neck from the major who would have the colonel down on him in turn. Bollockings all round and not good for the new boy to put up such a black on his first major exercise. He staggered back towards the fence. It was only a few paces, or should have been, but the fence wasn't there. Neither was the gravel track. A few paces further on should have been the main A-road but all he found was a rutted cart track. His head spun. He had lost his sense of direction. He turned and retraced his steps, back through the circle of the henge and out the far side. Meadowland extended as far as he could see. The air smelled sweet with summer flowers and skylarks rose from grass tussocks to sing.

The A303 should be off to his right and he lurched that way only to be confronted by more rolling grassland with ancient burial mounds sprouting from the land in the middle distance. Now he was very confused. He pulled his compass from a pocket and checked the reading. East was to his right where the Foxhounds should be waiting but he had already checked that direction. The A303 was to the south but there was just another track, wider and deeper with a stone surface but not the main asphalt road he was seeking. He stumbled back to the henge and sat on one of the fallen stones. He tried his radio but got nothing but static. He checked his watch again; now past 05.30. Why hadn't Serjeant Norton and his soldiers come looking for him? He'd been gone far too long. Why would they leave him alone after an obvious lightning strike? Another thought appalled him. Perhaps the strike had been so powerful that it had obliterated the immediate area like a nuclear bomb. Perhaps his rubber soled combat boots, the rain flowing down his body, and the electronics in the phone had earthed him sufficiently that he was the only one to survive.

It was a crazy idea but what other explanation could there be? The lightning strike could only have been local. After a few hundred metres he would be sure to find the road again. He decided to walk north in the direction of Imber, that way he was bound to come into contact with the emergency services and could inform his unit through them. How he was going to explain his change of route and the loss of four vehicles and thirty men was beyond him.

He started off at a slow pace as his balance had not completely returned to normal. It was strange that the air seemed so clean. Colours were vibrant and the scent of the wild flowers that he crushed under his boots was strong. His hearing too seemed more acute. Birdsong, which had never sounded so loud or so frequent, impinged on his consciousness.

After covering several hundred metres the landscape still had not changed. He cut away from the track and followed a compass bearing towards Imber. Fatigue started after about three miles and it worried him. He was used to running ten miles in full kit so three miles should have been a morning bimble but his legs were aching as badly as his head and teeth. A few hundred metres further on was a copse which sprawled either side of a track with a promise of a shady place to rest up for a few minutes. His Breitling was showing 11.00 hours and he grimaced. Over five hours to walk just a few miles? The lightning strike must have taken more out of him than he imagined.

The emptiness of the landscape worried him. He had caught glimpses of figures working in fields some distance off but no traffic. Nothing had passed him, no sound of car or truck. Every track he stumbled over was just that, a rutted dirt surface with grass growing between the wheel furrows. His map indicated metalled roads so he seemed wildly off course. Much of Salisbury Plain was given over to army training so it was unsurprising that people were few and far between. Maybe his compass had been damaged by the lightning.

He reached the copse and shrugged off his Bergen. He unclipped the flap, found his hexy burner and his mess kit and set about making some brew. The hexamine blocks burned hot and soon had the water boiling in his mess tin. He dropped in a tea bag, some powdered milk and sugar and let it brew as he studied the map and checked the compass. It seemed fine. South corresponded to where the sun was. He checked it with his Breitling, pointing the hour hand at the sun, dissecting the angle between the hour and minute hands which formed a point towards due north. It matched the compass. So where had he gone wrong? He scratched his head and orientated the map. He should be well on his way to Imber but there should also have been a metalled road running past where he was sitting although the copse wasn't marked. Possibly left off or hidden under the thick red and blue lines that marked the range areas. He matched the terrain to the map as far as he could see. Some ancient burial mounds were visible in the distance and these were shown but otherwise the plain was featureless rolling grassland.

The disappearance of the rest of his platoon was beginning to disturb him more and more. It was as if they were erased from the face of the earth. His fond hope that the damage would be limited to a few hundred metres had proven ill-founded. There was just nothing left of the vehicles, the men and the roads on which the five vehicles had travelled.

His headache was getting worse and he used the last dregs of tea to wash down some paracetamol. It was warm, even in the shade of the trees. Tiredness overcame him and his eyelids drooped closed.

A gunshot. A shrill scream. It jolted Chris awake. He sat up and peered around. It was coming on for sunset and the trees were casting long shadows towards the east. He had slept for hours, his headache and toothache had reduced to a dull throb. He scrambled to his knees as another scream pierced the still air. At the edge of the copse was a coach and four horses. Three other rider-less and saddled horses were off to one side. The coachman was sagging in his seat clutching an arm and two men were dragging a woman from the coach's interior. They were wearing breeches and one had a tricorn hat. Both had material covering the lower part of their faces.

Chris looked around for the cameras, thinking he must be caught up in a period film set. There were no cameras that he could see and no lighting or sound equipment either. He could understand if the cameras had long lenses and were filming from a distance but there should have been a full crew nearby but there was nothing.

The woman screamed again and sounded truly terrified. A good actress? Or was she really scared? Chris walked to the edge of the trees. The men were getting very rough with the woman, tearing at her clothes. One man was sitting inside on the coach floor with her wrists in his hands and his feet on her shoulders as another was pawing at the hem of her skirt. He decided enough was enough.

"Hey, what's going on?" he yelled.

The two men stopped what they were doing and looked round. He saw the dumbfounded looks on their faces as their masks dropped. The bigger of the two called a name that Chris didn't quite catch and a third man walked out of the shadows. Three horses meant three riders. The penny dropped.

Chris looked at the new masked man and then back at the original two. He took a deep breath. "I said, what's going on?" He walked out into the vestiges of sunshine and saw the men's mouths drop open. The third man stood still for a few seconds and then raised what looked to Chris like an old stick. Except it wasn't a stick, it was a pistol, an old flintlock, and it worked. There was a puff of smoke and then a flash and the ball caught Chris square in the chest. He stumbled backwards and fell.

The man inside the coach called, "What be *that*?"

The shooter shrugged. "Bain't be nothin' I ever saw. Maybe a goblin."

The third man pushed the woman to the ground and put a foot on her back. "You did it good. Is it dead?"

"Dead as mutton I be reckonin'."

"Let's get the stash and be on our way," the second man said. The woman had fainted and he turned her over and rubbed his greasy palms on her bodice. "Tain't in 'ere."

"You'm better check on yon goblin, Abe," the first man said and nodded at Chris's fallen body. No tellin' wi' goblins and the like."

"Ee be dead enough. The ball hit right centre."

"No yammerin', boy, do as I say for if I lay about you you'll be the worse for it."

"Keep your wig on, pa. I'll do your biddin'." He pulled a short knife and took a nervous few steps towards Chris's fallen body.

Chris had heard every word of the exchange. The ceramic plate of his body armour had stopped the ball but had knocked some of the wind out of him. As he caught his breath he thought of a plan that would scare the daylights out of them. If they believed in goblins, he'd give them one.

Hanging on his webbing harness was a green smoke grenade. Before the shooter could reach him he pulled the pin, released the lever and tossed it between him and the approaching gunman where it exploded with a dull thud. He grabbed his whistle from a pocket and blew a long shrill blast before jumping through the billowing smoke, waving his arms and shouting gibberish.

The gunman leapt back, real fear in his eyes, he turned and ran towards the horses. The man who had been inside the coach raced off after him. The third, the leader, was made of sterner stuff and turned to face Chris, pulling a flintlock from his belt. He fired as Chris dropped flat and the ball passed harmlessly over his head.

He rose to his feet doing his best imitation of Marley's ghost. The man, his courage used up, ran after his accomplices.

Chris let them go. He had much to think about; especially what old-time highwaymen were doing in the middle of Salisbury Plain in the 21st Century.

# 3

The four coach horses were restless, pawing the ground and snorting. Chris went to calm them, stroking the lead horse's neck. He glanced up at the driver, still slumped in the seat but in danger of toppling off and falling several feet to the ground. The woman had not moved.

The driver's arm looked in a bad way and he was by far the worst casualty. Chris heaved himself up, pulled the driver over his shoulder and brought him to the ground. He was a man who looked in his late thirties but he was very thin and light, barely seven stone, Chris guessed. He laid him down by the coach wheels and ran back to collect his Bergen and the trauma kit it carried. He was only a minute but the driver was conscious when he returned. The man moaned in terror and threw his good hand over his eyes. Chris pulled him upright and he let out another terrified wail.

"Oh do shut up," Chris snapped. "I'm here to help."

The driver pulled his fingers away from his face but his eyes were round with fear. "You speak."

"Of course I speak. Now I'm just going to give you a little jab in the thigh." He took out a self-injecting morphine ampoule and showed it to him.

"What trickery is this?"

"Good trickery, mate. This will make you feel better."

"Then you will eat me, tear out my heart and liver and feed upon it."

"Look, I'm a bloke, not a goblin."

"Aaaagh, a *bloke*. What is that? Some such other monster?"

"No, give me strength, a man, just like you, only not such a dick head."

"My name is not Dick, it is Thomas."

"Right, Thomas. Look up there."

Perplexed, Thomas first looked right and then upwards. As his face turned away Chris pushed the needle into his thigh and injected the morphine.

"What have you done?" Thomas asked, his eyes pleading.

"Yes, sir. What is it that you have now done to Thomas?"

The woman was sitting up on one elbow and watching his actions with a nervous fascination.

"I've given him something to dull the pain. In a moment it will begin to work and I can treat his arm. By the look of it, the bone's broken and it will need to be reset. We'll have to get him to a hospital as soon as we can."

"Hospital, sir? There is no such thing here. We have a doctor in Imber who will treat broken limbs."

"Imber? But that's ..."

"Just a short drive away. We were journeying there when the highwaymen struck. They have become too bold of late."

Chris bit back on his curiosity. Imber had a doctor? But it had been deserted since the 1940s. The people travelled by coach and horses and highwaymen infested the plains. What in hell's name was happening to him?

The drug was taking effect and he touched Thomas's shoulder but got no response. "Let me patch him up first to slow the bleeding. I'll put his arm in a sling to stop the bones from grinding together too much."

"Are you a doctor, sir? You are so strangely attired I scarce recognised you as a man. Tis no wonder Thomas mistook you for a denizen of the underworld."

Chris looked across as he worked. The last light was fading but he could see her face in the gloaming and it was a very attractive heart-shaped face under a silk bonnet which had come loose and was hanging behind her neck on its ribbon. She looked young, late teens to early twenties, he guessed. "No, miss. I'm a soldier. This is my uniform."

"Pon my soul, tis a strange attire. All green with a green face. Where is your red coat?"

Chris stopped tying the knot in the sling and rubbed his hand on the camo cream he'd forgotten he'd applied before leaving the camp. No wonder the men thought him a goblin. He pulled the useless headset and boom mike away from his head. "Red coat? Only the Guards wear those now on ceremonial occasions."

"You are mistaken, sir. We have a company of the 62nd regiment billeted at Imber. All the men wear red coats."

"Not where I'm from, they don't."

"And from where would that be, sir? You do have the strangest accent … and your phrasing is most peculiar. Just what pray is a *bloke*?"

Chris grinned. "How long were you awake?"

"Much of the time. I feigned the swoon to endeavour to ensure I would not be molested further."

Chris nodded his approval. "You're a very courageous young lady."

"You do me too much credit, sir. I was most afraid that my virtue would be taken … as well as my father's coin."

"They stole your father's money?"

"Yes. He will be most disgruntled and very angry. But come, sir, we must away to Imber before the night becomes too black."

"Who'll drive?"

"You cannot, sir?"

"One horse is no problem but I've never taken four in hand."

She laughed, a musical tinkle. "Then tis as well that I have acquired the necessary skill. Thomas taught me when I was but a girl, much to my mother's dismay for I was then quite the tomboy," she confided. "Put Thomas inside the coach then hand me onto the seat."

Chris picked up the lightweight Thomas and laid him on the floor of the coach before taking the girl's narrow waist in his hands and lifting her onto the driver's seat. She weighed less than Thomas and his arm tingled at the touch. He tossed his Bergen onto the roof and climbed up beside her. "Tally-ho, miss."

"You are a hunting man, mister …?"

"Chris … Chris Lennox. Lieutenant Chris Lennox. And no, I don't hunt."

"I am Miss Catherine Wadman and pleased to make your acquaintance, sir. You are a surprising man, Lieutenant Chris-Lennox. I thought every gentleman hunted."

"Do you mind if I ask you an odd question, miss?"

She took the reins in her hands spreading them between her fingers and taking up the slack. She turned to look at him, an impish smile turning up the corners of her mouth. "If that is as opposed to an *even* question, yes you may."

Chris smiled back. A smile to hide his nervousness. "What year is this?"

Her smile broadened and became quizzical. "A strange question indeed, sir." She smacked the reins on the horses' backs and they moved off at a fast walk. "It is the year of our Lord 1799 of course."

They drove on in silence, Chris too stunned by the news to talk further, the woman concentrating on keeping the team on the narrow track that passed as a road. She did give him an occasional sideways glance which registered on his peripheral vision but he was too absorbed to comment. 1799? It all dropped into place. It was science fiction. The lightning strike had thrown him back over two-hundred years. It was unbelievable, in fact he still did not entirely accept it even though all the evidence was there in front of his eyes, under his hands, even under his backside as the coach lurched and rattled its slow way through the deepening gloom.

It was a dream. It had to be. He was unconscious and having a vivid nightmare. He would wake soon and laugh about his trip back in time.

Except.

Except it was so real and so detailed. The sights, the smells, the ache in his arm where the lightning had struck, the ache in his head and teeth, the dull ache in his chest where the bullet had hit. He felt the hole, the shot was still lodged in the Kevlar. He pulled it out and turned it over in his fingers feeling the flattened side and the rounded reverse. It was a ball, not a bullet, and soft. He gouged it with a thumbnail. Lead. Too much detail; this was no ordinary dream.

"We are nearly arrived."

The woman was looking at him sideways again with a faint smile on her lips, as if she was wondering how to explain him to her father. That was a good question. Just supposing he really was back in 1799, how would *he* explain that? Would time travel even have occurred to them? Would they take him for a lunatic and have him locked up in some hell-hole for the criminally insane? The thought made him shudder. When was H.G. Wells due to publish his *'Time Machine'*? He was pretty sure it was about the end of the 19th century, still a hundred-odd years in the future.

In this case honesty definitely wasn't the best policy and he would have to dream up a cover story to hide his ignorance of the times and mores of the age. He was grateful for his parents' interest in history and that some of it had rubbed off on him as he absorbed it almost by osmosis. He had a basic idea of what would be expected of him in polite company, providing he was allowed to mix in such circles. Although his officer rank would mark him as a 'gentleman' his speech and actions might not.

His hand strayed to his right thigh and the Glock holstered there. That would raise a few eyebrows and no mistake. As the young woman concentrated on manoeuvring the carriage through the darkened curving street of Imber's only road, he slid the weapon out and pushed it inside his combat jacket under the chest plate of his body armour. That too would seem odd but at least armour was an historical fact, one he could explain away.

She pulled hard on the reins and the team turned sharp right through two imposing gates and onto a gravelled drive. Lanterns were burning in the windows of a house, its shape black against the just rising moon.

"This is my father's house and my home," she said as she pulled the horses to a halt. "Imber Court, the manor house. Father, Sir George Wadman, is Lord of the Manor and much respected in the village. He will be most disconcerted that highwaymen are so near to Imber."

The house doors opened and two servants rushed out holding lanterns high. One was dressed as a maid and with her hand on her chest looked mightily relieved.

"Oh, Miss Wadman! We were so fearful, you are so long overdue."

"Be quick, Mary. Thomas has been wounded. Roust the stable boy to run to Doctor Hawking and bring him with haste."

Mary curtsied but she had seen Chris in the lamplight and her face was a picture.

Catherine tutted. "In haste, Mary. All will be explained in due time."

"Yes, miss." Mary rushed away leaving the other servant standing with his mouth agape at the pair on the driving seat.

Catherine tutted again. "Matthew, don't stand there like a gargoyle. Thomas is inside, be pleased to take him out, but with care, his arm is badly broken."

"Yes, miss," the man said but he still had not taken his eyes from them.

"Now, Matthew."

The man nodded, dropped his lantern onto the steps and opened up the coach door. Chris swung down to help.

"Lieutenant, if you please," Catherine said and held out her hand to him.

Chris nodded and handed her down just as an elderly man and two women bustled through the house door.

"Catherine, what is all this? Are you in good health?"

Catherine dropped a curtsey. "Indeed I am, sir, thanks be to the lieutenant here who came to our rescue."

Taking his cue Chris bowed his head in what he hoped was a customary amount of deference to the Lord of the Manor. "Lieutenant Chris Lennox, at your service, sir."

"Indeed! What strange costume, sir."

The two women behind, one older and one younger, who both bore a strong resemblance to Catherine fluttered fans and gave each other a perplexed glance.

"Explanations will be given in due course, I am sure," Catherine said. "In the meantime we are preventing Matthew from helping Thomas from the coach. The poor man sustained a pistol wound and is bleeding. I have sent for Doctor Hawking to attend in haste."

"In that case we must repair inside and await his arrival," Catherine's father said. "Matthew, summon one of the grooms to help carry Thomas to his quarters."

"I can help," Chris said.

His offer was received with a puzzled frown. "And why, sir? The servants are capable enough to care for Thomas."

"I just thought …," Chris started before realising his faux pas, "Right, sir. I'll leave it to the servants."

"The lieutenant was kind enough to dress Thomas's wounds with his own napkins," Catherine said. "I daresay he feels some responsibility for him. Is that not so, sir?"

Chris nodded and silently thanked her for her perception. He was growing more aware that his appearance and, to them, outlandish mannerisms, were beginning to raise question marks. He would have to be on his guard as things were only going to get increasingly more difficult.

# 4

Inside, the drawing room was a blaze of light. Housemaids had lit more candles in the hanging candelabra and in sconces around the walls. To Chris's 21st century eyes, the room was still under-lit with gloomy corners that held vague outlines of furniture. Even though it was a warm night a fire was banked up in the wide fireplace where Catherine's father now stood with his back to the glowing embers.

He inspected Chris's combat suit from his boots to the armoured chest plate, then up to his camouflage painted face. When the inspection, which took almost a minute, was completed he grunted and clasped his hands behind his back.

"A strange costume. A strange costume indeed, sir."

"It's the uniform where I come from," Chris replied. He was not about to be intimidated.

"And from where would that be, sir? My daughter believes you to be an army officer but your attire is nothing I have ever experienced."

"Well, sir …?"

"I see I have failed in my manners. I am Sir George Wadman. This," he turned and waved a hand at the two women seated to his right, "is my good wife Lady Isobel Wadman and my younger daughter Miss Amelia Wadman. You have already met with my eldest daughter Miss Catherine Wadman."

Both ladies rose and curtsied and Chris returned a bow. Catherine, with a mischievous smile, curtsied more deeply. "Charmed, Lieutenant."

"Me too," Chris said and bowed in turn.

"Now that the introductions have been made perhaps, sir, you would honour us with some explanation of your appearance and the happenstance of your arrival here," Sir George said.

Chris had been dreading this moment. He took a while to compose his thoughts as Catherine and her father sat beside each other on a chaise longue on the opposite side of the fireplace. A maid brought in refreshments which gave him more time to concoct his cover story. Everyone settled and gave him expectant looks.

The welter of interlocking tracing on his arm had given him an idea. They looked similar to Maori tattoos. "I'm from a country called New Zealand. It was discovered by a Dutchman called Abel Tasman and since by our own Captain Cook. We are a small settlement and rather backward in some ways. In others we are quite advanced, especially in medicines and the use of new materials grown from strange plants that flourish there. The clothing I'm wearing is a case in point.

"The natives are unfriendly and we have learned to survive by hiding in the undergrowth when they are hunting us as we're outnumbered.

"Because we're a small community and so far from Britain, we've lost some of the niceties of English life and I confess our manners are perhaps not all that you may wish. Our language and accents too have obviously changed from the norm … the normal."

"But tell me, Lieutenant," Catherine butted in, "how it is that you survived a pistol ball in the chest?"

"Indeed!" Sir George muttered, "that is a trick of which I would like to hear more."

Chris made sure that the Glock was pushed deep inside his combat jacket then peeled apart the Virtus straps, the

Velcro fastenings making a ripping noise. "This is just armour covered with cloth made from the plants I mentioned. There is no real secret or trick, just old-fashioned protective armour plate."

"Your name, sir," Lady Isobel asked, ticking her fan at him, "are you of the Sussex Lennoxes?"

"Perhaps some years ago. I can't claim any recent family connection."

"Which is why you are now a Chris-Lennox, no doubt," Catherine said.

"The Dukedom of Richmond is a great one with which, I am honoured to say, I am somewhat acquainted," Sir George said.

Chris could see danger signs looming up fast. The Lennoxes were the Dukes of Richmond, after Charles the Second handed the title to his illegitimate son. "I doubt, Sir George, that the current Duke would have heard of me. I am just a soldier in the service of the Quee ... Crown."

"It is good that you still serve His Majesty," Amelia spoke for the first time, "even that you do come from a country whose name I could barely pronounce."

"Thank you, Miss Wadman. I've taken an oath of allegiance to my monarch and it's one that I take seriously."

"Come, let us get back to the business at hand," Sir George said. "How is it that you are now in our fair county and in such a position that you may render assistance to my daughter?"

"I was on my way to London from Plymouth to pursue my military career. I was struck by lightning near Stonehenge in the early hours of this morning and hadn't fully recovered from the shock. I was resting in a copse, taking a break from the heat, when I must have dozed off. I was woken up by the sound of a shot and Miss Wadman screaming for help. Naturally I ran to give whatever assistance I could. It was then that I was shot but the bullet did me no harm except to knock me down. I overheard the bandits talking about goblins. They seemed to accept their existence and I suppose my clothes confused them into believing I was one. It was then I decided to play on the idea and I was able to scare them off."

"They made away with the pennies, father," Catherine said, "but the silver coin is still well hid in the carriage."

"Miss Wadman was very brave, Sir George," Chris said, "I take my hat off to her."

"And so you must, she is a lady of breeding," Sir George said with a hint of asperity.

"I'm sorry, my apologies. To take your hat off to someone is just a colloquialism where I come from. It means one is impressed."

"Be that as it may. You must be aware of the finer qualities of such young girls," Lady Isobel said.

"I'll be more careful in future," Chris promised. He knew how carefully he must now tread. His story seemed to be accepted at face value but Sir George appeared to be a wily bird. He resisted glancing at his Breitling but the chiming of a long case clock in the hallway solved his problem.

"It's ten-o-clock, I mustn't impose on your hospitality any longer."

"Nonsense! Catherine said. "We are indebted to you Lieutenant, you must stay the night. The servants will prepare a room for you. I'm sure Sir George would agree that it would be unforgiveable to turn you out so late in the evening when you have done us such great service."

"Quite," Sir George said but he did not sound too sure.

"I am very grateful, Miss Wadman, but perhaps the local pub will put me up for the night."

"Pub?" Catherine said.

"Yes, public house, Inn, whatever you call it now."

Amelia giggled. "Fie, sir you have such strange language to be sure. But I do believe The Bell is full of soldiery this night. They have come to protect us from the footpads and highwaymen but it seems they find the ale very much to their taste."

"They are a company of the 62nd of foot. Their captain, the Honourable William Stewart, Member for Wigtownshire, will be dining with us tomorrow eve should you care to join us, sir," Lady Isobel said.

The name was familiar to Chris and he felt a sudden surge of excitement. "That is so kind of you, Lady Isobel. I would be delighted to meet the captain."

Sir George gave him a look that suggested he was not quite as happy with the invitation as his womenfolk appeared to be but he accepted the situation and cleared his throat. "That's settled then. Tomorrow eve, we dine at eight. Now I suspect you wish to retire and change into something more suitable. Matthew will see to your needs this night."

The footman had been standing in the shadows by the door and he stepped into the light, gesturing for Chris to follow him.

Trying not to forget his new found manners, Chris bowed to the ladies and Sir George in turn before wishing them good night.

As the door closed behind Chris Sir George turned to the ladies and scowled. "God's teeth, this is a rum do and no mistake. We know nothing of this fellow. He is damnably odd spoken, damnably odd dressed too."

"Damnably handsome too," Amelia added. "And so tall, scarce an inch off eighteen hands I'd wager."

Lady Isobel tutted and rapped Amelia with her fan. "That is quite enough of that unladylike language, Amelia. Sir George may wish to descend to the level of the ale house but I shall not abide such language from my girls."

"Amelia is quite correct in one thing," Catherine said, "he is very handsome."

Amelia cocked a delicate eyebrow at her sister. "Fie on you, Catherine. Whatever would your intended think of such a statement?" She waved her fan as if the shock would send her into a swoon.

"Mr Anthony Dean would most likely agree. He in his turn is such an agreeable young man, don't you think, Sir George?" Lady Isobel said.

"Young Anthony Dean? I daresay he is. A touch wet behind the ears but agreeable enough, my dear. Have he and Catherine set a date? Time is passing and at twenty-two years Catherine is in danger of becoming an old maid."

"Mr Dean proposed not a week ago, sir," Catherine said with mild disapproval. "The Dean farms take up much of his time."

"Yes, yes, the whole Dean family keep well occupied, even to being church wardens."

"I now tire of this conversation," Catherine said. "It may have passed your notice but my clothing is quite stained from where I had to feign a swoon and fall to the ground. Else I may well have faced a worse fate. If the Lieutenant had not happened upon the scene I have little doubt that I would have been ravished."

"We are indeed forgetting ourselves," Sir George said. "I must confess that in all the excitement I did forget the courageous role you yourself played in this night's drama and the strain it must put upon you."

"Then we should not forget the debt we owe to Lieutenant Chris-Lennox, sir. Without him you would have lost not only your purse but also a loving daughter as I would rather have died than be sullied by thieves."

# 5

Chris was up early the next morning and decided to explore the eighteenth century Imber. The servants were working but there was no sign of the family as he made his way out of the wide main door and onto the carriage drive.

The Imber he knew had the church, St Giles, still standing with its odd-shaped tower. He could see this now off to his left over the roofs of cottages which no longer existed in his time. Imber Court too was still there behind locked gates and in disrepair and the only other building in any fit state was The Bell Inn. Every other building had been wrecked, replaced by urban warfare buildings, or removed.

So it was with interest he walked the only street as it followed the stream known as Imber Dock as it curved around to his left. People were out and about and they gave him strange looks. He was no longer wearing his body armour or combat jacket but on this warm morning a green sleeveless T-shirt, combat trousers and boots. He had washed off the camo cream the night before with hot water brought up from the kitchens. There was no running water anywhere in the house; it was all drawn from a well. The toilet facilities were even more archaic with a pot beneath the bed.

The blue tracery running up his right arm from the lightning strike, as he suspected, all the way to his shoulder, was drawing prurient interest and he began to regret not putting on his only long-sleeved shirt. The locals were all covered from neck to wrist. It wasn't far to walk to the edge of the village and he turned on his heel to walk back past the smithy with its accompanying clang of hammer on anvil, towards the pub.

Several soldiers, their red coats adding splashes of colour, lounged around the building smoking clay pipes. Their chatter stopped as they saw him coming, suspicion evident in their body language.

One climbed to his feet and walked a few paces towards Chris. "Who might you'm be?"

From his dress Chris assumed he was a non-commissioned officer. "Lieutenant Chris Lennox. You can stand easy."

"Lieutenant, you say. Bain't be nothing like any Lieutenant we ever see, do ee lads?"

"Aye, serjeant. Queer lookin' cove," one said.

"Aye, that ee be. What you be wantin' 'ere?"

Chris pasted a smile on his face. "I'd like to speak with your commanding officer."

"What business be that o' yourn?"

"Officers' business, serjeant. Would you please announce me."

"The captain's at his breakfast. He'll not want to be bothered by the likes o' you."

At his full height Chris towered over the serjeant by a good eight inches. The man was broad and strong with hands the size of an orangutan's and just as hairy. A man used to getting his own way which had probably led to his promotion. A man not easily intimidated ... but it was worth a try.

"I am a lieutenant in the New Zealand Defence Force. If you wish to keep your position you will do as I say and do it now."

The man looked at him with comic amazement and then guffawed. "Do ee 'ear that, Lads? I'll be a-quakin' in me boots."

"Right cocky sparrow," another soldier said.

"That ... ee ... is." The serjeant's eyes had narrowed and he looked Chris up and down in the same manner that Sir George had the night before. "We be lookin' for footpads and scoundrels an' this one be more like a scoundrel than an officer."

"Aye, cuff his ears and send 'im on his way," the soldier said.

Chris sighed and as the serjeant stepped forward pushed his hand out in front of him in the universal stop gesture. "Please don't do that. It wouldn't be wise."

The serjeant's mouth opened and then closed with a snap. "Are you hearin' this, lads. Now ee's sayin' I be daft and all."

Three more soldiers climbed to their feet and formed a semi-circle behind the serjeant.

"A thrashin' be too good for him," one said and they all nodded.

"I wouldn't do that ..." Chris started but the serjeant's round house punch was already heading his way. He stepped inside the swing, caught the serjeant's arm against his side and flipped the man onto his back in the dirt. He retained his grip and knelt with one knee on the man's throat with his arm in a lock against the joint over Chris's other thigh. The whole move had taken less than two seconds and caught them all by surprise. Then the three soldiers started towards him.

"Stop there or I'll break his arm," Chris said. They did, looking at each other unsure of what to do and how to cope. The swiftness and strangeness of the judo throw had confused them.

"Get 'im off me, you lummoxes," the serjeant grunted through his squashed windpipe. Other soldiers joined the group, these armed with muskets, bayonets fixed.

"What the devil is happening here?" It was quietly spoken but had a galvanising effect on the soldiers. The original three jumped back and knuckled their foreheads as the others presented arms.

Chris turned his head and saw an immaculately dressed young officer wearing a sabre, still in its scabbard, and a silver gorget around his neck, with a powdered wig on his head but no hat.

Chris stood and dropped the serjeant's arm. The man scrambled to his feet and gave a more reluctant salute.

"Will someone do me the honour of enlightening me?"

"This vagabond attacked me, sir," the serjeant said.

The officer raised his eyebrows. "Tis a flogging matter ... if tis the case."

Chris took his chance and bowed his head. "Captain The Honourable William Stewart, I presume, sir."

"Pon my soul, the vagabond speaks daintily. How come you know of me?"

"I am Lieutenant Chris Lennox, sir, of the New Zealand Defence Force. I am a house guest of Sir George and Lady Wadman."

"The devil you say, sir. Might I enquire are you related to the Wadmans?"

"I rescued Miss Catherine Wadman from highwaymen yesterday, which is why I wish to speak with you."

"The devil you do. Well you had best come inside and speak over a tankard of the landlord's good cider. Serjeant, rouse the men from their lethargy and begin your patrol. I will seek you out later."

The serjeant knuckled his forehead but said nothing. The beads of sweat on his brow had little to do with the rising morning temperature but much to do with the thought of his punishment if found he had truly attempted to strike an officer. An action which could result in the death penalty.

Captain Stewart had an amused look on his face as he led Chris into the tap room at the front of the Inn. "Serjeant Biggin fears for his life, should you truly be an officer in His Majesty's army."

"It's not his fault. He had every right to be suspicious. My clothing causes a lot of interest."

"Indeed, sir. One could hardly call you a popinjay. Green is not a becoming colour. Now tell me of this attack on Miss Wadman."

Chris ran through the story as Stewart listened in silence, his tankard of cider untouched. When Chris had finished he slouched back in his seat and sighed.

"These highwaymen and footpads are growing ever more audacious. There have been instances of highway robbery along the turnpike to Salisbury in recent nights and now they dare to advance to Imber in broad daylight. There is a reward of two-hundred guineas for their capture such is the concern. Three men, you say."

"Three that I saw. Two were related, father and son I believe. They rode off towards Tilshead."

"I will send a despatch to the company at Tilshead to be on the lookout for these fellows. Now, sir, what of you?"

Chris spun the same yarn he had recited to the Wadmans the previous night. He saw the doubt in Stewart's eyes but the captain did not challenge his account.

"That is a very strange tale, a very strange tale indeed. I must admit to not having heard of New Zealand, or its defence force but you say you are loyal to the crown and hold the King's Commission."

"Not exactly the King's Commission. I was commissioned by my own people to defend them and by extension the realm. New Zealand is a new country that wishes to remain loyal to the crown. We face invasion from the Dutch and the French who want to claim the land as their own.

"The damned Frogs, you say. They are forever flexing their might."

"The natives too are fierce warriors. They've taught us by example, and we've learned to defend ourselves by hiding in the undergrowth and catching them unawares, hence our uniforms are made to blend with the greenery."

"That is a very ungentlemanly way to conduct warfare but I daresay it has its value. I am but temporarily assigned to the 62nd being newly returned from Swabia and Switzerland where I learned the value of less conventional tactics. But you will realise, sir, that your commission carries no weight here in Britain."

"I feared as much. But I'm a soldier and as such I could be of value to the army."

Stewart grimaced. "You would needs serve in the ranks or purchase your own commission. The 62nd would take you but an ensign's commission costs four-hundred guineas. Do you have that amount?"

Chris thought of the twenty-two sovereigns sewn into the hem of his jacket. Back home they were worth over two-hundred pounds apiece but he had a horrible feeling that they would not be worth anything near that amount back in the late 1700s.

Chris left Stewart on good terms with a promise to continue the conversation after dinner at the Wadmans later that evening. The thought of food had his stomach rumbling and brought on the thought of breakfast.

The door to Imber Court was opened to him and he was led into the dining room where the family were seated around a long mahogany table. He was welcomed in their formal way and was seated next to Amelia with Catherine opposite. They all eyed his choice of clothing and patterned arm with horrified fascination.

Chris pointed to it. I think this was caused by the lightning strike. The electricity ran down rainwater which soaked my arm, earthed me and probably saved my life. It acted like a lightning conductor.

Amelia broke the awkward silence that followed that statement as they struggled with the unfamiliar terminology. She flashed her eyes at him. "Have you had an enjoyable stroll, Lieutenant? Imber is quite remote but has much to recommend it for the air and countryside."

"Very pleasant, thank you, Miss Wadman. I did meet Captain Stewart for a brief conversation."

"Yes, excellent fellow, commanded the 67th as a brevet lieutenant-colonel," Sir George said. "He'll go far that young man. Good catch for any gel, eh, Amelia?"

"Fie Papa, I have merely eighteen years. I do believe there is time for me yet."

"Maybe there is time, my dear," Lady Isobel said, "but not so many opportunities for a young lady of good breeding. The Captain is of good family and would make an excellent match. I believe he has five-thousand a year."

"Captain Stewart is the son of the Earl of Galloway. Family money. Damned good income for an army officer. Most of those here are on half pay and stood down since the battalion was despatched to the Americas." Sir George said. "Your brother has written from London just this past week complaining that even staff officers such as he are on reduced pay. What of you, Lieutenant? Are you also in reduced circumstance? What is your income?"

"Chris was spellbound by the conversation and replied without thinking "Around thirty-one thousand a year."

"*Thirty-one thousand?* The devil you say."

Too late Chris realised his mistake. That sum would make him a millionaire by 18th century standards. He thought rapidly for an excuse as he felt all eyes on him. "Oh, that's just in local currency. I'm not sure how much that would be in pounds."

"Indeed, Lieutenant," Sir George said. "You are a man of many surprises."

Chris gave a faint smile of embarrassment and busied himself with choosing some food from the array of dishes at the breakfast table.

Catherine gave an amused little laugh. "You must forgive us our indiscretions, Lieutenant. Nothing we say here is in any way to be taken so seriously. It is also a family amusement to tease Amelia. She, I do believe, is already smitten by Anthony's brother, Mr Charles Dean. Is that not so, Amelia?"

"Another farm boy," Sir George muttered. "I had hoped for better marriages for my daughters."

"Now, sir, you know that is unkind. The Deans farm much of the land here, they are quite wealthy and neither Amelia nor I will go hungry, nor end up in rags," Catherine said.

"I suppose one must be grateful for mercies, however small," Sir George grumbled. "I can see the Deans taking over the Court, so great is their ambition."

"I am being forever teased, Lieutenant," Amelia said. "Do you think I should forgive them, or should I respond in kind?"

"Where I come from we have a saying that revenge is a dish best served cold, Miss Wadman. You must carefully consider your options and strike when it's least expected."

"Ah, at last, a man after my own heart," Amelia said with a broad smile. "I shall give this great consideration."

"I do believe you had just made all our lives a little more unbearable, Lieutenant," Catherine said. "We shall all now live in fear and trepidation of Amelia's revenge.

"But as to you, sir. Do you have nothing acceptable to wear? You cannot possibly be seen in such, such a …"

"Sartorial abomination?" Chris finished the sentence before her.

"If that means what I do believe it means, you are quite correct. I will have Matthew to open our brother's trunk. There may be something in there that will be fitting for tonight."

Chris sighed. The thought of wearing eighteenth century fashion really did not appeal.

# 6

Alone in his bedroom Chris eyed the clothing that Matthew had found for him. The son of the house was a few inches shorter than him but much the same chest and waist size. The local seamstress was summoned to lengthen the breeches and the cuffs of the jacket. She had been paid sixpence for her work and it was beginning to trouble Chris that he wasn't able to pay his way.

His situation was also increasingly worrying him. He was no science fiction fan but had always been intrigued by the possibility of time travel and, as a boy, had been hooked on the television series 'Quantum Leap'. That raised the question which had been at the back of his mind since the previous night, would anything he did in the 18th century change his world in the 21st. It was a dilemma. If he was truly back in the past and not merely in a lightning induced and very detailed coma, would it have resulted in the world that he knew or would it change that world beyond recognition? Would it still be _his_ world should he ever find a way back there? It was beyond him. He was now living in another, almost alien, society and he would need to adapt to his current circumstances. He was alone without the guidance of 'Quantum Leap's' helpful holographic mentor. That was fiction, this was now his strange reality. He decided that the future would have to take care of itself.

Later, Matthew helped him dress in the unfamiliar clothes. He had unpicked the hem of his combat jacket and taken out two sovereigns. One he now showed to Matthew.

"This is the currency where I come from, Matthew. What is it worth, here?"

"Is it gold, sir?"

"Yes, pure and solid."

"Then it be as a gold sovereign, sir and worth a pound."

"Just a pound?"

"Aye, sir, twenty silver shillings, two-hundred and forty pennies. A deal of money."

"Could you get it changed for me, into shillings?"

"Yes, sir. The landlord at The Bell would be pleased to make the exchange."

"You don't have a bank here in Imber?"

"Bless you no, sir. The nearest bank is in Salisbury. That is where the money goes to and comes from."

*Which would encourage the highwaymen,* Chris thought. *Easy pickings if they knew when cash was being carried.*

"That is the dinner gong sounding, sir," Matthew said as he brushed Chris's shoulders. "It is time."

"How do I look?"

"As a proper English gentleman should look, sir."

Chris grinned at the implied rebuke. "And not like a footpad or vagabond, eh, Matthew?"

"You did give us all rather a turn last night, sir."

"I'm sure I did."

"We are all most grateful to you, sir, for saving Miss Catherine's life and honour. It is the talk of the village."

"Jungle drums. News travels faster than a BBC broadcast."

Matthew gave him a puzzled look. "Beg pardon, sir."

"Never mind, Matthew."


The dinner gathering was much larger than he anticipated. Apart from the immediate family, Catherine's fiancé Anthony Dean was there with his parents and younger brother, Charles, the local doctor, whom, Chris recalled, was named Hawking, the vicar, Captain Stewart and another officer Chris did not know.

He was introduced to each in turn and he bowed stiffly to the ladies' formal curtseys and bows from the men. No one offered to shake hands and he kept his own firmly behind his back.

"I do believe I owe you a debt, sir." It was Anthony Dean initiating conversation. Chris was acutely aware that he was the centre of attention. A stranger in a strange village with an unlikely story to tell.

"Nothing you wouldn't have done in my place I'm sure, Mr Dean."

"Trouncing three villains single-handed is an extraordinary feat, Lieutenant. Miss Wadman tells me it was in every way extraordinary."

"Miss Wadman herself was very brave, Mr Dean. You are a lucky man to be marrying such a courageous and beautiful woman."

Catherine fluttered her fan and turned a delicate pink. "You do indeed honour me too much, Lieutenant."

"No more than you deserve, miss," Chris said with a smile, grateful to have turned the conversation away from his own part but the respite was short-lived.

"I wish to hear more of this extraordinary feat. Pray continue, sir." It was the other officer, a Lieutenant Foxley who seemed to have fuelled up on alcohol before arriving. He was slightly drunk and becoming obnoxious. Chris decided he didn't like him.

"Another time perhaps, Mr Foxley."

"I hear you also have a taste for street brawling."

"A little misunderstanding. There was no harm done."

"No harm indeed." Foxley snorted. "Biggin faces a flogging for the assault. One simply cannot have the ranks assaulting gentlemen."

"He wasn't to know …"

Foxley held up his hand. "Tis my decision. I decide the punishment and it will be carried out on the morn."

"Let us not discuss this matter before the ladies," Stewart interrupted. "Talk of floggings makes a poor appetiser."

"And speaking of such, dinner is served. Lieutenant Chris-Lennox, as you are the guest of honour this eve, would you be so kind as to escort me into the dining room if you please," Lady Isobel asked and held out a hand.

Chris took it and bowed. "It would be my honour, Lady Wadman."

As Chris led her in she whispered, "Tis Lady Isobel, Lieutenant, my father was the Earl of Lavingham. And be ware of Mr Foxley. I am told he is the best swordsman in the 62nd and most disagreeable in his cups."

Chris was getting the hang of the language and its subtleties. He registered the mild rebuke along with the need to be diplomatic in polite company. "I am grateful for your wise council, Lady Isobel and please accept my abject apology for my ignorance."

She gave him a tight smile. "Rank is most important here, Lieutenant."

"I'm beginning to understand that." Chris handed her to her seat. He was seated beside her with Catherine taking her seat on his left.

She leaned towards him and hid her mouth behind her fan. "Has my mother reproved you for your faux-pas?"

"Delightfully so."

"My dear Lieutenant, I do believe we have embarrassed you. I applaud your demeanour, it is quite noble in the face of such stricture."

"I do believe you're making fun of me."

"And you bear it well, sir. You bear it well."

The meal was a lengthy one and the long case clock was striking midnight when the ladies retired to the drawing room leaving the men with their pipes and brandy. The vicar and the Deans also left claiming early morning duties.

"Tell me, Lieutenant," Dr Hawking asked. He was by the fireplace lighting his pipe with a long spill. "What was it that you gave poor Thomas to relieve his pain? I was able to reset his arm with barely a whimper from him."

Chris started; he had deliberately drunk little alcohol as he needed to keep a clear head but the question still caught him by surprise. The concept of pain relief, other than drinking oneself senseless, was still way off in the future.

He made up an explanation on the spur of the moment. "It's a local native concoction taken from the Coca Tree. We've found it very effective in relieving pain ... but taking more than one dose is dangerous."

"In what way dangerous? Is it injurious to health?"

"Too much can prove fatal. We keep it in small containers with measured doses. The one I gave Thomas was the last one I had." Chris lied. He did not like doing it but there was no way he could explain morphine to a doctor who had never yet heard of chloroform and there was no way he was showing him the self-injecting morphine ampoules from his trauma kit. That technology, like his Glock pistol and wristwatch, was best kept hidden.

Hawking drew on his pipe and nodded. "Tis a pity. That is something I should like to study. By the by, twas an excellent job of securing the broken limb. Have you had medical training, sir?"

"Only what we term first aid. All our soldiers are trained in it. It saves lives on the battlefield."

"The ranks are the scum of the earth. Why should one bother to succour them?" Foxley said. He was slurring his words and his eyes appeared to have lost focus.

Chris bristled. "If you look after your men they will take care of you. It's common sense and common decency."

"Common? Common? Devil take it, of course it is common. They are common men, little better than animals. Why should we care if they are slaughtered? We slaughter sheep, does anyone care of that?"

"Perhaps, Mr Foxley, you wish to retire to your duties," Captain Stewart said from his seat by the fire. He could see that Foxley was beginning to lose control.

"Have you ever found me lacking in my duties, sir? I shall be ready at cock's crow to deliver my verdict on the serjeant's punishment."

"Then I ask that your decision is a lenient one," Chris said. "The man is guilty of nothing but excessive zeal."

Foxley staggered to his feet. "'Twill be my decision. The man is under my command and I will set whatever punishment I see fit."

"Perhaps you enjoy seeing a man flogged, Foxley. An unbecoming trait in any man."

"Damn your eyes, sir. I have no need to be lectured by such as you. You will retract that."

"Have a care, Chris-Lennox," Stewart muttered.

Foxley was now wild-eyed and dribbling brandy onto his tunic. "Apologise!"

Chris was sorely tempted to put the man on his back but he was aware of his position in the house and Lady

Isobel's subtle warning. He bit down on his natural instinct. "If I have caused you any offence, I apologise. Sorry, pal."

Foxley had no intention of backing down. "*Sorrypal?* Is that some abominable foreign insult?"

"No," Chris said, "but if that's the way you want to take it …"

"Then that is no apology. I demand satisfaction. My seconds will attend you on the morrow. Good night, gentlemen." Foxley turned and marched out with as much control as he could muster. He had a tight smile on his lips.

Chris stood there a little bemused. "Has he just challenged me to a duel?"

"I fear so," Sir George said. "He is a master swordsman. It will not be his first duel. I believe it is something to which he is accustomed."

"Foxley has already killed a man in a duel and maimed another," Stewart said. "It was taken as self-defence. The regiment did not wish its honour to be impugned and no case was brought."

"I fear this will not end well for you, Lieutenant," Dr Hawking said.

"Do I get the choice of weapon?"

"Yes," Stewart said. "His seconds will ask for your choice when they attend. Do you have some skill with blade or pistol?"

Chris grinned. "Some little skill, yes."

# 7

Before retiring for the night, Chris had made arrangements to meet with Captain Stewart at The Bell the following morning and he walked there after breakfast.

Stewart was his polite self but Chris could see that there was something troubling him and it wasn't long before he came to the point.

"Foxley's seconds wait to attend upon you, Lieutenant. It is with some regret I tell you this as I feel shamed that an officer under my command should act in such a disrespectful way to a stranger who has proven himself both kind and considerate to my friends the Wadmans, even to staking his own life in a rescue."

"Don't worry, Captain, I'm more than capable of taking care of myself."

"I must presume so, sir, taking account of your air of nonchalance but I must warn you that Foxley means to take both enjoyment and satisfaction from the duel."

"Foxley is what we might call a sociopath. I have come across men like him before. If he demands satisfaction then I'll have to give it to him."

"It is a strange place indeed from which you hail, Lieutenant. You must tell me of it sometime."

Chris laughed. "Stranger than you may think, Captain. But the real reason I'm here this morning is to discuss these highway robberies."

"How so?"

"I have an idea how the thieves may be caught."

"Indeed, sir. How do you propose you may do that?"

"I'll need twenty of your best men, men with patience and maybe the skills of a poacher."

Stewart smiled and it creased his eyes. "I have some who would fit that description. This intrigues me. I do believe I will do as you ask; damned if I know why but thus far any other solution has eluded us."

"You'll need to detach the men from the rest of the company and send them off on a patrol with the serjeant who Foxley means to flog.

"Serjeant Biggin."

"Yes, Biggin. He seems capable and it will give him some respite."

"Foxley is still sleeping off last night's brandy. I will set to immediately."

"Order them to the copse where Miss Wadman was held up. We will meet them there at midday and I'll outline the plan of action then. And tell them to keep the orders to themselves."

"More intrigue but I will do as you bid. Foxley will not be best pleased when he awakes to find his victim has flown the coop."

"Then that's something else he can demand satisfaction for, if he's in any fit state once I've finished with him," Chris said.

"Have a care, Lieutenant. Foxley is a very dangerous opponent."

"So people keep telling me."

"With good cause. I will send his seconds to attend you now, if that is convenient."

Barely a minute after Stewart had left two young officers entered and gave a stiff bow.

The elder of the two spoke. "Ensigns Blake and Willoughby, sir. Are we to assume you are Lieutenant Chris-Lennox?"

"That's close enough, boys. What can I do for you?"

They both looked at each other with puzzled frowns. "We are attending upon you on behalf of Lieutenant Foxley. He demands satisfaction for a slight to his reputation. You will withdraw your remarks, sir, in writing with a gracious apology, or Lieutenant Foxley will be obliged to meet you on the duelling field at sunrise on the morrow."

"I have said nothing that wasn't appropriate to Mr Foxley's manner and I don't see any need for an apology. If anything I deserve an apology for his boorish behaviour as does Sir George Wadman for the bad manners Mr Foxley displayed at his house."

"So be it, sir." The younger one said. "Lieutenant Foxley will await your pleasure in the meadow beyond the windmill at first light. What is your choice of weapon, sir?"

"I understand Mr Foxley is a passable swordsman."

Both boys looked at each other. Neither could have been older than sixteen years and Chris placed the younger at just fourteen.

"He is a-judged the best swordsman in the regiment. It is said he may be the best in the county and beyond." The older boy said.

Chris smiled. "Very well. I notice Captain Stewart carries an infantry sabre. That will be my choice. Sabres."

"You are quite sure, sir?" The younger one said. "Perhaps you would be wise to choose the pistol. Lieutenant Foxley has not such a reputation with a pistol."

"Then it would be no fun, Ensign. Now you go back to Foxley with a message from me. If I win he will commute Serjeant Biggin's punishment to being reduced to the rank of corporal. If he wins, he may do as he wishes. If he agrees then I will accept that as his apology to me and I will not require that in writing. Have you got that?

"We believe we do, sir. But have you no seconds to ensure fair play?"

"No …"

"Indeed he does." Two men had arrived unheard and had been standing in the doorway. "Misters Charles and Anthony Dean will be attending Lieutenant Chris-Lennox. We have heard the terms and shall ensure that they are kept to your wishes."

The two boys bowed. "We thank you, gentlemen. Until the morrow at dawn."

The two Ensigns left and Chris turned to face the Dean brothers.

"It is the least we can do after you afforded such gallant service to Miss Catherine Wadman," Anthony said. "I will be forever in your debt, sir, but I fear that forever may be short lived if what we have heard be true."

"Everyone seems so concerned for my well-being; I'm truly touched. Thank you, gentlemen. There was no guarantee that Mr Foxley would honour the terms should he run me though tomorrow."

"You seem to be taking the matter at hand lightly, sir."

"Dieu et mon droit, gentlemen. God and my right."

"Indeed. We can nought but wish you luck."

"With friends as good as you, what more can a man ask except …" Chris stood, "… is there a horse I could borrow?"

A look of panic spread across both their faces. "You are not considering …?" Charles stuttered.

Chris burst out laughing. "No, I just need a horse for an errand that I've promised Captain Stewart. I'll be there tomorrow morning, I'm not planning on running out on Mr Foxley."

Anthony gave a smile of relief. "There is a gelding that Miss Wadman rides occasionally. I am sure the lady will be delighted to offer the animal to you."

"As long as I don't have to ride side-saddle," Chris said and grinned at their puzzled looks. "Never mind, gentlemen. I'll ask Miss Wadman myself."

Catherine and Amelia were both in the drawing room when Chris found them working, Amelia on her embroidery and Catherine sketching with watercolours. They both stood and curtsied and he bowed in response. He found he was getting a liking for the gentle manners of the times.

"Oh, Lieutenant", Catherine said, "We have heard the terrible news. You are to fight Lieutenant Foxley in a duel. He has such a fearsome reputation we are concerned for your wellbeing."

Chris was touched by their pale demeanour and obvious concern. Catherine looked especially worried.

"Then please put your minds at rest. I'm sure no harm will come to me. I am a soldier and perfectly capable of defending myself."

"We are relieved to hear it, sir," Amelia said, smiled, picked up her embroidery and sat.

Catherine remained standing and looked unconvinced by his assertion. "You do not know of Mr Foxley's reputation, sir. Lady Isobel did warn you on his account. It is surprising to me that you let yourself be drawn into such activity so easily."

Chris grinned. "I couldn't resist the challenge, Miss Wadman. It seemed to me that Mr Foxley was a drunk who enjoyed throwing his weight around. Such people annoy me and it's about time someone took him down a peg."

"Such bravado, sir," Catherine snorted. "I dislike boastful men. I do not find it a becoming attribute."

"Then I'm sorry to disappoint you," Chris said.

"What is it you wish, sir?" Amelia said from the seat. She had gauged the rising temperature of the conversation. "I deduce from your demeanour that there may be some service we could offer you."

Chris was unsettled by Catherine's reaction and it bothered him that he should feel that way. Amelia's interruption saved him from adding words that he might later regret. "You are very perceptive, Miss Amelia. I came to ask Miss Catherine for the loan of a horse so that I can ride with Captain Stewart this morning. Mr Anthony Dean suggested you may agree to loan me a gelding."

Catherine's chin came up. "Anthony?"

"Yes. He and Charles have agreed to be my seconds. Mr Anthony wants to ride with Captain Stewart and myself. I think he takes his duty as a second very seriously. Mr Charles Dean needs his horse to ride back to the farm and neither could loan me their mounts."

"Lieutenant, I neither know nor should I care what you do. You have been in Imber for less than two days but in such time you have caused much stirring of our still waters. I do however care for Mr Dean and I have no wish to see him embroiled in some chicanery of your devising. I fear, Lieutenant that you are a disturbing influence in our small society."

Chris was shocked at Catherine's outburst. She had turned a deeper shade of pink than the previous night when she had been embarrassed by his compliments. He felt his own temper rise and clamped down on it. "Does that mean you won't loan me the horse?"

Catherine tossed her head. "Oh, sir, you are impossible. You may have the horse." She rang a small musical bell and Mary the maid came in and curtsied.

"Ask the groom to ready the gelding for Lieutenant Chris-Lennox."

Mary flashed Chris a smile before she left. At least she was still friendly. He was beginning to feel isolated. He was the alien in another world where he did not understand the indigenous people. He would be happier, he thought, walking through a minefield than negotiating the dangerous waters in which he now found himself.

Amelia too looked puzzled. "Catherine, dear, I fear you are too harsh in your judgement of the Lieutenant. Did he not save you from blackguards? Without his intervention we may now surely be mourning your loss. And that would sadden me greatly. I for one feel in his debt."

Catherine dropped her head with a slight bow. "You are right, Amelia. I am forgetting my debt of gratitude. Please accept my apology, Lieutenant. I allowed my fear of what may occur in the future to guide my tongue."

Chris thought he had decoded the underlying message. "Then you needn't worry any further. Once my business with Captain Stewart ... and Mr Foxley ... is concluded I will be moving on. I feel I've been a burden on your family's hospitality long enough. And don't worry on Mr Dean's account, he will be in no danger."

Chris left and went to his room to change back into his combat gear. He put on the Virtus Kevlar vest but left out the ceramic chest plate. He was adjusting his green Rifles beret with its silver bugle horn badge over his left eye when Matthew knocked and entered. He held out his hand.

"Your exchange from the landlord at The Bell, sir."

Chris took the small cloth bag from his hand.

"It is just ten shillings and sixpence, sir. The landlord had it that the sovereign was half the normal size so worth half the amount plus a little for the quality. My apologies for misleading you sir, I have never before seen a sovereign of any size with which to compare it."

Chris grimaced. His worldly worth had just halved to eleven pounds and eleven shillings. He gave Matthew the sixpence. "That is to repay the sum paid to the seamstress. I don't want to be in debt."

"That is unnecessary, sir. The household would gladly bear the cost."

Chris thought of Catherine's words. "Maybe not the entire household."

Chris collected the gelding from the stables and met Anthony Dean and Stewart outside the inn. They rode to the copse in silence each lost in their own thoughts.

Chris assumed that Stewart was worrying over whether he had made the right decision in allowing an unknown man to determine a plan for his soldiers. He knew the name of William Stewart and felt sure he had judged him to be a man open to new ideas. Perhaps Anthony was worrying that he would make a run for it and bring disgrace on his seconds. Maybe it was an uncharitable thought but he could not stop it from occurring.

He spotted the soldiers long before they walked the horses into the copse. Their red coats stood out like poppy flowers in a Flanders field.

Biggin met them and grasped Stewart's horse's bridal. Stewart swung a leg over his saddle and slid to the ground. "Have the men gather round, serjeant." He took Biggin aside and whispered a few words to him. Chris saw him cast furtive glances in his direction and decided Stewart was reading Biggin the riot act.

The horses were tethered to a tree as the soldiers grouped around. Chris ran his eye over them. Most were in their twenties with the odd one older or younger. There were missing teeth, plenty of scars and broken noses. Mostly their hair was long and unkempt. One had a tarred sailor's pigtail. There was a sullen air about them as they leaned on their Short Land Pattern Brown Bess muskets.

Stewart waved a languid hand over them. "Is this the best you could find, serjeant?"

"Aye, sir. Best in the time I had, beggin' your pardon."

Stewart turned to Chris. "Well, Mr Chris-Lennox. Will these do?"

Chris nodded. "I think they will do very nicely, sir. I don't think I've ever seen such a grisly bunch of private soldiers."

"Indeed, sir, they are some spectacle. The regiment's finest I am assured."

"Beggin' your pardon, sir, if I might speak,"Biggin said. "They be good soldiers. They be bored and wantin' back to Salisbury, sir."

"Then the sooner we catch the footpads and highwaymen we have been tasked to apprehend the sooner their wish will be granted," Stewart said. "And that is the very reason we are here. I trust your departure went unremarked."

"Aye, sir. A regular foot patrol."

"Excellent. I shall now hand you over to Lieutenant Chris-Lennox who has devised a stratagem."

# 8

Chris had briefed soldiers before on many occasions but this would be a new and trying experience. The men did not trust him, he could see that in their defensive body language. They may have heard the story of his gallant rescue but that did not carry much influence with the men. On top of that he was about to introduce them to a type of warfare of which they had no experience.

"All right, gather round." He indicated a circle and the nineteen men shuffled closer to a bare patch of earth he had scraped with a boot. "The area here," he waved a hand over the dirt, "represents the land from Imber to the Salisbury turnpike. Here," he made a mark with a broken stick, "is the henge. Here," he made another mark, "is Salisbury itself." He drew a line between Stonehenge and Salisbury. "This represents the turnpike and this," he drew another line, "is the road to Tilshead. We are here, on the Imber road." He made another mark. "Two nights ago highwaymen attempted a robbery right here where we are standing. They didn't take much money and so will be hungry for more. They'll be tempted to try again soon and we'll be ready for them. They won't try it here as I scared the daylights out of them."

"God's teeth, sir. How will we know where they will strike?" Stewart asked.

"We'll make it easy for them. The word will be put around that a coach carrying workers' wages will be travelling from Salisbury to Tilshead tomorrow afternoon. I've noticed how quickly word spreads in the villages so it should be all over the area by tomorrow morning.

"As you know, highwaymen prefer to hide in trees before staging a robbery. It gives them concealment from the coachmen as they approach. They also need a clear avenue of escape. You've told me, Captain, that there is only one suitable copse on the Tilshead road and to ensure that is where the highwaymen will be we'll arrange for the coach to throw a wheel in the middle of it and we'll be waiting for them."

"We'll be seen and they will make off," Stewart said.

"One moment and I'll address that. Mr Dean, would you be good enough to ride back to Imber and spread word of the money the coach will be carrying at The Bell? Also ask one of the young Ensigns to take a despatch to Tilshead with the same news."

"Of course, Lieutenant, if you so wish it."

"Here, take my seal," Stewart said and handed over a ring, "as proof that the orders come with my sanction."

"And if you would be good enough to return with two days' cold rations for these men," Chris added, "as they won't be returning to Imber tonight. Also some sturdy ropes. Don't trust anyone but your own servants with the job ... the task."

"As you wish, sir, though I am at a loss…"

"I will return to Imber with you this evening but these men will be moving on before sunset."

Anthony gave a slight bow, mounted his horse and turned back to Imber.

"About that matter of concealment," Stewart said.

Chris grinned and turned to face the soldiers. "Men, I'm about to introduce you to the brave new world of camouflage, concealment and the art of ambush."

Anthony returned three hours later with a dogcart loaded with bread and meats and with churns filled with water from the village well. He stopped at the edge of the copse but could see no one. The redcoats he assumed had moved off but he knew not where to and could not follow. Of Chris and Captain Stewart, there was no sign and his heart sank at the thought of appearing at the duelling ground without his duellist.

He drove the dogcart further into the shade to give the small horse drawing it some respite from the sun. All around was still, even the birds had stopped singing in the heat of the day.

He looked around and shouted but the woods on either side of the track absorbed the sound and the silence seemed to mock his efforts. He climbed into the back of the cart and ladled water into a leather bucket for the horse. He turned his back to climb down and as his foot hit the earth a musket rammed into the back of his neck.

"I have nothing worth stealing," he said, his voice firm.

"Then we'll take your cart."

The voice was rough and uneducated and Anthony felt a shiver of apprehension. "You will not get far. The army is nearby."

"Nearer than you think," Chris said and laughed.

The musket was removed and Anthony turned to see the men surrounding him, all laughing and cackling like hens with a cockerel. He looked around open-mouthed. Their red coats had been turned inside-out showing the dull linings. The men had branches of leafy twigs interwoven into capes around their shoulders, their faces blackened with dirt.

Chris pushed his way through the ranks of chortling men. "Sorry if we surprised you, Mr Dean, we were testing our new strategy for catching the thieves."

"And effective it appears to be, sir. I had no idea …"

Stewart walked from behind a woven trellis made from split branches that had concealed both him and the two horses he led by their bridles. "Stap me if I ain't now fully convinced that this might work."

Chris nodded. "It will work. As long as the men remember the principles of camouflage and concealment; shape; break it up, shine; dull it, shadow; don't cast it where it can be seen, silhouette; avoid the skyline, sound; keep quiet, and movement; don't make any which can be noticed. It is sudden movement which first attracts the eye. And that is equally important to the discipline of the ambush."

"We are much obliged, Lieutenant," Stewart said. "We will now make our way to the chosen spot and enter under cover of dusk."

"Remember, Captain, to position the men on one side of the copse," Chris said. "That will avoid anyone being shot accidentally by his own comrades. Put out hidden piquets at either end to foil any escape and string the ropes Mr Dean has brought low through the trees on the opposite side of the copse to the men. The ropes will fell the horses should the thieves try to ride through the trees."

"Pon my soul, sir, I do believe you have thought of everything."

"It will be a long day for you tomorrow. You will need to remain concealed at all times. But if you set up a base camp deeper into the trees, where it can't be seen from the road, the men can take turns to rest there. I will arrange for a carriage to be driven from Imber to the Salisbury turnpike and then along the Tilshead Road towards your position. It will arrive at sunset and stage a false breakdown. I will be there with it unless my meeting with Foxley goes badly."

"Yes, I had not forgotten your dawn tryst." Stewart held out his hand and Chris took it, each clasping the other's wrist. "Have a care, Lieutenant."

"I'll do my best. Any tips?"

Stewart gave him a puzzled look.

"Does Foxley have any weaknesses, or any favourite moves?"

"Ahh! Weaknesses ... I fear not. Beware the riposte from the parry. That is all I know. May it do you some good, sir."

As Chris walked to his horse Serjeant Biggin approached him. Chris watched him warily, unsure what the man had in mind. Biggin stopped a yard short and touched his forehead with a hairy knuckle. "Beggin' you pardon, Lieutenant, may I speak."

Chris nodded his assent.

"The captain tol' me what you done fer me, speakin' out against Lieutenant Foxley and how it dunned you into a duel. I hopes it goes well for you, sir."

"At the very least, serjeant, you may well lose a rank but that will be better than having stripes added to your back. Thank you for your good wishes. I'll do my best not to lose for both our sakes."

"Forgive me, sir, but I don't rightly understand why you be doin' this for an enlisted man."

"Where I come from, enlisted men are known as the backbone of the army and serjeants are the backbone of the men. I've been taught that you don't treat men serving under you with disdain. It's a novel idea but one that will take hold in the British army in time."

"Not in my time, sir, to be sure."

"You are probably right, Serjeant Biggin, but I will do all I can to see you are treated fairly."

Chris rode back to Imber accompanying Anthony driving the now empty dogcart. The small mare pulling it trotted at a good pace now there was no weight to haul.

Anthony rubbed the back of his neck. "That was indeed some trickery performed there. Where did you learn of it? It seems a mightily different stratagem."

"It's basic military training where I come from. We learned long ago that standing front-on, blasting each other with volleys, led to too many casualties. As I said, we are a small community and can't afford to lose men in such a way. That is also the reason we wear body armour; our lives are precious to us."

Anthony frowned. "I fear that will not gain universal favour amongst the generals with their sense of honour. I am no military man and can see the truth of what you say but I cannot see how such stratagems would work on a battlefield. The sheer size of an army would surely prove impossible to conceal."

"You're right to some extent. Large numbers are difficult to conceal. Those tactics work best with small numbers, that's why I asked Captain Stewart for just twenty men. The whole company would have been impossible to hide without them being detected by anyone passing by. The plan will only work with tight opsec."

"You do use the strangest of terms, sir. May I be so bold as to enquire …?"

Chris grinned, he had been carried away with the talk of tactics and had been going over the plan in his own mind, testing it for flaws. The jargon for operational security had slipped out.

"Opsec? It's a native word. It translates as fully secret. In confidence."

Anthony nodded his understanding. "I quite see the intelligence of it. You are a master of your trade, sir. Are you as accomplished with a sabre?"

Chris pulled a rueful grin. "We'll find out tomorrow morning."

# 9

The setting was as Chris had imagined it through a near sleepless night. Despite his apparent confidence, he had deep misgivings about his ability to defend himself against the experienced Foxley.

It was a cool morning with a thin mist hovering at knee height. The sun was just tinging the sky pink in the east. Foxley was standing in such an arrogant pose that it seemed he had already won the duel. He was in white shirt, dark breeches and stockings with his cloak over his shoulders to ward off the chill and dancing pumps on his feet, wet from the dew.

Chris was wearing his combat boots and Kevlar vest. It was stab proof and covered his upper body but not his arms which were prime targets for a sabre's edge. The boots would make him heavy footed by comparison and he wished he had something lighter to wear.

The Dean brothers and the two young Ensigns were in conversation in the centre of a rough circle marked with a sword tip through the grass. The field had been recently scythed and then grazed almost to the roots by sheep and presented a smooth surface. A coin was tossed and the younger Ensign, Willoughby, came to Chris with two sabres still in scabbards over his arm.

"The turn of the coin favours you, sir. You may have first choice of weapon."

Chris thanked him and pulled out one sabre. The shape and weight surprised him. It was curved and the sabre he was used to fencing with was straight. It was also much heavier. He flexed his wrist and tested the sword's balance. Then he tried the second sabre with much the same result.

"That sabre is mine, sir," Willoughby said. "I would be honoured should you choose it."

"Is it a good sword, Mr Willoughby?"

"A gift from my father. It is of the finest Toledo steel, taken from the Spanish at the battle of Manila in '62."

"In that case it will be an honour to use it. Thank you, Mr Willoughby."

"You may have need of its strength, sir. Good luck." Willoughby carried the second sabre to Foxley who took the hilt and flicked off the scabbard. He dropped his cloak and slashed the air several times before dropping the sabre's point onto the grass and leaning on it.

Anthony came over. "It is time, Lieutenant."

"I'm ready," Chris said. He could not help a thought enter his mind about a book he had once read called 'The Far Arena' where a Roman gladiator was thawed from a glacier and came to life to fight an Olympic swordsman. The gladiator had disembowelled the fencer and led him around by his entrails. Chris was classed amongst the top ten sabre specialists in Europe but would his sophisticated skills match the ferocity of a proven and battle-hardened duellist? He was about to find out. *Perhaps I should have chosen pistols.*

"En garde."

The elder Ensign waited while Chris and Foxley crossed sabres then using his own he placed it between the blades and heaved upwards to separate them, quickly jumping out of reach.

Foxley struck hard and fast, a downward slash at Chris's right knee. Chris parried and struck back at Foxley's left shoulder. Steel on steel rang like bells as they tested each other's skill. Foxley was good, Chris gave him credit. He was fast and dangerous in the attack, cunning and subtle in the riposte.

Chris watched Foxley's sabre point, as he had been taught, parrying each thrust and riposting himself when he had a small opening. This was nothing like an Olympic fencing competition and it was apparent that Foxley meant to do him serious damage. Despite his dancing shoes, Foxley's feet were relatively static as he preferred to use the swinging blade to attack rather than Chris's more nimble footwork. After a particularly savage attack Chris backed off to the edge of the drawn circle, tempting Foxley to pursue him, swinging savage cuts at Chris's upper torso. The blade hit his Kevlar vest but did not penetrate. Foxley blinked in disbelief and swung again. Chris ducked the cut and turned so that Foxley was now on the outer ring.

Chris needed more room and he backed away with Foxley standing provocatively with his sabre down by his side and a fierce smile on his face.

Chris felt something warm trickle down his arm and glanced at the blood seeping from a cut. He had not felt it in the heat of battle but Anthony had seen it.

"First blood, Mr Foxley. Are you satisfied?"

"If the jackanapes yields."

"Not a chance in hell, Foxley. You'll have to do better than this," Chris snapped.

"Then have at it, sir," Foxley said.

Chris had been assessing Foxley's technique. It was fast and hard but conformed to a regular pattern of slashes, ripostes and thrusts. He doubted if Foxley had ever seen the tactic he was about to employ. He backed away to the further edge of the circle as Foxley moved to the centre. It seemed as if Chris was avoiding further fighting and Foxley beckoned him back with a mocking grin.

Chris charged across the grass and leapt into the air thrusting the sabre down into Foxley's shoulder, twisting and landing with his sabre at the guard.

"God's teeth," Foxley screamed. He dropped his sabre and put his good hand to the wound which was pumping blood through his fingers.

Chris had his sabre point at Foxley's throat. "Do *you* yield, sir?"

"Lieutenant Chris-Lennox, are you satisfied, sir" Willoughby called.

"I am," Chris said and dropped the point.

"Mr Foxley, do you yield, sir?"

Foxley clutched his now almost useless arm. "Dammit, yes. I yield."

"Then honour is satisfied?" Ensign Blake asked.

"Twas a knavish trick, one that I shall remember," Foxley grunted.

"Come, sir. We shall visit Doctor Hawking," Blake said and led Foxley away before he could dishonour himself further by his comments.

Anthony and Charles came to Chris's side with broad smiles on their faces. Willoughby came to with a neutral look as became the second of a losing duellist. Chris bowed and handed back the sabre hilt first.

"That really is a fine blade, Mr Willoughby. It'll serve you well."

"I thank you, sir. You must teach me that trick with the leap and thrust."

"We call it a flunge."

"Another native word?" Anthony asked.

Chris grinned. "Not this time it's the short form of flying lunge."

Willoughby scabbarded the sabre and bowed. "I thank you, Lieutenant but I must confess that your speech often does confuse me."

"Make sure you clean the blood off the blade when you get back," Chris said.

Willoughby bowed again and turned to follow the now distant figures of Blake and Foxley.

"Foxley will not let matters lie, I fear." Charles said. "His reputation has been sullied and he is not a man to forgive and forget."

"That wound will take time to heal," Chris said. "He will be hors de combat for some time and it will give him an opportunity to consider the error of his ways. A lesson learned and one that was taught to me. No matter how good you are there is always someone better."

"Speaking of wounds you have blood flowing, sir" Anthony said and pointed at Chris's bicep.

Chris grimaced. "It's not too bad. I can treat it myself when we get back."

"It may need sutures, sir," Charles said.

"I can cope, Mr Dean. It's a minor matter."

"As you say, sir. Come we must get back to Imber Court. There are many there who will be delighted at this happy outcome."

The village was just stirring as they walked back. The soldiers had pitched bell tents behind the inn but no red coats were in sight as reveille had not been sounded. Imber Court, by comparison was buzzing with activity. The big front door opened as they approached and Matthew beckoned them in. His smile of welcome was replaced by one of concern as he saw the blood on Chris's arm.

"Just a scratch, Matthew," Chris said.

Catherine and Amelia were standing inside the hall, their hands to their faces.

"You have been hurt, Lieutenant," Catherine said between her fingers. "Mary quick, bring hot water and some towels."

"There's no need ..." Chris started but he was propelled into the dining room and pushed into a chair. Anthony and Charles, seeing the women taking charge, bowed and left. Amelia ran out to supervise Mary's assignment leaving Chris and Catherine alone.

She smelled faintly of rose water and her hair was hanging in ringlets on either side of her face. It brushed his shoulder as she leaned forward to inspect the cut.

"Is this proper, you and I being alone?" Chris said.

She pulled back as if stung but quickly regained her composure. "Quite proper, Lieutenant. You are wounded and it is of concern to me that you are treated with haste."

"Why are you angry with me?"

"'Tis not anger, sir, merely concern for another who did me a service."

"Do I frighten you, Miss Wadman?"

"There is very little on God's good earth that gives me cause for alarm."

"Forgive me, but that doesn't answer my question."

"You forget yourself, sir. I have barely made your acquaintance; you are being too forward."

"I apologise if I am but it's the way of ..."

"Your country?"

Chris was about to say 'my time' but checked himself. "Perhaps. My upbringing is very different to yours. We have progressed to another code of manners."

"I cannot say that it is an improvement, Lieutenant."

"I can see why you might think that."

"Now sit still, sir. Your agitation is reopening the wound."

Chris realised he *was* agitated. Her nearness was having an effect on him and he felt the hair rise on the back of his neck. He was being stupid. She was of another time, was engaged to a man who was becoming his friend and was intent on a good marriage. What would a vagrant from the future have to offer? He stamped on the thought. Was it a proprietary feeling of part ownership of her life? Or was he really falling for the beautiful woman with the beautiful manners and a touch as soft as the look in her eyes?

She was watching him now, standing back, an odd expression on her face, halfway between concern and irritation. Chris felt the tracery on his arm tingle as if a current was running up it, it seemed to crackle and fizz and sent pins and needles down to his fingers.

Mary rushed in and broke the tension which seemed to flow out of both him and Catherine in a simultaneous rush of expended energy. She carried a tin bowl of hot water and a towel over her arm. Amelia followed close behind with soap in a wooden dish.

Catherine turned away picked up her fan and wafted it. She had turned the delicate shade of pink again.

Amelia was all business as she bustled around Mary who mopped at the cut. She shot a glance at her sister. "Are you unwell, dearest? Does the sight of blood give you the vapours?"

"I am quite well, thank you, Amelia. It is merely a little warm in here. I will leave you and Mary to attend to Lieutenant Chris-Lennox whilst I go to the garden for air."

One half of Chris was glad to see her go. The other half was desperate for her to stay. He wanted her to go before he said something he may regret and he wanted her to stay just so she would be near to him. Idiot, he thought, you really are. Now life was becoming more complicated than ever.

# 10

The cut was not as bad as it appeared and Chris tactfully refused to have it washed with soap. In the privacy of his room he sprinkled the cut with Baneocin powder to prevent infection and rebound it with a pad and pressure bandage from his trauma kit. He pulled on his long-sleeved shirt so that Mary and Amelia wouldn't be upset that he had overridden their ministrations.

When he came back down Sir George was waiting for him with Anthony and beckoned them both into his study.

"Mr Dean tells me you require the use of my carriage and four this day, sir. May I enquire as to why you have need of it."

"We, Captain Stewart and I, are setting a trap for the highwaymen tonight. I need a carriage to bait it and yours is the only one sufficient to accommodate the size of the lure we've set."

"I have heard a tale of a large amount of money being carried this day. Stap me but who would be so stupid as to trumpet such a movement in advance?"

"That would be me," Chris said and gave a sheepish grin. "I'm pleased that word has got around so quickly."

"So there's little truth in it?"

"Pure fabrication, Sir George. But I need the carriage to add meat to that particular bone."

"A bold stratagem, indeed. What chance of success?"

"A good chance, Sir George, if all goes well."

"You have the carriage with my blessing but who is to drive it? Thomas is in no fit state to handle a puppy, let alone a team of four."

"I have made enquiries of my stable hands," Anthony said. "There is one who professes some skill with a team."

"So be it. I'll have the carriage readied and you bring your man," Sir George said. "When shall you depart?"

"We'll take the road to Salisbury than cut back onto the Tilshead road," Chris said. "Captain Stewart tells me that the journey would take around four hours. We agreed to arrive at dusk, say nine-thirty this evening, which means we need to leave here at around five-thirty at the latest."

"Very well. Have you a weapon, sir?"

"I have but ...," Chris said thinking of the Glock, "it may not be suitable."

"I have a Dragon you may use."

Chris raised his eyebrows. "Dragon, Sir George?"

"Yes, sir, are you not familiar with the pistol?"

"I must have missed that one."

"I'll have Matthew familiarise you with it. Very comforting to have close by. The Post has great use of them, that is why the highwaymen avoid the Post coaches and attack private conveyances. The one blunderbuss and two Dragons that they carry are enough to put any miscreant to flight."

"Then I'm very grateful for your offer, sir."

"Nonsense! If it helps rid the plain of ne'er-do-wells it is a small price to pay."

"Will you warn your stable hand that this may get dangerous, Mr Dean?" Chris said. "I'll do my best to keep him safe but fighting has a habit of getting messy."

"Have no fear, sir. He will be well compensated for his time. I have promised him a crown for this night's work."

"More than generous, sir," Sir George said. "More than a whole week's wage for a single night."

"Danger money," Chris added.

"Devil take it, sir, that is a notion I have no wish to see gain credence."

"It will," Chris said under his breath.

The day had clouded over and by the evening it was beginning to drizzle. Chris put on his combat jacket and beret. Anthony's driver was already sitting on the driver's seat wrapped up against the rain with a heavy oiled cloak, tricorn hat, gloves and a scarf which covered the lower half of his face.

Chris climbed inside and banged on the roof to let the man know he was ready to roll. The carriage lurched forward and out of the gateway.

Chris pulled the Dragon from his belt and checked it. It was a muzzle-loading flintlock with a brass barrel flared at the muzzle, a brass trigger guard and iron workings. The pan was primed with gunpowder and Matthew had rammed various pieces of odd-shaped metal down the barrel with the main charge and wadding to prevent the load from falling out. It was a mini-blunderbuss and he could remember seeing pictures of cavalrymen using them, which is where they had acquired the name Dragoons. It was a very close range weapon, "wait 'til you see the whites of their eyes," he said to himself in a hopeless impression of John Wayne.

The journey dragged as the carriage lurched and rumbled along the now muddy tracks. It had been a dry spell and the mud was not deep enough to cause them any problems. Cocooned as he was inside Chris did not have the luxury of conversation with the driver, a dour and uncommunicative sort who failed to respond when they stopped to rest and water the horses.

He checked the Dragon twice more, unconvinced that the powder would stay, neither in the primer pan nor in the barrel, but it did. He resolved to have more confidence in 18th century technology. They made the turn from the Salisbury road onto the Tilshead road with Stonehenge on the left as they passed. Chris wondered what had been in the stones that had thrown him back two-hundred odd years. It was the stuff of nightmares and he began to feel homesick for the comforts of his own time. Would he ever be able to return? If so, how could he do it? He didn't have a time machine, it had been a random force of nature. But while he was here he would do his upmost to make the best of it.

Thanks to his parents' love of history he knew most of the important dates of the past, plus the basics of the language and a grasp of the mores of the age from Jane Austen's works.

Now, as the time approached, he began to worry that the ambush wouldn't be set correctly, the soldiers insufficiently hidden, that the highwaymen wouldn't appear at all. He was used to having constant radio contact with his men and the lack of communication was troubling. He had to put his faith in Stewart. He knew from his history that the man was capable, having recently served in a campaign in Europe, and was heading for General's rank but would Chris's own interference change history? It was a troubling thought. A butterfly flapping its wings in the Amazon rainforest, causing a hurricane in Florida? The Chaos Theory. It was too much to grasp.

His musings had taken his mind off the journey and he was surprised when the setting sun, which appeared beneath the trailing edge of the cold front, was blotted out by trees. The coach ground to a stop and the horses snorted and stomped in relief.

Chris climbed out of the coach and ordered the driver down. He had loaded a broken wheel into the boot before they left and he pulled this out and leant it against the side of the carriage.

Chris looked around. There was no sign of the soldiers. Either his training had worked or they had packed up and moved to drier quarters. He sincerely hoped it was the former.

The driver lit the carriage lamps and watched him, his face in shadow.

"You'd better get inside the carriage and keep out of sight. It'll be safer and things could get hairy."

The man cocked his head and Chris gave him a fleeting grin. "That means dangerous."

Time passed slowly and Chris sneaked a peek at his watch. The luminous hands showed 9.45 and it was almost fully dark under the trees.

A flicker of movement caught in his peripheral vision and he swung his head. A night flying bird maybe; a nightjar or tawny owl. He turned his head back and checked with his peripheral vision again. Nothing; could have been imagination.

A twig cracked, gunshot loud.

"Who's there?"

A towering shape, not ten yards away, moved slowly towards him; a man on horseback. "*Stand and deliver.*" Dry, throaty, contemptuous, sure of himself.

Chris pulled the Dragon.

"*Stand!*" Another voice closer and lower, a man on foot.

Two men, one load in the Dragon.

Torches flared and muskets cracked in volley. The horse and rider screamed and went down. The man closest to Chris levelled his flintlock at his head. Chris pulled on the Dragon's trigger ... nothing; he had forgotten to cock the gun. Too used to the Glock's double-action. Gunpowder flared at the flintlock's pan.

The coachman erupted from the carriage and hit Chris in the chest. Both went down in a welter of limbs and his head thudded on a stone.

A pistol cracked; another scream close by. Chris's head spun and for an absurd moment he thought he smelled rosewater. The coachman climbed off him and he shook his head, his vision still clouded. Stewart ran around the horses, a smoking flintlock in one hand, a blazing torch in the other.

"Hurrah, sir. We have them all."

"Oh, great," Chris mumbled.

"Are you wounded, Lieutenant?"

Stewart carried the torch close enough for Chris to feel the heat from the flames. The light hurt his eyes and waved the flames away. "Bang on the head. I'm seeing stars."

"Ah! The moon will rise soon." Stewart said, "and then we will discard the torches." He tucked the flintlock in his sash and heaved Chris to his feet. "By god, sir, your stratagem has worked. We have two highwaymen dead and have captured a third who foolishly attempted to ride through the piquet. Come morning we shall take him and the bodies to Tilshead for identification. There may be more of the blackguards at large."

Chris nodded and gave the back of his head a gentle probe. There was no blood on his fingers but a lump was forming the size of a pigeon's egg. He had no doubt that the coachman had saved his life. The lead ball had fanned his face as he fell. He turned to thank him, but there was no sign of the coachman.

Stewart pulled him away to check on the soldiers who were busily cleaning up. The highwayman's horse lay on its side, its rider still in the saddle one leg trapped beneath the animal. The musket fire had done terrible damage and the other leg was severed at the knee. Chris felt sorry for the horse, glad that in his world horses no longer faced such dangers.

"Here," Stewart said and pulled on his arm. A few paces along the track the prisoner was sitting on the gravel with his hands bound and two watchful soldiers standing guard with fixed bayonets. They presented arms as Stewart approached. He waved the muskets down. "See here, Lieutenant, a live scoundrel who may yet direct us to his nest of vipers."

"You believe there may be more?"

Stewart nodded. "Footpads and highwaymen keep close company. I believe we chance to root out the entire nest ere the morrow is out."

Chris could see that adrenaline was still pumping through Stewart's veins. The soldiers too had grins on their rough faces. They both gave Chris respectful looks. He had proven himself in their eyes.

"We shall strike out at first light to rendezvous with the Tilshead company. They have local intelligence and may know from whence these blackguards come," Stewart said.

Chris gestured at the man on the floor. "What will you do with him?"

"He will go before a Justice of the Peace and thence to the Assize at the Guildhall in Salisbury. Justice will be done. He shall hang for certain."

Serjeant Biggin approached and knuckled his forehead. "Beggin' your pardon, sirs. We have squared away the remains. The horse we dragged into the wood ready for the knacker's cart. The bodies we have wrapped in sack cloth and tied to the saddles of the remaining horses."

"Well done, serjeant," Stewart said. "We shall build a good fire and sit out the night wrapped in our cloaks. Tis more congenial now that the rain has gone."

"It may be best if I take the carriage back to Imber. There'll be some worried people waiting for news."

"Tosh, man," Stewart said. "Tis too dark to see the road. Stay until dawn."

"You said the moon will be up soon. If you let me have two men with torches until moonlight does the work ..."

"If you are so determined. Serjeant, order two able men to lead the Lieutenant's carriage."

Chris found the coachman huddled inside the carriage. His head came up as he pulled open the door. "We're leaving for Imber now. We have two soldiers to light the way until you can see by moonlight. It's a much shorter journey than the circuitous route we took on leaving. Barely two hours at a walking pace. We should be back at Imber by one-o-clock."

The driver said nothing, just nodded, a vague shape in the blackness. He staggered to his feet and yelped in a high-pitched fashion as his left foot buckled.

"Looks like a sprained ankle," Chris said. "Here let me help you down ... Miss Wadman."

# 11

Chris lifted Catherine onto the driver's seat and climbed up beside her. The two soldiers walked ahead, one on either side of the track to mark its width. It wasn't very many minutes before a near full moon came up deep orange and climbed quickly.

The two soldiers doused their torches, saluted goodbye and turned back towards the copse. Chris had remained silent until then but heaved a theatrical sigh. "What on earth possessed you?"

"Need you sound so reproving, sir?" Catherine said. "Coming from one of so short an acquaintance."

"You could have been killed."

"And so might you, sir. Indeed your brains may now be more addled."

"And I see you have a hole in your hat which could have aired your head."

"A small price to pay, sir, to be rid of such an encumbrance of debt."

"So now we're even? That's fine. Thank you for saving my life."

"Ha, sir, gratitude at last. I did not think I would see the day."

"Do you have such a low opinion of me?"

"I have no opinion of you in any way."

"But you masqueraded as a coachman," Chris said "and put yourself in danger when there was no need. You must have had a reason."

"I am not without reason. Despite what men may think of women we do have reason, sir, sometimes reason to spare."

"That's not what I meant, and you know it."

"You wish me to have but a single reason, Lieutenant? Then I shall give you one. I did not wish for my father's carriage to be damaged by an oaf of a groom."

"Carriages can be replaced, Miss Wadman, you can't. Your family will be very worried about you."

"They have no knowledge. I excused myself to bed with a headache. Only Mary knows as she negotiated with the groom for his cloak and hat and the promise of another shilling if he would remain out of sight for the day. He was happy to sleep in the barn and be paid for his lazing."

"Deviousness, thy name is woman."

"Fie, sir, to add to your sins you misquote the Bard."

"We call it paraphrasing."

"Whatever you call it, it lacks respect."

"Well, Miss Wadman, I can see there is no pleasing you tonight."

"Then you had best please yourself, sir. I have no intention of being pleased by such a man as yourself who's sole ambition in life appears to be to end it in as bloody a manner as is possible. You have resided in Imber scarce three days and you have gambled with your life three times. I do not wish to be associated with such disreputable adventurism."

"Then you won't have to worry any longer. Tomorrow I'll move to the inn. There are some ends to tie up with Captain Stewart after today's work. Then I'll be moving on to London."

"Not before time, sir. Not before time. But say nought of this night's work to anyone. You must pledge an oath."

"Must I?" Chris gave a deep sigh he couldn't see any reason not to. If Catherine wanted her escapade kept secret that was down to her. "Very well, Miss Wadman, if that's what you wish. I promise I won't say a word about your clandestine adventure."

Catherine gave him a sharp look but said nothing. They were nearing Imber and she drove the carriage straight to the stables where Matthew and a groom were waiting. She declined to let Chris help her down but allowed Matthew to carry her to the house where she slipped inside and hobbled to her room.

Matthew returned with a troubled look on his face. "How went the day, sir?"

"Fine, Matthew, just fine. We caught the highwaymen and Captain Stewart is hoping to round up some more in Tilshead in the morning. I'll be leaving too. Can you arrange for a room with the innkeeper?"

"Of course, sir, if that is your desire."

Chris shrugged. "It's as Miss Wadman desires. I think I've offended her."


Stewart arrived at the inn late the next morning as Chris was settling in to a basic room overlooking the courtyard. He called from the window and Stewart beckoned him down. He was in high good humour.

"By god, sir, we got them all, sir, every last scurvy knave. Thieves' kitchen tells barely half a tale."

"Well done, Captain. That must be a relief for you."

"Come, a tankard of cider to wash down the dust of the ride. There is more to tell."

Stewart settled himself in a window and gulped his cider before wiping his mouth on a lace cuff. He looked at Chris and beamed. "I have good news. The Justice of the Peace has awarded you the two-hundred guineas bounty. I could not claim any credit for the stratagem."

"That's very generous of you, Captain, but we must share it between us and the men."

Stewart nearly choked on his drink. "God's teeth, sir. Are you deranged? This isn't the navy to share a prize. Give them so much as a crown and they will be in their cups for a sennight."

"Is Serjeant Biggin trustworthy?"

"As much as any man I would suppose."

"Then I would propose to pay Biggin twenty guineas, one guinea for each man. He can keep the balance and pay out a little at a time. How much do you pay your soldiers?"

"They are on a shilling a day."

"So an extra day's pay per week for twenty-one weeks should make them all happy and keep them sober."

"Indeed, sir, you are full of unusual stratagems. I cannot say I fully agree but the naval precedent is made and I can see no reason to dissuade you from your course. However should it prove irksome I will call the payments to an end and retrieve what is left from Biggin."

Chris grinned and held out his hand. "Then we have a deal, Captain?"

Stewart laughed and took the proffered fist. "We do, sir, even should I be the laughing stock of the regiment."

"What about your share?"

"God's teeth, I have no need of the money. Take it, sir, you have earned it. Which brings another matter to mind. I have sent a despatch to Horse Guards commending your service. Sir George's son, Major Henry Wadman, is an Aide-de-Camp to His Royal Highness the Duke of York and has his Highness's ear. It may do you some good as you may be seeking a King's Commission."

"I'll be honest with you, Captain Stewart. I don't have enough money to buy a commission. Even with the remainder of the two-hundred guineas it would be only half what is needed.

"I came with what in my country was worth over four thousand pounds but here I've learned that they're worth just eleven pounds ten shillings. I can pay my way here at the inn but I must find a way to earn some cash."

Stewart frowned. "That may be problematical, it may not. But in the meantime, sir, you need some fresh attire. Tomorrow we will go to my tailor in Salisbury and have you measured for a new suit of clothes. You may spend some of your bounty to good effect. Thirty guineas will see you fitted out handsomely."

Wheels turned slowly in Imber. Chris was bored out of his mind. People treated him with deference but went out of their way to avoid speaking. He caught the occasional glimpse of Catherine but she seemed determined to avoid him too; although the mere sight of her lifted his spirits. He met Amelia and Mary one morning as he was walking the fields and passed a pleasant half hour in their company. Amelia was far more friendly than Catherine and Mary looked on him with big moon eyes, almost as if he were some kind of demi-god. Amelia teased her good-naturedly about it and made the poor girl blush bright crimson. Amelia sent some books to the Inn for him but they were not to his taste and he read only a few pages.

Doctor Hawking also took pity on him and invited him in for light refreshments one afternoon. It was apparent that Hawking wanted to pick his brains about the pain killing attributes of the Coca Tree and of first aid.

Hawking lit a long-stemmed clay pipe and Chris had to smile. "That's not good for your health, you know."

Hawking took the pipe from his mouth and frowned. "It is most beneficial, I believe, in calming a troubled soul."

Chris rubbed a finger in the soot in the chimney. "This is how your lungs will be affected."

"But that is the result of burning wood and coal, sir, not tobacco. See, he showed Chris the contents of his tobacco pouch, "it is clean and made from good leaf."

"It's a habit forming drug, Doctor."

"You say you have no medical training yet you profess knowledge of medicine and things medical. How is that possible, sir?"

"It's common knowledge where I'm from but I can easily prove that tobacco is habit forming."

"How so, sir?"

"Would you agree to a small experiment?"

"If it serves the cause of science."

"It's a simple idea but one you might find difficult."

"I am a man of medicine and, I like to think, a man of science. Speak on, sir, I am intrigued."

"Then put your pipe away for a month without touching it."

"That is merely a matter of self-will."

"And that's the experiment. Can your self-will override the call of the tobacco."

"Ha, sir. I see the way of it. I will take part in your experiment merely to prove you wrong. Stap me if you don't have the most outlandish ideas. But I like you, sir, yes indeed, your company is most invigorating."

Almost a week after Chris received his new clothes from the Salisbury tailor a messenger arrived from London with a despatch for Stewart. It wasn't long before he sent a runner to find Chris who was watching the blacksmith making rims for farm cart wheels.

"Major Henry Wadman is coming here to visit," Stewart said without preamble. "He wishes to meet with you, sir and to that end I am tasked with requesting of Sir George that he hold a supper party so that you both may meet with due privacy. I shall attend Sir George immediately. "You, sir, must look your best for the morrow. He will come on the Post coach at four hours past noon."

"Why would he want to see me?" Chris asked.

"That I cannot say. There are happenings that we cannot discuss here. Serious matters Lieutenant Chris-Lennox. Serious matters indeed."

# 12

Chris dressed carefully. He had bought Hessian boots to go with the breeches as the idea of stocking hosiery did not appeal. The linen shirt had ties at the neck instead of buttons and frilly lace cuffs. The double-breasted frock coat was the height of fashion the tailor said but Chris had the feeling that Beau Brummel, then a Lieutenant in the 10th Hussars, would not have approved of the fussiness of the cuffs and neckwear. He gave a mental tick of approval to his parents for their thorough schooling in history.

It was a smaller supper party than on the previous occasion. Neither the vicar nor the doctor were there, nor Charles Dean or his parents, although Anthony was present. Foxley was also notable by his absence. Chris had seen him around the camp from time to time with his arm in a sling. Foxley had avoided eye contact but had some modicum of revenge by demoting Biggin to the ranks instead of to corporal.

Sir George made him welcome and introduced him to his son, Henry, who bowed formally but sized Chris up like a buyer at a racehorse auction. Chris could see the family likeness to both Catherine and Amelia but Henry was older and more careworn.

Catherine was formal and icily polite but Amelia took pity on him and requested his arm as they went in to dine. "What ever has poor Catherine done," she said from behind her fan as he seated her. "She is not herself and walks like a puppy with a thorn in its pad."

"I noticed. It seems like a slight sprain."

"I cannot but help notice that your attire has greatly improved, Lieutenant."

"With Captain Stewart's help. He recommended his tailor to me."

"I see the captain and my brother are deep in conversation and they appear to be casting glances in this direction. I do believe the captain has more interest in you than he does in me."

"If I didn't know that they're discussing military matters I would say you are mistaken, Miss Wadman. You are a far more attractive picture."

"I do believe you are flirting with me, sir."

"And you're teasing me."

"You are far too serious and far too perspicacious and therefore no fun to tease. Fie on you, sir."

Chris laughed. "But *you* are still very pleasant company, Miss Wadman."

"Please do call me Amelia. Miss Wadman is so formal now that I feel we have become such firm friends. What is your Christian name and may I also address you by it?"

The question put Chris in a quandary. Catherine had assumed that his surname was hyphenated as it wasn't the fashion to give a forename. He could hardly call himself Chris Chris-Lennox, it would seem odd. Sir George was holding court at the head of the table and it gave him the idea. "My name's George."

Amelia beamed. "As my dear papa. Such a worthy name, George."

"Amelia, you are too forward," Catherine hissed from across the table.

"Not at all, *Miss Wadman*," Chris said. "Amelia is charming company and whose friendship I cherish. She has made me feel very welcome and has my gratitude."

"How is your wound, sir? I wondered whether it might keep you from this soirée."

"It's healing nicely, thank you for asking, and nothing would keep me from such warm company."

"I thought perhaps your adventuresome nature may have taken you elsewhere."

Chris bowed, a slight incline of his head. "There's still time, Miss Wadman."

Lady Isobel, ever the vigilant hostess, had noticed the sudden drop in temperature in the frosty exchange. "Let us not dwell on future partings, let us rejoice in Henry's return to Imber, albeit for too short a stay."

"Of necessity, mama," Henry said. "I needs be back at Horse Guards within a sennight. His Royal Highness commands it."

"Then let us eat and make merry whilst we have your dear company," Lady Isobel said.

After the women had withdrawn the men pulled chairs together at the head of the table.

"Major Wadman brings some grave news, I fear," Stewart said.

"Indeed, Captain, the gravest. I have intelligence from the Indies. The 62nd has been decimated by yellow fever and has ceased to function as a regiment. Those that survive have been despatched to the aid of other regiments. This is sore news indeed for the Wiltshires. Twice in living memory disaster has befallen them what with Burgoyne's surrender at Saratoga with the loss of so many fine officers.

"Captain Stewart, by command of his Royal Highness the Duke of York, you will command the 62nd until such time as it pleases him. You are to be promoted to brevet Lieutenant-colonel once again, with immediate effect. Here is your warrant, sir." Henry handed Stewart a heavy parchment.

Stewart stood to take it with a bow. "I am greatly honoured that his Royal Highness should consider me worthy of the rank."

"Oh, do sit down, sir," Henry said. "His Royal Highness well knows of your capabilities. You are the man to begin the work of refurnishing and training a second battalion of the regiment until such times as the duke sees fit to repost you."

"What of the survivors in the Indies?"

"They will be transported back by ship in time."

"In time for what?" Chris asked.

Henry speared him with a hard look. "You, sir, are the gentleman who devises strategems, are you not. I have read the despatch from Captain Stewart and circulated it around Horse Guards. It has raised much interest ... and raised eyebrows. Not all approve of our soldiers lolling in the dirt."

"The art of concealment, Major Wadman, is an important facet in modern warfare."

"Indeed, sir. Are you now to write the book on military tactics?"

Chris smiled. "Perhaps, with time, these ideas will become accepted."

Henry laughed. "In a duck's arse, sir. The generals are aghast at the very notion. Massed ranks and volley fire are the way the British fight, upright and man to man, not crawling on their bellies like vipers."

"Snakes can prove deadly, Major."

"That may be so, sir. It is not something to which his Royal Highness would add his public support. The mere notion would offend any decent officer."

"But privately?" Stewart asked.

"This must not go beyond this room. I must swear each of you to secrecy. Have I your word, gentlemen?" He faced each man in turn and received nods of assent. "Then I can reveal that his Royal Highness wishes to form an experimental detachment, one that can live, work and, if necessary, fight, from concealment.

"Imber is ideally located as a place such a formation can be raised and kept without undue notice amongst the wider nation. The populace are already aware of the stratagem so will raise not an eyebrow if such tactics are continued here."

"Who will command such a formation?" Stewart said. "I have no one officer in the regiment with the knowledge or necessary skill."

Henry pulled another parchment from his despatch case. "This is a warrant from his Royal Highness to commission any such officer whom I see fit. The name is left blank but the authority has been invested in me to complete the warrant. His Royal Highness has already signed the parchment."

"Then it must be Lieutenant Chris-Lennox," Anthony said. "He is the one, the only one, who understands such concepts."

"Indeed," Sir George added, "his stratagem rid us of the scourge of the highwaymen and footpads. There is none better qualified."

Chris gave a slow nod. "I can see where this is heading. I can see where this has been heading for some time. Major Wadman, it would be my duty to accept such a commission but I don't have the money to pay for one."

"Pah, sir. This is in His Royal Highness's gift. All he asks in return is your loyalty and your success in the venture."

"I've already sworn an oath of allegiance to the Crown, my loyalty is not in doubt. My success, however, may depend on other factors."

"Such as, sir?" Henry said.

"I get to choose the men."

"Granted," Henry said.

"I also get to choose the weapons."

"Surely the weapons choose themselves. There's no finer musket than the Brown Bess."

"Have you heard of the Baker Rifle?"

Henry frowned. "Of course but it is hellish difficult to reload and expensive to buy."

"I want thirty."

"God's teeth, sir, I hope you know what you're about."

"Do I have a deal?"

"Very well, sir. Is there any other demand?"

"It seems to me that this detachment will be off the record. I'll need money to buy food and equipment and to pay the men. How will this be financed?"

"Through the 62nd. Provision will be made for additional costings under the guise of rebuilding the regiment. But be warned, sir, that there is not a bottomless pit of money. If more cash is needed you will raise it yourself through whatever means you may this side of the law," Henry said.

"To whom do I report?"

Henry nodded at Stewart. "To Lieutenant-colonel Stewart in the first instance, who will pass the despatches directly to me. The two companies of the 62nd here and at Tilshead will be withdrawn to Salisbury leaving only those men that you choose from the 62nd. Others will be sent from good regiments should you request more personnel."

"I'll need sixty men and two officers. They need to be young men. All those who succeeded in ambushing the highwaymen would be ideal as a start and I like the look of young Ensign Willoughby. I will trust Colonel Stewart's judgement on the other officer."

"All granted," Henry said. "Will you now sign, sir?" He called Matthew and demanded a quill and ink which appeared quickly. "I will fill in your name. I understand it is George Chris-Lennox."

"I would prefer simply George Lennox."

"As you wish, Captain George Lennox and to any other such rank as His Majesty may, from time to time hereafter be pleased to promote or appoint you." Henry painstakingly drew the characters and handed it to Chris to counter-sign. He sanded the parchment and rolled it. Then he did the same with a second which Chris was also asked to counter-sign. This one was handed to Chris with a smile of satisfaction. "There we have it. You are now commissioned in His Majesty's army. May God help you."

"There is one thing I haven't asked. Why does his Royal Highness need such a clandestine detachment?"

"Your orders will be issued in due course, sir. Ensure your training is carried out diligently for your service will be both dangerous and arduous."

# 13

In the privacy of his room the next morning, Chris wrote out a 21st century training programme. He wrote it with a ballpoint as the thought of labouring with quill and ink made him cringe. He would find a way to explain the script should anyone query the fine lines.

After reading it through it came home to him how much of a task he had taken on. The soldiers outside were nowhere near as fit as his regular army men. They were wiry and strong but most smoked and drank to excess and probably had not moved faster than a quick march since childhood. Fitness would be an issue that would not prove very popular.

The training itself would not be difficult. Most of the men he had selected, and would select when the cadres from other regiments arrived, would be countrymen used to digging, and reformed poachers who were proficient at avoiding gamekeepers. He had found that his original twenty men had taken to that part with gusto and humour. Some others may not be so keen to take off their red coats but he would deal with that problem when it arose.

The thirty Baker Rifles were a step into the unknown. He knew their history, they were far more accurate than the Brown Bess but they were difficult to reload, taking almost twice the time that it took to reload a musket, due to ramming a ball down the tight rifled barrel. The black powder used as propellant coked up the barrels. The musket users got around this by using a slightly smaller ball in the smooth-bore barrels but the rifles had to have balls that fitted the rifling. An intractable problem that could only be overcome by developing a tactic to protect the riflemen. And first he had to find the men with the shooting skills to use them.

There was a polite tap on the door. Chris put away the ballpoint but kept the notepad open on the table. "Yes, who is it?"

"Ensign Willoughby, sir. I have been ordered by Colonel Stewart to report to you for instruction."

"Come in Willoughby and pull up a chair."

Willoughby came in with his tricorn under his arm and knuckled his forehead.

"Sit, Willoughby. You don't have to salute me, not in private, only on parade or in front of the men. You must also never salute, or receive a salute in the field in the face of the enemy. That will mark you as a target."

Willoughby sat stiffly at attention, his boyish face creased in a frown. "Targeting officers? Surely that would be ungentlemanly."

"Not everyone learned their manners on the playing fields of Eton. War isn't a game. The kind of warfare we will be training for will be harsh, brutal, professional and direct. You'd better steel yourself for it."

"I will do my duty, sir."

"Of that I'm sure, otherwise I wouldn't have asked for you to be one of my platoon commanders."

"*Platoon,* sir?"

"Yes, a formation of thirty men, one officer and one serjeant. We will split each platoon into two sections one with sixteen muskets and the other with fourteen Baker Rifles."

"I do not understand, sir."

"You will. Here." Chris tore the page from his notebook and handed it over. "That is a training schedule. Can you read it?"

"In truth I cannot. The spelling and letterforms are quite beyond me."

"In that case find someone who can write and send them to me. I'll dictate to them and they can make several copies so that we'll all be singing from the same hymn sheet."

"A church parade then?"

"It's a colloquialism, Willoughby. Not meant to be taken literally. I can see I'm going to have to watch what I say in future.

"Now, is Colonel Stewart around?"

"He is preparing to strike camp but he is still at Imber the last I knew of it."

"Good. I need to consult him. When you leave, Willoughby, call on the seamstress and the blacksmith. I want to see them both this afternoon."

Stewart was sitting astride his horse watching the first of the bell tents being struck.

"Leave me six of those tents, Colonel, I'll need them," Chris said.

"As you say. Is there anything more?"

Chris nodded. "Can you find some sailcloth?"

"The 62nd once served as marines, you may have noticed some of the men still wear the tarred pigtail, and I have contacts in Portsmouth from whom I may enquire. The navy guards its sails with a ferocity akin to that of a tiger with its cubs but I will see what can be done."

"Thank you, sir. There is something else."

Stewart raised his eyebrows. "Why am I not surprised?"

"I need sixty new uniforms; waistcoats, shirts and breeches, plus several bolts of green serge."

"The devil you do, sir." Stewart pulled a face. "The quartermaster will be most inconvenienced to be sure."

"As soon as possible ..."

"Your demands grow more outrageous by the minute," Stewart said but laughed. "Very well, I shall send a despatch to Salisbury this very day.

"Now, sir, I have some intelligence for *you*. Despatches were sent to the Officers Commanding the 49th, 55th, 69th and 71st regiments requesting one corporal and nine good men from each to come here by all possible speed. The men were requested to be those adjudged able to receive new instruction and be able to act upon it. I daresay those officers may see fit to rid themselves of their troublemakers and near-do-wells."

"Sometimes they make the best soldiers," Chris said.

"Then I wish you good fortune. I will be marching the company to Tilshead this day and thence to Salisbury on the morrow. I needs make my goodbyes to the Wadmans."

"Before you go, have you had any thoughts about my second officer?"

"Indeed I have not. Foxley would not suit your needs, besides he is still hors de combat and simmering like a pot on the trivet. I myself have need of Ensign Blake. There may be an officer with the Tilshead company whom I could detach but I shall not know for certain until I am there to assess them."

"I need a volunteer, someone with an open mind."

"Therein lies a dilemma. I shall do what I can."

"That's good enough for me," Chris said.

"Would you care to accompany me to the Wadmans? It is time for morning chocolate. I do believe in preparation for Miss Catherine's forthcoming nuptials. I have heard it said that it has a deal of potency to aid a newlywed woman to conceive."

"An old wives' tale, Colonel. Chocolate has a way of adding poundage, a moment on the lips but a lifetime on the hips."

Stewart laughed. "The devil you say. Doctor Hawking was remarking on your assessment as to his pipe smoking. Now it seems you would question another staple of medical belief. Confound it, sir, are you to undermine every facet of it?"

"Only those things I know for certain. Where I'm from it's proven fact that tobacco is addictive and injurious to health and chocolate is good to eat or drink but also fattening."

"You are debunking two of life's great pleasures. Next you will be telling me that cider or ale will do me ill."

"Taking most things in moderation, Colonel, will do you little harm."

"I am relieved you may think so. Now come with me to Imber Court before I lose the will."

Stewart dismounted and handed the reins to his groom. They walked the short distance to the house and were shown into the drawing room where Lady Isobel and the two daughters were seated. They went through the greeting ritual bowing and curtseying before they were invited to sit on the opposite side of the room.

"I understand we will be losing your company, Colonel Stewart," Lady Isobel said.

"Indeed, milady. I have recently informed Captain Lennox of my departure to Tilshead this day."

"So soon?" Amelia said. "There will be no time to dine you out."

"Needs must Miss Amelia. The army is a hard taskmaster."

"And what of you, *Captain* Lennox? Will you also be leaving?" Catherine said.

"I'm afraid I'll have to disappoint you, Miss Wadman. I'll be staying for a while longer."

"Oh what fun," Amelia said, "we shall enjoy your company, shan't we, mama?"

"Most certainly. Captain Lennox will always be welcome in this house."

"You're very kind, Lady Isobel, but my duties will keep me busy and I'll have little time for socialising."

"*Such* a pity," Catherine said.

Amelia gave her sister a sly smile. "Indeed it is a pity but we shall make it our duty that you do not languish without entertainment for too long, Captain. You must be allowed some recreation."

"Speaking of recreation," Chris said before Catherine could respond, "I've noticed that Miss Catherine has quite an artistic talent with watercolours. Could I ask a favour?"

Catherine raised an eyebrow. "And pray what might that be, sir?"

"I need to design a new type of uniform for my men. If I could describe it could you draw it for me so that I can show it to the tailors?"

"Oh, do say yes, Catherine," Amelia said. "It will give you something to occupy yourself. You have been moping so dreadfully."

"I have not been moping. I have much on my mind with the forthcoming nuptials."

"Has the day been set?" Stewart asked.

"We are thinking perhaps October when the harvest has been fully gathered. It will be a double celebration," Lady Isobel said. "We will be sure to send you an invitation, Colonel."

"I shall be honoured to attend, my duties allowing. Now I must offer my goodbyes, there is much to oversee."

Stewart rose and bowed and Chris stood with him. Lady Isobel took Stewart's arm to escort him out and Amelia with an impish grin took the other leaving Chris and Catherine alone.

He took a few paces towards her but stopped short. "Would you be so kind?"

"I daresay I could find the time, Captain, if I must."

"Oh, please, Miss Wadman, can we call a truce to this animosity? I don't know what I've done to offend you but whatever it is, I apologise unreservedly. I would like us to be friends again."

"Being friends again implies we were friends at all. You have not offended me, Captain but if I am being truthful, I find your presence discomforting."

"Then I'll go and not bother you further."

"No, stay. I must apologise in my turn. I should not have been so indiscreet as to say that which I just did. I will take your instruction as to the sketch."

"That's good of you." Chris advanced a couple of paces and the nearer he got the more tension he felt. The pins and needles effect came back to his arm, a gentle fizzing that wasn't painful but was disconcerting as it went across his chest and up his neck. He had noticed that the blue tracery on his arm hadn't faded. He had not needed to shave neither had his hair nor nails grown in the time he had been in Imber. A peculiar situation which he hadn't had time to analyse.

He could see Catherine tense up at his approach and he stopped. "I would like the jacket to be short without tails and dark green in colour. There should be black frogging on the breast and black pantaloons. Black shakos for headgear and the gaiters should also be black."

"My, my, sir, you do paint a dull and uninteresting picture. Is there to be no colour other than green?"

"Could you do that for me this morning? I have a meeting with the seamstress this afternoon and I would like to show her the picture."

Catherine gave an affected sigh. "Has your life always been such as this whirligig of time. You scarce seem to breathe between one happenstance and another."

"Life in the fast lane; it always has been for me."

"Sometimes I struggle to take your meaning, sir. What is a fast lane?"

"It's a common adage where I'm from. It means there is little rest between *happenstances*."

"Indeed, sir. That is apparent with you. But, as you wish, I will have the drawing prepared by noon if you would care to call back."

Chris nodded, bowed and backed away. Catherine didn't look at him as he left. He had the impression that she was fighting to keep her composure but it was just a fleeting impression, which could easily have been relief at his leaving.

Good as her word Catherine had a passable sketch ready when he called to collect it that afternoon. Mary met him in the hall and handed it to him, saying that Miss Catherine was indisposed. He wasn't surprised but asked Mary to wish her well.

The seamstress and blacksmith were waiting near the remaining bell tents; Stewart and the company having already decamped to Tilshead.

Chris showed the sketch to the woman. "I have sixty uniforms arriving from Salisbury soon. I want all the pantaloons and waistcoats dyed black. There will also be sailcloth coming from Portsmouth that also needs to be dyed black. Can you do that?"

The woman looked dumbstruck but she nodded. "I would need have two large coppers, sir."

"I can get those. Mr Smith, I have a special assignment for you. I would like you to fashion wheel rim iron about the length of your arm from the wrist to the elbow with a slight curvature and a small hole at either end. I will need two hundred of them and I need them before the summer is out."

"It will mean working day and night, sir, but I'm sure I can, sir. The cost will be eight pence per strip, better than eight guineas all told."

"The regiment will bear the cost or I will. Make a start as soon as you can."

"May I ask why you require them, sir?"

"You may not ask, Mr Smith, but I'm sure you will find out soon enough."

# 14

Days grew into weeks and passed quickly. Forty men from the other regiments had arrived and were soon engaged in the tough training regime that Chris had instituted. They did not like it one bit and through a gradual weeding out process Chris ended up with fifty better trained and fitter men who could march 140 paces to the minute for an hour without pause.

The Baker Rifles arrived one afternoon and he and Biggin, reinstated to serjeant, pulled them from their crates. They were .75 calibre early models based on the German Jager Rifle design.

"My, these are real beauties, beggin' your pardon, sir," Biggin said as he turned a rifle over in his hands.

"It's the way warfare will be going. The Kentucky Long Rifle was instrumental in defeating our forces in America. Come on, let's take two into the field for a little experiment. Pick up one of those canvas vests with the iron facings the seamstress made."

"I've been wonderin' 'bout those, sir. What they be for and all."

"You're about to find out. Get two men to make up a scarecrow and put the vest on it. As if it's a real man."

Puzzlement crossed Biggin's face. "Sir?"

"You've been used to shooting at a sheet spread wide for volley fire. With these rifles you can aim at a single man and hit him. My compliments to Ensign Willoughby and ask him to parade the detachment."

"Very good, sir," Biggin said and saluted.

Chris watched him go with a half smile on his face. Biggin was turning into a very able platoon serjeant.

The lack of a second officer to help Willoughby was troubling him. He had received a message from Stewart that he needed all the officers he had to rebuild the regiment after its decimation in the Americas. Stewart was putting out feelers to other regiments but so far had found no volunteers. It seemed the word had got around about Chris's peculiar ideas of uniform and training which went against their code of honour and their dress sense. Chris knew it would be an uphill battle but one he hoped to win in the end.

He was concerned about the leak of information. He surmised the men he had sent back had talked like gossiping fishwives but he consoled himself with the thought that they had no idea of what the end result was going to be.

Biggin came back and saluted. "The scarecrow be ready as ordered, sir."

Chris nodded and took two of the rifles, powder and ball out to the field. The men had positioned the scarecrow, complete with turnip head just a few paces into the field. He shook his head. "Take the scarecrow back a further hundred paces."

"That be a hundred and twenty paces, sir."

"That's right."

"Will you be shooting at 'im, sir?"

"Yes." Chris waited for the men to return then loaded the rifle, primed it, checked the flint and pulled back the hammer. The rifle weighed just shy of nine pounds but was barrel heavy. He adjusted his stance and took aim.

Biggin was dubious. "Mighty long way off ee be, sir, beggin' your pardon, sir."

Chris gave him a sideways grin, steadied himself and squeezed the rigger. Ninety metres away the turnip head exploded.

Biggin's jaw dropped.

"Replace the head. In case you think it was an accident, I'm going to do it again."

He picked up the second rifle as the two soldiers tasked with repairing the scarecrow scurried back.

The second shot was as spectacular as the first and drew a ripple of awestruck murmurs.

"That's what these rifles can do at twice the distance with a good rifleman."

"I never seen the like of it," Biggin said.

"Get used to it. I want a butts set up at the bottom of the field and everyone in the detachment will try their luck. Now where's Ensign Willoughby got to with the men?"

"They be a-comin', sir."

As he spoke, Willoughby led the detachment in a quick march around the bell tents and into the field. Chris had one of the soldiers reload the rifles and watched as he struggled with the ramrod. It took him almost a minute to reload just one.

With the turnip replaced Chris did the same demonstration and hit the scarecrow's head for the third time. Then he went for the piece de resistance.

"Many of you have been wondering about the vests the blacksmith and the seamstress have been making. The scarecrow is wearing one of them. You all saw just what this rifle could do to a head. Now watch what it can do to an iron clad vest."

Chris aimed at the scarecrow's chest and fired. The scarecrow fell back into the grass. Not so amazing for the soldiers, many had seen their muskets have the same effect on men.

Chris signalled for Biggin's two soldiers to retrieve the dummy. They carried it back and placed it at Chris's feet. He bent down and prised a lead ball from where it had lodged between the blacksmith's iron bars.

"This is my version of armour for your protection. The iron bars are less than a musket ball width apart, three on either side of the chest. It's not fool-proof but, as you can see, it will stop musket balls from penetrating. Not everyone will have them. Men carrying muskets will have priority. The men whom I select as riflemen will only wear them when I deem it necessary. Any questions?"

Chris looked around the faces. There was much scratching of heads but no one spoke.

"Very well. I want work to start on the butts tomorrow. Mr Willoughby's platoon will be the first to try the rifles. Then the platoon led by Serjeant Biggin. I want a list made of every man who can hit a scarecrow at a hundred and fifty paces.

Biggin and a second serjeant called Pocock marched the men away leaving Chris with a puzzled Willoughby.

"You cannot expect the men to hit such a target at such a distance, surely," Willoughby said.

"Not only do I expect it but I intend to increase the distance out to two-hundred paces once they're used to handling the rifles. The men who can master that distance will be my riflemen and will receive additional training."

"I am in awe, sir, of your expectations."

"Come on, Willoughby. Hasn't everything I've said come true? We are slowly turning out the finest and fittest soldiers in the British army."

"I cannot gainsay that, sir. This enforced isolation however is also having an effect on the men. Some wish to be reunited with their women."

"Very well. Arrange for carts and give everyone a weekend off. But impress on them the need for secrecy. I don't want them talking about what we do here, is that understood?"

"I understand your order but not the reason for it."

"Opsec, Willoughby, operational security. What we are doing here is vitally important to any future war effort and I don't want news of it leaking out to the French. They may have spies in the inns." Willoughby did not know of the orders he had received from Horse Guards by despatch rider with instructions to keep them confidential.

Still non-plussed but suitably impressed Willoughby made his way back to the lines to pass the order.

Giving the men some time off was good for morale. Chris had noticed a dropping off in performance in recent days and had guessed at the reason. You could only flog willing horses so much.

Discipline in this man's army was strict. Floggings for even minor offences were commonplace along with other punishments such as standing on a tent peg in bare feet for hours. Men were hanged for striking a senior officer and some of the NCOs played on it. Chris had no stomach for it and had gradually instituted a more humane system which doled out punishments which were less physically abusive but still kept discipline in check. There was a danger he would appear weak but having men fully fit was more important.

He went back to his quarters at The Bell to prepare for a planned evening supper with Doctor Hawking. The chambermaid brought hot water for him to wash. He still had no need to shave and it was beginning to bother him. It was as if the lightning strike had damaged his hormones.

Hawking welcomed him with a warning look and he was surprised to see Anthony Dean there.

"Mr Dean, what a pleasure. I thought the doctor and I were going to be dining alone."

"When the doctor mentioned you would be dining together I begged an invitation but I shall not be staying. There is something of importance I wish to discuss, with your permission."

"That sounds very mysterious."

"I have been in correspondence with Colonel Stewart. He is most exercised that he is not able to locate a suitable officer for your detachment."

"Go on …"

"This month I rode to London with the post and purchased a Lieutenant's commission in the 62$^{nd}$."

"With what end in mind?" Chris asked but he already had a terrible inkling.

"That, with Colonel Stewart's permission, I may serve with you,"

"But you're just about to get married, man."

"I shall discuss it with Miss Wadman. I am sure she will agree …"

"Then I'm sure you don't know your future wife's mind very well." Chris snapped.

"… she will agree to bring forward the nuptials to the end of August. The harvest is proceeding ahead of time and will be completely taken in given that the good weather continues."

"My apologies, sir. I don't wish to disparage your relationship with Miss Wadman but I am concerned that you are letting yourself in for more than you know. You've had no military training, it will take months to bring you up to standard."

"I shall be a very assiduous student."

Chris shook his head. "You really don't understand. I don't have the time to train you. I have received orders to strike camp by the first week of September. The detachment will be posted to a destination far away from here."

"Then what will be, will be. It is a matter of honour, sir. You saved Miss Wadman's life and I am indebted to you."

"That debt has already been repaid," Chris said. It slipped out and he regretted the mistake. He could not break Catherine's confidence. She had saved his life in turn and wanted her bravery kept secret.

"How so, sir? Is a life so easily cast off."

"It has been repaid by your kindness and that of the Wadmans. I don't need any further repayment than having such good friends."

"My honour cannot accept such a paltry return, sir." Anthony said and bowed. "I am at your service whether you wish it or not."

Chris was beaten and he knew it. There was no point in fighting a losing battle. "Very well, Lieutenant Dean. Be on parade at sunrise tomorrow for your instruction."

# 15

Chris and the doctor had become good friends. He was waiting in his small parlour with his pipe in his hand, his feet on the firedogs and his eyes half-closed.

"I could not but help overhearing you conversation with young Anthony Dean."

"You know about my correspondence with Horse Guards, doctor, having written my despatches for me."

"I know of the despatches you dictate but not of those that you write with that small stick and roll into those I scratch."

"Ah! You know about that too. There's not much that goes on around here that isn't common knowledge in minutes. What do you make of it?"

"That there are intrigues afoot that you do not wish others to know of."

"You'll have to forgive the secrecy on my part, doctor. I picked up some intelligence during my travels and passed it on to Major Wadman. It has matched news from France which sounds ominous. Horse Guards is determined to move much more quickly than we anticipated."

"So you will be leaving us at September time."

"Yes before the autumn gales set in. We will be sailing to Portugal from Portsmouth."

Hawking pulled a face. "Portugal? The devil you say. Now I see why you were so displeased at Mr Dean's machinations."

"God help him. His heart's in the right place but he hasn't a clue about military life."

Hawking shrugged. "He appears to be under Colonel Stewart's orders. He no longer has any say in the matter."

"That's why I gave in with the best grace I could. I've been out-manoeuvred."

"But still you are troubled, my friend," Hawking said.

"I have an awful feeling that Miss Catherine Wadman will assume I instigated the ploy. We've only just broken off hostilities over another matter."

Hawking gave a sage smile. "I know of Miss Catherine's ways. I have not been the Wadman's family doctor for twenty years and more without learning of them. I delivered her bawling into the world, a lusty infant with a mind of its own."

"Not much change there then," Chris murmured then changed the subject. "I see you're back with your pipe, doctor and it's less than a month."

Hawking laughed. "As in so many matters you have proven to be correct. I bow to your superior intellect. Twas the first week that the longing took me but I fought it until this past weekend when there was a case of suspected typhoid in Tilshead. A false alarum as it happened, but scare enough for me to need tobacco to calm me.

"Tobacco is addictive you say. An interesting theorem and one that I'm bound to say appears to have some truth to the matter. Come we'll continue to discuss things medical and military over a delicious spatch cock prepared just this eventide."

"Typhoid is usually caused by polluted water supplies. Best you should know if it does happen."

"Indeed, a fount of all knowledge. Come, sir, before you ruin my appetite."

"I'm much more of a military man than a medic, doctor but I'll be delighted to discuss both. I could make a start on the amount of calories you propose to consume."

"I've no idea what you are about but I daresay it will be to debunk another of life's small pleasures."

Chris called on Catherine the next day. From her demeanour he knew that Anthony had broken his news.

Amelia gave him an uncertain smile. "So good of you to call, Captain. Will you sit?"

"No, thank you, Miss Amelia. I have something to say to Miss Catherine."

Amelia turned to Catherine. "Do you wish me to stay, dearest?"

"No, Amelia, you may leave. I trust that Captain Lennox is an honourable man."

"Very well, I shall leave you in peace but I shall be outside the door."

Amelia left with a swirl of satin and taffeta skirts. She gave Chris a small smile as she passed and nodded. He waited until the door was closed.

"It seems that Mr Dean has given you his news."

"Indeed, sir. Have you come to rub salt in my wound?"

Chris was getting the familiar tingling that grew the closer he got to Catherine. He tried to shake off the feeling but it persisted.

"I've come to assure you it was none of my doing, Miss Wadman. I tried to dissuade Mr Dean from his venture but it was too late, the die had already been cast, his commission obtained and his orders given. There was nothing I could do."

"Be at ease, Captain. Mr Dean did fully explain his motives and although I do not agree, I must abide by them. He feels he owes you a debt that can only be repaid by his serving alongside you in whatever adventure you may embark upon."

"I told him that the debt was repaid in full but couldn't break your confidence. It was still too late and nothing could have changed the outcome."

For the first time Catherine looked at him and he could see tears gathering at the corners of her eyes. He felt the sudden urge to put an arm around her but stopped himself.

Catherine stood and took a pace towards him. The tingling at the back of his neck went into overdrive and it was all he could do to stop himself from either taking a pace back or sweeping her up in his arms. He must have been radiating something as her eyelids fluttered and she held up a small hand as if to push him away.

She swallowed. "Captain Lennox, I have a favour to ask of you."

He swallowed in turn. This really was ridiculous. It was as if she was a magnet and him the iron filings. He had never before felt so drawn to another person. "You only have to ask," he finally managed to say.

"Will you do your best to protect Anthony? He is very dear to me and I would loathe to lose him so soon after we are wed."

"Miss Catherine you know I'll do whatever I can to keep him safe but I can make no promises. War is an ugly business and the fortunes of it smile on very few."

"You are cold comfort, sir but I must thank you for your honesty. I truly believe you will do your best. That is all I can ask."

"I would rather *he* came back than me."

"I would rather you *both* came back safe and whole, Captain. That is my dearest wish."

"Then you know I'll do everything I can to make that wish come true."

"I do, Captain."

She put out a hand to him but he did not trust himself to take it. He bowed and turned on his heel. He did not see the look of pain that crossed Catherine's face.

Catherine looked downcast and Amelia took her hand. "What ails you, dear?"

"Tis nothing."

"Tis something. Of that I am more than certain."

Catherine gave her a wan smile. "I have a conflict, dear Amelia. One that I shudder to even think on."

"A conflict?" Amelia gave a little laugh and fluttered her fan. "Oh my, a conflict indeed."

"You must not mock me, dear Amelia, for I am a lost soul, one who does not know whether she is ruled by her head or her heart."

"Would a handsome young officer be at the bottom of this conflict? One cannot but help notice your uncustomary lack of witty repartee when we are in his presence."

"Oh, dearest Amelia, am I so transparent? I would not wish to hurt the feelings of my betrothed. Anthony is such a kind man, and I am as devoted to him as to a brother. I will not do him an injustice, or sully my reputation in his eyes. But you are right. When Captain Lennox is in the room I can scarce draw breath."

"Hence the conflict betwixt your head and your heart. Fear not, tis only I, who know you so well, who can discern the pinking of your cheeks. Catherine, dear, how can this be that you are become so infatuated?"

"In all honesty I do not know. Something draws me to him. Perhaps it is the newness, the lure of the unknown and exotic. Yes, he did save me from the highwaymen and quite likely a fate worse than death. He can be also uncouth in many ways, his manners sorely lacking, and his dancing worse than a carthorse hitched to a haywain. But, Amelia, when he is not there he fills my thoughts. I long to see him, sometimes just the merest glance will suffice to still my need. I trouble myself to seek out his whereabouts just so that I might cast my eyes upon him. To speak with him I utter the most dreadful platitudes even when I am not being fully saucy. I fear I must distance us, durst my feelings overcome me. He must think me unbearably rude."

"Surely not. I do believe the gallant captain has a great regard for you."

Catherine raised her hand to her sister's shoulder. "Do you truly think so?"

"He will not speak of it, Catherine. He may be lacking in some respects but he is as gallant as any gentleman. He would not wish to cast any shadow on your reputation."

"He is right, if that is his mind," Catherine said. "His arrival has given me cause to study my thoughts and my emotions and I conclude that despite occasional dalliances in Salisbury and London, in this small village my mind was contained and restrained to its inhabitants. Now I grow more acutely aware of that which lies without the bounds of Imber and can know how narrow my ambitions were become. My love for Anthony I now know to be affection and respect due to our mutual upbringing and not that love which makes the heart race. In spite of all, I would not break my promise to Anthony should it break my heart."

Amelia put her hand over Catherine's. "For myself I am happy with my lot and very fond of Charles. I would that for your happiness you should marry for love but what is then to be done for you, dearest sister?"

"What *can* be done? Perhaps I am being childishly romantic. I shall endeavour to suppress my feelings and hope that it is mere infatuation which will wither with time. Until then I shall bear it the best I can. No word of this must be mentioned to Captain Lennox. I would rather he stay in ignorance of it than feel obliged to compromise his honour."

Chris felt dreadful. He had come so close to alienating the woman he now knew he loved, crazy as it seemed. Even if he was back in his own time he'd baulk at making a move on another man's fiancée, especially a man who was a friend. Here, in this time and place, it was unthinkable. He was a stranger with little in common with the people who currently inhabited his world.

Not for the first time he cursed his misfortune at being in the middle of Stonehenge in a lightning storm. Even so, he was beginning to get the feeling that it was all pre-ordained. Things were falling into place like the colours on a well-used Rubik's Cube. History was being made; a history that he'd read about, some of the knowledge of which he had passed on to Henry Wadman. A history that he, Chris Lennox, was making for real.

He wasn't sure how he would cope in future. He was unsure how he would cope with the wedding when it came. Watching the woman you love marrying another man wasn't going to be easy yet it was something he couldn't possibly avoid and had no control over. In the meantime, he hoped throwing himself into work would help to keep his feelings suppressed.

# 16

All the green coats had come from the tailors in Salisbury which had made Chris's civilian suit. He paraded the men and officers for fittings with the local seamstress making adjustments to the serge. The work was done to Catherine's sketch and a very good job had been made of the design. To Chris's eye, the officers' tunics looked similar to that of Russian Hussars except the frogging was black cord and not gold braid. The men's jackets were longer and plainer and cut to button over the bulletproof canvas vests. The black and green made a dull showing with the heavy black leather buckled boots but Chris was pleased with the result.

The men were now divided into two platoons; one with Anthony Dean at its head and the experienced Serjeant Pocock as second in command, the other with Ensign Willoughby and Serjeant Biggin. There was a section of fourteen riflemen in each platoon, those who had passed his exacting standards of marksmanship. The rest were armed with the tried and trusted Brown Bess musket. He had encouraged a certain amount of rivalry between the two platoons and this had speeded up the training programme but got out of hand on two occasions when over-enthusiasm nearly came to blows. Overall, Chris was proud of his detachment; they were ready.

It was now nearing the end of August. Catherine and Anthony's wedding was scheduled for the next Sunday, the banns having been read on the previous three weeks, and the detachment was due to strike camp the following Monday for the march to Portsmouth, a distance of nearly sixty miles which would take three days with the equipment they would carry with them. There would be no animals to help carry the loads and the officers would march on foot with the men.

There was comradeship but as yet no esprit de corps. It was Chris's job to develop it.

He stood the company at ease and took a rifle from the nearest rifleman. He held it above his head so that they could all see it. "Men, the time is coming when we will have to leave here and go to war. We don't yet know what we will be facing but we do know that you are all ready to face whatever comes your way with skill and courage. These," he jerked the rifle upwards, "will be our colours. The enemy must not be allowed to take a single one. I know you will all do your duty to protect them and do it bravely. We are the Rifles, the rifles are ours, and the enemy shall not have them. What do you say?"

"*The Rifles, the Rifles!*" The chant went up and Chris could see the fervour in the men's eyes. He had a cynical thought that it could also be too much rum in their grog, the quartermaster corporal was known to have a heavy hand after a hard week.

"Mr Dean, be so kind as to dismiss the men for weekend leave. Everyone to be back at Imber by dusk on Sunday or they will have to answer to me. And remind them they are to speak to no one of what we do here and to wear the red coats they came with."

"Three cheers for Captain Lennox," Biggin shouted. Three rousing cheers he got. The men were pumped, full of adrenaline. They were going to fight and maybe die but it was for their King, their country and for their detachment … the Rifles.

Chris called his two junior officers to his room at The Bell. He had a recently delivered despatch in his hand.

"Our orders, gentlemen. I've ordered some brandies from the landlord, you may need them."

There was a knock at the door. Willoughby opened it, took the mugs from the chambermaid and handed them round. "Not good news, I surmise, sir."

"Depends on your point of view, Mr Willoughby. I don't doubt that word has leaked out that we are being sent to Portugal and you already know this. What you don't know is that Bonaparte has taken power in France and is putting pressure on the Portuguese who have a treaty with Great Britain. The Portuguese are in a bad way without a viable head of government. Their Queen is considered too unwell and her son, Prince John, is reluctant to accept the regency. There will be another war on the Iberian Peninsular and we have the task of assessing the military situation and the strength of French forces there. We will be gone some time so you had better say your goodbyes this coming weekend."

"By god, sir, are we to be spies," Anthony asked. He seemed shocked by the idea.

"It's called reconnaissance in depth, Anthony. It will be a hard task and all the training for the past months has been about tactics and concealment. We will need to keep the French in ignorance for as long as possible. There will be a time when they finally discover our presence and they will move heaven and earth to try to stop us. We have to avoid serious conflict and evade capture. If we are found we must fight our way out with as much ferocity as we can muster. Some of us may not return but if we are successful, the information we bring back will be invaluable.

"Horse Guards has given us four months and weather permitting will have a frigate standing off the Portuguese coast for two weeks in January to watch out for our signals to be taken aboard. If we don't make those signals within that time the frigate's captain will assume that we have failed and will sail back to Portsmouth without us.

"Our kind of warfare is new and untried. If we succeed history will judge us. If we fail we will die forgotten and unmourned except by our nearest and dearest."

"I perceive there is much riding on our success, sir," Anthony said.

"More than you realise, Lieutenant. Anyway, I have a proposal to make and a toast. As we're all now friends and bound together, I propose we drop all the rank and titles and call ourselves by our Christian names in private. Anthony I know but not yours, Willoughby."

"It is Richard, sir."

Chris grinned. "It will take a while for the formality to wear off, Richard but please do call me George."

"As you wish but it does feel peculiar."

"Now to the toast. It's two actually. One to the success of our mission and the other to Anthony's forthcoming marriage."

"I shall happily drink to both," Anthony said. "And to our safe return, all three."

"Amen to that," Willoughby said.

"May you have a long and happy life with Catherine," Chris said. "You are a lucky man," he could not help adding.

Anthony gave him a genuine smile of thanks. "I am sure we shall be more than happy and I thank you for your good wishes. I shall pass those on to Mrs Catherine Dean."

Willoughby raised his mug. "To Lieutenant and Mrs Dean. Long life and happiness."

Chris foraged under his pillow and came out with a document rolled and sealed. "There is just one other thing before we part this evening. I have the honour, and I'm delighted to announce, that Ensign Richard Willoughby has been promoted to Lieutenant with immediate effect by order of His Royal Highness the Duke of York. Congratulations, Richard, you have the distinct honour of being the youngest Lieutenant ever appointed in the British army in peacetime."

Willoughby's face turned red as he took the document. "I am astounded, George. What could I possibly say?"

"Nothing. You have earned the distinction. I know you will live up to the responsibilities that go with the rank. You're a good young soldier, Richard … but there's room for improvement yet. That goes for you too, Anthony. You must both remember that my orders must be obeyed instantly and without question at all times if we are all going to come through this in one piece."

"We shall always do as you ask," Anthony said.

Chris nodded. He did not add the fact that he hadn't seen real combat either, having been too young for Iraq and Afghanistan. "Finish your brandy gentlemen, I have a lot to do. We'll meet again tomorrow and remember these orders are confidential."

The two young men downed their drinks and left pushing past the chambermaid on the stairs.

She had overheard every word and knew of someone who might pay for the news.

Foxley rode into Imber with Stewart on the eve of the wedding and made straight for The Bell. He had not wanted to come, he detested the place as the scene of his defeat. He still seethed at the thought of the knavish trick that had beaten him. He would remember it; a hard, painful lesson learned.

Stewart had demanded his attendance so that he might pay his respects to the Wadmans. Stewart, he believed, was too much taken with the family, an impression strengthened after Stewart turned straight into Imber Court on arrival.

The ride from Salisbury had brought on a thirst and his first desire was to quench it. The second was to see the little chambermaid in the woodshed behind the inn where she had pleasured him on former occasions. Foxley did not endure celibacy well and his enforced abstinence due to the pain of his wound was another reason he hated the man who had given it to him.

It was Saturday evening and the inn was busy with men in from the fields but not as busy as when the soldiery had been billeted nearby. He had noticed the six bell tents as he passed but no sign of a piquet or any men. Strange there was no sentry posted.

He slapped dust from his uniform and found a seat in a quiet corner. The chambermaid brought him a tankard of ale. He grabbed her wrist and pulled her close. "Will we make a stitch in the woodshed this eve?"

She winked and pulled her hand away. "It may be more than strumming I have in mind, sir."

"What else could *you* have in mind?"

"I have news," she looked around but other men were intent on their own conversations or in their own drinks, "but not here. Wait until nightfall."

It wasn't a long wait, the nights were drawing in, but Foxley downed three more tankards before he staggered out to relieve himself and then push his way into the lean-to where the logs were stored.

It wasn't many minutes later when the woman slinked in. He grabbed her from behind and bent her over the logs, throwing her skirts over her back.

"Gently, sir, it has been a while since I was last strummed."

"Then you will play a pretty tune, Abigail."

He was not gentle but it was over quickly and he fell back gasping and buttoning his breeches.

She rolled over and pulled down her skirts. "I have news, sir. Will you pay for it?"

"I will pay you a shilling as is my custom. Of what interest is your news to me?"

"Tis about the soldiers who are here, sir, and where they be headin'."

"They are of the 62nd and will be come to Salisbury, I have no doubt. Why should I pay for such intelligence?"

"No, sir, they go elsewhere and it is not just the 62nd, there are other regiments here. They have been diggin' and shootin' and changin' their coats to green."

"Green? The devil you say. And for where are they bound?"

"Another shillin', sir, would improve my memory."

Foxley gave her a crooked grin, dug into his pouch for two coins, pulled open her bodice and dropped them in. "There, paid in full. I am not a man to quibble about such niceties."

"They go to Portugal, sir, I believe that is what was said but I know of no such place. There was talk of the French and how Boney had taken power and there was to be a war comin' soon."

"When was this posting to happen?"

"This very week, sir. They decamp to Portsmouth and thence to Portugal to spy on the French, returnin' in four months. Captain Lennox ordered that the details be kept secret, save for the men themselves."

"Where are the soldiers, the camp would appear to be empty?"

"They are given leave to be with their women and will return tomorrow eventide."

"Lennox is a fool. I would never trust the hoi polloi to return, let alone in time. He will be led by the nose."

"The men do seem to favour him, sir."

"Do they, by god. Spying? That is beneath contempt, the man's a cad. What of these green coats?"

"Specially made in Salisbury to a design by Miss Catherine Wadman. I am told it is so that the soldiers can hide and not be seen by the French."

"Hide? The man is a coward and an upstart. The British Army does not hide from the French."

"Captain Lennox says the French may not find them and that the news he will bring back will be of good use to Horse Guards."

"Oh my, you do have big ears, little Abigail. But what if the French do find them?"

"Then they will fight, sir, as hard as they might."

An inkling of an idea was forming in Foxley's head and it brought a crooked smile to his lips. He shook his head as if to clear it but the smile lingered.

"Now roll over, little Abigail, for I feel the need to strum another tune."

# 17

The wedding was a quiet affair by 21st century standards. The immediate families and close friends attended the church but the rest of Imber, over two-hundred people, waited outside in the early autumn sunshine.

Anthony and his best man, his brother Charles, walked to the church with Stewart, Willoughby, and Chris. Foxley trailed behind with an odd grin on his face. He had been icily polite but had spoken little.

Catherine, Lady Isobel and Sir George arrived in an open topped landau with Amelia as her only bridesmaid. Catherine was dressed in a powder blue gown with matching bonnet laced with autumn flowers. Amelia had a silver dress decorated in the same way.

Chris's heart thumped so hard he winced as he thought those around him might hear it as Catherine walked down the aisle. She gave him a long look and a strained smile as she passed. He took it as a sign that she was happy with her lot. Chris knew that marriage in this era meant the woman gave up her life and freedom to her husband's whim. An irrevocable step for any woman, especially one as strong-minded as Catherine appeared to be.

He had harboured the thought that maybe, deep inside, she had a soft spot for him. Why else would she risk her life for him? But her subsequent attitude had quashed that idea. He was doomed to suffer unrequited love and for the first time in his life, he really felt what that over-used term actually meant.

The ceremony was a short one with the giving and taking of vows. There was no exchange of rings, just one for Catherine, something that Chris found odd until he remembered it was an American 20th century custom gaining popularity in Europe after the second world war. After signing the register, the brand new Mr and Mrs Dean drove off to Imber Court in the landau followed by a hail of good luck shoes thrown by the crowd.

All the officers were invited back for the wedding breakfast but Foxley did not join them, preferring, he said, to find his own amusement.

"Foxley's in strange temper this morn," Stewart said when they were assembled in the dining room at Imber Court.

"I did not take to that fey smile on his lips," Willoughby said. "Most disconcerting."

"Lieutenant Willoughby, I do declare you are developing an opinion," Stewart said.

"He's right, though," Chris added. "Foxley's look is far too superior. It's as if he knows something that we don't."

"Foxley has always had a supercilious air about him, nought odd there," Stewart said. "He will have some whore to attend to. No doubt that is his reason. Come let us not concern ourselves with Foxley, we have merrier diversions to entertain us."

Catherine and Anthony entered the room arm in arm and were soon swamped with good wishes. Chris held back. He was happy for them but it was coated with a pang of jealousy that he needed to digest in order to make his congratulations sound as sincere as they should be.

Catherine saw him, made an excuse and came over. "Do you not wish to congratulate us, Captain?"

"Of course I do. I wish you every happiness in your marriage."

"And yet you are stealing my husband away before the ink is dry on the marriage lines."

"It's not my doing, Mrs Dean. We're under orders from Horse Guards."

She turned so that he was between her and the rest of the room before laying a hand on his arm. "You will remember your promise."

Chris swallowed and nodded, his arm tingling and his heart thumping at her nearness. "To keep Anthony as safe as I can, yes of course."

"No, sir, to *both* come back safe and whole."

He put his free hand over hers but she pulled away. "That is my dearest wish."

Anthony clapped him on the shoulder. "Ha sir, on your orders I am to have but one day and one night with my wife and yet you keep her from me," he said with a grin. "Come, dearest, we must sit and dine with the guests."

Catherine curtsied and went to the table with Anthony.

"Mrs Dean makes truly a beautiful bride, does she not?" Willoughby said from his side.

Chris gave him a sharp look. "How old are you, Richard?"

"Fifteen years, George, old enough to appreciate beauty when I see it, as I know you do."

"A cat can look at a king, Richard."

"So it would seem, sir. And an officer can look at a queen it would also seem."

"The Chinese have a belief that if you save a person's life then you are responsible for that person until the favour is returned. I believe I've taken on a similar responsibility with Mrs Dean and I would prefer not to have any further comment on it." Chris said it in a jocular fashion and hoped Willoughby saw it in the same light. The boy was growing up, fast, not just bodily but also in maturity.

Willoughby gave him a snappy bow and a cheeky grin. The lad understood more than he was letting on.

They were about to join the others when Matthew approached with a worried look on his face. "If you please, Captain Lennox."

"What is it, Matthew?"

"Tis Mr Foxley, sir. He is taking advantage of Mary, sir, in the scullery. If you would be so kind. I dare not approach Sir George at this moment."

Chris nodded, his face grim. "Show me where."

Matthew led him away at a walk so as not to disturb the guests but soon broke into a trot as they entered the servants' quarters. "There, sir." He pointed.

Chris heard muffled screams and burst into the scullery where Foxley had Mary pinned against a wall, one hand covering her mouth and the other up her skirt. He turned his head.

"Be gone, Lennox, tis no business of yours."

"I'm making it my business. Get away from her." He Grabbed Foxley by his collar and heaved him off.

Foxley snarled an oath, swung a fist at Chris's face. He blocked it and threw Foxley onto his back.

"By god, what is happening here?" Stewart had come in unnoticed with Willoughby. "Lennox?"

"You'd best ask Mr Foxley, sir."

"Well Foxley?"

Foxley climbed to his feet, his face scarlet with rage. "I was merely dallying with the maidservant. Twas no business of Lennox to put his hand on me."

"He was taking advantage of her, without her consent, Colonel Stewart."

"She is just a peasant, sir, with whom I should do as I wished," Foxley snapped.

"You arrogant bastard," Chris snapped back. "She is a woman, a human being who has a right not to be groped by ignoramuses like you. There is no droit de seigneur in this country and there never has been."

"Be that as it may," Lennox," Stewart said, "I saw Foxley attempt to strike you, a senior officer. I will not have that in my regiment. He brings the 62nd into disrepute with his behaviour. And here, at Sir George Wadman's house, forcing himself on his servant, I shall have him cashiered." He shook a finger at Foxley. "I will have your commission, sir. Be gone from here and attend me at Salisbury on the morn. Good day, sir."

"I shall go, sir but you have not heard the last of me. You Lennox have crossed me once again and I shall not forget it. Be ware, sir for I have a long memory and do not forget a slight." He brushed past Chris and stalked through the door.

"I shall not be sorry to see the back of Mr Foxley," Stewart said. "I have been waiting for such an opportunity to see him gone for he has long tried my patience."

"Gone with a grievance," Willoughby said. "And a threat to Captain Lennox."

"I shouldn't worry too much about that," Chris said. "I can take care of myself. Now, how is Mary?"

Matthew had his arm around Mary's shoulders and she was sobbing softly. "Our thanks cannot be payment enough, Captain," he said.

Mary gave Chris a wan smile, disengaged herself from Matthew's arm and bobbed him a curtsey. "Thank you, sir, with all my heart."

"I won't see anyone mistreated, Mary, especially a woman. I hope you're not too shaken by what's occurred."

"No, sir, thank you sir, you did arrive before Mr Foxley could have his way with me."

"Then I suggest we say no more of it," Stewart said, "lest it mars the family's happy day. Come let us re-join the revelry with a word to no one."

After the meal, Catherine and Anthony left for the farmhouse on the estate that was to be their new home, a gift from Sir George as part of the wedding dowry.

Stewart pulled Chris to one side and drew a despatch from his coat. "More orders from Horse Guards, sir. Details of with whom you are to rendezvous when reaching the Portuguese coast. Local insurrectionists. Pah, sir, I would rather sup with the devil but needs must."

"I have a long spoon, Colonel."

"And you will need it. There's no knowing how these blackguards will jump. They would sell their mothers if it was to their advantage. Have a care, sir, in your dealings with them."

"Thank you, sir. Has everything else that I requested been done?"

"Yes. Each man will have a waterproof oilskin issued on shipboard and a bandage with cotton pad wrapped in oilskin and laced tight, though for the life of me I cannot understand the significance of that particular item."

"We call them first field dressings. It's to plug wounds and stem bleeding. We've found that blood loss and shock will kill a man faster if wounds are not bound quickly."

"My word, sir. You have a care for soldiery better than none other."

"I've always found that if you take care of your men they fight all the better."

"The rope and the cat work well also," Stewart said. "But I hear you do not believe in either."

"A flogged man can't fight well and a dead man can't fight at all. It's common sense to me."

"Well have a care, sir. There are some that would disagree and think that it would encourage outright dissent in the ranks."

"Some verbal dissent should be encouraged. The British soldier is never happier than when he has something to grumble about. The time to worry is when he goes quiet. But please don't mistake my leniency for stupidity. There is only so far I'll go. I'll take counsel but final decisions will be mine and mine alone. That is a line I won't allow anyone to cross."

Stewart nodded and held out his hand. "I do believe you are ready, Captain. This is the last you will see of me before you depart these shores. I wish you god speed."

Chris gripped the hand and looked into Stewart's eyes. He knew the man and knew he had an ally; one who, if history was right, would prove to be pivotal.

"Thank you, Colonel ..."

He was interrupted by a rapping on the table and he turned to see Sir George and Mr Dean senior staring at him. "Ah, we have your attention now, sir, do we not," Sir George said. "We have a further ceremony to conduct this day. On the morrow Captain Lennox and his detachment will be leaving us. You may all have noticed that he does not carry a sword about his person and he arrived here in Imber without one. That is an omission that we are about to correct. No British officer should be abroad without a blade to accompany him about his duties.

"Last month we sent to Sheffield for a blade of their finest steel, which, with Colonel Stewart's good offices was delivered here this morn. Come Captain." He beckoned Chris forward and took a decorated scabbard from beneath the table and laid it on the cloth. "Pick it up, sir. It is yours, presented by two grateful families, the Wadmans and the Deans, in recognition of your gallant service in saving Mrs Anthony Dean from blackguards."

Chris was stunned. "I don't know what to say."

"Use it well." Sir George said. "By all that's holy I believe you know how to use it to good account."

Chris grinned his thanks, picked up the infantry sabre and drew it from its scabbard. It gleamed in the sunlight and he could see the Wadman family crest finely engraved on the blade with the initials G.L. for George Lennox beneath. The Dean family name was engraved on the reverse of the blade. He swung it; the balance was perfect.

"Thank you all, it's a wonderful gift. I shall carry it with pride and hope to do it the honour it deserves."

"You shall, sir, we have little doubt of it," Sir George said and beamed. "Come let us feast and make merry for the morrow will be a sadder day."

# Part 2

## To Arms

# 18

The weather had finally broken and it was drizzling when the detachment made its way into Portsmouth dockyard. Chris was shown a half-empty warehouse near the quay where the men could rest out of the weather while he and Anthony went to find their ship.

HMS Aquilon was a Hermione class frigate with thirty-two 12-pound guns on one deck. It was what the navy called a fifth-rater which had been built in 1782. It was as long as a man-o-war but not classed as a ship of the line being faster and less heavily armed than the multi-deckers.

He was met at the gangplank by a marine guard who viewed his dark cloak with mistrust but saluted Anthony's red coat. A master at arms was called who saluted and enquired their business.

"I'm Captain Lennox and this is Lieutenant Dean. I believe the captain is expecting us."

"Aye, he is, sir. If you'll come this way. You'd best be mindin' your heads."

Chris saluted the quarter deck as he came aboard and Anthony doffed his hat. It was a tradition as old as the Roman navy and it pleased the master at arms that two landlubbers knew of the practise. He led them astern, under the quarterdeck and to the master's cabin beneath the poop deck.

Chris had to angle his head the whole way as the headroom was below his near six foot height. The master at arms knocked and waited.

"Enter."

He pushed open the door. "Captain Lennox and Lieutenant Dean, beggin' your pardon, Captain."

"Very well, show them in."

"Aye, aye, Captain. This way, sirs."

The cabin was large with glazed windows overlooking the harbour filled with its hoards of small boats, sailors and shore men going about their business in what appeared to be complete chaos. As his eyes adjusted Chris could see a blue uniformed figure seated behind a table with quill pen in hand and charts and papers spread across its surface.

Chris saluted a crisp army salute. "Captain Lennox at your service, Captain."

"Lieutenant Dean, sir," Anthony added.

The captain was a Master and Commander and older than Chris had expected. He had the lined face of an experienced sea-farer and looked as he was the kind of officer who had worked his way up in the navy to command his own vessel.

"Be seated, gentlemen. You shall have my attention shortly." He wrote on for a few more minutes before sanding the document and pushing it to one side with a sigh. "Much of my time in port is concerned with writing lists. Lists of men, of guns, of powder and of stores. The Admiralty demands its pound of flesh even to the bone."

"My sympathies, Captain," Chris said with a grin. "I hope we are not adding to your burdens."

"To the contrary, Lennox. You are giving me the opportunity to put to sea far sooner than we might have had the pleasure of expecting. I have my orders from the Admiralty to deliver you to the coast of Portugal with all possible speed."

"My men are nearby and ready to board at your convenience, sir."

"Very well. How many do they number?"

"Fifty men and three officers. Lieutenants Dean and Willoughby and myself."

"I daresay you will find the accommodation less to your liking than you are currently enjoying but they will be adequate for the time you will be aboard. You sir will share with the Lieutenant of Marines, your juniors with my lieutenants second class. The master at arms will show you your places."

"And the men ...?"

"They will draw hammocks and sleep betwixt decks with the tars. This is a well-found ship, sir, clean and well run. I should hope that your soldiery will behave itself or they will have good naval discipline to answer to."

"This will be a strange experience for them, except for those who have already served aboard ship as His Majesty's marines. There are four in the detachment and we have tasked them to keep the rest of the men informed as to traditions and the correct behaviour aboard."

The captain smiled for the first time. "I am impressed, Lennox, that you have taken such trouble. I welcome you aboard the Aquilon and trust your voyage will be a pleasant one."

"Thank you, captain ...?"

"Charles Cunningham, sir. We sail on the morning tide so be pleased to have your soldiery aboard in good time."

In the warehouse the men had changed from their wet red coats into their new green uniforms, having packed the old ones into sacks that Pocock had found. Chris called Biggin and Pocock over. "Keep everyone out of sight until it's dark. The ship we're boarding is HMS Aquilon, about five-hundred paces along the quay to the left. Be sure that the men understand what is required of them. I've given assurances to the captain that the men will abide by all regulations and traditions at all times. I wouldn't want to be let down."

"Beggin' your pardon, sir," Biggin said, "but they all been told. They know which end of a rope is which."

"I'm glad to hear it. Now post sentries and don't allow anyone access to this warehouse unless I say so. Those not on sentry stag should rest until it's time to move out."

"Aye, sir, tis all in hand."

"Very good, serjeants. Return to your duties."

"There is just one thing, sir, beggin' your pardon, sir, there is an officer waitin' to have conversation with you," Pocock said.

"Why didn't you say so earlier? Where is he?"

"With Mr Willoughby, sir, yonder by the barrels."

Chris found Willoughby with a heavily cloaked Major Wadman. "I wasn't expecting you, sir."

"Thank you, Willoughby," Wadman said and Willoughby took the hint to walk out of earshot. "I have news, sir and it may not be to your liking."

"I thought it might be important to bring you all the way from London."

"We have information that the Frogs may be mustering west of Cadiz. The Spanish are very feeble in defence of their realm. They have signed an alliance with the French and are doing nothing to dissuade them from their machinations. Several Frog ships of the line have been espied in the Gulf of Cadiz, we believe trying to run our blockade of the port to land more troops and to bolster their own continental blockade against us. We shall have to disembark you nearer to Albufeira than we hoped."

"It's as I thought," Chris said. "Bonaparte has his eye on Spain and Portugal. It wouldn't surprise me if he made an attempt on the Spanish throne at sometime in the next few years."

"Confound it, sir. From where does this knowledge of yours come? We have our spies and they have confirmed all that you have divulged so far but even they cannot divine the mind of that little Corsican upstart."

"It's simply conjecture, Major. But from my experience, men of Napoleon's ilk are never satisfied until they conquer every nation that poses a threat to them. Spain and Portugal are weak now but they may well grow stronger in the coming years and he won't want to risk a threat on his southern border, especially in the light of the pact between Britain and Portugal."

Wadman grimaced. "The War of Roussillon did not go well for either Portugal or Spain. It is that which led to Spain's treaty with the French. They may not be so ready to wage another war so soon. However, I can see the logic of what you say, sir, but what is to be done?"

"I believe we still have some years before Bonaparte is strong enough to make his move. The omens point to a war on the Iberian Peninsular and it is one we daren't lose if we are to keep him in check."

"You make grave assumptions, Captain. Such preparations will prove a drain on the Exchequer and there will be many voices opposed to such plans with so little but assumption to go on. I shall speak with His Royal Highness the Duke of York for his opinion. He is much taken with your grasp of matters military and may well see your analysis in the same light."

"The fact that the French are landing troops at Cadiz may go to prove their motives on the peninsular. It's early days but a toehold will soon become a foothold and then a stranglehold," Chris said.

"Bleaker and bleaker by the second but I cannot fault your logic, sir. I may further add that the troops in question are Bonaparte's Grenadier Guard; the best he has."

Chris grimaced. "So he *is* getting serious. Thank you for the warning."

Wadman nodded. "There is another matter that I must warn you of. Colonel Stewart has informed me that Lieutenant Foxley has absented himself. Slipped away like a fox in the night. The Colonel has no knowledge of his whereabouts, having searched the ale houses and whore houses he is known to frequent, nor of his intentions but he fears the worst. The doxy from the inn at Imber has boasted of earning an extra shilling from Foxley for intelligence that was overheard in a conversation between yourself and your juniors. Be of great care, sir."

# 19

The ship left Portsmouth in a brisk southerly that kicked up a medium swell. Chris had no experience of sailing and was soon hanging his head over the side with some of his men. They were allowed on deck in relays to get air and to exercise, much to the amusement of the tars who first watched open mouthed at the physical jerks that Chris put them through and then with gales of raucous laughter as the ranks broke for men to spew over the side.

Captain Cunningham called Chris to the quarterdeck on the second day out. "Tis no disgrace to suffer mal de mer on your first voyage, Lennox. Even Vice-Admiral Nelson is prone to it, I am told."

"A great man," Chris said.

"Aye that he is. Now, Lennox, what is the purpose of all this jigging on my gun deck?"

"It serves two purposes, Captain. The first is to keep the men's muscles in tone and the second is to prevent them from becoming too bored. My serjeants also keep them further occupied with weapon cleaning and kit inspections every day."

"I must confess I have never seen the like. I am not at all sure I am in favour of a gentleman cavorting in front of the men in such fashion."

"I am a firm believer in not asking my men to do anything which I'm not prepared to do myself."

Cunningham raised his eyebrows. "The devil you say, sir."

"From the talk in the wardroom I'd say you are a man after my own heart, Captain."

"Flattery, sir?"

"Not at all. I've been told that you have been known to lash yourself to the wheel in a gale and guide the ship safely through."

"But the once, sir, did I feel the need to do so. You make a fair point, Lennox."

"Could I ask a favour, sir?"

"Ah!" Cunningham grimaced but there was humour in his eyes. "I now see the way of it. What is it you require?"

"I'd like to give the men some target practice. Could we tow a boat at half a cable length with a scarecrow seated at the stern?"

"A single scarecrow? My marines would not trouble it at that distance. That's very nearly one-hundred paces in a rolling sea."

"I think you may be surprised, Captain."

Cunningham grunted. "As long as I am not surprised with holes in my pinnace. Very well. I shall give orders to the sailing master on the morrow. The glass is set for a fair day with a stiff southerly. It will test your men's mettle."

Cunningham was as good as his word and the sailing master came to ask Chris for his instructions the next morning. Chris explained what he needed and the man grinned a gap-toothed smile.

"How will you know if the scarecrow is hit, Captain?"

"We might be able to borrow the officer of the watch's telescope."

"That mayn't be possible. We be entering waters riddled wi' Frenchies and they need to keep a good watch lest we be surprised. I have another notion, sir, beggin' your pardon."

"Fire way, Mr Lee."

"If we put a sack of flour where the scarecrow's chest may be. We could see the powder fly from it."

"You can spare the flour?"

"Oh, aye, sir. We have more than we need for this short voyage and we'll use a half empty sack as it will be easier for the powder to flow. Once across Biscay we'll have the winds set fair. Maybe another six days sailin' will see us on the return."

"That's a good idea, Mr Lee. Thank you."

"We'll be usin' the Captain's pinnace, sir. I hopes your men are as good a shots as you believe or there may be a price to pay for the damage."

"Perhaps your sailors could jury-rig a mast and lash the scarecrow to it and away from the hull."

"Aye, that we can. The better for the tars to see as they be layin' odds against the scarecrow's chest gettin' hit at all, sir."

"Gambling, Mr Lee?"

"Just a friendly wager between friends, sir."

"What are the odds?"

"Three to one against a hit."

"And if you were a betting man where would you put your money?"

The grin again. "Oh against, sir. We be enterin' choppy waters as we round Ushant. That scarecrow will be doin' a jig to the devil's fiddle like no other. We bain't be losin' no flour from that sack, you mark my words."

"I'll put a crown on a hit, Mr Lee. You know we are using Baker Rifles and not muskets?"

"You could be usin' one of our twelve-pounders with grape and it would make little difference, beggin' your pardon sir. You be wastin' your money."

"Then it will give the crew something to sing about the next time they weigh anchor."

Chris flipped him a coin. Lee caught it deftly and bit it.

"Thankee, sir."

"Can you cover that at three to one?"

"Aye, there not be many as will bet the same way as you, sir."

"Very well, Mr Lee. Be kind enough to get the pinnace launched so that we can get going."

"Done as we speak, sir. I'll be getting' the mast rigged and the sack brought up from the galley."

Lee left and Chris had a sailor call Biggin to the cabin. He came in and knuckled his forehead.

"How are the riflemen, faring?"

"Not well, sir. Many still be green around the gills wi' all this tossin' around."

"Some fresh air will do them good. Have them muster on the gun deck with their rifles, powder and ball. There's some shooting practice to do and the sailors are rigging a target off the stern.

"Two-man teams, each to fire one shot in turn until all twenty-eight have shot. The sailors don't think it's possible to hit the target but I'll give a half crown each to any team that does. Pass the word."

Biggin's face lit up. "Aye, sir, that'll get their minds off the sickness."

"Oh, and Biggin, load the two spare rifles … just in case we need them."


The sailors had done a good job of the scarecrow. They had found an old blue jacket and lashed the sleeves to a crossbar on the rough mast. The head was made of a brown sack stuffed with wadding and painted with two eyes and a red slash of a mouth. The chest was a white flour sack; smaller than Chris had anticipated as the crew had folded it down on the remaining contents.

If Chris remembered correctly, a cable was about a hundred and eighty metres and half a cable should have been ninety metres or around a hundred paces. The distance to the pinnace looked far longer than that and Chris wondered if the crew had let the line out further than intended. The white blob of the flour sack, although easily seen seemed miniscule as the small boat bobbed and twisted in the ship's wake, sometimes disappearing altogether in the deepening swell until only the tip of the makeshift mast showed.

The ship's deck itself was prone to sudden shifts of height coupled with a corkscrew effect like a continuous figure of eight. One of Chris's corporals, a man called O'Dell, was first in line and he eyed the target with misgivings as it dipped and rolled.

"Plant your feet firmly and take your time, corporal," Chris said. "It's all in the timing."

"Aye, sir," O'Dell said but he did not sound confident. He raised his rifle and squinted his eyes, adjusting his footing as he had been taught.

Chris could see the man calculating the time between rise and fall as he regulated his breathing. O'Dell was one of the better shots in the detachment; if anyone could do it, he could. The rifle exploded and a chip flew from the mast two feet above the scarecrow's head.

Cunningham had come up to Chris's shoulder unheard. "A miss I believe, sir."

"Twenty-seven or so to go, Captain. There's time."

"The wind is blowing up, Lennox. There may not be as much time as you hope."

O'Dell's team mate also missed and so did the others one by one until all that was left were Biggin and Pocock holding the spare rifles. Anthony Dean and Richard Willoughby had also been drawn to the stern along with all the ship's officers. Chris noticed that the rigging was clustered with grinning seamen all bent in watching them miss their target.

Biggin looked across at the officers. "Beggin' your pardon, sirs but both me and Serjeant Pocock believe this is beyond our skills to hit yon target."

"You are the better shot, Captain Lennox," Anthony said. "You must try your luck."

"We have two loads left. If I miss it's down to you, Richard. You did well in the butts."

Willoughby nodded. "I shall do my best, sir."

Chris gave him a crooked smile and took Biggin's rifle. He raised it and sighted on the target, closed his eyes for three seconds and when he opened them he was pointing to the left of the scarecrow's mean position. He moved his rear foot further behind him and did the same again. This time the sights aligned on the mean centre of the figure eight the pinnace was performing. He waited for the roll of the ship to lessen and for the pinnace to bob through the centre of its arc. He squeezed on the trigger until the pinnace crested a wave and the white blob of sack was firmly in his sights. He fired just as the ship rose and the bullet hit the mast between the scarecrow's painted eyes.

Cunningham was looking through his telescope. "Another miss, I believe."

Chris gave him a rueful look. "He'd be dead enough but you're right, sir. It's a miss on the prime target. Are you ready, Mr Willoughby?"

"Yes, the honour of the detachment is on your shoulders," Anthony said.

"No pressure, then," Chris muttered. "You know what needs to be done. Just take your time."

Willoughby gave him a cheerful smile, the confidence of youth. He took Pocock's rifle and went through the same routine as Chris had but taking longer so that he had to rest the rifle as the muscles in his arm began to tire. The sailors were chanting in the rigging trying to distract him but he had his eyes firmly set on the target.

The pinnace rose and fell several times and the ship rolled from port to starboard. Finally he fired. Everyone looked to see the small puff of white flour.

Cunningham took the scope from his eye and smiled. "Another miss, I believe.

"Master, haul in the pinnace so that we may be sure there are no holes in the sack."

"Aye, sir." Lee turned to face the crew now dropping onto the gun deck like windfall apples in autumn. "Set to you lubbers, haul in the Cap'n's pinnace."

The small boat was hauled alongside and hoisted aboard in double time by the grinning sailors. The scarecrow was unlashed, brought to the quarterdeck and laid at Cunningham's feet.

"As I said, not a hole in the sack but by god, sir, there are better than eighteen holes in the head and blue jacket. That is indeed fine marksmanship, the best I have seen.

"Bosun, an extra measure of grog for the soldiery this night, they have earned it in my opinion."

"That's thoughtful of you, sir," Chris said.

Cunningham gave him one of his now familiar looks. "It has kept the crew amused and they shall be sharing out their bounty to which, I hear, you contributed handsomely.

Your greenbacks deserve some reward. You have a fine command."

"I do, Captain and they will be sorely tested in the coming weeks."

# 20

"Sail ho!" The shout came from the crow's nest on top of the main mast.

"Where away?"

"Four points off the starboard bow."

"I cannot see it," the officer of the watch shouted.

"A minute, sir, tis below the horizon from the deck."

"Ah, I see the mast top pennant now. What do you make of her?"

"Three-masted, sir, maybe a seventy-four."

"Bosun, call the Captain to the quarterdeck."

Cunningham was quickly up from below his telescope in his hand. "What is it man?"

"Sail four points off starboard, sir. Maybe a Frog fourth-rater. Lookout thinks a seventy-four gun two-decker.

"God's teeth, we will be outgunned if we cannot outrun her. Master cram on all the sail we have, let's see if we have the legs of her."

"She has the windward side, sir."

"Aye it will be a close run thing. She will be after blockade runners and in familiar waters. Give me every last stitch of canvas the masts will carry."

Chris had heard the excitement and climbed the quarterdeck starboard ladder.

"The French?"

Cunningham handed him his telescope. "On the horizon, sir. A French frigate but more heavily armed. We will try to outrun her."

"And if we can't?"

"Our orders are to land you safely on Portuguese soil but we also have other orders to attack and harass the enemy wherever we find them. If we cannot outrun our friend then we will fight her."

"Even though we're outgunned?"

"Outgunned, sir but not outclassed. We can fire three broadsides to her two and her officers are likely inept. The best were executed in the terror."

Chris peered through the scope. "She appears to be gaining. I can see the hull now." He offered the telescope back to Cunningham.

"I have no need of the glass to see that now, she is gaining but it will take until the morrow for her to get within chaser range. We shall see what her captain is made of then," Cunningham said. "Now let us repair to the wardroom, there is nothing to be done until then."

Much to Chris's surprise the food on board had been edible and plentiful washed down with large quantities of wine and brandy. Most wardroom dinners were boozy occasions and this night was no exception. Chris always drank sparingly; he was always worried about dropping unguarded comments in answering the often searching questions about his history. He made up so many stories about his fictitious life in New Zealand that he was in danger of forgetting the details. It wasn't that the officers were trying to trip him up but their curiosity was endemic.

On the eve of almost certain battle the wine flowed more freely than ever and Cunningham plied him with more than he was comfortable drinking.

"Dash it, man, tomorrow we may all be dead or lolling in a Frenchman's brig. Drink up and be damned."

Chris grinned and gulped down a mouthful. He didn't get drunk easily but was beginning to feel light-headed.

The Lieutenant of Marines, with whom he shared a cabin, clapped him on the back. "That'll make a man of you, Captain. Best Madeira ever I tasted."

"It's the only Madeira I've ever tasted," Chris admitted. "But it does seem very fine."

"Never tasted Madeira," Cunningham roared. "This New Zealand must be the back of beyond."

"It's off the beaten track, that's certain but it has its compensations."

"I fail to see how a land without Madeira can compensate one," the first lieutenant said. "You say it is in the southern ocean. I have heard that the albatross flies there, an omen to sailors."

"There are many types of albatross," Chris said. "They fly over the sea for most of their lives but come to dry land to mate and raise their young."

"Indeed, sir. That is news to me for I believed they were born in flight and never set foot on mother earth."

"I've seen it, I know it's true. The young are very ungainly and many die falling into the sea before they learn to fly."

"Learn to fly, sir?" The lieutenant said. "But surely it is natural for them. If this be true then I believe that man may learn to fly if it is simply a matter of learning."

"Man will fly one day."

"Come now sir, I was merely jesting."

"Why do you say so, sir?" Cunningham asked.

"In 1783 two Frenchmen, the Montgolfier brothers, ascended in a hot air balloon. Not far it's true and the balloon was tethered to the ground but fly they did. It's not beyond the bounds of reason that men will travel in heavier-than-air craft one day."

"I had not heard of this," the marine said. "I believe it is not possible, a tale concocted by the French."

"What keeps a bird aloft, Lieutenant? You've shot game, you know a bird lies heavy in your hand. How does it fly?"

"Why, it flaps its wings and rises."

"Flaps it's wings against what exactly?"

"Damned if I know, sir. A bird just flies."

"It's the same principle as propels this ship. Wind in the sails drives us along. Wind, or air under the wings propels the birds."

"By god, sir, you are quite the scientist," Cunningham said. "I can see the sense of it but how did these Frogs get themselves to fly?"

"Hot air rises. We have all witnessed ash rising from a fire. That is due to heated air being lighter than cooler air. They filled a large envelope with heated air and it rose up with them in a gondola beneath it."

"A conjuror's trick no doubt. I cannot see any useful application in it," Cunningham said.

Chris smiled but had the feeling he was getting into this conversation too deeply and regretted starting it. "Perhaps you're right, sir. Merely an entertainment but it caught the imagination."

"We have seen how your imagination works," the first lieutenant said. "I do believe you imagined that your greenbacks could hit the chest of the scarecrow."

Chris laughed with the others. "You're right, sir, I was mistaken but there were some useful lesson for the soldiers to learn."

"I have seen how you teach your men, Lennox. Not by rope's end but by calculation and example. I cannot sanction it in this man's navy where strong discipline must be upheld by liberal use of the cat and I wish you well in your endeavours ashore but you may find your approach also mistaken."

"Maybe you're right, Lieutenant but all my men are volunteers, not pressed men. I haven't yet felt the need for flogging, they work better without it."

"That may well be put to the test on the morrow," Cunningham said. "I have seen the quality of the greenbacks' marksmanship and I wish your riflemen to be in the rigging should it come to battle."

"How will you take them, Captain?" the marine asked.

Cunningham grinned and gulped another mouthful of wine. "By guile. Come the morn we shall know more by her position but, with luck, we shall be ahead of her as dawn breaks. We shall then see what the Frog's made of, by god."

# 21

As the rim of the sun cracked the eastern sky all the gun crews were closed up and ready for action. The French frigate was behind them but slowly drawing nearer. They had tried ranging shots with bow chasers but the shot had fallen short on each occasion. Now the gun billowed smoke again and the ball flashed through the rigging above head height before the sound of the cannon was heard.

Cunningham was on the poop deck with his telescope fixed on the ship behind. "Frog's got the range now. Helmsman steer two points to starboard, keep her off the larboard stern so she can bring only one chaser to bear."

"Aye, sir. Two points to starboard it be."

"That will allow her free water to come along the larboard side, Captain," Lee, the sailing master, said.

"Tis where I want them, Mr Lee. If I allow a stern-on shot their chasers can throw a ball along the length of the deck. At this position a ball will only pass through a stern quarter."

"Ah! I see the way of it. What will you do when she's alongside? Her cannon are twice our number."

Cunningham gave him a bleak smile. "We shall take a leaf from Vice-Admiral Nelson's book and surprise the Frog. See, she has not changed her course, she is planning on taking us on the larboard side."

"We shall have the wind with us, sir."

"Indeed we shall, Mr Lee. Have your top men aloft and ready to reef the topsails."

"Then we shall lose way more readily to the Frog."

Cunningham gave him another look. "Just do it, Master and be ready on my command."

Lee doffed his hat. "Aye, sir, at once."

A shot smashed through Cunningham's day cabin below his feet, the boom of the cannon almost instantaneous. He walked to the quarterdeck where his officers were assembled. "Take post, gentlemen, the hour is almost upon us. Captain Lennox, your riflemen to the rigging if you please. Lieutenant of Marines make ready a boarding party. Helmsman, be ready on my command."

"What the devil is the captain about," the marine whispered in Chris's ear.

"He obviously has a plan," Chris whispered back. "Let's hope it works. I have my muskets ready below decks to help with the boarding party."

"My thanks, Captain. Twill be a hard fight, the Frogs outnumber us two to one but our tars will give good account of themselves, of that I am certain."

Another boom and crash as a second ball hit the stern splintering glass and wood and dismounting the rear stern twelve-pound gun as it exited the hull.

"Master at arms, open the larboard gun ports if you please and run out the guns," Cunningham yelled.

"Aye, sir, all guns ready, sir."

"Master, reef the topsails."

The ship slowed perceptibly as the sails were reefed. Cunningham swung to watch the French ship close. "*Helm hard a larboard!*"

"Hard a larboard, sir."

The ship wallowed crazily for a brief second then swung to the left across the bow of the racing French ship.

"Master at arms fire when your guns bear."

The ship had rolled to starboard and the guns were pointing skyward but as she rolled back each gun blazed in turn, raking the Frenchman's bow from first the starboard and then the port quarter. The heavy iron balls smashed the length of the main gun deck killing crewmen and disabling the forward guns. One ball brought down the foremast in a crash of canvas and timber.

"Hard a starboard," Cunningham ordered. "Let her run alongside and give her a broadside with the starboard battery."

As the ship straightened the riflemen in the rigging had a clear view of the enemy's decks and began to pick off the officers on the French quarterdeck and the men manning the two bow chasers. They went down one by one under the accurate fire.

The French guns along half the main deck had been destroyed but the ones sternward of the top deck were still functioning and these opened up as the two ships closed together. Wood and metal exploded in a maelstrom of flying pieces as the balls struck home. Sharpshooters in the rigging began to shoot into the British sailors.

Chris screamed at Biggin, who was lashed half-way up the mainmast to get his riflemen to engage the enemy marines. He waved an acknowledgement and soon the shooting onto the deck slackened.

"By god, we have a fight on our hands," the marine said and grinned a maniacal grin at Chris. "Are your greenbacks ready for this?"

Chris nodded and shouted. "Serjeant Pocock stand to and be ready to board."

Pocock's lined face came up from below followed by the muskets, each wearing the metal-faced jackets the blacksmith had made.

Chris was wearing his own body armour. He had bought two Dragon pistols and these were stuffed in his belt. His new sabre was in his hand as he took his place at the head of his men.

Cannons blasted and pieces of wood, metal and men flew as the grappling irons were pulled tight and the hulls crashed together. The marine officer and his men were the first over the side. Sailors were swinging on ropes and dropping like apes into the fight; ferocious but undisciplined.

Chris waited for a lull in the onslaught and for a gap to appear on the Frenchman's deck. "Forward the Rifles," he shouted. They climbed the side, landed on the deck in two ranks facing the quarterdeck. The first rank knelt. The French captain was surrounded by blue-coated marines who fired a ragged volley. Two of Chris's men went down.

Pocock was calm in control. "Front rank, *fire*." Twelve muskets roared and half the French marines dropped to the deck. "Second rank advance. Second rank, *fire*."

By luck, the French captain was still standing and Chris leapt up the starboard ladder to get to him. A blue arm smeared with blood raised a pistol at him from the mess on the deck. He fired his Dragon left handed and the hand dissolved in a red mist.

It had given the Frenchman time to draw his own sword and he lashed at Chris with it. The man was already wounded in the leg and it was a clumsy stroke that was easily parried. The next stroke was more determined and he fought it off with a parry and riposte.

All around him was a sea of bodies, some dead, some badly wounded. An arm caught at his leg and threw him off balance. The French captain struck and stabbed hard into Chris's chest plate.

Chris blinked in annoyance, knocked the blade up, stamped the hand away and came back at the captain whose mouth had dropped open in disbelief. The man backed away from the ferocious attack until he was up

160

against the ship's wheel and could retreat no further. He parried several cuts but one caught his sword arm. He threw his sword down as Chris's sabre tip reached his throat.

"Surrender your ship, sir."

"*Mon dieu, mon bateau est envahi par les démons.*

"*Je me rends lui. Oui.*"

"I take it that's a yes, then," Chris said. He waved his sabre at the heaving mass of men still fighting on the decks. "S'il vous plait."

The captain nodded, defeat on his face but hatred in his eyes. He cupped his hands and called. "*Mettez vos armes, les hommes. Je l'ai abandonné le navire.*"

The fighting slowly subsided and the British disarmed the French sailors one by one and herded them into a group in the centre of the top deck.

Cunningham was leaning on the ship's rail with a broad smile on his face. "Well done, gentlemen, the day is ours."

"We have a good prize, sir," the marine lieutenant replied. His arm was down by his side with blood dripping from his fingers but he was still pumped full of adrenaline. "It's named the *Hercule*. She should fetch a pretty penny."

"Aye, the navy could use a good fourth-rater. She'll serve under the British flag there's no doubt of it."

Chris ushered the French captain in with the rest of his men where the remaining British marines were standing guard. Already the sailors were clearing the mess of fallen men, rigging and spars from both the ships.

"You'd best get that wound attended to," Chris said and pointed to the blood.

The lieutenant glanced down as if seeing it for the first time. "Ah! Tis but a scratch I believe."

"Best it's seen to quickly. I have medication in the cabin that will help."

"As you say, sir but ..."

"My serjeants will take care of the prisoners. I see your marines have had a hard time of the fight."

"So many of your greenbacks are still standing, yet I saw them in the thick of the maul."

"I have them well-trained. We can talk about it later, let's get that wound plugged."

He helped the man over the rails and back to the cabin. He took out the trauma kit keeping his body between the kit and the marine so that he wouldn't see it but he need not have worried the man's eyes were closed and he had fallen back against the bulkhead.

Chis levered him out of his tunic and tore off his bloody shirt sleeve. It was a cutlass wound and it was deep, slicing into the muscle at the top of the shoulder. He opened the trauma kit for the morphine ampoules and stopped short. There should have been five but there were six. The one that he'd used on Thomas the coachman was back in its place, as were the bandages he'd used.

He had no time to wonder about it. He took out the ampoule and plunged the needle into the marine's thigh. He barely moaned as Chris cleaned the wound, dusted it with anti-septic powder and used some superglue to close it before tying a pressure pad in place.

The man would be sore in the morning and would need stitches but his arm would be safe from the ship's surgeon busily amputating smashed limbs on the wardroom table. The screams of the wounded were echoing around the ship.

He pushed the marine's legs onto the bunk and left him to wake in his own time. He closed the lid on the trauma kit still with six ampoules in their slots. He went to help the ship's doctor in the wardroom. His syrettes of morphine would save a lot of agony.

# 22

The elation of the previous day had now descended into sombre contemplation as the bodies of the dead were committed to the sea in a short but moving service. Chris had lost one man dead and another wounded who was put onto the captured *Hercule* with the first officer and skeleton crew to sail back to Portsmouth with their prize. Some of the Frenchman's crew, of differing nationalities, had agreed to take the King's Shilling and make the journey as imprest British sailors, a practice frowned on in public but nevertheless common amongst commanders in the field. The French captain had given his word of honour not to return to the fray but Cunningham confided that the man was no gentleman and would renege on his word once returned to France. He felt the man's value would be greater if held until an exchange of prisoners could be arranged. He sent despatches to that effect with the ship.

Anthony and Richard had come through the fight without a scratch as had all the riflemen. Cunningham was effusive in his praise, going as far as saying that the fire from the rigging had turned the tide of battle.

Running repairs were ongoing and the wardroom, scrubbed clean of blood and body parts, had canvas sheeting where the glass had once been. It was a darker room in daylight but still a place where the officers could relax and swap their war stories. Much of the conversation was on the value of the bounty their prize would bring. Each man was due a share, from the cabin boys and powder monkeys to the captain. Chris and his greenbacks were included too.

Cunningham was in high good humour at the head of the wardroom table. He tilted his glass at the assembled men. "Here's to good fortune and calm seas. May we make it safely back to Portsmouth where we shall discover the value of our labours."

"I'll drink heartily to that," the marine said. "And to the King, god bless him."

He had his arm strapped up in a sling and looked pale but on the mend. The ship's surgeon, seated next to Chris, had marvelled at the 'native' medicine that had brought such relief to stricken men. He was now as full of questions as Doctor Hawking and Chris was glad that they were just a day away from their landing on the Algarve coast.

He had checked the trauma kit again that morning to find that all dressings and ampoules were still there even though he had used them the night before. He was baffled. The cut on his arm inflicted by Foxley had healed within days but the lightning-burned tracery had not faded. He still had no need to shave, going through the motions each day but finding no growth. His hair was still the same military length, his nails needed no trimming. It was as if time had ceased as far as his body was concerned. He ate, he drank, he peed and he defecated all as normal but nothing grew.

Sharing a cabin with the marine had also proved problematic. It was difficult concealing the 21st century kit that was packed into his Bergen. Every item that would raise eyebrows he pushed to the bottom. His Glock and holster and his wristwatch were obvious but there had also been questions about his rubber-soled boots, the way water ran off his combat jacket and the multi-bladed safety razor in his wash kit. Toothbrushes and toothpaste were unheard of but he was damned if he was going to bed each night without cleaning his teeth. He could have used salt water but there was only so much anachronistic living he was willing to give up. Yes he would be happier away from the questions and his rather inadequate answers.

"Captain Lennox!"

The shout jolted him out of his reverie. "Sir! Sorry I was miles away."

Cunningham guffawed. "Indeed, Lennox, and soon you shall be. We shall be landing your greenbacks in the longboat after dusk on the morrow. I trust you will be ready to disembark."

"Willing and able, Captain."

Cunningham rose unsteadily and took a sealed oilskin pouch from his table. "Your final orders, sir, direct from Horse Guards and the Admiralty."

Chris took the package. "More orders? I had assumed I'd already been given them."

"I am not privy to the contents so cannot comment but I wish you well in your endeavours. The good Lord willing we shall be back in January to take you off the same beach where we shall land you.

"It has been a privilege having you and your officers aboard my ship, sir and I shall be saying adieu to you with much regret."

"We will be sorry to leave you and your brave crew, Captain, but you'll forgive me if I say us lubbers will be happier on dry land."

"I hope the dry land is as happy to receive you. Have a care, sir, I hear there are brigands abroad on that godforsaken coast."

"We are aware of them, Captain and we thank you for your concern."

"I raise another toast, before we grow too maudlin. To the greenbacks ... and their safe return."

Chris, Anthony and Richard acknowledged the toast and the good wishes of the sailors. These were stalwart men who did not easily wear their hearts on their sleeves and all three were moved by the tributes paid to them.

Richard, the youngest officer aboard, even younger than the two midshipman, did the honour as Mr Vice and raised a toast to the King's navy, especially those officers and men aboard HMS Aquilon.

Cunningham beamed his approval. "Well said, Lieutenant, you have the makings of a diplomat."

"I'm sure I should do my best, sir, at what ever endeavour is set me."

"I am sure you would, sir. From whence do you hail?"

"I am from the 62nd, the Wiltshires."

"They breed them true in that county, I see."

"Thank you, sir. Wiltshire men are strong and bold, serving God, king and country the best way that we may."

"Then I shall not say what was in my mind of thick arms and thicker heads as I have heard it of many counties," Cunningham said with a grin. "Before we go about our duties I have one more toast. To our wives and sweethearts ... may they never meet."

Chris unwrapped the oilskin package when he was back in the cabin. The marine excused himself and left on his tour of inspection. The marine unit had fared badly in the exchange with the *Hercule* and his small command had been reduced to just ten men as the wounded had been sent to help guard the prisoners on the returning prize.

He asked how the greenbacks had survived so well and Chris had shown him the iron reinforced waistcoats that had stopped many of the French musket balls. The man had been intrigued but could not see the fad gaining support amongst the wider military community. The marines, he said, would not be allowed to fall to such low tricks."

Chris grinned at the memory; the marines would, two-hundred years in the future. It was a pity so many lives would be lost in the meantime due to notions of honour and hide-bound senior officers keeping to outdated practices.

With that thought he read the paper folded neatly inside the oilskin and frowned. Another mission added to the one he already had, and a dangerous one at that. Horse Guards were definitely trying to get their money's worth.

"What do you think of this Lennox fellow, Wellesley?"

Arthur Wellesley looked across the room at the Duke of York. "I cannot say I am much taken with his ideas, sir. Men rollin' in the dirt, not my idea of soldierin' Might give the Frog a belly laugh."

"Major Wadman feels it has merit, don't yer know, and that Stewart fellow also. He has been pondering on it with His Majesty's equerry, Colonel Coote Manningham, who is also rather taken with the notion."

"We'll see how this expedition to Portugal runs out, sir. Personally I think the chap is battin' on a sticky wicket with the tasks he has been set."

The Duke sat his bulk in a window seat with a sigh. "I admit that his orders are formidable but we cannot allow the idea of dressing in green and hiding in holes take hold until it has been properly tested. The French are growing in strength after that damned alliance with Spain and it is putting Prince John under pressure to rescind our agreements with Portugal. The prince is reluctant to take on the regency but the Queen has been getting the religious vapours. He must act soon and perhaps Lennox's little enterprise can give him the disposition he needs."

"The Admiralty have been building up the navy, near one-hundred-thousand men now, I do hear, with the imprest men. The army is yet far behind in its preparations and we need time to grow and train the regiments," Wellesley said.

The Duke puffed out his cheeks. "This adventure in Portugal may buy us some time. Tie the Frogs up for some weeks, if luck be with us. And keep them wondering when next we may strike at their underbelly."

"Do you believe that Lennox can successfully carry out his orders, sir?"

"I suspect he will last no longer than a fortnight once he comes upon the French Grenadier Guard."

"Or they come upon him."

"Exactly, Wellesley. However should he succeed we will have a novel tactic to play upon the Frog."

"A gamble then, sir."

"Most decidedly so, Wellesley. Most decidedly so."

# 23

The cove was lit by a just rising moon as the ship's longboat and pinnace ferried Chris's men ashore onto a shelving sandy beach surrounded by towering sandstone cliffs. In daylight, the cliff faces would be red but in the cool moonlight they shone a dull orange.

Chris waded the last few paces ashore with his kit over his shoulder and a Dragon in one hand. He had no idea whether they would face a hostile reception and he made sure all the men had loaded and primed rifles and muskets in their hands.

Those first on the beach had secured a perimeter laying down behind bulky packs and covering the two paths that led down to the sand from the cliff top. It took three trips to get all the men ashore and the sailors waved a silent farewell as they pulled back to the ship, a black outline on a paler sea.

Chris had strapped on his Breitling beneath his combat jacket and now took a furtive look at the time. 22.00 right on the money. Cunningham had proved to be one hell of a navigator.

There was a muffled warning from the piquet and pebbles rattled down the left hand path. Chris was only too aware that they were in a rat trap. Enemy soldiers on the cliff tops would be able to pick them off with ease. With nowhere for them to hide and the sea at their backs it could prove to be a death trap. He silently cursed whomever it was at Horse Guards or the Admiralty who had selected this particular beach to land on. He knew it was a last minute decision due to the proximity of the French further east towards the Spanish border. Even so, it seemed an obviously flawed decision to land on a beach with no room to manoeuvre.

More pebbles rattled down and several weapons went to full cock.

"Fingers off triggers, men," Chris hissed. "Pass the word along the line."

Anthony dropped into the sand beside him. "Shall we expect the enemy?"

Chris could see the pale blur of his worried face and sought to reassure him. "We are expecting our guides and interpreters but it pays to be cautious. Go back to your men and be ready to leave."

"And if it is not they?"

Chris gave his shoulder a quick squeeze. "Then be ready to fight. But be careful we don't want anyone shot by accident and we don't want to make any noise that will give away our presence unnecessarily. No one's to fire unless I give the order."

"As you say, sir," Anthony said and squirmed away.

"Who goes there?" It was Willoughby with the piquets as two forms materialised from the narrow path into the moonlight.

"Don't shoot, I beg, it's Chalmers from the British embassy in Lisbon."

"You must give the word, sir."

"Oh, yes, of course. The word is … York."

"You may approach, sir but do so slowly with your hands raised."

"Is all this really so necessary?"

"It is my orders, sir, if you would oblige, and your companion also. We must see that your hands are free of weapons."

"Well, really, this is most ungentlemanly but very well. Anxo, your hands up."

"I understand, senhor, they are already raised."

"Approach slowly, gentlemen."

Willoughby ushered the two men through the piquet line and Chris walked to meet them.

Willoughby did the introductions. "Captain Lennox, this is Mr Chalmers and a Portuguese gentleman ..."

"Anxo Costa, Captain. I am your guide and I am at your service whilst you are in my country."

Chalmers gave a courtly bow. "I bring greetings from his Excellency Ambassador Fawkener."

"Was it you who selected this beach for a landing?"

"It was I," Anxo said.

"We need to get off it and into cover."

"Have no fear Captain. I have men on the cliff top keeping watch. It is a quiet beach away from other habitation, we shall not be disturbed."

"Where are the French?"

"The last I heard they were a day's march to the east," Chalmers answered. "They should not trouble us."

"The last you heard is not very comforting, sir.

"Lieutenant Willoughby. Take your men to the head of the path and secure it with a defensive position. Senhor Costa will go with you to make sure his men know who you are. Pass the word to Lieutenant Dean that he's to follow once you send a runner back. On the double."

Willoughby gave his grin. "Aye, sir, on the double."

Willoughby and Costa moved off, collecting soldiers on the way. Chris waited until they were out of earshot. "You have news for me, Mr Chalmers?"

"Indeed, sir, I do. His Excellency has bid me to tell you that Mr Foxley arrived in Lisbon not three days gone and is even now, we believe, ensconced in the French Legation. We have no intelligence as to why he should be there and what exact knowledge he could impart."

"But you fear the worst?"

"Indeed, sir but he has not been seen since his arrival and one wonders whether he is still a guest of the Frogs or whether he has slipped away."

"I can't understand what Foxley's doing, although I could guess at why."

"The man would appear to be a traitor, sir."

"Yes, it would appear that way. Now, the runner has returned, it's time to get off this beach."

Foxley was disgruntled and silently seethed. He had thought his information would have entitled him to more consideration than the French had shown him. Damned Frogs did not know the meaning of gentlemanly behaviour. He had paid for his own passage from Dover to Lisbon on the expectation that he would be well-rewarded. True he had been given several hundred French francs but that was below what he imagined was his due. In addition, they had bundled him from the back entrance of the legation covered in an evil-smelling cloak and into a carriage that had seen better days for the long and arduous ride south and east towards the Spanish border. He had hoped for some time visiting the houses of ill-repute beside the docks.

His companion, a sour-faced French revolutionary, complete with tricolour sash and bicorn cockaded hat, had barely uttered a word over the two days other than to order him from the carriage in his poor English at the change of horses and for light refreshments which in no way matched his appetite.

Perhaps the French did not trust his story and were to put it to the test. If he were honest with himself, which was a seldom enough occurrence, his story did indeed sound unbelievable to a suspicious ear. Why indeed should the British put ashore a small contingent of soldiers in a friendly country? How indeed would they know of French intentions in the region? How indeed did he, Foxley, come by the intelligence?

He did not know exactly to where they were travelling. His guard-cum-companion would not say. He kept his beaded eyes forever on him and also kept his hand close to the horse pistol stuffed in his sash. It was not something that allowed Foxley to contemplate his immediate future with equanimity.

After a particularly jolting passage where every lump in the unevenly padded seat sent a shock up his spine he thought to try a conversation.

"Somewhat of a washboard, this road, monsieur."

The man stared back and grunted.

"And warm for this time of year, by god." Foxley pulled at his cravat with a finger. "Damned warm."

"It is the south."

"Are we to go much further this day?"

*"Vous trouverez bien assez tôt."*

Foxley understood well enough but thought it wise to profess ignorance. "Sorry, monsieur, what was that?"

The man grunted again and gave Foxley a baleful glare. "Soon, you will know."

"Much obliged, I am sure, although that tells me precisely nothing."

"You must not ask the questions. It is *interdit* ... forbidden."

Foxley slumped into a brooding silence as the coach rattled on for another two hours. Then there was a shout and the horses were reined to a halt.

The revolutionary put his head out of the window and rattled off a stream of French. He grunted again and jerked a thumb at Foxley "Out now."

"Where are we?"

"*Allez, vite.* You get out."

Foxley gathered his bag and opened the door onto a ring of savage faces and the glinting steel of bayonets.

# 24

Foxley swallowed hard. From the tall bearskins with their angled belt, red hackle and gold head plate, the blue white-fronted and red trimmed coats to white breeches, these men wore the uniforms of French Grenadiers. Judging by the infantry sabres dangling on their left hips they were an elite unit and were armed with the long Charleville musket. Each one towered above him and their heavily moustached faces showed no hint of friendliness or compassion. For two sous, each man would run him through without a second thought. Or possibly just for their amusement. Foxley could not help the thought from entering his head.

*"Attention, mes braves."*

The men stood back, shouldered arms and stood to rigid attention. Foxley could not help but be impressed by their discipline.

"Welcome Monsieur Foxley" The officer, similarly dressed but with gold epaulettes and no cross belts, gave Foxley a mock salute. "We have been expecting you."

Foxley relaxed as it no longer seemed he was about to be run through. "Indeed, sir. Whom do I have the pleasure of addressing?"

"Colonel Fouquet of the First Grenadiers. I am at your service. But first let us see the pipsqueak citizen on his way." He waved his hand and the soldiers quickly unharnessed the horses, turned the carriage by hand on the narrow track and re-harnessed a fresh team. Foxley's travelling companion had not set foot outside but pushed his head through the window. *"Vive la revolution."*

Fouquet slapped a horse's rump and the carriage lurched away. *"Au revoir, monsieur le révolutionnaire."* He turned to Foxley with a smile. "Come sir, our camp is but three-hundred paces away, you must dine with us and tell your tales. We have received despatches from Lisbon but we need to put meat on the bones."

The camp was well ordered with rows of bell tents with attendant campfires disappearing into the gloaming. It seemed to Foxley that there was a full regiment of twelve companies camped there in the Portuguese countryside.

The mess tent was huge and held upwards of sixty officers of various ranks. Foxley was led to the top table and greeted as an honoured guest by the brigade commander. Fouquet, a battalion commander sat beside him and poured him some wine. "We will drink to our Commander-in-Chief, Napoleon Bonaparte, our petit caporal, before we eat. You have no objections?"

Foxley shook his head. "No, colonel, I shall be honoured to join you."

"You are a strange Englishman, Monsieur Foxley, who disowns his nation so easily. But, come, we shall drink and eat and then talk. There has been an English ship sighted off the coast and I wish to hear more of this invasion."

Chris was feeling more comfortable. The land at the top of the cliff was dotted with scrub and patches of thicker foliage with some stunted trees. It was difficult to see in the dark but they dug in on one side of the track and set the piquets. Fires were lit but kept small inside pits where the flames would not show. Anxo had assured him that there were no enemy troops within a day's march so the smell of wood smoke was a risk he could afford to take. No point in going on hard routine if there was nobody nearby to discover them.

The nearest village, Vilamoura, was an hour's march away to the east and Albufeira even further to the west. He had sent men back to the beach to erase their boot prints from the sand anyway. There was also no point in taking any unnecessary risks.

Chalmers stayed with them and would leave at first light with news of their safe arrival to be despatched back to England on the first available packet boat.

Anthony Dean heard the arrangement and gave Chalmers a sealed package. "For my wife, sir. Could you use your good offices to see it safely delivered."

Chalmers nodded. "My pleasure, Lieutenant but it may be some time before it reaches her hand."

"I have a correspondence too," Willoughby said and handed Chalmers a sealed paper. "For my father and mother, so that they should not despair of their son."

Chalmers turned to Chris. "Have you no correspondence, sir. No friend nor family to whom you may write?"

Chris shook his head. "No one in this time or place."

"Come, George, there must be someone who would wonder at your circumstance and whose mind you need set at rest," Anthony said.

"Not really, Anthony. All my friends you see around me. My family are far too far away to easily reach."

"Then you must write to Catherine. She would be most pleased to receive a note of your good health and welfare."

"No, Anthony, I could not possibly …"

"Come, I insist, sir. Write your message and include it with mine."

"I shall remind Anxo Costa that he must continue to send despatches from you once I have departed," Chalmers said. "The organisation of which he is the regional chieftain, is spread across southern Portugal to Lisbon. They are royalists, opposed to the French dogma of revolution which some Portuguese find attractive, and Anxo is as trustworthy as any.

"We shall receive all correspondence at the embassy and despatch them in the diplomatic bag to Horse Guards. I am to remind you, sir of the necessity of sending regular despatches."

"No need, Mr Chalmers, it's already imprinted on my soul. If you'll excuse me, gentlemen, I'll go and write this note that Anthony insists on. If only I could think of anything worthwhile to write about."

"Knowing you are safe and well will no doubt please her. She has a regard for you, sir, due to the great service you stood her," Anthony said.

Chris gave him an uncertain smile, left them seated around the flickering fire and crawled into his bivouac. His ballpoint's metal-cased refill had long since dried and he now used a pencil with the point shaped like a chisel so that it would write like an italic pen nib, broad and narrow strokes to emulate the characters that Dr Hawking had written for him.

He had noted some of the flowery phraseology that was used in written correspondence of these times but writing to Catherine was his worst nightmare. How would he start? *Dear Catherine* or *My Dear Catherine. Dear Mrs Dean* perhaps would prove the safest option but was that too cool, even for these times? Would she feel insulted that he wasn't more personal or would being more personal insult her? It was a quandary he could do without.

He had been given paper for his 'regular' despatches and used half a sheet of this, tearing the coarse material along a fold. The battery in his torch, another thing he had kept well hidden, was still fresh and he used this but masked the beam with his free hand so that it wouldn't shine beyond his shelter. He decided on a compromise opening salutation.

*Dear Mrs Catherine Dean,*

*I hope this finds you in good health. We have safely arrived at our destination and everyone is in good spirits. Your husband, Anthony, is faring well, as is our young subaltern, Richard Willoughby.*

*I am writing to you by the good offices of Anthony who bade me to correspond as I have no other to whom I could write. I do hope you will not be offended by this intrusion.*

*We are all missing our friends and family and are looking forward to returning home as soon as our duties will allow.*

*I remain your devoted friend,*

*George Lennox.*

Short and to the point, without giving too much away. No mention of their destination or their mission. More importantly, no mention of how he felt about her. He thought twice about deleting 'devoted' but maybe this would be taken as just good manners and she would read nothing more into it. Should he also have written 'devoted servant'? Then again, he had deliberately left off his rank so as to appear less formal. All-in-all it was a mish-mash but the best he could come up with.

He had tried to forget her, to cast her to the back of his mind but he could picture her face as she read the note, as sharply as if she were sitting in front of him. They had left Imber more than four weeks earlier and his memory of her had not faded. He tried harder to remove her face from his mind's eye and succeeded for a brief instant. It wasn't enough. Anthony's gesture, far from being kindly as intended, had inadvertently left him fighting his secret demon again.

It bemused him. He hadn't felt this way about previous girlfriends, such a flaring of need that was hard to control. Perhaps the lightning strike had changed more in him than just stopping his growth hormones. Perhaps it was the fact that she was unattainable. Catherine wasn't his, he had no right to her and never would have. The thought sent a pang of loss through him.

He folded the paper and tucked the ends in to form an envelope. Chalmers could take it when he left at first light.

Now he had work to do to check on the piquets, make sure that Biggin and Pocock had organised the guard rosters, and that they knew where to find his bivouac in an emergency. The minutiae of army life; details that could keep them alive ... and take his mind off the image of Catherine.


"So, Mr Foxley, this British expedition is less than sixty men, you say."

"That is what I have been led to believe, Colonel."

"What could they hope to achieve?"

"I am not privy to that intelligence, sir. All I know is that, what is known as the detachment, has been ordered to Portugal on a secret errand. They are to be spies, sir, but to what end I cannot fathom. They also do not wear the King's uniform but an abomination of green serge."

Fouquet grunted and pointed to a rough map of the south coast of England and the Iberian Peninsular. He traced a line with his finger as he spoke. "A frigate was seen to depart from Portsmouth with soldiers aboard some three weeks gone. The English frigate that was recently sighted was under sail from this southern coast not a day's march from here." He tapped the map hard. "Are we to believe that the landing has already taken place?"

"You have admirable information, sir. That time of departure from Portsmouth would indicate an arrival about now."

"Then we will march westward and scour the country. Even as few as sixty men cannot stay hidden for long. Prepare yourself, Mr Foxley, we have a long day ahead."

"I, sir?"

"Yes, you, sir. We have further need of your services in identifying these brigands. If they be not soldiers but spies, they may be dealt with as such with summary execution."

# 25

First light and stand to. Each soldier was in his defensive position should there be a dawn attack; a favourite tactic when biorhythms were at their lowest ebb. The Portuguese countryside appeared peaceful, warblers were singing in the scrub, many on their autumn migration back to Africa for the winter, others would stay in the milder climate of southern Europe.

Chris never tired of hearing so much birdsong. The 21st century was a desert by comparison. And the sweet smell of wild shrubs and flowers untainted by the industrial revolution and the internal combustion engine. The air was fresh and as pure as he had ever experienced.

He gave the nod to his two lieutenants and the men stood down for breakfast. They had brought their own supplies of oats and dried meats but would be living off the land for most of the duration of the mission. It was one of the reasons he had wanted countrymen and former poachers in his Rifles, they knew how to live in the wild and weren't averse to digging holes and trenches.

Chalmers came to him yawning and scratching his crotch. "God's teeth, sir. I do believe I have been sleeping with an army of fleas."

Chris gave him a crooked grin. "You'll be leaving us soon and I've had your horse saddled and made ready."

"You are not one to let the grass grow beneath your feet, Captain. An admirable trait. I have broken fast and will be on my way betimes. Do you have any further despatches?"

Chris fished in his pocket and gave him Catherine's note. "Put this with Lieutenant Dean's letter, would you."

Chalmers turned it over in his hand. "It is not sealed, sir. Do you wish a seal to be added?"

"There aren't any secrets in there, military or otherwise. Tying it with Mr Dean's message should be sufficient."

"As you wish, sir. The sun is rising and I must be away. Fare you well, Captain Lennox."

"You too, Mr Chalmers. Safe journey."

Chalmers walked to his horse. He had two Portuguese guides waiting for him, each astride small but hardy ponies. All around soldiers were packing away their kit and covering any sign of the bivouac site by burying rubbish and filling in the holes dug for the fires and latrines. He could smell wood ash where the soldiers had doused the fires, his sense of smell heightened in recent weeks, but he hoped that the wet ash stink would fade over the next few hours.

Anxo stepped up beside him. "What is your wish, Senhor Captain?"

"We go west, Anxo, towards the Monchique Mountains."

"It is three days march, sir, and the territory may be hostile. Not every Portuguese has a love of the English. Many now seek to emulate the French Revolution and declare a republic. We will need to proceed with care."

"We'll avoid the villages and keep to rarely used tracks. If it's impossible to avoid habitation we'll lie up during daylight hours and pass by at night."

"As you command, Captain. Should I send men ahead to judge the lie of the land?"

"A scouting party. Yes, thank you." Chris looked around, saw Biggin and beckoned him over. "Serjeant, take three men and accompany Senhor Costa's scouting party.

You are to keep out of sight, avoid all contact and report back to me if you come across any enemy activity."

Biggin nodded, knuckled his forehead and scampered away pick his riflemen.

Anxo gave Chris a look through narrowed eyes. "I see you do not fully trust us."

"It's not a matter of trust, Senhor, it is a matter of security. My soldiers will protect your men should they run into trouble."

"I hope they are fleet of foot as my people move very quickly at the scent of danger."

"They are fleet enough, Senhor Costa, fleet enough."

He turned to check that every man was ready. "Lieutenant Dean, advance to contact but be on the lookout for returning scouts. Lieutenant Willoughby set a rearguard of six riflemen. Forward the Rifles."

Colonel Fouquet's battalion of six companies and a half squadron of Horse Grenadiers had marched out of the encampment at dawn with drums beating and flags flying. Foxley had been given a horse and he rode behind Fouquet's staff officers in the centre of the column. The drums stopped beating after several hundred paces, except for one that tapped out every other pace. The flag, Foxley assumed the battalion's colours, was also furled inside a leather case and carried by an ensign.

The pace was spritely and by mid-morning they had covered six English miles by Foxley's calculations, with just two five-minute stops.

Fouquet called another halt and sent for the cavalry *chef d'escadron*. The man galloped up towing a small cloud of dust in his mount's wake. He reined the horse to a sliding stop and threw Fouquet a salute. *"Oui, mon Colonel."*

"Fouquet replied in French and Foxley strained his ears to catch the words.

"I trust you have another mount, Captain, for that one will be dinner for my soldiers should you persist with such exhibitionism."

The cavalryman laughed. "Indeed I do, Colonel but your men will starve long before this animal will go down under me. What is your wish?"

"Take your horse soldiers and ride ahead along the coastal track. See what you make of it. Skirmish formation if you please, we have no wish for unpleasant surprises."

"You are expecting an enemy formation?"

"None that you might recognise as such. Bring anyone you find in green clothing to me."

"Green, Colonel? Are you suffering a touch of the sun?"

"You will be suffering the touch of my crop for such insolence," Fouquet said but he was laughing. "No, I am reliably informed that our foe is so attired. Subversives, Captain, green men, and should be treated with care as they may well bite."

"Then they will feel the edge of our sabres for their impudence."

"Bring back one alive, should you find them, as I wish to question the brigand."

"As you wish, Colonel. Until later." He wheeled his horse and galloped back to his men before signalling them to follow him. The entire unit thundered past the foot soldiers covering them in clouds of dust, ignoring the shaken fists and ripe comments.

Fouquet turned in his saddle, pointed at Foxley and shouted. "My nephew, Captain Perrot, the Horse Grenadier, late of the 9th Dragoons, Mr Foxley. He will flush our game or you may call me mistaken."

# 26

It was not ideal cavalry country, Perrot conceded. In places the underbrush was too thick to ride through and there were many gullies and small canyons, each of which had to be searched.

So he was looking for green men. The idea amused him. However, his uncle was not given to flights of fancy and he should take the warning of an implied threat seriously.

His men were riding in two skirmish lines, one a hundred paces behind the other with a twenty pace gap between each horse. It was enough to flush small game and partridge but nothing larger than small mammals. He rode in the centre between the two lines so that he could easily communicate with his subordinate officers. He checked the sun, it was moving to the west, well past midday and yet no sign of green men.

The track here was close to the cliff edge overlooking a small bay and he called a halt to water the horses. He jumped from the saddle, stretched and walked into the underbrush to empty his bladder. He had only taken a few paces when he stopped and sniffed the air. He called over his shoulder. "LeClerc, can you smell anything?"

"Nothing, other than horse sweat and your piss?" The man replied.

"Use your nose, you old goat. Come over here."

"What is it, Captain?"

"You tell me."

LeClerc took a deep snort. "Burnt wood."

"And recent, do you think?"

LeClerc took another great sniff. "I would say so. Maybe a few hours, maybe more."

Perrot took a few more steps into the brush and came to a flattened area. "Look, LeClerc, the ground has been recently dug."

LeClerc shrugged. "Maybe woodsmen, Captain."

"There are no woods here to speak of. A few stunted willows is all."

"Then what, Captain?"

"Green men, LeClerc, subversives, and in numbers judging by the ground. Send a messenger to Colonel Fouquet that we have found sign and are in pursuit. The rest to horse, the quarry is afoot and cannot be far ahead."

Corporal O'Dell jogged up to Chris's side and pointed back the way they had come.

"Beggin' your pardon, sir."

Chris followed his pointing finger and saw the flash of light glinting from accoutrements as horsemen crossed the ridge two miles behind them. "Cavalry. My, my, I wasn't expecting them."

"They be upon us shortly, sir," O'Dell said.

"About ten minutes, I'd say. Not a lot of time. Everyone into the brush. Spread the word, O'Dell, quickly now."

O'Dell ran forward waving his arm. Willoughby came up to Chris with the remainder of his riflemen. "I do believe they have not yet seen us."

"We're lucky, the brush is thick here. We can see them far more easily."

"What are your orders, sir?"

"We'll try to disappear. Have your riflemen brush our tracks from the path. We'll lay up in a defensive position just over the ridge to our right and hope they'll ride past."

"They are at the canter. On the scent I do believe."

Chris screwed his eyes and studied the group. "Just a dozen. Probably an advance party. There will be more following. Quickly, now, set your men to work, we have only a few minutes."

As the men broke saplings and brushed away the boot marks Chris pushed his way through the undergrowth and followed the rest of the detachment up the rise. Anthony had spread the men on the far side of the rise with the rifles at either side and a block of muskets in the centre of the line. The riflemen were grouped in pairs, the way he had trained them. He nodded his approval. "Well done, Lieutenant. Keep everyone concealed and let's hope they pass us by."

"Aye, sir. We have not the numbers to form a true square. If the cavalry get amongst us we will fare badly."

Willoughby and his men scampered over the rise. "They are almost upon us. I have left two riflemen concealed where they may watch and warn us if we are discovered."

Chris unwound a scrim net face veil from around his neck and draped it over his head. He dropped to his knees and crawled forward to find himself a place where he could see the line of the track. There were two indentations in the foliage where his soldiers had pushed through. He hoped the riders would miss the significance. He could not see Willoughby's two riflemen, they were well-hidden with camouflage cut from the surrounding shrubs.

Dull thudding was getting louder and he could hear the faint jingle of harness as the riders approached. They were going at a steady canter but the lead rider was low on the neck of his horse following the trail of boot prints. Chris cursed himself. Their sudden disappearance would ring alarm bells, he hadn't been so clever after all.

They rode past stirring up dust but did not get far. The lead rider raised his hand and called out.

*"Arrêt."*

Chris did not need to know much French to get the gist of that as all the riders pulled on their reins, milling in a circle behind their young sub lieutenant. He rode forward a few more paces and then back again, laying low on the horse's neck as he studied the ground. He looked up and gestured to the other riders. *"Aucun d'entre vous les hommes peuvent-ils voir les pistes?"*

His voice carried and Chris watched the men below shaking their heads. It seemed no one had seen where the tracks had disappeared. The milling horses had covered any sign that might have been left.

The officer stood in his stirrups and looked around with his hand shielding his eyes. He sat and turned his horse to continue along the track but this time at a walk as he tried to rediscover the prints.

Another thought struck Chris. Biggin and his riflemen had passed ahead of them with the Portuguese scouts. The cavalry would pick up their tracks within a few metres. No sooner had the thought entered his head than the Frenchman gave a shout of triumph. *"Ici, ils sont, allons."* He waved an arm in the air in a typical Gallic gesture.

Chris made a decision and called out. "Rifleman, take down the officer's horse."

"Aye, sir," a steady voice said. The brush below Chris stirred and O'Dell stood, levelled his rifle and fired.

The officer slumped in the saddle as the other riders pulled up in shock. The officer slid to the ground.

O'Dell had dropped back down but not quickly enough, one of the guardsmen had seen the cloud of blue powder smoke and screamed as he pointed up the slope. Intent on retribution they wheeled their horses and spurred them into the brush. It was slow going, the horses leaping forward and upward one bound at a time like giant rabbits, riders jerking in the saddles as they drew their sabres and screamed their battle cries.

O'Dell's companion stood now and watched. The French troopers saw him and screamed even louder. The horses got more traction as the scrub thinned and gathered speed. The rifleman took careful aim and brought down the leading rider with a shot between the eyes. Both he and O'Dell turned and ran for the ridge with the riders now closing fast, sabres raised.

There was a rustling in the undergrowth behind Chris as the remaining riflemen marched forward, Anthony with them. O'Dell was struggling now as the thick brush caught at his legs; his younger companion had passed him and he was now in danger of being struck by a flashing sabre.

O'Dell stumbled and a guardsman lunged at him. He was just a few metres from safety, a few metres from Chris who hoped the Dragon had the range. He fired the pistol as the guardsman lashed downwards. The man faltered as a few pieces of buckshot hit him and his cut missed.

O'Dell rolled away from the horse's hooves but the guardsman wasn't finished, he raised the sabre again.

A volley of rifle fire crashed out and seven more riders fell from their mounts but not the one threatening O'Dell. He lunged again. This time he did not miss, catching the rifleman on the back. His horse stepped sideways and the next cut hissed through air but he spurred the animal closer. On the ridge, the muskets had moved into line and were preparing to fire a volley but they would be too late to save O'Dell.

Chris leapt forward and yanked on the horse's bridal pulling it away from O'Dell. The grenadier swung his sabre but lost his balance. Chris pulled his second Dragon and fired into the man's chest.

The ridge was enveloped in a cloud of acrid blue smoke from the musket fire. The muskets had fixed bayonets and were advancing down the slope finishing their gruesome work. Chris tried to wave the smoke away but it crawled up his nostrils and made his eyes run. He turned to O'Dell who was on his feet.

"Corporal O'Dell, I said shoot the officer's horse, not the man himself."

O'Dell gave him a pained grin. "Beggin' your pardon, sir, I thought you said take the officer of horse down, sir."

Chris knew the man was lying but also knew that there was no Geneva Convention and killing Frogs was meat and drink to these tough men. He gave O'Dell a fierce glare. "Serjeant Pocock. Get a dressing on this man's back."

Anthony was beside him his face flushed with excitement. "By god, sir, we got them all."

"Don't celebrate too, soon, Lieutenant. This was just an advance party, the main body will have heard the fighting and will be over us like Chimps at a tea party before dark."

# 27

Perrot heard the distant gunfire and wondered about it. His lightly armed Horse Grenadiers could not have put up such a volume of noise. He called his officers to him.

"It appears the advance guard has made contact. It also appears that the enemy are heavily armed. We should proceed at speed but with caution to assist our comrades."

"How far do you place the combat, Captain?" LeClerc, his serjeant-major, asked.

"A league or so, maybe less. The wind is from the west and carries sound more readily. Certainly no nearer as the sound is dull to the ear.

"Prepare the men for battle. Carbines and pistols primed. We must keep the horses fresh so will start at the trot in columns of two."

"There will be nothing left for us, our comrades will have decimated the enemy before we arrive," a sub-lieutenant said with a wide grin.

Perrot was more cautious. "Perhaps so and we may meet them as they return but we should be ready to give assistance when we come upon them."

"But we are the Horse Grenadiers and invincible," the officer said. The others cheered.

Perrot looked at each one in turn and smiled. "Your spirit is unquenchable. Let us see what good French steel is capable of cleaving this day. We Horse Grenadiers have not yet been tested, so let us make history. Unfurl the standard, today we live or die for France."

Chris knew they had to move quickly but could not leave the dead lying where they fell and did not have time for a burial detail. He ordered the remaining horses to be caught and had the bodies lain across the saddles. The strongest looking beasts carried two bodies lashed in place across their backs.

Chris said a prayer for the dead. He wasn't religious but his men expected it of him. The horses were in a ring, snorting and stamping, the smell of blood seemed to excite or disturb them. He took a surreptitious look at his Breitling. Cleaning up was taking too long, nearly half an hour had passed.

He checked on O'Dell. He had given him morphine and he was comfortable and able to walk. The cut across his back had sliced through muscle but missed his spine. It would need stitches later but for now the bleeding had been slowed.

He was feeling bad about killing the French grenadier. His training had taken over and he had acted instinctively but now doubts were creeping in. What if the soldier had been General de Gaulle's ancestor? Would de Gaulle ever be born? Would 20th century France settle for a Vichy government under the less than charismatic Marshal Petain? Had he changed the course of history? Or had he changed history to what he knew in the 21st? He had been determined not to let these thoughts colour his actions but he could not help but wonder what kind of world would develop from his meddling in these distant times.

"Captain!" It was Pocock and he pointed at the rocky rise to the east. "Cavalry, sir. At least forty riders."

Chris gave a grim nod. He watched the horsemen turn to form two ranks twenty men wide. Sabres were resting on shoulders, glinting in the setting sun. They were preparing to charge.

He called to Biggin who had returned with the advance party and was with the horses. "Let them go, serjeant. Give them a good smack and send them on their way."

The ten horses galloped off towards the east, keeping to the track and kicking up dust. Chris could see the cavalrymen break their discipline to turn their heads to watch them gallop past and then settle back in their saddles determined to avenge their dead.

"Riflemen take post," Chris ordered. "Muskets, stand to and be ready on my command."

Anthony came to stand beside him. "Forty against fifty. We shall give good account of ourselves."

"The advantage is always with the defence. Now go to your men. You have your orders."

"Indeed, sir." Anthony saluted and turned away.

In the distance Chris saw light winking on a lens. Their commander was watching through a telescope and now knew who was in command of the British detachment. How often had he warned them not to salute in the field. They would all need reminding.

"They are advancing at the walk, sir," Pocock called.

"Very well. Wait for the trot. Riflemen pick your targets with care."

"They are at the trot, sir."

"Riflemen shoot in your own time. Muskets, set your fires."

Three hundred metres away the cavalry was going to a canter. Two officers flew from their saddles as heavy rifle balls struck home. A third, a corporal, had his arm shattered.

The pairs of riflemen changed places. To their front the musket group set fire to the undergrowth. The arid vegetation caught immediately and fanned by the strengthening evening breeze blossomed into a fiery barrier a man's height high and double the width of the cavalry's lines. They could not go through it and could not easily go around it. Men reined in their mounts and turned in confusion, the attack broken before they reached the charge. Rifles cracked and more men fell. The ensign carrying the flag went down beneath his horse taking the banner with him.

Chris watched as the commander rallied his men. One NCO dismounted and retrieved the flag. He was hit before he could remount his horse but another guardsman snatched it from his hand before he fell.

The commander was leading his remaining troops to the top end of the fiery barrier. Chris had foreseen this manoeuvre and had ordered the muskets to either end once they had finished their fire-raising.

The fire was now raging eastward at an ever increasing speed. The smoke had thickened leaving the rifles unsighted. They withdrew back to the far side of the ridge to reload. They had done incredible damage. All but one officer was down and the majority of the NCOs with them. The cavalry were still dangerous and should they breach the line of muskets could cause untold trouble. Chris counted twenty-one men still in the saddle, more than enough to break through their lines. These were tough, hardy men, the cream of the French army, they would not easily back down. They were forming a disciplined line with the commander in front. Chris pulled one of the spare rifles from Pocock's back.

The cavalry were turning into the attack. His muskets would not stop them.

He sighted through the swirling smoke at the commander and fired. The man rocked in the saddle but did not fall. He did pull on the reins and his mount stopped. The remainder of the line pulled up in confusion. One large red-faced rider leaned over and grabbed the commander's bridle turning the horse back. The rest of the horsemen followed in disarray.

The muskets fired at their retreating backs but the distance was too great for the smoothbores and little damage was done. A ragged cheer went up from the British line.

Chris watched the French retreat with a thoughtful look. They would not be back tonight but he had the awful feeling that all they'd done was ruffle the cockerel's feathers. They would return in larger numbers before too long. That was a fight he did not relish.

Perrot rocked in his saddle and clenched his teeth on the awful pain, The bullet had hit his lower right chest and exited through his back. It had chipped a rib but passed between the diaphragm and bottom of the right lung. Blood was seeping through his fingers as he clutched the hole tightly, not pumping, which was a good sign that nothing vital had been hit.

LeClerc was leading his horse by its bridle until they were over the crest and out of sight of the green men, then he pulled up with the other guardsmen milling around. All had looks on their faces, a mixture of anger, anguish and the shame of the defeated.

LeClerc dismounted and gently lowered Perrot onto the ground. He pulled his fingers away and inspected the holes front and back. "I think you will live Captain, if we can get you to a surgeon quickly enough. The bullet passed right through but there will be pieces of your uniform in the hole."

*"Merde."* Perrot muttered. "My tailor will be heartbroken."

"So will the ladies in the Rue Pigalle if I do not get you back in one piece."

"I am not that easily done with, you old goat. Get a bandage on me and hand me back on my horse, if you please."

As LeClerc worked Perrot analysed what had just happened. Riderless horses were standing close by or slowly walking in small circles, unsure of their surroundings. They were well-trained animals and would easily be rounded up. He counted the empty saddles. Too many, far too many. He had lost all his brother officers and half his non-commissioned officers. His command of sixty grenadiers had been reduced to a mere handful. And yet it should not have been so. They were out of musket range when most of the riders had been felled. Not by a volley but my single shots. His own wound had been caused in the same way. A single report and the hard slap in the side. His own men had not fired one weapon. There were no obvious targets and all were well out of range of their carbines and pistols. Then the flames. What kind of warfare was this? It was beyond his experience. He knew the ancient Greeks and Romans were adept at using fire but he had not seen the like in modern times. Not on a battlefield against cavalry.

He had seen the enemy commander receive a salute; a man strangely attired in green of varying hues wearing a Breton style beret. He would know that face again should ever they meet.

Now he had his immediate future to consider. His Horse Grenadiers had been outfought and he humiliated. He would report to his uncle the colonel and it was not a meeting he viewed with any enthusiasm. Failure was not an option for the elite regiment.

LeClerc coughed and it brought him out of his reverie.

"The men await your orders, Captain."

Lost without their immediate commanders the soldiers were standing watching him, waiting.

Perrot struggled to his feet on LeClerc's helping arm. "I wish a despatch sent to Colonel Fouquet. I shall pen it now. Betwixt times, send two scouts back to the battlefield to ascertain whether the enemy still hold it. Make it under a flag of truce as we wish to retrieve our dead and wounded. If the enemy has left the field take efforts to discover their whereabouts and direction but keep well back, they appear to have muskets that have a far greater range than our own Charleville weapons.

"LeClerc, I shall leave you in command to see to our fallen comrades whilst I visit the surgeon. Have a care that you follow my orders fully. I want to know where those green men go, for I intend my revenge to be terrible."

# 28

The fire had died away as its fuel ran out on the rocky slope of the ridge. The battlefield had been cleared of bodies. The British laid them in a line and covered their faces with the dead men's own tunics as two cavalrymen rode towards them waving a white cloth.

Chris turned to Willoughby. "How's your conversational French, Richard?"

"Passable, sir, passable."

"Find out what they want and send them on their way."

"They will want to recover their dead, sir."

"As long as that's all they want they have my permission. Just keep an eye on them. Take Serjeant Pocock and six muskets with you. Keep the rifles hidden, no point in giving the game away."

Chris went to Biggin. "What did you find, Serjeant?"

"Beggin' your pardon, sir. Me and Mr Costa 'ere went right ahead and found us a small village, a hamlet more like. The natives are friendly and loyal, or so Mr Costa believes, to the Portuguese queen. They have a well with clean water that they are willin' to share."

"The village is called Bartolomeu de Messines," Costa added. "I know them well."

"We need to get off the coast track and head inland or we'll be sitting ducks for cavalry."

"That's right, sir, beggin' your pardon, sir, this is nigh on two leagues northward."

"That's far enough for tonight. It will be dark in two hours. The French won't pursue us until morning and until they've had time to mop their bloody noses."

Biggin guffawed. "Aye, sir. I 'ave never seen the like. Put the wind up ol' Froggie right enough, beggin' your pardon, sir."

"A cheap victory, Biggin. They'll be back for more. Mr Costa are your people ready to travel?"

Costa nodded. "Of course, at your command."

"Good we leave soon but I have a despatch for the embassy if you could arrange for two of your men to carry it. Biggin, my compliments and ask the lieutenants to see me as soon as they have completed their current duties."

"To attend you, sir. Yes, sir."

Biggin scuttled off and Costa went to brief his two messengers. Chris scribbled a quick note for Horse Guards about the unexpected presence of French cavalry. He had just folded the note when Anthony and Richard arrived. He begged some sealing wax from Anthony. He had safety matches in his Bergen and rummaged them out. He needed an instant flame to melt the wax and decided this was the time to introduce the two officers to some more New Zealand Maori magic. He struck the match and wasn't disappointed by their astonished looks. "Simple chemistry, gentlemen, a combination of paraffin and red sulphur. We've no time for flint and tinder." He dripped wax onto the paper and used the reverse of one of his sovereigns to make an impression of St George and the dragon. He waved Costa over to take the package.

Anthony pulled a note from his pocket. "Would you see that this is also delivered, Senhor." He saw Chris's quizzical look. "Newly wed, sir. A note of undying love to warm Catherine's heart whilst we are separated."

"Nice thought," Chris said. He sat them on rocks next to a bare patch of earth. "Everyone did well today. No one injured except for O'Dell."

"He is beginning to burn up with fever," Anthony said and may not march for long."

"I'll see to him shortly but first I want you to understand our position. Today we had a small victory, small but welcome, it's given the men confidence in their weapons and in their officers. However, I didn't plan on being discovered so soon and by cavalry which puts a completely different complexion on our situation.

"We can't fight a large formation, we don't have the numbers. What we do have is guile, as Captain Cunningham put it. We'll hide by day and march at night. It will slow us down but it's a damn sight safer." He drew a rough map in the dirt. "Here is the coast. The track we have been following goes to the far west. We are about to turn inland, sooner than I'd hoped, but necessary now. Biggin and Mr Costa have found us a village where we can rest for tonight and replenish the water canteens. Remember to have the men boil the water before drinking it as it may be contaminated. This night will be the last night we will have fires as we'll go to hard routine once away from the village. Perhaps we can buy supplies from the villagers but, if not, set the poachers amongst the men to work on small game. Have the meat cooked and dried." He drew another line on the map. "This is where we're headed, into the Monchique Mountains and to the Setubal road. Horse Guards has heard rumours that the French are building fortifications there. If we discover them we have orders to to map them.

"From now on the rear guard will drag branches behind us to cover our boot prints, I don't want a repetition of today. We have to disappear, gentlemen, as if we were never here.

"Richard, have you seen off the French?"

"Indeed, sir. They have taken their dead from the field but two still linger on the ridge beyond the rocks although they no longer display the white flag."

Chris gave a thoughtful nod. "Right. Two reasons for that, maybe. One they are there to warn of our advance on them or, more likely, they will be following us to see where we are headed."

"And if it is the latter," Anthony asked.

Chris gave him a taut grin. "I'll think of something. Now, get your men ready to move out. I'm just going to check on O'Dell."

"The men much appreciate your high regard for their wellbeing," Willoughby said. "They are much in awe of you, I have overheard them speak so."

"Let's hope their trust in my awesomeness isn't misplaced. Get going, we haven't much time."


Perrot completed the ride back to the regiment's camp without falling from his horse, although on two occasions his outriders prevented any such dishonour from occurring.

They pulled him from his mount and half-carried him to his cot. The surgeon was summoned and came quickly.

Perrot had stripped off his tunic and his manservant was peeling his shirt away from the dried blood that plastered it to his torso. The surgeon eyed the holes, thoughtfully rubbing his chin.

"I will need hot water and clean bandages, quickly. I shall have to probe, Captain but it appears the ball passed through."

Perrot ground his teeth as he wriggled into an upright position. "Do your worst, *maître boucher*, do your worst. Pierre, where is the cognac?"

The surgeon stood upright and puffed out his cheeks. "You slander me, Captain. I was trained at the Sorbonne. Master butcher, indeed."

"My mood will improve with some cognac. Pierre get your lazy backside moving."

A half-full tankard was thrust into his outstretched hand and he swallowed most of the contents in one long draught. He wiped his mouth on the back of his hand and thrust the tankard back at the luckless Pierre. "Fill that, properly this time, and then run to beg an audience with the colonel with my compliments and apologies. He needs come to me as I am somewhat indisposed for the moment."

Pierre handed him back the tankard and bobbed a bow. "At once, my captain."

The surgeon was unrolling a leather bundle full of surgical instruments. "I shall have need of some of that brandy to disinfect my *butcher's* knives."

Perrot had just downed another large swig. "Now I am concerned about your qualifications, monsieur. Any gentleman, butcher or not, should know the difference between vintage cognac and mere brandy and what a waste it would be to soak such instruments of torture in the good grape."

"Suit yourself, Captain. It's the cognac or a dose of blood poisoning."

"You drive a hard bargain, monsieur. Very well, here." He thrust the tankard at the surgeon and collapsed back on the cot, staring at the canvas roof.

The surgeon rinsed his probes and forceps and advanced on his patient.

"Before you start, monsieur."

"What now, Captain?"

"Will I be scarred?"

"Undoubtedly."

"Very good. I shall have a souvenir to show the ladies."

"What misfortune has befallen you, nephew," Fouquet said from the tent opening.

Perrot was now more than a little drunk. "We are facing demons, my Colonel. Green clad demons."

"So the story from Foxley is more than a fairy tale."

"Indeed, sir. They are a most ferocious foe, they snap and bite like a pack of wolves."

"Did you get amongst them?"

"No, sir. They downed my men with devilry and flame. But wolves can be caught, sir, wolves can be hunted down, wolves can be shot. My god, sir, it will be my honour."

After the episode with O'Dell and the assassinated officer, Chris decided to take personal command of the rearguard. As they moved inland, dragging torn branches of broom with them, the country became more wooded.

They marched for half an hour until the sun was almost on the horizon. The main body of men were five-hundred paces ahead as they stopped in a small copse of wind-stunted trees. Chris signalled the men to drop into cover.

It wasn't many minutes later that he could hear the soft jingle of harness. Two mounted horse grenadiers walked their horses into the copse. The horses' hooves were wrapped in cloth to dull the sound but the men had neglected to muffle harness trappings.

Chris waited until they were level before giving an order. The men closed in from either side so quickly the grenadiers had no time to react. Bayonets were pushed up at them and bridles seized. One reached for a pistol but a bayonet jabbed him in the ribs and he froze.

Chris signalled the men to dismount and they did so reluctantly. He did not want to kill them in cold blood and they could not afford to take prisoners which left him with something of a dilemma.

Pocock sidled up to him as the French were being disarmed with ribald comments from the soldiers. "Beggin' your pardon, sir. What do we do wi' the Frogs now, sir?"

Chris scratched his head. Maybe humiliation was better than death, maybe not in these days but he felt he had no option. "Take their boots. We'll give the horses a smack and send them back the way they came. These two Frogs won't be able to follow us on foot. Just to make sure, tie them to a tree, tight enough that it will take them until nightfall to release themselves."

"Aye, sir, if that be your orders, sir, but they be after our blood soon enough."

"Don't worry, serjeant. There will be a time to kill in the days to come."

# 29

The hamlet was as Biggin had described it. It was a small farming community, not unlike a smaller version of Imber. There was an orange grove on one side and olive trees off to another. Chris noted with satisfaction that there was a copse of Spanish Oak nearby where they could make their camp. He was unsure how far he could trust the villagers and was happier away from the buildings.

The light was fading fast and he had the men dig defensive shell scrapes under the trees and camouflage their bivouacs. Anxo had bartered food and water, enough for several days which would be supplemented by trapping and foraging.

Chris wanted to put as much distance between them and the coast as they could the next day as the French cavalry could cover ground very quickly. The mauling they had been given would make them more careful and they now had a wider area to search but they would come across the hamlet in time. By then he hoped to be well into the mountains.

O'Dell was worrying him. The man was running a temperature and there were already signs that the wound was becoming infected. He had completed the march to the hamlet but had needed the help of two other soldiers to make it. Chris doubted that he would be able to continue. He checked on him again and shook his head. If anything O'Dell was in a worse condition. He called Anxo over. "My corporal can't continue, Senhor. Will the villagers agree to take him in until we return?"

"I do not know, Senhor Captain. We will need to have the village elders' permission and they will require some form of payment."

"I understand. It's not without its dangers and will be an act of good faith on their part."

"You are right, sir. If the French discover him here they may take retribution."

"See what you can arrange. As reluctant as I am to leave him behind, we can't take him with us, he is too sick."

"I will appeal to their Christian conscience, Captain, perhaps that might sway their judgement."

"It's worth a try."

"Will you accompany me, Senhor? It may give my argument more weight if a British officer is with me. Might I also suggest you discard the strangely coloured tunic. It may disconcert them."

Chris had an officer's serge tunic in his Bergen. "Give me a minute." Anxo nodded and he walked to his bivouac to change. He buckled the sabre around his waist and pushed a Dragon into the belt. He had taken to wearing the sabre on his back, as in the sword and sorcerers films, because he found it cumbersome dangling beside his leg. Now he had to be the archetypal British officer, the green uniform notwithstanding, to impress the locals. He returned to Anxo's side. "Lead on McDuff."

Anxo gave him a quizzical look but led him into the hamlet and a small stone building that appeared to be the local meeting hall. There was a mule tied outside with a saddle on it's back and dust on its coat. Chris cocked a thumb at it.

"The local priest," Anxo said. "There is no church and he rides here to advise the villagers and take communion each Sunday."

"Is today Sunday? I've lost track of the days."

"It is, Captain. Do you wish to take confession?"

Chris gave a wry smile. "Church of England, Senhor. We don't make confessions."

Anxo sighed. "More is the pity, Captain, that you cannot have your sins expunged as we do."

"I think I can live with mine. Is the service over?"

"Yes. The hour is now late. The priest and elders will be conferring before retiring. The father will stay the night and return to his home on the morrow." Anxo pushed open the heavy wooden door and they entered a candlelit room. There was a table at one end with a middle-aged priest and five elders sitting around it. They all looked up as the pair entered.

Anxo bowed. "Please forgive this intrusion, senhors. I have come with the British officer who wishes a boon."

The priest stood up and beckoned them in. "Welcome. Please join us."

Chris did not understand the words but the man's face was sincere. Anxo pushed him forward as one of the elders drew up two roughly made chairs for them to sit on.

The priest looked from one to the other but he spoke directly to Anxo.

"What is this boon?"

"The British have a wounded man, father. They wish to leave him to be tended by the village until they can return for him. They will pay for his keep."

"It is dangerous," one of the elders said. "There are rumours that French soldiers have come from Spain and that we will be overrun. If they were to find him here, well …"

"And where will he stay?" another said. "We have nowhere here."

"Where do your injured farmers stay to recuperate?" The priest asked.

"In their own casas, father, tended by their own families."

"There is the widow Nunes," another said.

"That would not be proper," the first man said. "A strange man alone with another man's wife."

"Bonifácio has been dead these three years gone," the second man said. "I would think he is much past caring."

"I believe the widow Nunes would *much* appreciate the extra funds, don't you think," the priest said with a twinkle in his eye.

"But there is still the danger ..."

"God will be watching. And I know of old there are many places that you hide your wares from the tax collectors," the priest said. "Places you could also hide a man. Should we Christians turn away a soul in need?"

Chris had been watching the exchange with an eye on the body language. He noted some reluctance on the part of the elders but the priest had a reassuring manner. His tone of voice suggested he was gently persuading the others to take O'Dell in. He gave Anxo a sideways look and the man gave him a pronounced wink in return.

"We should ask widow Nunes what she thinks of having a strange man in her casa," the first elder was grumbling. "What will her neighbours make of it? And the man is a soldier. We all know what soldiers are like."

"Saint John, chapter eight, verse seven. Remember what our Lord said, Roberto. Let he who is without sin cast the first stone," the priest said and gave him a meaningful look. "I will speak with the widow Nunes. I believe she is more than capable of defending her honour against a mere British soldier.

"Senhor Costa, ask the officer how much he is willing to pay for his soldier's care."

Anxo nodded and turned to Chris. "They want to know how much you are willing to pay."

"What do you suggest? What's the going rate around here for room and board?"

"These are simple people. Pay too much and they will be suspicious of your true motives. I would suggest five centavos per day. Pay some now and the rest when we return."

Chris did a quick calculation in his head. If he put the gold escudo on the same par as a sovereign then five centavos would equal ten pence, a good day's wage for a working man. "Agreed, Senhor but add that I will also pay a bonus of another two centavos per day if O'Dell is in good health when we return."

Anxo relayed the message and saw slow smiles appear around the table. The priest asked a question. "The padre wants to know when you will be returning, Captain."

Chris spread his hands and shrugged. "Maybe six weeks, maybe more." He wasn't about to let that information out; it breached opsec.

Anxo interpreted the reply and there was a brief exchange and some nods around the table. The priest stood and offered his hand with a smile. "It is agreed, Senhor."

Chris took the hand and returned the smile. "Thank you, padre. I'm most grateful."

The priest gave him a shrewd look and spoke in accented English. "It is unusual for an officer to have such care for the welfare of his soldiers. You wear green, not red and you have the aura of a good man, Captain. I trust God will guide you in your endeavours to aid Portugal and our sovereign lady."

Chris was a little surprised by the man's command of English and his apparent knowledge of their mission. The surprise must have shown on his face

The priest nodded at Anxo. "We are old friends, Captain."

"Now I understand what he meant by appealing to Christian consciences," Chris said with a wry grin.

"Your path will be fraught enough without having to tend to the needs of the injured. Bring your man down to us tonight. We shall ensure his comfort."

"Thank you again, padre. And you're right, there are many dangerous days ahead. There is a war coming. We'll do what we can to delay it, and that's why we're here, but come it will in the next few years."

"How do you know this, my friend?"

Chris shrugged. "I read the signs, padre. The French are expanding their sphere of influence and both Portugal and Spain are weak; like the oranges in your trees, ripe for picking. Bonaparte has seized power in France. He is an ambitious man and his ambition will make him ever more hungry for conquests."

"You paint a bleak picture, Captain."

Forewarned is forearmed, padre. Unfortunately I can see the future of countries but not of myself and my men. We are about to go into the unknown."

# 30

Fouquet was angry. Angry and frustrated. For two weeks they had scoured the countryside from the Spanish border to the tip of Cape Sao Vicente and as far inland as Sao Marcos da Serra without any sign of the green men. He had split his command into half companies and positioned them along the main routes east to west and north to south. He dare not make his units any smaller. The ferocity of the enemy was now legend. His men were not fearful of battle but he could see no point in handing any numerical advantage to the foe.

He sat in his tent and brooded with a map spread out on the ground in front of his chair. Perrot lounged in a corner, his side still heavily bandaged and his face pale. He grunted as he moved.

"Your horse grenadiers have nothing to report?" Fouquet queried.

Perrot moved and grunted again. "We have ranged further north in the past days but we have not sighted anything other than peasant farmers. No one knows anything. We have asked, we have cajoled, we have bribed, we have threatened, we have thrashed but to no avail. The peasants know nothing that they are willing to impart to us, even to the threat of death. I do believe they know nothing worth the telling."

Fouquet threw down his quill pen and ran a hand through his long hair. "These are not ghosts. Ghosts do not decimate my cavalry. How can they disappear so completely? We have searched every village for leagues in all directions. Where can they be?"

"Perhaps we are searching in the wrong place," Perrot said and picked the map off the floor with an awkward lopsided movement. "Here, Colonel, let us analyse our past course of action. We may yet see some light emerge."

"Very well, Captain." Fouquet took the map and spread it on his folding table. He waved a hand over it. "Where do you suggest we may now look?"

Perrot stroked his chin. "We have to ask the question why did the British land here at all? What is there to attract their attention?"

"There is nothing south of Monchique," Fouquet said. "There are the new revetments on the route from Portimao to the north. And the new fort that we have been ordered to garrison once it is completed, but otherwise ..."

"With no other choice perhaps it is the area near to the fort that we should be watching."

Fouquet gave a Gallic shrug. "What do we have to lose? If you are fit to ride take a full squadron of your horse grenadiers to set up a base camp. I will follow with my battalion. The rest of the regiment should stay south to guard the coastal routes. Those routes will be needed to re-victual the garrison once it is in place as our illustrious navy cannot venture any further west in strength than Cadiz due to the British blockade. I shall request permission from the Brigade Colonel but I do not see that he could entertain any objection."

"And what of that fool Foxley?" Perrot asked.

Fouquet gave a crooked smile. "He shall attend to me. I may yet have a use for him and some exercise may keep him from my cognac. Make your preparations, Captain. If all is well we shall march at dawn."

Moving only at night had slowed the detachment's progress much more than Chris had anticipated. Each morning at first light they had found an area to bivouac and dig in amongst trees and other vegetation which, pegged down, camouflaged the flimsy shelters. They had lived off cold food for some days before finding a secluded canyon where they could light fires without fear of the flames or smoke attracting attention as there was no nearby habitation. There he had checked the men's feet, much to their puzzlement and consternation. Many were averse to showing their often filthy toes in public.

Chris had given orders that feet were washed and blisters treated as often as circumstances allowed. After their initial reluctance the men could see the sense of it and he heard little grumbling. But they were getting bored. The long periods of inactivity was wearing on them. Sleeping during the day in holes in the ground, under leaking groundsheets in the occasional downpour, was chafing on all their nerves.

After the first couple of days they saw no sign of French troops. Anthony reckoned they had left them behind and they would see no more of them until they returned south.

"The Frogs will keep to the wider routes," he announced as they sat together for the evening meal before breaking camp. "They will not venture into these hills."

"Maybe so," Chris said, "but we must keep out of sight anyway. Senhor Costa has news that the French are questioning villagers across the south for any sight of us."

"They will not find us," Richard said.

"Maybe not but if the villagers don't see us they can't tell the French. It's better that we stay hidden," Chris said.

"The men grow more stale by the day," Anthony murmured. "They believe we can now afford to live a more comfortable existance."

Chris shot him a sharp glance. "Then it's as well that I'm the one making the decisions. You must stamp on that talk immediately. We are safe because of the precautions that we're taking. The French may not be near now but there's no guarantee they won't be here anytime soon. From my calculations, we're just a night's march away from where Horse Guards believes the French fortifications are being built. We'll have to maintain our tight security and be even more alert."

"I have grit where no gentleman should ever have to suffer grit," Anthony said. "I have insects crawling on my body at night and I have been bitten more times than I can hope to count."

"Welcome to a soldier's world," Chris laughed and clapped him on the shoulder. Anthony was just beginning to learn of the privations of soldiering. Even the 21st century soldier had to contend with mosquitos, ticks and lice. He had an aerosol can of bug juice; another of his futuristic secrets, that would kill most things that crawled and bit. He was reluctant to bring it out but Anthony's morale was obviously at a low ebb. He could not afford for his officers to start feeling sorry for themselves. The NCOs and men could cope, they were more used to it.

"What about you, Richard? Are you suffering too?"

"Somewhat, sir. I sometimes fear I could scratch the skin from my bones."

I have another native remedy that will ease the problem." Chris delved into his Bergen and got a hand on the small can. "It can often affect the eyes so I want you both to close them. It also hisses like a snake but don't be alarmed it doesn't bite although it will feel cold on the skin. Who's first?"

"I propose it should be Richard, as he is the younger," Anthony said.

Chris grinned. "Guinea pig time, is it?"

"That is a most expensive pig, sir." Richard said. "I would pay no more than five shillings."

Chris sighed. "Just unfasten your collar and cuffs, Lieutenant, and keep your eyes closed. You too, Anthony."

He sprayed each man in turn, firing the cold jet down their backs and up their sleeves. "Now loosen your belts, there is another area that needs to be treated."

"You do not mean …" Anthony said.

"I do. Your nether regions need the same treatment but don't worry, it might burn a little but nothing will drop off, except for a few ticks."

"I do not find this at all humorous, sir," Anthony complained.

"You'll thank me for it later." Chris completed the treatment and put the can back in his Bergen. "If any of the men are suffering badly let me know so that I can treat those too."

Richard paused as he fastened his shirt collar. "I would hazard there will be no further volunteers." He pointed to where some of the men had lined up grinning and chortling. "We have been observed in our undress. I believe our dignity has suffered a terrible blow."

"But tomorrow they will still be scratching like flea-bitten dogs and you won't," Chris said. "Who do you think will be laughing then?

"Now it's almost dark. Be prepared to move out and do it silently. I've a feeling that this walking holiday is about to get much more interesting."

# 31

The French had chosen the site for their fort well. The mountains closed in at this point, making a narrow valley where the stone paved road snaked through rock walls. The fort sat on an outcrop with battlements overlooking the road. There was a smaller tower half completed on the other side and revetments guarding both buildings. The fort wasn't large, barely more than a castle keep but it looked solid. With cannon mounted on the battlements, it would command the road. With a chain strung across between the two buildings, nothing would pass without first gaining permission and secondly paying a toll. It would allow the French to control all the traffic to and from the south.

He counted several dozen men working, looking like ants on an anthill with mules carting materials back and forth from a line of tents on flat ground to the left of the road. The French engineers had cleared much of the greenery from around it but some still survived, lapping up to the encampment. Sentries were posted but they looked bored with their muskets either over their shoulders or stacked with the barrels fixed together and the butts on the ground while the soldiers smoked.

Chris studied the structures through a borrowed telescope and sucked his teeth. If they was half as dangerous as they looked the Portuguese were in for a tough time. Why hadn't this shown up in his school history lessons?

Anthony took the scope from him and peered through it. "A monstrous edifice, by god. And we are to map it?"

"Those are the orders. Richard is a dab hand with a pen. He'll draw the plans."

Costa crawled up beside him. His men had been taking messages to Lisbon and now one had returned with despatches. He handed two to Chris and one to Anthony.

"Thank you, Anxo. It amazes me how your men are able to find us."

Anxo gave him a broad grin. "We mark the trail so only they may follow it, Captain."

"I guessed as much. There was no other explanation. Now what do we have here?" He broke the seal on the first letter and read the message. He sucked his teeth again.

"Is the news bad?" Anthony asked.

"Horse Guards has upped the ante. The ship will be coming back in November, not January. We have less time than we thought. No reason given."

"The navy is a law unto itself," Anthony said. "Anxo, is your messenger with us still and is he able to return to Lisbon?"

"After he and his escort are rested. Do you wish another communication to your wife?"

"I do, I have it here." He handed the package to Anxo and waved his new delivery. "This is from her."

Chris slipped the second letter into his breast pocket. He recognised the faint aroma of rosewater. "I have a despatch for Lisbon too. It's in my pack at the bivouac."

The bivouac was sited in a depression surrounded by small trees and bushes. The men, apart from the sentries, were sleeping in holes covered with groundsheets and scattered with earth and leaves. The whole site was invisible, even from a close inspection.

Chris wormed his way back from the ridge and then ran doubled over to his narrow foxhole. His Bergen was propped in the far corner. He undid a side pocket and found his despatch. He had written it earlier that day and contained a description of the fortifications and the number of men working on it. The intelligence had been correct and the fort posed a clear danger to the stability of the region and would control a main supply route to the north. Napoleon, it seemed, was working on a two-pronged strategy to squeeze Lisbon from the north and the south.

Anxo followed him back a few minutes later. He stuffed Chris's despatch inside his shirt but had a troubled look on his face.

Chris cocked a questioning eye.

"You must come and see, Captain."

The noise reached him first, the jingle of harnesses and the thud of hooves on hard ground. He crawled into place and Anthony handed him the scope, not that he needed it.

Below a full squadron of Horse Grenadiers was riding into the camp, wheeling into line and coming to a disciplined halt. Behind them were the beginnings of a column of infantry that stretched out of sight.

"French Grenadiers," Anthony said. "Unless I am much mistaken, a whole battalion."

Chris ran the scope over the cavalry and picked out the officer with his arm bound to his side. It was the officer from their previous battle; still alive but looking a little the worse for wear. He moved the scope to the approaching infantry. The first two companies were wheeling into the camp and he could now see the command detail of staff officers riding together with the furled battalion flag. One man in civilian dress caught his eye and he drew in a deep breath. *Foxley*.

He watched as all the six companies marched in and formed ranks behind their commander. They looked tall and proud in the blue, white and red tunics and high bearskins. Each man carried a musket at the shoulder and an infantry sabre, which marked them as an elite unit, although they were known to rarely use the swords in battle. The commanding officer, a half-colonel, Chris assumed, swung a leg over his saddle pommel and surveyed the area. He pointed here and there and finally right at the ridge, it was almost as if he could see the hidden watchers.

"I think we are going to have company soon," Chris said. "The Frog colonel has an eye for defence; he'll be sending some men up here to hold the high ground."

"What shall we do," Anthony asked.

Chris gave him a tight grin. "Stay put in the trenches we've made. They would have to fall into one to find it but they're unlikely to venture into the undergrowth. They'll stay in the open areas, it's less work for them."

Anthony was watching the troops below. "Yes, a half company has been detached. They have mules and tents. It seems that they will pitch camp here. Others have moved to left and right."

"The colonel's securing his perimeter. Security was pretty lax until he arrived."

"We shall be trapped," Anthony said and bit his lip."

Chris grinned again, this time to try to ease Anthony's fears. "Ever heard of the saying to catch a tiger by the tail?"

Anthony shook his head. "I cannot say I have."

"That's what the French are about to do. Don't worry, Anthony. Spread the word amongst the men that we'll stay out of sight during daylight but get ready to move after dark. No noise from anyone. The French mustn't know we are here. Are your people all right with that, Anxo?"

"Of course, Captain."

"Go now, both of you and pass the orders. I'll join you in a short while."

The two men left and Chris continued to watch the French soldiers settling in and setting out their lines. As he watched, a string of mules made its way from the original tent line through the revetments towards the fort. Some mules were loaded with gunpowder kegs, others with large wheels and the barrels of artillery pieces. The French were on the verge of mounting cannons onto the fort's battlements.

Tramping feet brought his attention back to his own situation. The half company of Guards was swinging from the main road onto the steep path that led to the ridge. It was little more than a goat track and it slowed the soldiers down as they went into single file, dragging the reluctant mules with them.

Chris reckoned he still had a few minutes before the first of them arrived and watched as the cannons were unloaded alongside the fort's walls. The engineers were rigging pulleys from a gantry on the battlements so that the cannons could be hauled up.

*"Merde,"* a muffled oath drifted through the undergrowth. He had left it late to get into his trench. He ran doubled-over to the bivouac, threw himself into the undergrowth and crawled into his foxhole, pulling the groundsheet back in place over his head.

He was breathing hard from the sudden exertion and the adrenaline rush. He lay still and listened to hear if any alarm was given but apart from some voices giving orders and some complaining at receiving them there was no alarm raised.

He settled with his back to his Bergen and took out the note Anxo had given him. It was from Catherine. He held it for a while, fancying he could feel her hand in it. He was reluctant to break the seal but couldn't stand the suspense for long. There was a little light filtering into the hole and he held the note where he could read it.

*Dear Captain Lennox,*

Captain Lennox? So formal?

*My grateful thanks for your welcome letter. It was kind of you to inform us ...*

US! was that the royal *us* or her way of telling him she had treated his letter as a family communication.

*... of your safe arrival and that the officers and men are faring well. Here at Imber, we are suffering a period of heavy rain which has dampened what remained of the late harvest. The mood has dampened also now that we no longer have your company to entertain us. Amelia is particularly downcast at the absence of any invigorating repartee and wit at our dining table.*

*We* (we?) *hope you are all safe in God's keeping and we look forward to your prompt and happy return to us.*

*Perhaps you may use your good offices to persuade my husband to avail me with some tidings of his wellbeing as I have, as yet, received none and fear that he is unwell.*

*I trust that this favour will not prove an onerous one.*

*With our good wishes,*

*Catherine Dean (Mrs).*

Chris read the letter through twice more. Anthony had sent at least three letters that he knew of. If Catherine had not received them, but had received his own, who on earth was Anthony writing to ... and why?

The rest of the letter was equally puzzling but in a different way and he was trying to read between the lines. Was the use of royal pronouns a subterfuge or were they genuinely intended as plurals? Was it really Amelia who was missing his repartee and wit? Or was it a mischievous reference to his lack of either in Catherine's eyes. In which case the letter was a coded message for him. He could dream and for a few minutes, with the faint aroma of rosewater in his nostrils, he did.

# 32

The clouds had thickened overnight and covered the moon. The only light on the ridge was from two fires the French sentries kept burning. The Grenadiers had pitched their tents in a row backing on to the bivouac area but several paces above it. The sentries patrolled the ridge and like good soldiers did not turn to face the tents at the end of their respective beats but faced outward, the direction any perceived enemy might approach. This made it easy for the detachment to creep out unseen and inch their way silently to the foot of the ridge where they knelt, invisible in the night.

Chris had a plan. It was so bold it was outrageously dangerous. He was about to stage the world's first commando raid. He called an orders group and outlined his plan in terse whispers.

"This is madness, Senhor," Anxo whispered back. "It cannot be done."

"Once we have taken down the sentries on the revetments you can take your people further along the road. We'll rendezvous after we've completed our tasks. You don't have to be part of it."

"However mad I think you are, Senhor, I will not abandon you. I will send the messengers onward but the remainder will fight with you."

"Thanks, Anxo. Anyone else have anything to say?"

"No, sir, beggin' your pardon, sir, but it is about time we stuck it to the Frogs, sir," Biggin said.

"Anthony, Richard? Do either of you have anything else to add?"

"I would deem it an honour to accompany you on your task, sir," Willoughby said.

Chris squeezed his shoulder. "Thank you but I can't spare you. I'll take two riflemen with me armed with just their bayonets. Serjeant Pocock detail two of your best men for the task."

"It seems an unnecessary danger, sir," Anthony whispered. "Should we not just withdraw? We are so vastly outnumbered we surely cannot prevail."

"Buck up, Anthony. This is why I joined the army. A fight against the odds is much more fun. We'll make history tonight, one way or the other. Besides, my part in this is on the orders of Horse Guards; I'm honour bound to carry them out."

"Then so be it, George. My hand, sir. May God go with you this night."

Chris took the hand and shook it. "May God go with you all. Good luck and, with luck, I'll see you in an hour."

Chris and his two men slipped back towards the main French camp. Once again, it was as if fate was controlling his actions. The subsequent orders from Horse Guards had requested he obtain copies of any French documents that may throw light on their intentions in Portugal. Written orders, marked maps or anything else of sufficient interest were required. And now a complete French battalion had dropped into his lap where maps and written orders were sure to be found.

Chris wondered whether the officers at Horse Guards imagined him doing a frontal attack on French positions and, by defeating the enemy man-to-man, take the documents as spoils of war. He thought they might suffer apoplexy if they knew he was about to creep in; a thief in the night, a wretched spy. He grinned at the thought.

226

Apart from the calls of the sentries and the pawing and snorting of horses in the dark the camp lay silent and asleep. Chris led the two men as they slipped through the lines of tents towards the grand marquee that housed the battalion colonel's quarters. Two sentries stood by the main opening but they were resting on their muskets and appeared to be drowsing. The riflemen took them down silently and efficiently. They dragged the bodies into the deep shadows behind the tents, took the bearskins and muskets and replaced the guards. In the light of a nearby brazier they could be seen as the tall dark shapes of the original grenadiers.

Chris slipped between them and into the marquee. It was separated into one large briefing room and a smaller sleeping area which was curtained off. He could hear heavy breathing coming from there. A folding table was to one side with a candle guttering on it, almost burnt out. He was grateful for the meagre light it gave. The table was littered with documents, a bottle of cognac, an unlit lamp, a snuffbox and a pistol. He quickly sifted through the papers. The maps were self-evident and he rolled one of them to stuff into his tunic. The other papers were covered in small neat writing and he wished he had allowed Richard to come with him to translate the French. He had no idea of the importance of any of the documents. He shrugged and rolled some of the most important looking to join the map.

As he turned away his hand caught the lamp and it crashed to the floor.

Chris heard a grunt from the other side of the curtain and the creak of a cot.

"*Qui est là? Parlez ou je vais vous faire fouetter.*"

227

He tipped over the cognac and the candle and ran for the door as flames flared. The curtain was snapped back.

*"Gardes, que diable se passe?"*

The two riflemen turned at the shout as Chris charged between them. "To the right, this way."

*"Réveillez le camp, ma table est en feu."*

The three of them ran away from the now glowing tent into darkness. They passed another tent as a man came out waving a sword. Chris had no time to think he just reacted and punched the man hard in the face with the heel of his hand. He felt a nose crunch and the man let out a strangled howl as he staggered back. "God's teeth."

It was Foxley. Chris could not resist another hard jab and caught Foxley's chin with enough force to put him on his backside. He stood on Foxley's sword wrist. "A little something in advance, you traitor."

Foxley's voice was thick but there was no mistaking the venom. *"Lennox.* You will die for this."

He was talking to air, Chris and the two riflemen had already disappeared between two tents and towards the cover of the bushes. Behind them the camp was in turmoil as torches were lit and sentries roused men from their sleep. A musket cracked and someone screamed.

The detachment edged forward to the revetments and disposed of two sentries. The other guards were asleep in a tent and they were captured at bayonet point, bound together and gagged.

Of the four cannon that Chris had seen transported to the fort, two were still by the outer wall assembled and ready for the French to hoist them to the battlements. Willoughby ordered the guns wheeled to the road and placed on either side where it passed through the bottleneck. Inside the fort Anthony and Pocock found the magazine which was stacked full of gunpowder, cannon balls and canister shot. They took some gunpowder kegs and canister and broke open several other kegs spreading the gunpowder all around and laying a trail out of the door and into the open.

Ten riflemen ran to the far side of the track to the small tower taking kegs with them and did likewise in the circular room at its base, breaking some kegs but leaving others intact in a pile on the floor alongside a spiral staircase that led to the roof and a winding mechanism designed to carry a heavy chain.

On the road, the muskets lined up in two ranks behind the cannons and the riflemen, together with Anxo's Portuguese, dispersed into firing positions further along the sides of the valley.

Anthony and Richard stood together at the centre of the line. "Our tasks are completed," Anthony said. "What is now to be done?"

"We wait," Richard said and smiled in the dark at the other's nervousness.

"You believe George will come safely back to re-join us?" Anthony asked.

"I do and we must await his return."

"I cannot help but wonder at this turn of events, Richard. These actions were not ordered by Horse Guards; merely the mapping and positioning of the fortifications. Surely we are exceeding our orders."

"I rely on George's good judgement. He will have good reason."

"Even so I do believe we are committing an act of war which may yet rebound to our cost."

"Be at ease, Anthony. The Frogs would not hesitate to do likewise should they have the choice. Is it not they who have invaded a sovereign country, an ally of England? Are we not protecting a friend in need?"

"I suppose …"

"Suppose not. Horse Guards will be well pleased with our work this night or I'm not a true Englishman."

"I oft wonder if Horse Guards marches to the beat of a different drum."

"You will grow used to the ways of the military. You are new to this life and not yet inured to its vagaries."

A flare of torches in the camp caught their eyes. A musket cracked and someone screamed.

# 33

More musket shots and another scream, voices raised and flames now licking upward from the marquee. A bugle sounded the alarm and more men tumbled half asleep from their tents.

Chris and the two riflemen crept away from the noise and confusion, keeping to the cover of scrub. Sentries were more alert now and they took care to avoid passing the beats too closely. With all their precautions, they did not escape the attention of one sharp-eyed grenadier who challenged them. They did not respond, moving quickly away. The man fired his musket towards the dark shapes melting into the night. He missed but called out his serjeant and the rest of the guard.

They came with lanterns held high and followed in the direction the guard pointed. They moved quickly, able to see the snags and gullies that Chris and his men could not. They had to move more slowly to avoid breaking a leg or twisting an ankle and the French were gaining on them.

They reached the first of the revetments and ducked inside. The two riflemen still had the muskets taken from the sentries but had discarded the bearskins in the chase; their value as souvenirs diminished when measured against the possibility of a musket ball in the back.

The French had paused, swinging the lanterns back and forth to try to catch a glimpse of the fleeing men. The serjeant pointed ahead and snapped an order and the chase continued at a fast walk.

"Better slow them down," Chris said and took a musket from a rifleman's hands. "You two make a run for the fort."

The second man left his musket propped against the revetment wall, tapped his friend on the shoulder and they squirmed their way out. Chris gave them as much time as he could the lanterns were swinging his way and now giving enough light that he could see the white facings on the uniforms. He cocked the musket, aimed and fired.

He had no idea if he hit anything, the muskets were notoriously inaccurate at anything over thirty metres but he heard shouts and curses and made a run for the second revetment. There was a volley of shots but no ball came anywhere near him. He tucked himself behind the next wall and waited for the French to reorganise. They did so surprisingly quickly, making a rush at the first revetment. Finding nobody, they moved forward.

Chris fired the second musket dropped it and ran. A musket cracked and a ball slammed into his back knocking him on his face. It punched the breath out of him and he lay still gasping for a few seconds. It was all the time he could afford. Already, heavy footsteps were pounding close behind. He staggered to his feet and half-ran, half-limped along the hard surface of the road. Another musket cracked a ball snapped at his sleeve as it passed. The French were yelling cries of triumph; they were almost upon him.

Ahead he could just make out a ragged outline of rocks with the fort towering above him and the line of muskets. He swerved to one side and dropped flat. A series of flashes rippled along a line and several French soldiers dropped screaming. Another series rippled out. Two volleys fired in perfect timing. The remaining French grenadiers fell back dragging their fallen comrades by the arms, their heels bouncing on the stony ground.

Boots crunched on gravel and Anthony pulled Chris to his feet. "Are you able to walk, sir?"

Chris was still gasping for breath but nodded. "That was close."

"We thought you were hit, George."

"I was, right under the shoulder blade. I think I'll live though. The musket must have been poorly loaded and the ball didn't penetrate." *(Thank god for Kevlar).*

"Luck of the devil, sir. Now come behind the line ere they return."

"They'll wait for dawn. I would in their shoes. Their commanding officer will want to see what he's up against."

Fouquet was in a foul mood. The burning table had fallen against the marquee wall which had gone up in flames in turn. Only swift action by his grenadiers had saved the whole marquee by hacking away the wall and dousing it with buckets of water. The whole tent now stank of burnt wood and canvas and all his papers and maps were destroyed. Partly dressed with his tunic hanging from one shoulder he paced the grass and waited for information to come to him. From the shouting and musket fire someone must have seen something.

Perrot was the first to arrive but he had nothing of interest to tell only that one of the sentries had mistakenly fired on another and killed him. Foxley staggered up, his face a bloody mess. Fouquet cocked an eye at him.

"Lennox. It was Lennox. I had him by the throat but was set upon by his ruffians."

"The green men?"

Foxley nodded. "It was they."

"Invading our camp like thieves in the night?" Perrot said. "Incredible."

An officer ran up and saluted. "My Colonel, the men have something afoot towards the fort and are in pursuit."

"Thank you, Monet. Bring me what they find."

"At once, my Colonel." He turned on his heel and ran back the way he'd come.

"What do you think would interest the green men in my tent that they should take such risks, Mr Foxley?"

"Richer pickings. They are thieves and scoundrels. Have you inspected your purse?"

"My purse is untouched, as are all my valuables, except my damned marquee."

"Perhaps they were disturbed," Perrot said.

"Perhaps," Fouquet muttered. There was the crack of musket fire near to the fort. "Ha! It would seem that my grenadiers have caught up with the felons." More shots sounded then, a rippling volley. "My god, a full engagement."

"Those were British Brown Bess muskets," Perrot said. "British powder is less refined than our own, it burns more slowly and makes a deeper sound when ignited."

"British, yes, but few in number I think, which would chime with Mr Foxley's intelligence," Fouquet said. "They shall not escape me this time. Captain, pass the order to call the men to arms at first light. This time my grenadiers will make short work of them."

"Take the cannons back to where the road is at its narrowest point. About three hundred paces. Load with double canister and standby," Chris said. He did not like what he had to do next but it was necessary if they were to make any attempt at a clean escape.

Biggin and Pocock nodded and set their men to work wheeling the gun carriages further along the road away from the fort and tower.

Richard had mentioned Anthony's misgivings to him and he had to agree. They could have slunk away. He was exceeding his original orders in that mapping the fortifications was all that was asked for but that would not have got them the documents. Anthony did not know about the second set of orders delivered by Henry Wadman at Portsmouth with the codicil at the bottom which, similar to the orders given to Cunningham, gave him carte-blanche to use his own judgement in harassing the enemy wherever he found them.

The sky was beginning to grey in the east and he could hear trumpets blowing orders in the French camp. It would not be long now. He checked behind him that the cannons were in place. The muskets were at ease in two ranks behind the cannons, manned by Pocock and Biggin. They depressed the gun barrels to their lowest level and propped the trails up with rocks. Each gun was good for only one shot but Chris was hoping that was all they would need.

Richard was standing by his side twitching with suppressed excitement. "Are you ready, Lieutenant?"

"Indeed I am, sir."

"You are clear on what you have to do?"

"Yes."

Drums were rattling out a marching beat, still faint but getting closer.

"Then take your post and good luck," Chris said. He took his matches from a pocket and struck one in a cupped hand. Richard held a long piece of fuse over the flame until it sparked into life. Chris glimpsed his nervous smile in the dying flame before he turned away.

Chris watched him walk into the gloom before turning in the opposite direction and climbing the rocks to the base of the fort. The end of the gunpowder trail was twenty paces from the main door. With his matches in his hand he sat and waited. Now it was just a matter of time.

# 34

Richard Willoughby could do nothing to dull the butterflies in his stomach. He was nervous but it was not the nervousness of fear but of excitement. George had entrusted him with a dangerous task, one which, if done carelessly, he would be lucky to survive. He did not fear death. His youth imbued him with a feeling of invincibility.

He watched the approaching ranks of French Grenadiers in the growing light. He could see the white facings on their tunics but he had to wait until he could see the moustaches on their faces.

The drums were rattling and they marched in perfect step twelve abreast across the whole width of the road as it narrowed into the pass. Rank upon rank extending back into the gloom and the plume of dust thrown up by their pounding boots. It was a magnificent sight, enough to make the sturdiest heart quail on any normal battlefield. But this was no ordinary battlefield.

The British had twenty-six muskets and two cannons against hundreds of experienced veterans. They were outmatched by any standard. Richard had a twinge of doubt. Had George miscalculated? Was Anthony correct? Should they have turned away and hidden as they had done on so many previous nights? It was George himself who had said the first casualty of any battle was the plan for it, that they should expect the unexpected and be prepared. He shook the thought from his head. This was not unexpected; this was exactly how George had described it in his briefing. All he, Richard Willoughby, Lieutenant, late of the 62nd, had to do was his duty.

The faces of the front rank of grenadiers were becoming clearer. He blew on the fuse to brighten the spark and plunged it into the gunpowder trail at his feet. It caught with a flash and a cloud of blue smoke. He watched for a few seconds as it burned its way towards the tower door and then fizzled out. His breath caught in his throat.

On the road below the French were reaching the twin rocks along either side of the road. He dropped to his knees so that the soldiers below could not see him and scrabbled his way to the break in the powder trail. A careless boot had scuffed across it. He blew on the fuse again and dropped it into the gunpowder. Beneath the fort opposite, George would have ignited its powder trail which would now be nearing the magazine. His own powder trail was burning rapidly. Time was now short. He had to run desperately for his life.

Chris lit the powder and ran down the rocks jumping from one to another like a mountain goat. He and Willoughby had to be behind the cannons with the rest of the men before the charges blew or they'd be in danger of becoming two more of its victims. He cast an anxious eye at the tower but could see no sign of Willoughby.

The French were massing between the rocks at the mouth of the pass. As the light improved he could see an officer, his sabre over his right shoulder, leading the ranks. He knew that the French could now see them and their thin line of defiance. Not a thin red line but a green one.

Where was Willoughby? He was cutting it very fine. The French gunpowder burned quickly and if he had timed it right it would explode very soon.

There was a command from the French ranks and a roar of voices. Muskets were raised to the hip and the first ranks began a slow march forward. Eight ranks passed between the rocks before the fort exploded. It was a massive blast that hurled stones and wood skyward. To the left the tower also exploded in a sheet of flame. Rocks hurtled sideways into the massed ranks of grenadiers and began to cascade down on them from above. Dozens were knocked down in the huge twin blasts and many more crushed by falling stones. The pass protected the first eight ranks of soldiers from the worst of the blast but not from the cannons and musket fire. Biggin and Pocock fired both cannons as one, the canisters split apart and drove hundreds of musket balls through the French. Two great swathes cut through the ranks. Riflemen firing from the trees further along the pass picked off the few NCOs still standing and another volley from the muskets dropped many more.

Rocks and stones had blocked the pass at its narrow mouth so the French could not retreat. The survivors came forward, muskets at the hip, bayonets glinting and determination on their faces. There were barely twenty of them but they came on into the musket fire. They got off a ragged volley before the riflemen brought them down.

Chris looked at the carnage and felt sick. Such brave men and he was responsible for their massacre. Ninety-six here and who knew how many more killed and maimed by the explosions. He had lost two men in the last French volley, both hit in the head and killed instantly. They had to go, and go quickly, before the French could reorganise. The pass was blocked to cavalry, which had been his main concern but the infantry would climb over the blockage and be behind them in no time.

Pocock and Biggin had spiked the two cannons and were organising a party to carry the two dead men. The rifles, under Anthony's command, would cover the muskets' retreat and he could leave the organising of that to them. They would leave no one behind and that meant he had to find Willoughby if the explosion hadn't blown him to pieces. He scaled the left bank of the pass and edged his way along. He found Willoughby with a huge stone pinning his legs. He was conscious and in pain but his face broke into a ravaged smile when he saw Chris.

"I've come for you, Richard." He pushed against the stone but could not move it.

"Tis useless, George. My legs are crushed and I have but little time."

"The French will kill you if they find you. After this they won't be keen on taking prisoners."

"I know it, sir but I will not be taken easily. Give me your Dragon. I will take good account of myself."

"I can't leave you like this."

"You must, sir. There is nothing that can be done for me but you must see to the other men. I am but one life; theirs are many and in your care."

Chris knew he was right but it was breaking his heart to leave the gallant young man. He pulled a Dragon from his belt, cocked it and placed it by Richard's hand.

"Thank you, sir. Be sure to inform my father and mother that I died well for England."

A deathly silence had fallen over the battlefield after the explosions but now men were shrugging off the trauma and were beginning to reorganise. Chris could hear shouted orders and knew that time was running out. He gripped Richard's shoulder and could not stop a tear from rolling down his cheek. "Give them hell, Lieutenant."

"Be of good cheer for I shall die a soldier. I am cold now, George, but soon the sun will rise." His voice was getting weaker and his face screwed up in agony. Chris took a morphine ampoule from his pouch. "This will help to ease the pain."

"No, no thank you. I will endure it. Go now before the Frogs are upon us."

Chris left him, cursing the fate that had thrown him into a war of such crudity. No medics, no helicopter, no radios to call in assistance. He had to leave a comrade to die knowing that the French would give no quarter or that he might die unburied. The commander's curse; a curse that decreed he sacrificed the one in order to save the rest. He hoped that Richard's sacrifice was worthwhile.

He slid down the bank and ran to catch up with the rearguard. Anthony met him by a stand of trees. "Is Richard not with you?"

"Chris shook his head. "He's gone."

Anthony let out a deep sigh. "I feared as much."

Above them a rifle cracked and there was a distant scream. Chris took Anthony's arm. "Call the rifles down and let's get out of here. It seems the French are crossing the barricade and we need to go. Detail a rearguard of eight to cover our withdrawal."

"At once, sir," Anthony said, and appeared grateful for something to do to take his mind off Richard's death.


Fouquet was angry and appalled. "The best part of two whole companies lost this day and we are no further on. The pass is blocked by rock and I cannot release your cavalry, Perrot."

"It will take the engineers until the morrow to clear a path," Perrot added and slapped his palm on his thigh. "Damn these green men to hell."

Fouquet swung around to Foxley who was standing to one side moodily staring at the dust cloud and the wreckage of the fort. "Just fifty men you say, sir? Fifty men wreaked havoc on one-hundred and twenty of France's finest soldiers? How can this be?"

Foxley shrugged. "I had thought Lennox a fool with foolish ideas but unless I am much mistaken he took ship with just fifty men."

"What sort of men do we speak of, Foxley? Are they giants or devils? Satan's spawn could surely do less damage than has been done this day."

"They appeared merely ordinary. I heard rumour that they were the dregs of such regiments that seconded them. Thieves and poachers whose officers were pleased to see the back of."

"These are the dregs of the British army?" Perrot said and whistled. "Then I should be fearful of meeting the very best they have."

"These are the tactics of the gutter," Fouquet said. "What army clads its men in green who will not stand to fight? The sooner the world is rid of them the better."

An officer came in and saluted. "We have discovered one of the green men, my Colonel."

"Bring him to me."

"He is dead, sir. It took five men to lift the stone from his body."

"Even so, I would wish to see who it is that opposes me. Bring in his body."

The officer returned a few minutes later with four soldiers who carried a groundsheet with a body in it. They laid it on the ground and Fouquet indicated they should open it. He stared at Richard's face and stepped back. "My god, tis but a boy. They are sending boys to do such terrible damage."

Foxley walked over and peered into the sheet. "His name is Willoughby. He was an ensign of the 62nd."

"An officer." Fouquet beckoned over the officer who had brought the body. "How did he die?"

"He was crushed by a stone, sir, but he took a grenadier down with a pistol before he was bayonetted."

"My god, such courage in one so young. Perrot, ensure this Willoughby receives a Christian burial. I will not have it said that the First Grenadiers do not honour valour, even though we abhor their tactics. Bury him away from our own dead and mark his resting place with a cross. Be assured we shall not be so gracious to the living when we find them."

# 35

The weeks of fitness training was paying off. The detachment put several miles between themselves and the battleground by mid-morning when Chris called a halt. They had carried the two dead men with them but now took the time to bury them in a peaceful grove with a view over a wooded valley. Chris said a few words over the graves and left the men to rest for a short while as he wrote another despatch detailing the battle and the destruction of the fortifications for Anxo's men to take to Lisbon.

Anthony came and sat beside him. "I also have a despatch for Lisbon."

"For Catherine?"

Anthony hung his head. "Sir, I have a confession."

"That you have been writing to Horse Guards and neglecting to inform your wife of your well-being?"

Anthony looked up in surprise. "How the devil did you know, sir?"

Chris took Catherine's letter from his pocket. "I received this in reply to the note you asked me to write."

Anthony waved it away. "I hope it is not so but does she bear me much ill-will?"

"Not in the slightest. She is most concerned about you and asks for my good offices to persuade you to write her a letter. It can't be that difficult."

"In truth, sir I know not what to write. That is why I wished you to write in my stead, to inform her that all is well with us."

"Good god, man, what on earth is wrong with you? You left your bride of a day and you can't write to her?"

"In truth, our wedding night did not go well and I left on poor terms. Now I have little idea how to make amends.

I see the rams in the fields with the ewes, the bulls with the cows but a man with a woman ..."

"You were too ... *enthusiastic*."

"I fear so, sir. Perhaps with more time I should have more consideration."

"Do you love her, Anthony?"

"Yes, with all my heart."

"Then it's time you need. Write to her now. Apologise for whatever you think you have to apologise for. Tell her how much you miss her. Good god, man, I'm no agony uncle, you work it out for yourself. Be quick as I want to get the messenger away soon."

Anthony gave him a taut smile. "Thank you, sir. I shall do as you bid."

"Before you go, why are you sending despatches to Horse Guards?"

"Twas my brother-in-law's suggestion. He wishes me to validate the intelligence of your messages."

"So Henry Wadman was behind it?"

"Indeed, sir. Did I do wrong?"

"No, don't worry about it, Anthony. Go and write the most endearing letter to Catherine you can. I'll speak to Henry when we get back to England."

So they didn't trust him. Chris was sure the Duke of York would be behind Henry's subterfuge. Getting Anthony to spy on him was a low trick but he had to smile at the thought of it. In one way he was impressed. A mister-nobody turned up from a country none had heard of with tales of native medicines and scientific discoveries that baffled them and knowledge of French intentions that even their best spies could not corroborate. It was no wonder they didn't trust him and a good sign that the 18th century equivalent of MI5 was on the ball. Perhaps he shouldn't take umbrage, not too much umbrage, but his knowledge of the scheme was bound to come out once Anthony sent in his next report. It would seem strange for him not to call Henry out in a duel. That really would put the dampers on any friendship with Catherine. That was a worry for another day; he may not live long enough to get back to England.

A sharp whistle sounded from one of the sentries and Biggin came running up. "The Frogs, sir, beggin' your pardon, sir."

"How far?"

"A half-hour's march, sir. They be makin' good time."

"Fuelled by a desire for revenge, no doubt. Thank you, Serjeant. Get the men ready to leave." He called Anxo over and gave him his despatch. "Mr Dean has one too. Collect it from him and get the messenger on his way. I don't want the French to have sight of them."

"Of course, Captain."

"Which direction do we take from here, Anxo? Whichever way, we need to head back towards the coast as soon as possible."

"We shall march north for a day. Maybe the French will think we are heading for the fishing village of Sines. There is a lago … a lake to the east near to Santa Clara. The country is very rough and will not be good for cavalry. We shall go there and then turn south, back towards Bartolomeu."

"Sounds like a good plan. Let's get organised."

The sentries were called in but the eight-man rear guard stayed in place kneeling on a wooded crest where they could watch the track into the valley below. Chris joined them and peered at the approaching troops through the borrowed telescope. The French commander had sent out a skirmish line ahead of his main force and they were moving quickly.

The senior rifleman, a corporal, stood and leant on the barrel of his weapon. "You want that we should harass them, sir?"

"Not yet, corporal. There will be a time for that. Keep an eye on them and let me know if they get any closer. Right now I want them to think we are headed north."

The man glanced up at the sun. "Beggin' your pardon, sir but we are … headin' north, that is."

"But not for much longer. Do you have everything you need for the task?"

"Aye, sir, except for Mr Willoughby leading us, sir."

Chris thought he detected a note of criticism but wasn't sure. He decided to ignore it.

"We will all miss him, corporal. A brave officer and my good friend."

"Beggin' your pardon, sir. Did he die well?"

"You can rest assured he died a true soldier. His last wish was for the safety of his men. He was a credit to his regiment. You could do worse than follow his example, corporal."

"I meant no disrespect, sir."

"Then I'll look to you and your comrades to honour his memory in the best way you can."

"So be it then, sir. Me and the lads here all."

"I'm relying on it. Now, the French have advanced another two hundred paces while we talked."

"We'll watch the bastards, sir. Beggin' your pardon."

Chris turned away to hide a grin. He made his way at a trot to catch up with the main body. No longer encumbered with the dead they were making better time and it took a while to reach them.

He knew Anxo was right. About a day was all they had before the cavalry were let loose. He had studied the French colonel's map, it was rough and poorly detailed but did show the main roads, if the tracks they were travelling could be termed as such, and knew there were few other than goat tracks leading east to west. They were hampered by the mountainous territory which kept them in the valleys. They would need to break out before the cavalry reached them.

They took a five minute break which allowed the rearguard to catch up before moving on again at a fast pace until darkness began to fall.

They dug in on a slope where they could watch the track. The ground was hard and rocky and all they could manage were scrapes barely deep enough to lie in. They piled loose rocks in small untidy heaps to provide additional cover. They had to look haphazard and not man made to fool any observer.

They had not passed a single village all day and their water supplies were running low. Lack of rain had all but dried up the natural springs and most of the streams were dry. Chris ordered water rationing of half a cup per man. It wasn't enough but would keep them alive until they could reach the lake Anxo had mentioned. From here on it could only get harder.

# 36

The piece of cord tied to his wrist jerked Chris awake. The alert sentry tugging on the other end of it had spotted something. He rolled onto his stomach and crawled to where he could see the track, shaking Biggin as he passed. He put his mouth to Biggin's ear and ordered a stand to. He checked his Breitling; forty-five minutes to dawn. It was a clear sky with a myriad stars, the previous cloud having melted away overnight and it was cool enough to bring on a shiver.

As his eyes adjusted he could see movement. Deer maybe. The sentry slithered over and gave him a reality check. "Frog skirmishers, sir. There be two dozen of 'em, I reckons," he whispered.

Not many of the men knew their numbers so the sentry's estimate might be off but there were certainly enough to cause a problem. They must have started out in the small hours to be here. An indication of how determined they were. How far back was the main force? He wouldn't allow his own skirmishers to get too far ahead and doubted if the French commander would either. So they were close.

Another dilemma. Should they attack the skirmishers or let them walk past? Would they have enough time to do so and not be engaged by the main group? Were their positions concealed well enough to fool the French in the warm light of day? If they let the French pass ahead of them, what then? The road would be used by supply groups, despatch riders and soon after, the cavalry.

It was the last thought that decided him. He squirmed back to Biggin. "Let them pass and we will follow them until it gets light enough to take them down if need be. We have to move out quickly so leave anything that isn't already packed. Pass the word."

It was a gamble. He hoped that the skirmishers would be focused on the track ahead or, if they did turn around, mistake them for another skirmish line in the poor light. It was all he could think of.

The whole detachment made it to the track with little sound apart from an occasional dislodged pebble. The skirmishers were about two-hundred paces ahead. As yet, there was no sign of a larger body approaching from behind. Chris signalled for them to close up to a hundred paces behind the skirmishers.

Dawn was about to break, the sky was brightening in the east and with the rising sun came a stiff breeze. Luck was with them as the breeze was blowing in their faces and carrying any sound they might make away from the French. The small valley began to widen out and the ground became more even. The French skirmish line spread further apart. Their bodies now turning to dull grey in the half light of pre-dawn.

Anxo touched Chris's shoulder and pointed to the right where a goat track meandered between scrubby bushes and disappeared from view. He signalled a stop and found Anthony. "We're leaving our Frog friends. Take your men to the right. Quietly now, it would be a pity to wake the Frogs at this late stage."

Chris signalled the remaining riflemen to kneel and make ready as the Portuguese and the muskets peeled away. Then two-by-two, they followed.

Chris breathed a huge sigh of relief as the last man reached the cover of the scrub. They had got away with it for now.

They found the lake that Anxo knew and camped there to rest and recuperate. Water was plentiful, running down from the higher ground and they made the most of it to wash themselves and their clothing.

The following weeks started busily with harassing attacks on French patrols but the days became less fraught now that they were in wild country away from the main routes. On occasion, they saw small bands of French cavalry riding in the distance or a platoon of Grenadiers checking small villages but none of them came close enough to engage.

Somewhere in their escapade September had turned into October and the weather was becoming colder and wetter making their lives more miserable. It brought Chris's mind to the thought of getting to the coast and the ship back to England.

French activity had died down with fewer and fewer sightings. The Portuguese messengers had also failed to find them; Anxo thought it too dangerous for them to risk the journey in the early days and their route markers might have faded or been overgrown so much they could not now be followed. Chris wasn't too worried he had little to tell Horse Guards and there was little he wanted to hear from them except perhaps that the ship to take them home was about to set sail from Portsmouth.

In these quiet days his mind had turned more and more to Catherine and his feelings for her. He had hoped that this long absence from Imber would help him to see sense. She was a married woman, married to a friend. He was a fugitive from another time. Nothing could ever come of it but he could not shake her image from his mind. He rubbed his right arm. The tracery was still as vivid as the day the lightning struck. His hair had not grown and he had given up even the pretence of shaving.

Anxo and his men had slipped away some time before, they had their own lives and families to consider. They agreed to rendezvous at the end of October outside a village called Gomes Aires on the River Mira which fed the lake and was an easy route to follow to the village.

This was rough but beautiful country, sparsely inhabited but with an abundance of small game for the poachers amongst them to trap. Wild lime trees were plentiful and reduced the risk of contracting scurvy on the low vitamin-C diet they were living on. His small command, if not exactly prospering, were surviving. Daily drills and exercise was helping to keep them fit although most had lost weight. Biggin and Pocock kept him informed of the men's mood and he was becoming perturbed, first by the rumblings of discontent and even more so by the absence of them. The British soldier was always at his most flammable when he stopped complaining. Anthony tried to keep cheerful but the absence of any reply to his letter to Catherine was eating at him and his prevailing mood was fretful and irritable.

It came to a head one morning when four riflemen refused Anthony's direct order to dig new latrines. Already in a bad mood, he drew his sabre and threatened the men with court martial and flogging as soon as they were back on British soil.

"We bain't be goin' back," one man said. "We be stuck here forever."

"Aye," another said." You wavin' yon skewer won't do ee no good, sir."

"I should cut you down where you stand."

"Will you be takin' down all four?" a third man said. He had been cleaning his bayonet and he held it forward as he rose to his feet.

"Aye, we may be diggin' a hole for you, sir," the fourth man said.

Anthony was nonplussed. "Are you threatening me, rifleman? Is this mutiny?"

"Mutiny? Now there be a terrible word to be bandyin'," the first man said.

"We have grievances, Lieutenant Dean. Them navy men had grievances at Spithead and they were listened to and paid more for their trouble. So the crew on the Aquilon were tellin'."

Biggin had seen the trouble brewing and had brought Chris to witness it.

"I'm willing to bet they didn't tell you what happened at the Nore," Chris called. "Now put away your weapons, all of you."

"Ah, Captain Lennox, sir, we have grievances, sir." The third man said. "We be stuck in this place too long and we grow tired of it. No word from home and no end in sight. Poor food and nought but water to drink."

"Put away the bayonet, rifleman and all of you sit down. I'm not going to listen to you under threat."

The man suddenly looked sheepish, bobbed his head and slid his bayonet back in its scabbard. Anthony gave Chris a puzzled look but sheathed his sabre. "Captain Lennox, sir ..."

Chris raised his hand. "One moment, Lieutenant, please. Now, men, I understand your problems and I sympathise. I may be wrong but I don't believe the poor food and lack of a rum ration are the real reasons for your discontent. Which of you is going to speak up. Not all of you, this is not going to be a debate, just one man."

"Beggin' your pardon, Captain, but that best be me," the first man said.

"Jed, isn't it? Jed Carter?"

"Aye, sir, you know my name, sir?"

"I know all your names. I make a point of knowing who serves under me. State your case, Carter."

"We grow homesick, Captain. With little to occupy us we dream of home and our wives and little-uns. We rather be givin' the Frogs a bloody nose, standin' together and fightin', sir, even should we die, but we be doin' nothin' here for too many a day."

"So instead you pick a fight with Lieutenant Dean, is that right?"

"We meant no disrespect, Captain. The thought of diggin' more holes and the chance it meant we be 'ere for more time because of it. More than we could stand, sir."

"You know me to be a fair man, Carter?"

"Aye, sir, that we do, none has treated us fairer."

"Then you will know that I will consider this fairly but I can't let this insubordination pass without punishment."

"Mutiny was spoke of, sir."

"In the heat of the moment and I won't pursue it … unless it happens again. You will all do double guard duty for the next ten days. Furthermore you will act as rearguard when we move out tomorrow and until we reach our destination."

A smile lit up Carter's face. "We are to move on the morrow, sir?"

"Yes, Carter. I had already decided you men had enough of a holiday and should get back to work. Make sure you're ready."

"Aye, sir, twill be a pleasure, sir."

Chris looked across at Anthony. Are you satisfied, Lieutenant Dean?" Anthony chewed his lip and then nodded.

"It's settled then."

"Beggin' your pardon, sir, but please to tell us what happened at Nore," Carter asked.

Chris grimaced. "They turned the cannons on the mutineers, Carter, and hanged the ringleaders from the yardarms. Theirs was not deemed a proper grievance.

"Perhaps the crew of the Aquilon also didn't tell you that the three ringleaders of the Spithead mutiny were taken from Plymouth Citadel and shot." He gestured for them to look around and they saw Biggin and the muskets lined up behind them. "I'm happy we could come to a fairer conclusion."

He turned away and Anthony came with him.

"Would you have Biggin turn the muskets on those men, sir?"

Chris took him to one side, out of earshot of those nearby. "Where I come from we don't shoot men for disobedience. They get punished, sometimes severely if that disobedience is in the face of the enemy, but we don't kill them.

"Let the men believe I would, then, maybe, they will think twice about disobeying an order at any future time. I hope there won't be another occasion, Anthony."

# 37

Gomes Aires looked peaceful. Chris studied it from a tree-lined hill and could see nothing untoward. There was a wide track that ran through the centre of the village, which crossed the rapidly flowing river over a rough stone built bridge that could take the weight of heavy wagons. The French map showed the track joining two other centres of habitation, with a crossroads off to the east that joined a major route south to Faro. It was not a place he would have picked for a rendezvous, it seemed too public, but Anxo had not yet let him down.

He grimaced and handed Anthony the telescope. "What do you think?"

"It is not necessary for you to seek my opinion, George."

"Still, I value it. You've learnt a lot in these past months."

"I thank you for your faith in me. It has been hard pressed of late."

"We're all under pressure and we have different coping mechanisms. The riflemen needed to blow off some steam and you learnt that irritability causes more problems than it solves. You're wiser for it. Now, what do you think?"

"I think we should wait for dusk and then send in a reconnaissance patrol of three men."

"Why?"

Anthony grinned. "So this is a test?"

"Of observation and tactics. I agree but why did you come to that conclusion?"

"Judging by the position of the sun, we have been here an hour, yet there has been no movement in the village. The turnpike is well-used but carries no wagons this day."

"Perhaps it's a public holiday."

"Perhaps but I have also learnt from you to be wary of the unusual or the unexpected."

"Good man. We'll lay up here for now and keep watch until dark."

"I wish to lead the patrol tonight."

"Biggin or Pocock should do that."

"I do believe that I lack the respect of the men and wish to foster it."

Chris was aware of his promise to Catherine and had kept Anthony away from the more dangerous assignments. He now knew he could no longer keep him wrapped in cotton wool, it was having a detrimental effect on Anthony's reputation amongst the men. It had been evident in the recent incident that the soldiers had little respect for him, it was a mood that had been growing since Willoughby's death.

"Okay, Anthony. Choose your men and get prepared. Take pistols and nothing that will jingle as you move. I want to know where the people are and what they're doing. Check the main buildings and the church."


"Is everything in order, LeClerc? Perrot enquired. He was sitting with one buttock on a rough table with a pistol resting on his thigh.

"Yes, my Captain. Half the squadron is hidden in the trees on this side of the bridge. Ten Grenadiers hold the peasants in the church and some are in the buildings along the main street."

"That's good. Any sign of our visitors?"

"No, not yet but as you ordered no one will venture outside unless on your command."

"Perhaps we have learned a trick or two from the green men, eh, LeClerc. Hiding in corners like little rats. What do you say, Senhor Costa?"

Anxo raised his bloodied pain-racked face from the table. Both his hands were pinned to the wood by bayonets. His mouth was tightly gagged but he was beyond screaming.

"Oh, nothing to add, Senhor? How tiresome. But then we know all there is need to know. The green men are to rendezvous with you here, is that not so?"

LeClerc reached over and raised Anxo's head by his hair. "I do believe he's gone all quiet on us, Captain."

Perrot smiled a puckish twist of the lips. "One would have thought him beyond shyness, now that we know each other so well."

"My Captain!" A guardsman whispered to him from the small window. "There is movement outside."

"Ah, at last. Very well, light the lamp and leave it on this table. Then everyone into hiding, stand where you cannot be seen from the window but let them see poor Senhor Costa in his painful predicament."

Anthony and his two men edged over the bridge. The moon was up and it cast shadows for them to hide in. They reached the first of the small stone houses with its rush roof. Jeb Carter peered through the window and shook his head. "Empty, sir."

The church was in a small square in the centre of the main street and they walked towards it keeping their backs to the house walls but checking through each window as they passed. A sudden beam of light shone through a window two houses ahead. Anthony held up a hand.

"We have something at last."

"Tis strange, sir, as if all be swallowed up," Carter said.

"Until now," Anthony said. "Be on your guard, men, for I have no faith in this turn of events."

They inched forward until they were hunched beneath the lighted window. Anthony took a quick look, gasped and squatted down, his face white. "Tis Mr Costa in a parlous state, he is sorely wounded," he whispered.

Carter also dared a look and spat. "Tis a trap, sir."

"In all honour I cannot leave our friend to suffer this. One of you return to Captain Lennox with my compliments and inform him of the situation. One shall accompany me as we attempt a rescue."

"Tis madness, sir," Carter said. "We should all return and let the captain decide what is best."

"Those are my orders, will you disobey them a second time? The room appears empty but for Mr Costa. We should be able to make a speedy resolve."

"Then who lit the lamp, beggin' your pardon, sir?"

"Possibly just one guard. We can be away before the alarm is raised."

"Aye, sir, as you say. Samuels here can run back to the captain. I shall be with you ... for good or ill."

As Samuels scuttled off towards the bridge, the two men cocked their pistols. Anthony took a deep breath and tried the door. It swung open to his touch. He leapt through it with Carter on his heels. A musket butt slammed into his spine and another against Carter's head. His pistol exploded as he fell.

Samuels heard the report and started to run. A door opened behind him and two grenadiers tumbled into the street. Muskets cracked and Samuels felt a sharp burning pain in his side. He stumbled but kept running, a hand clutched over the wound.

Inside the house, Anthony was dragged to his feet and held by two soldiers. He could not feel his legs and they dangled uselessly beneath him. Carter was left on the dirt floor, a bayonet at his throat.

Perrot raised the lamp to get a better look at his prisoners. "And who do we have here?"

Anthony found the strength to look him in the eye. "Lieutenant Anthony Dean of the Rifles, sir. Whom do I have the doubtful pleasure of addressing?"

Perrot raised an eyebrow. "*Lieutenant* Dean, indeed." He reached behind him and grasped two letters, both with the seals broken. "And what have we here? A despatch from the British Horse Guards and a letter from a Mrs Dean to her husband." Perrot held the note to his nose and gave a delicate sniff. "I do believe it is scented with rosewater. How say you, LeClerc?" He thrust the note to LeClerc's who slapped it on his face and gave one of his huge nasal intakes.

"Reminds me of sheep droppings, Captain."

"Ha, LeClerc, it is as I supposed, you have no romance in your soul." He waved a hand in LeClerc's direction and looked at Anthony. "I suppose you have no French so I shall translate. He says it smells of sheep shit."

"How dare you, sir. That is a private communication. You are no gentleman, sir."

"And you are nought but a bandit. I have no consideration for bandits or their ilk." He tossed the letter on the floor and trod on it. "That is all you deserve for your cowardice. You green men do not fight as true soldiers but as thieves and scoundrels. I shall have you hung on the morn."

"You will soon discover how we fight, sir."

"Ah, the rest of your vagabond band will be close by no doubt. Let them come. This time they will more than meet their match."

# 38

Something was bothering Chris and he realised what it was almost as soon as Anthony had left on his scouting mission. No dogs. Not a single one. It was unusual to say the least as most villages usually had several half-wild animals running around to give notice of any strangers.

He called Biggin and Pocock over. "I think Mr Dean is walking into trouble. We'll follow him down. I'll take four riflemen into the village, the muskets will guard the bridge; nobody is to cross it. The remaining riflemen will take position in the trees on the high ground. If I'm wrong, we won't be any the worse but if I'm right we'll need all the firepower we have."

"Too quiet is it, beggin' your pardon, sir. I myself thought so," Pocock said.

"No dogs, Serjeant, that could be even more meaningful than no people."

"I be ponderin' on that too, sir," Biggin added.

"You have your orders. Get into position as quickly as you can but don't make an exhibition of it. Stay quiet and stealthy."

Chris had made a promise to himself never to use the Glock but he had an awful feeling he might need it. He rummaged in the bottom of his Bergen and pulled it out with its holster and spare magazines. He strapped the holster on his right thigh and loaded and cocked the pistol.

The four riflemen were waiting for him at the bottom of the hill and they slipped over the bridge but turned to the rear of the houses. They had not gone more than a few paces when Chris tripped on a heavy lump. He bent down and ran his hand over stiff fur. His hand came away wet.

The dog had been bayonetted and left to die. "So much for animal welfare," Chris muttered to himself.

A pistol exploded some way ahead. There was a commotion in the street on their right and musket shots rang out. There was answering rifle fire from the hill behind them and cries of pain. Whoever was in the street had just received a rifleman's greeting.

Chris led the men forward at a trot until they reached a house where light spilled beneath the door and voices could be heard. One was Anthony's. He tried the door and it opened silently outward. Most of the light was blocked by the large shape of a Horse Grenadier with his back to them watching the action inside the room. He was leaning on his carbine and chortling, obviously enjoying the show.

He was slow to notice the rush of cool air on his neck but started to turn. Chris hit him hard on the chin with the handguard of his sabre and burst into the room. The riflemen were hard on his heels, firing as they went.

Perrot was the first to react and raised the pistol in his hand. Chris threw the sabre at him but LeClerc stepped in the way. The sabre spun end over end and the pommel hit LeClerc in the face. He staggered back into Perrot and they both crashed to the floor.

The two grenadiers holding Anthony let him drop and pulled their sabres. Two more by the door were raising their carbines. The riflemen had all discharged their weapons but leapt at the grenadiers using their bayonets attached to the rifles. At such close range the carbines could not miss and two of the riflemen were shot down. One grenadier had a bayonet through his throat but the other parried the thrust and buried his sabre in the rifleman's chest.

It was three against two. Behind them Perrot and LeClerc were struggling to their feet and two more grenadiers were pushing their way through the front door.

Chris wrenched the Glock from the holster and screamed at his rifleman. *"Clark! Get down!"*

The man dropped on his face. The two coming through the door had carbines so he shot them first, twisted and put a double-tap into LeClerc. Perrot had dropped his pistol somewhere and was searching for it his previous wound making him slow. Chris spun back as the remaining three grenadiers advanced on him with sabres raised. He remembered the word, *"arrete,"* but they did not stop, coming at him in a rush. The first took a head shot and collapsed like a sack of potatoes; the next stumbled over the falling body and took two bullets in the chest. The third halted, his sabre raised above his head, but a look of incomprehension on his face.

Chris could see what was running through his mind. One weapon, five dead, what were his chances? He was a grenadier there was no choice. His battle cry was cut short as two parabellums took him down.

There was a noise from behind and Chris spun into the double handed isosceles stance. He looked at Perrot over the foresight. "Yes, Captain. Is it your turn now?"

"Mon dieu … how?" Perrot had found his pistol but it was still uncocked and dangled uselessly from his fingers.

"Drop the pistol or you'll be next for a personal demonstration."

Perrot looked at the pistol in his hand and threw it carelessly on the table. "You are the green men's commander. Lennox."

"My, my, you are well informed."

"He has our despatches," Anthony said from the floor. And a letter from Catherine which he crushed underfoot so that I may not read it. He took them from Mr Costa."

Chris had only just noticed Costa skewered to the table. "Enjoy inflicting pain do you, Captain?"

Perrot shrugged. "It was necessary, besides he is merely a peasant, why should you care for his health?"

Chris could feel the rage bubble up inside him and bit down on it. "Because he's a friend." He dropped the barrel away from Perrot's face and shot him in the leg. "That's the pair, now, Captain. Another to complement the one I put through you in September. I'm going to leave you alive to reflect on your behaviour. Perhaps you'll learn some better manners."

Perrot did not hear, he had fainted.

Chris holstered the Glock and pulled the two bayonets out of Anxo's hands. He too had passed out and could not feel the pain. Rifleman Clark was on his feet staring at Chris open-mouthed.

"Carry this man out."

"Aye, sir. But what of Mr Dean and Rifleman Carter?"

"Carter? Where is he?"

"I be 'ere, sir," Carter said and sat up rubbing his head.

"And you, Anthony? Can you walk?"

"I do believe not, sir. I took a blow to the spine."

"Will you help me with him, Carter?"

Carter pushed himself to his feet and tried a couple of wobbly steps. "Aye, sir, as well I might."

There was a distant clatter of hooves. "I don't think that's the milkman's horses," Chris said. "We have to get out now."

Chris scooped up the torn letter from the floor and the despatch from the table. He pulled Anthony over his shoulder in a firefighters lift, ignoring his yelp of pain. It was a good sign that he could feel something. The rifleman followed suit with Anxo and they left by the rear door. As the cavalry thundered down the main street they were met by volley fire from defensive positions beyond the bridge. Riflemen sniped from the treeline and French officers and NCOs went down like skittles. The bridge was too narrow for a cavalry charge and the banks of the river too steep for them to cross. The charge was broken up in disarray with horses at the rear ploughing into horses at the front that went down with their riders, some into the river where they were washed downstream by the turbulent water.

The muskets reloaded for another volley and the pairs of riflemen on the hill changed positions to take out the remaining command structure.

The Horse Grenadiers would not easily give up and they tried two more advances, both of which failed with terrible bloodshed. Chris watched the carnage from the corner of the last house until the cavalry completely withdrew. He could do nothing to stop his muskets from going amongst the fallen French and finishing them off with bayonets; their adrenaline was still rushing and bloodlust was in their hearts.

His small party crossed the bridge, walking over the fallen men and horses with the stink of death in their nostrils mixed with the pungent tang of gunpowder.

Biggin and Pocock met him with grins of relief on their faces.

"Have we lost any more men?"

"The grins disappeared from the mouths but their eyes still shone with the excitement of battle.

"Two muskets, sir. Many were hit by balls but saved by the iron weskits."

"We have three dead rifles in the house with the lamp. That's another five men we can't afford to lose. I've wounded to attend. Send a party to retrieve the bodies, we leave no one behind. Be quick before the Frogs decide to return to the attack."

"They never learn, do they, sir, the Frogs?" Biggin said.

"They will, Serjeant."

With the remaining riflemen acting as rearguard, they made a tactical withdrawal into cover at their old laying up point. Chris gave both Anthony and Anxo doses of morphine and bound Anxo's hands. Carter seemed to have mild concussion and was sent to rest for the night with a bandaged scalp. The other wounds were all minor and were treated by the men themselves.

Anxo came to and gave Chris an apologetic grimace. "I am sorry, Senhor Captain that I told the French of our rendezvous here."

Chris gave him a sympathetic grin back. "I'd have given them my inside leg measurement if they'd asked. I don't blame you."

"Thank you, Senhor Captain."

Get some rest, Anxo. We'll have to move on further south in the morning."

Anthony was also awake. "I fear I can no longer move my legs, George."

"You've taken a blow to the spine and it may have dislocated some of the vertebrae and put pressure of the nerve. It may recover with time. I wouldn't worry too much as the medicine I've given you will make things seem a little numb. Here," he fished in his pocket for Catherine's letter, "you may still be able to make sense of this. It's not so badly damaged."

"Thank you, George. You are a true friend." He took the letter but did not attempt to open it.

Biggin found them. He had Chris's sabre in his hand. "Beggin' your pardon, sir, but I was a-thinkin' you may need this."

"Thanks, Serjeant. It was a gift; I'd be lost without it."

"We also brought back the rifles, sir, so that the Frogs won't get them."

"And the French officer."

"We left him lie, sir, beggin' your pardon. Seemed no point in wastin' good powder on the like o' him."

"That's good. I don't like wanton killing, even if the man deserved it. Bring me a brand from the fire, I have to read a despatch from Horse Guards and Lieutenant Dean has a letter from his wife."

"I shall read it later," Anthony said. "When my mind is more at ease. I do believe I made yet another error in my judgement tonight, George."

"We all learn by our mistakes, Anthony; don't beat yourself up over it."

"I should have listened to Carter's advice but instead I tried to prove myself to you and the men. Twas derring-do that undid me. Bravado of its worst kind. It brought you into danger and caused the deaths of so many."

"It was a trap, Anthony. The Frogs knew we were coming. Whatever you did, we would have had a fight on our hands. Sleep on it, you'll feel better in the morning."

"I fear I will not, sir. I fear it will lay heavy on my conscience forever."

# 39

"My god," Fouquet said. "I would not be surprised if we faced the guillotine upon our return to France." He threw a despatch onto his table. "It is our recall, Perrot. We are to return from whence we came, covered not in glory but with our tails between our legs.

"The little corporal himself has signed the order. With the fort destroyed we have nowhere to garrison. We have lost the best part of two companies of grenadiers and a whole squadron of horse grenadiers. Our masters in Paris believe that we face at least a whole regiment of English, for how else might we have sustained such casualties? They believe the English will continue to aid the Portuguese at whatever cost to themselves and the strategy in the south is to be abandoned.

"How could I tell them that, according to Mr Foxley, we face barely fifty men? It is intolerable, Perrot. And there are you, my nephew, my sister's son, twice wounded and twice the defeated commander. There may yet be dire consequences."

Perrot struggled into a more comfortable position on a chair. His leg was splinted to the thigh. "We cannot leave without taking revenge. That would compound the dishonour. We must make amends or we may indeed be kissing the bottom of Madame la Guillotine's basket. What say you, Foxley?"

Foxley had been brooding in a corner, a cup of cognac in his hand. "I came to you with good intelligence, my hope was that you would use it to good effect and lay the scoundrel Lennox in his grave. Captain Perrot is correct, we cannot leave without exacting due recompense."

"Ha, you would say such, Foxley," Fouquet snapped. "But I have my orders. The brigade colonel is intent on seeing them carried out without delay."

Foxley grunted with annoyance. "But you read the captured despatch from Horse Guards. The ship departed Portsmouth not these two days gone to embark these wretched green men and carry them back. If you could but delay your departure, we could be awaiting them by that same bay where Perrot first found their sign. Did not the despatch say so much?"

"You wish me to disobey a direct order, one from Bonaparte himself? You must be mad, sir."

"No, sir, not mad, but angry. I have given up my position in order that I may be of service to France. This man Lennox is dangerous and will cause more calamity if allowed. Yes, just fifty men does he command and yet he has made fools of the cream of the French army. He is dangerous, sir, mark my words, and it would be foolish to let him live."

Fouquet sighed and sat with his legs splayed wide. He threw his head back and sighed again before pointing at the despatch. "We have to be in Cadiz within the week. Our ships are there and will not delay their departure, timing being of the essence so as to avoid the British blockade. My command must be on board when they sail, myself and Perrot with them, that is imperative.

"However, Mr Foxley, as you are so keen on retribution perhaps you should stay to see that duty done."

"I cannot do this alone, sir."

"Perhaps we could arrange for a few stragglers to accompany you; perhaps six men from the Horse Grenadiers. How say you, Perrot?"

Perrot shrugged. "That is about all the number left unwounded from my squadron. They would welcome an opportunity to avenge their comrades should the luck come their way."

"Excellent," Fouquet said and smiled a chilling twist of the lips. "It is an opportunity for them to redeem themselves. Should they succeed they would rid us of this so dangerous Lennox, fellow. Should they fail no one would be the wiser about the fate of six deserters who would otherwise be shot. Foxley, you have convinced me.

"Now, leave us, Mr Foxley, we have other matters to discuss that do not concern you."

Foxley bowed stiffly and left with his secret smile. He had what he wanted.

Fouquet put a hand into a small canvas bag and took out a brass cartridge case from the several in there. He held it up for Perrot to see. "And what are these strange objects, nephew?"

"I do not know. They appeared to fly from nowhere amidst the shooting. I swear, sir I am not mistaken that the man Lennox killed LeClerc and five others alone with but the one pistol."

"That is impossible. No one can reload with such speed. There must have been other pistols secreted about his person."

"Then the man is a magician as well as an assassin. I am sure my eyes did not deceive me."

"He let you live."

"Yes, to torture me. The physician has said I may always walk with a limp from now onward."

"Very well, nephew. We shall take these items with us to Paris to see what they can make of them." He held one to his nose and wrinkled it. "My god, smells of burning. I can make head nor tail of it. Let us hope others can."

They had seen no sign of the French for some days as they made their way south west through the Serra do Caldeirão mountains to Bartolomeu to collect O'Dell. Tracks were few and narrow and mostly the going was difficult. The men were growing tired. The long walks and lack of excitement was wearing them down and Chris was glad that the end of the expedition was in sight.

At Bartolomeu they found O'Dell in good health, his wound almost healed and more than happy to greet his friends again. Chris gave the widow Nunes her money with a little extra on top and she gave him a saucy smile in return which suggested that O'Dell may have been a little more than a boarder.

The despatch retrieved from the French, sent some weeks earlier, gave a date for the sailing of HMS Aquilon from Portsmouth. Since his meeting with the priest, Chris had kept a record of the days in his notebook and by his calculation, the ship would be nearing the Portuguese Algarve coast now, which gave them two weeks to get to the small bay to the east of Albufeira where they had landed in September.

The information contained in the despatch was dynamite. The French would be able to calculate the date of the ship's arrival as easily as he could and be ready to intercept the Aquilon and to put a cordon along the coast road. He had sent Pocock and two riflemen ahead to scout the way and these had not yet returned.

They camped within the confines of the village. Anxo said that the local gossip indicated that the French army were withdrawing back to Spain and that his men had seen no sign of any patrols for days. Chris thanked him for the story but wondered whether it was an elaborate plot to lull them into revealing themselves or to blunder into an ambush. He wasn't about to lose concentration and drop his guard at this late stage.

Anthony had some feeling back in his legs but could still only walk with a shuffling gait for short distances. The men had taken turns to carry his makeshift stretcher when he could walk no further. They bore it with good grace and Chris had noticed a warming in relations between them since his brave but foolhardy attempt to rescue Anxo. The Portuguese himself showed his gratitude by serving as Anthony's aide, as much as his ruined hands would allow.

Anthony had never mentioned the letter from Catherine, although Chris had seen him reading and re-reading it over the past days. He felt a pang of … what? Jealousy? Hopelessness? Need? He savagely suppressed it. The first was unthinkable, the second undesirable and the third unattainable.

He had no time to think about his own life; others took precedence, he was responsible for all their lives.

Anthony shuffled over and sat awkwardly on a log by the campfire. "How fare you, sir?"

Chris gave him a tight smile. "It's two days march to the cove where we landed and the Aquilon should be offshore by then. We'll be setting sail for home soon."

"That is indeed very good news, George, but why so long a face?"

"The cares of command, which you'll find out about yourself, one day."

"I do doubt that, sir. On return, I shall tender my resignation from the army. I wished to be of service to you but it seems I have been nothing but a burden."

"You're no burden, Anthony, but I can't say I'm surprised at your decision. I think you're more cut out for farming than soldiering."

"I do believe you are right, George. This was an adventure which I would not have missed but the strictures of military life become wearisome with time. I cannot else but marvel at your grasp of military strategy and the merest intricate detail of survival. I shall write so in my next communication to Major Wadman and write that all of the detachment owe our lives and the success of this expedition to you."

"Don't be too lavish with that praise, Anthony. The serjeants and the men have all earned their share. We couldn't have done everything we have without them and their outstanding courage."

"Do not chide me, sir. I shall not be so lax as to forget them. Now what is the real reason for your gloomy demeanour?"

Chris nodded. "You're getting to know me too well and you're right. We may be two day's march from the cove but the French know about the arrival of the Aquilon. Pocock and his two riflemen haven't yet returned from their scouting mission. I'm relying on their report and without it I'm just a little concerned that the French could be planning a nasty surprise."

# 40

The Aquilon was showing a white light towards the beach. It was the signal that all was well and that the embarkation could proceed.

The men were in cover in the scrub at the top of the cliff. Chris signalled back with a lighted torch hidden beneath a cloak. He was still worried. His scouts had not returned. They might have got lost, always a possibility in the rough country but they knew, if all else failed, to head south west to the coast road and from there to turn east along it until they reached the cove. They were good men and with Pocock in command well able to take care of themselves.

Now he had a decision to make. Should he wait for the missing three men or embark the remainder? Many lives against three. He signalled the ship to send the longboat.

"Anthony, take Biggin and the muskets to the beach. I'll stand guard here with the remaining rifles until you've embarked. When you reach the ship report to Commander Cunningham with my compliments. If it is safe to do so, I'll wait for the missing men until dawn but it will be his decision when to send in the longboat to take us off. We can't be allowed to endanger the ship for three men."

"I wish to stay with you. Serjeant Biggin is well able to command the muskets."

"No arguments, Lieutenant. It's an order. You'll have trouble negotiating the track into the cove if we need to evacuate in a hurry and I don't want you slowing us down unnecessarily."

Anthony clutched his arm and gave a grim nod. "I see the way of it, George. You wish me safely gone and I thank you for your concern."

"It's nothing personal, Anthony, I'm just looking after my own skin."

"That is one thing I would never believe of you, George. I shall obey your order, with regret."

"Ask Cunningham to show the light again when he's ready to launch the long boat and we'll be on the beach to meet it."

With Anthony safely aboard the ship, he could breathe a little more easily. The missing men worried him and he still feared that they may have been taken by the French.

He sat it out until just before dawn when the Aquilon showed the white light again. Cunningham wanted to be away with the ebbing tide before it became too light with his ship so close to the shore.

Chris ordered the first riflemen to the beach while he stayed with a rearguard of four, reluctant to leave until the very last minute. Then a man tugged at his sleeve and pointed along the greying track. The vague outline of three men were rounding a bend and approaching at a walk. He turned to the rearguard. "Get to the beach now. I'll bring these three with me." He stood and waved them on, now anxious to get everyone out.

"Come on," he hissed, "on the double." The men kept their heads down and appeared not to have seen him. He raised his voice to call them in. "Get a move on, the ship's about to leave."

The leading soldier raised his head and smiled. "Without you, I trust," Foxley said.

The other two men raised their rifles and hooves thudded as three cavalrymen rode around the bend, their sabres unsheathed.

"Don't kill him, you fools," Foxley shouted, "he's mine to deal with."

The horsemen rode past and stopped behind Chris in a swirl of dust.

"I believe we have some unfinished business," Foxley said and bared his teeth in a feral grin.

"And I thought you'd already learned your lesson," Chris replied.

"Taken with a trick? I think not and you shall not catch me out with that again."

Chris was incredulous. "You want another duel?"

"You slighted me, sir and I demand satisfaction."

"With these Frenchmen to help you?"

"Ha! They know not to interfere. I do not need their assistance."

"And if I should beat you?"

Foxley showed his yellowed teeth. "Then they will abide by my order to set you free. However I have no intention of losing to you a second time and this shall be to the death."

"No pressure then," Chris murmured. He had his Sabre in its scabbard on his back. He knew he had no chance of fighting off all three cavalrymen, the two dressed as riflemen and Foxley before one of them got to him. Maybe taking on Foxley was the best bet and he would have to trust that Foxley wasn't lying about them letting him go.

"Right, Mr Foxley. Let's see what you've got." He pulled the sabre from its scabbard and saluted with it.

Foxley grinned his maniacal grin, threw his stolen shako and tunic to the ground and flexed his fingers. He drew his own sabre and went straight to en garde.

"Before we start, what have you done with my three soldiers?"

"Stripped and tied in the scrub. We shall finish them after I have dealt with you. We could not risk them screaming like stuck pigs and giving away the game. Have at you, sir."

He lunged forward with the point of his sabre aimed at Chris's throat. He parried the strike with a counter-thrust. Steel rang on steel and sparks flew in the grey light of a November dawn. Foxley was quick and lunged forward, the tip of his sabre burying itself in Kevlar but not penetrating. Chris knocked the weapon away with a twist of the wrist and caught Foxley on the shoulder. First blood. A minor cut that Foxley hardly felt. He drove forward swinging the sabre both backhand and forehand, driving Chris onto the back foot as he parried the onslaught. He kept his hand low and the sabre point face-high, waiting for a lull in the attack as Foxley ran out of steam. He did and backed away as Chris went onto the front foot. He made a rapid shuffle forward and flicked the point up towards Foxley's head. He made contact with a cheek and the cut welled with blood. Foxley felt that and put his hand up to feel the warm wetness. He snarled and backed away.

"Touché," Chris murmured.

Foxley lurched forward swinging wildly, angrily and powerfully, backing Chris into the horses. He tripped and fell between the hooves as the animals shied away. Foxley gave a screech of triumph as he hacked downwards at a leg. Chris rolled away but the blade sliced through his trousers. It was a flesh wound which bled but did not slow him down. He rolled again and jumped to his feet as Foxley came in for the kill. He knocked the blade aside and hit Foxley in the chest with the handguard, knocking him back for a brief respite. Their positions were now reversed and Foxley had his back to the horses as they snorted and pawed the ground. Chris backed away to put some space between them. Foxley was in no hurry and paced slowly after him, a glint of triumph in his eyes. "I have you now, Lennox." He started his run and leapt into a flunge, the tip of his sabre striking downward, but Chris was already thrusting forward and drove his sabre deep into Foxley's chest.

Foxley stood there with a bemused look and slowly the sabre trickled from his fingers and he slumped to his knees. He looked at the blade embedded in his chest and then up at Chris, surprise slowly turning to shock.

"You copied the flunge but hadn't seen the defence against it. A little knowledge is a dangerous thing, Mr Foxley." He pulled the sabre free and Foxley fell forward, supporting himself on one arm as the other attempted to stem the flow of blood from a severed artery. His grimace of pain turned into a terrible grin as blood spilled out of the corner of his mouth. He pointed a bloody finger at Chris. *"Tuez-le ... et le rendre douloureux,"* he shouted then fell on his face.

The cavalrymen spurred their horses forward with sabres raised over Chris's head. Rifle fire rippled from the undergrowth and the men fell from their saddles.

Chris clawed the Dragon from his belt and spun around to face the two on foot behind him but they were both spread-eagled on the ground. The bushes parted and Anthony limped out with Biggin and half the complement of Rifles.

"I throw myself upon your mercy, sir, for disobeying your order. You may do with me as you wish."

Chris tried to look angry but could only muster a wry smile. "Extra duties for the lot of you but I'm damn glad you're here. Pocock and the other Rifles are somewhere nearby. Serjeant Biggin, muster a search party to find them. The rest of you get those green uniforms off the dead

Frogs, they'll be needed, and collect up the rifles. Unsaddle the horses and set them free."

"What will you do with the dead?" Anthony asked.

Chris took a look out to sea where the ship's lantern was madly semaphoring for their return. "We don't have time to bury them. We'll leave them for Anxo's people. Arrange the bodies with respect, Foxley's too. He can be buried with his new friends."

"He called for the grenadiers to kill you as painfully as possible. The traitor does not deserve such consideration."

"Perhaps not but we are civilised people and we'll treat his remains with Christian dignity."

Anthony bowed. "As you wish, sir. Tis another lesson I have learned, to be magnanimous in victory."

"As a society we have a long way to go yet but we'll get there … in time."

A yell came from along the track and Biggin emerged leading three half-naked men, shivering in the morning air. "Found 'em, sir, beggin' your pardon, sir." He could not keep the laughter out of his voice as he pointed at the three. "Bundled up like faggots o' firewood, they was, sir."

Chris suppressed a grin. "Get them down to the beach with their clothes."

"Aye, sir. The longboat's a-waitin', sir and the tide be ebbin' fast," Biggin said.

"Then we had better not keep Commander Cunningham waiting any longer."

# Part 3
## Step Forward

# 41

Chris would never make a sailor but he enjoyed the rough passage home more than the voyage out. He had his sea legs, was no longer seasick and he was going back. Back to England, to Imber and to Catherine's company. That thought alone buoyed him up. Just to see her again would be a tonic.

Cunningham too was in high good humour. The prize money for the captured Hercule had been gazetted and he was due seventy-five pounds in prize money. Chris's share was three pounds, twelve shillings and his men were each awarded five shillings and sixpence, the equivalent of a week's pay. When they would receive it was another matter as the Admiralty often took several years to pay out. Still it cheered the lower decks and the wardroom.

It was a cold grey morning as the longboat towed the ship onto its mooring at the dockside in Portsmouth. Chris was huddled in his cloak as he watched the mooring lines taken ashore and made fast. Anthony stood with him, his weight now supported by a stick made for him by the ship's carpenter.

"Home, George, such a pleasant sight even should the day be so grey."

Chris had seen Henry Wadman standing in the lee of a wall and wasn't so sure the sight was as pleasant. "It seems your brother-in-law has come to welcome us back."

"Then I shall give him my despatches personally and he may make haste to Horse Guards with them. He may also take my commission for I am done with the army."

"You'll go straight back to Imber?"

"With all possible haste. I have much to set my mind on and much to make good."

"Mrs Dean's letter?" You never mentioned the contents. I hope it wasn't bad news."

"It gave me much to ponder on. I thank you for your good offices in these matters. Mrs Dean was most grateful for your solicitude. It seems we are always to be in your debt, sir."

"There's no price on friendship, Anthony. There is nothing to repay."

"Only that which cannot be counted in money."

Chris watched the gangway being fastened in place. "I see Major Wadman is beckoning. Let's see what he has in store for us."

"I have orders for you," Wadman said without preamble. "The men will disembark and dress in their red coats for the march back to Salisbury. Everything is in the warehouse behind us. The rifles will be left and the men reissued with the Brown Bess."

"We aren't going back to Imber then," Chris said.

"Twas only a temporary posting in order to pursue the highwaymen. Now that they are no longer a menace it is unnecessary." Billets have been made available and the men will be under the command of Lieutenant-colonel Stewart."

"I shall be returning straightway to Imber," Anthony said. "I am resigning my commission forthwith." He handed Wadman a sealed package. "Tis all there, my last despatch and my written resignation. I must away to see my wife, your sister Catherine."

Wadman pursed his lips. "You must sell your commission as others must. There is a broker in Cheapside who will serve for you. I had some anticipation of this and advised Colonel Stewart of your likely decision. You may have unpaid leave of absence until such time as a purchaser for your commission can be found."

"I am grateful, Henry."

"Be grateful that His Majesty is in no great need of officers in this current stance. There are too many languishing on half pay. Leave your green in the warehouse and be gone to Catherine while you may."

Anthony bowed and left with a smile of relief.

Wadman weighed the package in his hand and gave Chris a studied look. "I must take me back to Horse Guards with this latest intelligence. You, sir, must travel with your men to Salisbury and await orders there. Much is yet to be discussed and decided."

"The men have acted impeccably and with courage. Will they have time to recuperate?"

"They will be allowed their ease until Colonel Stewart shall have a use for them. You may command them as you see fit and await further orders."

"What is going on, Major? Why the secrecy?"

"That is not your fortune to know, Captain."

"Above my pay grade, huh?"

"Pay? That is a trifling matter and it is for Horse Guards to decide. Now I must away to London."

Chris caught his sleeve. "Is Catherine, Mrs Dean, in good health?"

"When last I saw her but pale and I suspect pining for the return of her husband."

"That would explain it," Chris said.

Wadman gave a half-smile. "Be of good cheer, Lennox. Good news may yet come your way." He hurried away, not giving Chris any time to question his remark or to face him over Anthony's spying. That would have to wait.

The men were disembarking and lining up along the quay. Chris called Biggin and Pocock and repeated the orders that Wadman had given. They both gave him questioning looks but did not comment. They led the men into the warehouse and found the sacks with their red coats piled in a heap in one corner. Two marines were there to collect the rifles and hand out muskets. The riflemen were reluctant to let their weapons go but they obeyed, touching their foreheads in a goodbye to the guns that had served them so well.

Biggin came to stand alongside him. "Beggin' your pardon, sir, but what are we about now? We be the Rifles, sir, and cannot be without them or our green coats."

Chris shrugged. "I know as much as you do, Serjeant. It's in the hands of Horse Guards. You and the men have behaved with courage and determination. I have said so in my despatches. I'm sure no one will be forgotten."

"It has been a rare expedition, sir. We gave the Frogs a bloody nose all right, beggin' your pardon, sir."

"That we did, Serjeant Biggin. That we did. Now if everyone is ready we have a march to barracks in Salisbury to contemplate in raw November weather."

"Back in time for Christmastide we be, sir. My woman will be best pleased to have her man home for the burnin' of the yule log."

"It's a time to remember those we lost. One of my first duties will be to call on Lieutenant Willoughby's parents."

"A fine young officer, sir, beggin' your pardon. Twas hard he had to go when others less worthy did survive."

Chris gave him a sharp look, he could read Biggin's mind. "No one was less worthy or more worthy. Each man did his duty for King and country and I will not have it said otherwise. Is that clear, Serjeant?"

Biggin gave a reluctant nod. "Aye, sir. Tis as you say. The men will harken to your words, sir."

"We are the Rifles, Biggin. Swift and bold in all things and in all things we protect our own."

Biggin showed his tobacco stained teeth in a cheesy grin. "Beggin' your pardon, sir, but that does cheer me. Swift and Bold, aye, that we be and more."

"Pass the word then, Serjeant. Tell the men to be proud and we'll march out of Portsmouth as if we own it."

Stewart made Chris welcome on his return to Salisbury and had made adequate provision for the soldiers with clean billets, each with a pot-bellied stove for warmth. It wasn't until his men mingled with the other soldiers that Chris realised how much they had grown in authority and maturity. The other soldiers sensed it and treated them with respect. They were returning warriors and had tales to tell around the fires at night that made men's eyes bulge with admiration and no small amount of disbelief amongst the older veterans.

Chris was bored. With December fast approaching, he had been kicking his heels, wanting desperately to visit Imber to find out how Anthony was faring and to catch a glimpse of Catherine. Stewart did his best to keep Chris amused with odd jobs and boozy mess dinners which began to eat into the money he had left from the two-hundred guineas reward and the sovereigns he had brought with him. The army pay had not materialised and neither had the bounty from the Hercule. Most of the officers had independent means but lack of cash was becoming a problem for him. It was strange that his non-metal possessions reconstituted themselves but nothing made of metal did. The Glock's magazines remained half-empty and none of the sovereigns had reappeared.

He needed to find a way to make money ... and soon.

# 42

For no reason Chris could quite understand the Wiltshire Regiment's temporary headquarters were built outside the city's ditch and rampart but with access through the nearby Winchester Gate. He could only assume that the burghers of the city were averse to having rough soldiery billeted within the city limits.

He had borrowed a horse from Stewart but the distance to Silver Street on the west side of the market square was short enough so he dressed in his civilian clothes to walk.

The vibrancy of an eighteenth century city always entranced him, although he could happily live without the stench and the obvious squalor that was everywhere. He walked the length of Winchester Street into Blue Boar Row, careful where he put his feet as the road was full of ordure and rotting vegetables thrown carelessly from windows. The market place was a large open square with a pillory, stocks and whipping posts on the north side, the Guildhall and jail in the southeast corner and the south and western sides taken up with market stalls selling, meat, fish, greengrocery and oats.

He passed the cheese cross and walked through St Thomas's churchyard, preferring the peace and quiet to the raucous noise of the traders in the square. The shop he needed was a clockmakers on the corner of Silver Street and the High Street. It was a small business in a city that specialised in cloth, cutlery and leather but it excelled in making and selling high quality long case clocks. Chris had seen the name *'Burdens of Salisbury'* on the face of the clock at Imber Court.

A small bell tinkled as he pushed open the door into a shop full of the melodic tick of big clocks. A small man looked up from his table at the rear of the shop. "Could I be of service, sir?"

"Are you the proprietor?"

The man bowed. "I have that pleasure, sir. Josiah Burden at your service."

"Mr Burden. I have something that may interest you." Chris slid the Breitling from his wrist and offered it to Burden.

The man blinked and took it with care, as if it might bite him. "Whatever is this, sir?"

"It's called a wrist watch. From Switzerland."

Burden took a Lupe from his pocket and screwed it into his eye. He studied the watch face. "Remarkable, sir. The manufacture is ... the workmanship ... I have never seen the like."

"No, it's the only one in England, I can vouch for that. In fact, that is the only one in the world. It is unique."

"The bracelet is so finely worked, I can scarce see the joining of the links."

"Can we discuss business, Mr Burden?"

"Of course Mr ...?"

"Captain, Captain Lennox, attached to the 62nd."

"Ahh! Colonel The honourable William Stewart commanding. I have the honour to have been of service to the Colonel."

"And to Sir George Wadman, I understand."

"Yes, yes. You have the acquaintance of Sir George?"

"That's where I learned of your company, Mr Burden."

"Please be seated, Captain. How may I be of service?"

Burden showed Chris to a chair beside his table. He still held the Breitling in his hand as if it was completely made of glass. He laid it reverently on the table.

"How much do you sell your clocks for?" Chris asked.

A faint look of pride crossed Burden's features. "From one-hundred and fifty to three-hundred guineas, Captain. They are fine timepieces."

"I don't doubt that, Mr Burden. Sir George wouldn't have favoured you with his patronage otherwise." He pointed at the watch. "Now how much would you say this timepiece is worth, bearing in mind it is the only one of its kind? It's an elegant piece of jewellery in its own right but also keeps time to within one minute each week."

"One minute, you say. How is that possible?"

"Swiss ingenuity and, I'm told, tiny diamonds in the workings."

"Indeed, sir, that is astonishing."

Chris knew that Burden was playing for time and decided to give him another jolt. "Do you have some water, sir?"

Burden nodded, went into a back room and returned with a jug and glass. He gasped with horror as Chris picked up the watch and dropped it into the water. "You have ruined it, sir." He fished in the jug and brought the watch out.

"Look closely, Mr Burden. There's a hand that counts the seconds and it's still moving. The watch is waterproofed to many fathoms."

Burden's jaw dropped. "I am lost for words, sir."

"The small window on the dial also counts the days."

Burden screwed the Lupe back into his eye socket and studied the watch face. "Indeed, sir, it is the correct day. And what is this number, 1884?"

Chris could hardly tell him it was the date the company was founded, still eighty-five years in the future, but he had given it some thought on his walk. "It's the number of days it took to manufacture the timepiece. The Swiss watchmaker was so proud of his accomplishment that he incorporated the length of time on his masterpiece. Now, Mr Burden, your answer. How much is it worth?"

Burden gave a wry smile. "Should I hazard an estimate I would say it would fetch at least six-hundred guineas with the London clientele. Possibly more."

"You are a shrewd business man, Mr Burden. And if I was to offer the timepiece to you, how much would you pay for it?"

"It is beyond my means, Captain."

"Then let me make a suggestion. I will loan the watch to you for say, one-hundred and fifty guineas. If you're able to interest one of your London clientele in buying it, I will allow you twenty percent of the sale as commission on top of the loan repayment. If you can't sell it I will simply repay the money and neither of us will be any worse off."

"That is a very generous offer, Captain. I am honoured that you would entrust me with such a rare obligation."

"Your honesty is a byword, Mr Burden."

Burden beamed. "I trust that is so. Many have remarked upon it."

"Then we have a deal?"

"Yes, Captain. I shall bring the hundred and fifty guineas." He went again into the back room and returned with a small leather bag. "Do you wish to count it?"

"I'm sure it's all there. Now two more things you need to know. The watch doesn't need winding, just gently shake it every other day to keep it running. The small knob on the right side is merely to adjust the hands and the date panel. If you unscrew it ensure that it is fully re-tightened or the waterproofing will fail."

"It is truly a marvel."

"It is, Mr Burden, more of a marvel than you know. Please take good care of it."

With his immediate money concerns abated, Chris was in high spirits when he returned to the camp. They were dampened when he saw Stewart waiting for him with a troubled look on his face.

"Ah, Lennox, come sit with me."

"What is it, Colonel? You look agitated."

"Sit down. There are bad tidings from Imber. Lieutenant Dean has had a fall. He has taken to his bed and is calling for you. I have a letter from Mrs Catherine Dean asking if you may attend at your earliest convenience."

"Of course, I'll leave immediately."

"No, sir, you cannot. I have also received a despatch from Horse Guards. They demand our attendance there forthwith. We must leave for London on the noon coach."

"But what of Anthony and Mrs Dean?"

"Write them a note and I will ensure they receive it on the morrow. Duty calls, sir and we cannot delay."

# 43

The ninety miles from Salisbury to London would in summer conditions take around ten hours. But in the depths of winter with the first of the snows the journey took over twelve and it was well past midnight when Chris and Stewart walked into Brooks's Club in St. James's Street. Stewart was a member and signed them both in for the remainder of the night. Gambling was going on, even at that late hour and Stewart went to watch at a noisy table playing whist for high stakes.

Chris had spent a part of his original two-hundred guineas on a green dress uniform. He had dressed in it for his trip to Horse Guards and now it raised some interest around the salon. A distinguished middle-aged man approached him and looked him up and down.

"My god, a dandy in uniform; 'pon my soul. Who and what are you, sir?"

Chris gave a stiff little bow. "Captain George Lennox, attached to the 62nd. And you sir?"

"William Cavendish, sir. Fifth Duke of Devonshire. I had no idea that the 62nd wore such frippery and in such dowdy colours. What is the purpose of it?"

Stewart came up to Chris's shoulder. "That, your grace, is intelligence you would needs ask of his Royal Highness the Duke of York."

"Confound it man, am I not to get a straight answer to a question? I'll wager neither of you could tell me what that upstart Bonaparte will do next."

"He has left Egypt and returned secretly to France," Chris said. "He may already be in Paris."

Cavendish gave him a surprised look. "The devil you say, Lennox. Will you wager on it?"

"I would, your grace, but you would be wasting your money."

Stewart smiled. "Captain Lennox is newly arrived from abroad where he had occasion to relieve the French of secret despatches indicating that Bonaparte has indeed arrived in Paris."

"It wouldn't have been a gamble, your grace, I'd have taken your money under false pretences."

"A brave man and an honest one it would seem. Do you wager at all, say on the toss of a coin?"

"I rarely gamble unless the odds are on my side. As a soldier I prefer to stack the cards in my favour. Perhaps not toss a coin but spin a coin on a hard surface and bet on which side turns uppermost."

Cavendish gave him a shrewd look. "I see no difference but I am game. Let us find a table."

Stewart tugged at Chris's arm. "What are you about, Lennox? I smell some devilry afoot."

"His grace appears to be a gambling man and I won't deprive him of a little sport."

"I know you. You do not take idle risks."

"It's more than that. The duke took exception to my uniform and he has to know that green jackets are not to be taken lightly. I hope I'll earn some respect as well as relieve his grace of some of his money."

Cavendish found an unoccupied table and slapped a coin on it. "Now sir, what is the wager?"

"Ten guineas I can call it right."

"Very well, what say you?"

"I'll call tails."

Cavendish spun the coin and it whirred on the hard surface and clattered to a standstill. "By god, sir, tails it is.

My turn and I shall call heads." He spun the coin again and it came up tails. "Now sir, how shall you call?"

"Tails again."

"Three times, sir? That is long odds indeed." He spun the coin for a third time, and again it came up tails. "This I cannot believe. This run cannot hold, I shall call heads again." He spun the coin for a fourth time, and again it landed tails. "By all that is holy. Tails four times. Surely this cannot continue. What do you call now, Lennox?"

Chris bit his lip the odds were lengthening. "I'll stick with tails."

"The devil you say, sir. Very well for fifty guineas, tails called." He spun the coin and it landed tails again."

"This is most extraordinary, I cannot believe my eyes. Your luck cannot hold, Lennox. This time I shall call tails." He spun the coin again, and again it landed tails. "Huh! I have won one back. I do believe I have taken your thunder, Lennox. What do you say to doubling the wager?"

"Very well, your grace but my limit is one-hundred guineas. I do not believe in winning, or losing, any greater amount at any one sitting. That way I keep my friends and reduce my enemies."

"Honest and sage into the bargain. I like this fellow, Stewart. Now, sir, what will you call?"

"Heads," Chris said.

"You are the most admirably daring fellow, Lennox. Six times it has come up tails and now you call heads when the wager is doubled. Very well." He spun the coin and watched it as it clattered to a stop. "Pon my soul, heads. How do you do it?"

Cavendish's exclamations had drawn a crowd of onlookers from the other tables.

"I'll wager the green suit cannot win another," one man called.

"A hundred guineas that he can," another man said. "He has the luck of the devil."

Cavendish smiled at Chris over the hubbub that had sprung up. "Well, Lennox, we appear to have created quite the stir. You are sixty guineas to the good. What say we make this last turn double or quit. I daresay you may stretch your rule to a further twenty guineas on this one occasion."

"It's your call, your grace."

"I shall defer to you, Lennox. The call is yours."

"Then you give me a hard choice." Chris weighed the odds against losing most of his recent loan. "Then I'll call heads again."

Cavendish spun the coin. In the suddenly silent room the whirring noise was eerily loud. It clattered to a stop and all eyes peered at the table.

"Bless me, it is heads," Cavendish said. "Well done, Lennox, you have not called one wrongly."

"And made me an easy hundred," a voice called amid laughter. A hand clapped Chris on the back and the crowd made its way back to the tables.

Cavendish showed Chris and Stewart to a quiet corner near to a fire and pulled up chairs. He muttered to a wigged and livered footman who left the room, ordered drinks from a servant and treated Chris to a basilisk stare. "Now, Lennox, I know when I am bested. What is your secret? No man can be that lucky."

Chris nodded, he knew he would have to explain. "It's simple physics, your grace. If you toss a coin the odds are fifty-one to forty-nine that the side which is uppermost when the coin is tossed will end up uppermost. Fairly even odds. But when you spin a coin, the heavier side, most often the head, will fall to the bottom eight times out of ten. It's a matter of guessing when the coin will turn but otherwise the odds are with the tail turning uppermost."

Cavendish squawked a laugh. "Well I'll be damned. I like your nerve, Lennox. Tis a trick that may stand me in good stead some day and I thank you for it."

The footman returned with a chamois leather pouch on a tray and offered it to Chris.

"Your winnings, Lennox. Never let it be said that William Cavendish does not straightway pay his debts."

"I don't feel I should accept it, your grace. The odds were in my favour."

"All is fair in love, war and gambling. You did warn me that you only gambled when the odds favoured you and I chose not to accept the warning. The fault is mine and I shall be most disgruntled should you not receive your winnings with good humour."

Chris smiled. "So accepted, with thanks."

Cavendish switched his gaze to Stewart. "What are you two about? I wondered on the strange uniform but having now made Lennox's acquaintance I find it is no mere foible and there is something afoot."

"We cannot say, your grace," Stewart replied. "We are summoned to Horse Guards and betimes shall know more on the morrow."

"Then I shall wish you good fortune. However should you need my counsel you have but to ask."

Chris spent an uncomfortable night tossing in a strange bed. He could not get the thought of Anthony and Catherine out of his mind. Anthony's injury was serious. Several vertebrae in his spine had been dislodged by the

French musket and these were pressing on the spinal cord causing his lameness. A fall may have damaged the spinal cord even more causing complete loss of his legs. He also knew that Anthony's mental condition wasn't the soundest. The death of Willoughby and the men's reaction to it weighed heavily on him. Being new to army life had also taken its toll with the ferocity of close quarter battle coming as a shock to the young farmer. Even in these hardier and more callous times, it wasn't easy for a civilian to take up arms without proper training.

And then there was Catherine. Would she feel abandoned in her time of need? Anthony had asked for him, she had taken the time to write to Stewart. He knew she would never have done that unless her need was desperate. They had a bond. He had felt it the first time he had lifted her onto the coach driver's seat; the thrill that had run up arm and down his back. Was it simply pressure of his flexed muscles on the lightning burn? If so, why did he continue to feel so attracted to her?

And overlaying all this was a need to keep himself in check, to never display his feelings to her, or to anyone else. It had to be his secret and he would have to find the strength to keep up the charade for as long as it took.

As long as it took? He had now been in this alternative universe for several months. The feeling of unavoidable fate was still with him. Would he ever escape back to his own time and what would he find there? Perhaps they had buried his charred body, played the Last Post over his grave, had his parents drop their tears on his coffin. How could he go back to a world that may no longer exist for him?

A knock on the door brought an end to his dark thoughts. It was time to make the journey to Horse Guards where his fate might take another twist.

# 44

Horse Guards was not that much different in the late 1790s to as it was in the 21st century, although the buildings were cleaner, and not yet surrounded by other developments. No monuments had yet been erected around the sandy parade ground, which had seen service as Henry VIII's tilting yards.

A battalion of foot guards was parading with attendant screamed orders and rattle of side drums as Chris and Stewart made their way up a wide staircase to an office with a balcony that overlooked the parade ground.

Henry Wadman met them at the door. "His Royal Highness the Duke of York is within and should be treated with the deference deserving of his position. I know Colonel Stewart is aware of the protocols but I am not sure our friend from the settlements is so informed."

Chris gave him a hard stare. "Major Wadman, you and I will need to have a serious conversation at some future time."

Wadman gave him a half smile in return. "I shall look forward to it, sir. Now please remove your headgear and leave them with the servant. You will take your lead from me. When dismissed, you will not turn your back on His Royal Highness until you reach the door." He swung open the double doors and marched into the room with the two soldiers close behind. He stopped and bowed and they did likewise, waiting for the duke to acknowledge them.

Chris looked around. The duke, a rotund figure in red military coat and black cravat was standing at a desk with another man in military uniform. One man in mufti was standing by the full-length windows watching the Guards parade beneath.

The duke turned and waved them forward. "Come in, come in, do not stand on damned ceremony. Wadman, who have you brought?"

"Colonel The Honourable William Stewart of the 62nd and Captain George Lennox, Your Royal highness."

"Ha, Stewart and Lennox. Come here, we need you to see this." He waved a paper. "This is our order to form an experimental corps of Riflemen. Colonel Manningham here shall command and you, Stewart, shall be second in command. How do you say, what?"

"I am honoured, Your Royal Highness," Stewart said, "but may I ask what of Captain Lennox, sir. Twas he who first hit upon the tactic of using rifled weapons in disciplined warfare."

"Tut, Stewart. We have other plans for Lennox. Here, let us read this aloud. We shall be requiring Harry Calvert to issue this on the seventeenth day of January 1800 and it will be addressed to Officers Commanding; the 2nd Battalion Royals, the 21st, 23rd, 25th, 27th, 29th, 49th, 55th, 62nd, 69th, 71st, 72nd, 79th, 85th, and 92nd Regiments.

"We read,

*"Sir, I have the honour to inform you that it is His Royal Highness the Commander-in-Chief's intention to form a corps of detachments from the different regiments of the line for the purpose of its being instructed in the use of the rifle, and in the system of exercise adopted by soldiers so armed. It is His Royal Highness's pleasure that you shall select from the regiment under your command 2 serjeants, 2 corporals, and 30 private men for this duty, all of them being such men as appear most capable of receiving the above instructions, and most competent to the performance of the duty of Riflemen. These non-commissioned officers and privates are not to be considered as*

*being drafted from their regiments, but merely as detached for the purpose above recited; they will continue to be borne on the strength of their regiments, and will be clothed by their respective colonels.*

*His Royal Highness desires you will recommend. 1 captain, 1 lieutenant, and 1 ensign of the regiment under your command, who volunteer to serve in this Corps of Riflemen, in order that His Royal Highness may select from the officers recommended from the regiments which furnish their quota on this occasion a sufficient number of officers for the Rifle Corps. These officers are to be considered as detached on duty from their respective regiments, and will share in all the promotion that occurs in them during their absence.*

*Eight drummers will be required to act as bugle-horns, and I request you will acquaint me, for the information of His Royal Highness, whether you have any in the Regiment qualified to act as such, or of a capacity to be easily instructed. Etcetera, etcetera.*

The duke waved the paper with a flourish. "Now what do you say to that, eh?"

"I am most gratified, sir, that you have chosen me." Stewart said.

"Tosh, man. You have been in this from the beginning with Lennox. How could we not choose you? Now, away with you and Coote Manningham, you have much to discuss. We do not wish for this experimental corps to be languishing for long. It must be within the order of battle in eight months. There is a room you may use to start your work. Wadman will show you the way." The duke waved his hand and the three men backed to the door before bowing and leaving.

"Now, Lennox, what are we to make of you?"

"I am a soldier, Your Royal Highness, I will do as I'm ordered."

"Yes, yes, you misunderstand us, deliberately we think. What say you, Wellesley?"

The tall man with a sharply hooked nose turned from the window. "As much a politician, I'd wager."

"Indeed. Wellesley has broken his service in India to be here. Excellent service to be sure. It will soon be Sir Arthur Wellesley, eh, what."

Wellesley bowed. "If it pleases His Majesty to confer such an honour."

"Balderdash, man. You have earned the honour or our name is not Frederick. Now back to the matter in hand. Lennox, are you in any way related to Colonel Charles Lennox?"

"No, sir, I don't believe I am, certainly not closely related."

"Damned man near took our head off in a duel this past May. We refused to return fire, honour was satisfied and perhaps," the duke frowned and rubbed his chin, "we should not, in afterthought, have accused him of ignoring an insulting remark. By the by, we are relieved that you are of no kin as there will be no ill-will."

The duke waved his hand at the pile of papers on his table. "These despatches from you and Lieutenant Dean. It is they that have finally persuaded us that we have to raise a Corps of Riflemen. Manningham has been harking on it for some year or so. If half of what is detailed here be true, the corps shall be a unique turn in soldiering."

"I can't vouch for Lieutenant Dean's despatches, sir, although I'm sure he has been diligent, and mine are as accurate as I could make them."

"You had the fortifications at Monchique destroyed?"

"I did, sir. It was obvious that the French were building a main supply route from Cadiz. I believe they were planning a two-pronged attack on Portugal, one from the south through Cadiz and the other from the north with the collusion of Spain. The fortification at Monchique would allow them to control the route from the south."

"Lieutenant Dean reports that you saved him from the Frogs and single-handedly took down six of them."

"I think Lieutenant Dean was dazed from the assault on him. I had four riflemen with me, three of whom were killed in the encounter."

"Yet he is quite adamant that the riflemen were already hors de combat. We do not appreciate false modesty, Lennox."

"I won't argue with the lieutenant's recollections, sir."

Wellesley walked to the table and picked up one of the documents. "This details your account of the battle with the French Horse Grenadiers. You say that you decimated an entire squadron with just forty men."

"The ground favoured us. The Rifles took down the squadron command and the muskets volley fired into the main body which was attempting to cross a narrow bridge. The French made it easy for us."

Wellesley picked up another paper. "This is the document you retrieved from the French. It details some numbers lost to them. You were indeed well occupied."

"We were lucky."

The duke grunted. "Is it false modesty again, Lennox? We have it down to tactics, sir and that is why we are to commission you to devise a suitable programme of training for the Corps of Rifles. We are pleased to promote you to lieutenant-colonel with immediate effect with an income of, ooh, what say you Wellesley, five-thousand a year?"

"That would seem adequate, sir."

"We shall have the money paid into your account from the Civil List."

Chris shrugged. "I don't have an account, sir. Being newly arrived and in somewhat straightened circumstances, I haven't had the opportunity to open one."

"Then we shall open you an account at Coutts. It is in the Strand."

"That's most kind, sir but if I'm to be responsible for training an entire corps I'll need a staff."

"Of course, you may choose your own men but you will be responsible for clothing and equipping them from your own income. You have men in mind?"

"The soldiers who accompanied me to Portugal. They are experienced, courageous and loyal. Most are already trained on the Baker Rifle and those men will make an ideal training cadre."

"So be it. We will have letters of authorisation made ready for you."

"Will I be able to promote the men myself?"

"You may do as you wish within your own command but you must remember this is a detachment and men may not retain their rank should they re-join their regiments at some future time."

"Thank you, sir. I'll need to get started on this. With your permission."

"Just two more things, Lennox," Wellesley called. "No more hiding in holes, it ill becomes British soldiers to be seen cowering like so many rabbits. And no more iron weskits, it is undignified."

# 45

Chris hurried back to Brooks's Club to retrieve his belongings. The whole episode with the Duke of York was rattling around his head like an express train and he needed to give the ramifications some thought.

He was now a lieutenant-colonel with an income. Not that five-thousand a year would go far if he had to equip, feed and pay his own men. He would need all the surviving men to form the training cadre. He intended to promote them all to NCO rank with Biggin and Pocock promoted from serjeant to serjeant-major. At a quick calculation it would cost him nearly fifteen-hundred pounds a year in wages alone.

He went to settle his bill and was hailed by William Cavendish. "Leaving us already, Lennox?"

"Yes, your grace. Back to Salisbury, for now, anyway."

"Another wager before you leave?"

Chris grinned. "Not a wager, sir. I have a far better idea that may appeal to you."

They found the chairs by the fire were unoccupied. Cavendish called for drinks and with a look of impish interest he begged Chris to continue.

"I have a proposition to put to you. I've just returned from an audience with His Royal Highness the Duke of York. He has commissioned me for an important task which requires me to finance a body of men. My means are limited and I wondered if you might consider agreeing to supplement the cost of the cadre."

Cavendish raised his eyebrows. "To what advantage?"

"None, except that of serving your king and country."

"At what cost?"

"Say fifteen-hundred pounds ..."

*"fifteen-hundred?"*

"… per annum."

*"Per annum?"*

Chris grinned. "There is an element of risk."

"I should say there is. Why do you think I should consider such a venture?"

"Have you heard of the Baker Rifle?"

"No, Lennox, I certainly have not. Just what the devil is a baker's rifle?"

"A weapon that is about to be purchased in quantity by the army. In two month's time the Board of Ordnance will hold trials at Woolwich which Baker will win due, in no small measure, to the fact that I have already tested the rifles in action and His Royal Highness is much taken with them. The gunsmith will need to expand his armoury to cope with the increased business and that expansion will need financing. I'll wager, should you invest in the company, you should, over a period of time, return an excellent profit that will more than compensate you for your fifteen-hundred … per annum."

Cavendish beamed at him. "That is more to my taste, young man."

"You'll find Ezekiel Baker at his gun shop in Whitechapel Road. There is no need to mention to him where you gained your information. It should remain between us."

"Huh! Machinations. I like this even better. I shall write a promissory note for your fifteen-hundred and have it despatched to …?"

"Coutts, in the Strand. To the account of Lieutenant-colonel George Lennox."

"From captain to colonel in one day, that must indeed be cause for celebration."

"It is but you must excuse me. I have just seen my colleagues enter and I must speak with them."

Stewart was with Coote Manningham and they walked over. Cavendish bowed and took his leave with an artful wink at Chris.

"I do not believe you have been introduced to Colonel Manningham," Stewart said.

"No but I know of him by reputation. It is an honour and a pleasure to meet you, sir."

"And I you. Were it not for your expedition to Portugal I doubt that I could have persuaded His Royal Highness of the benefit of a Corps of Rifles.

"Stewart and I met in the Indies. He has an eye for new tactics and I was much taken with the rifle's use by the colonists in the Americas who did cause much distress amidst our soldiers with the rifle's range and accuracy. Until now I have been waging a near impossible campaign to have the rifle adopted and a regiment trained in its use."

"You should know that His Royal Highness has charged me with training the corps and promoted me to lieutenant-colonel," Chris said.

Stewart clapped him on the shoulder. "Yes, we were informed by Major Wadman of your task and promotion. Congratulations, my dear fellow."

"It's an honour that weighs heavily. The training should be decided between all three of us and I'm more than happy to bow to your wisdom in matters of tradition. There is one area of discipline on which I am adamant. The use of flogging must be kept to an absolute minimum, used only in extreme circumstances, if at all."

Manningham nodded. "I have read of your methods and the encouraging results thereof. Both Stewart and I are in agreement, given the quality of the soldiery we are expecting from the fifteen regiments of the line, that the need for corporal punishment shall be greatly reduced."

"Then we are all in agreement," Chris said. "I understand, Colonel Manningham, that the Board of Ordnance is due to conduct a test of possible rifles at Woolwich in February."

"Yes, indeed. I was with them but yesterday at their offices in Horse Guards to discuss the parameters of the contest. We must agree on a standard for the army."

"Having used the Baker Rifle in battle, I am somewhat of an authority on the weapon. Might I suggest you take cognisance of a barrel with a quarter turn in the rifling and a calibre of below point seven."

"Indeed, sir. Might I enquire as to why?"

"It will become clear in the trials but I have found that a larger ball means more weight for the soldiers to carry and the barrel will need sponging more frequently. A quarter turn induces more spin to the ball with the resulting increase in accuracy up to three-hundred yards."

"Lennox is a mine of information," Stewart said with a grin. "I do believe he be more academic than soldier. He out-wagered the Duke of Devonshire on the spin of a coin simply on the *physics* of it."

"Gentlemen, we must reconvene this discussion at another time," Chris said. "As Colonel Stewart is aware I have a responsibility to one of my officers which needs my attention. If you'll forgive me I must get back to Salisbury."

"I too will take my leave, sir," Stewart said. "The officer in question is also a friend of mine and I wish to know how he fares."

"Very well," Manningham said. "There is little that can be accomplished before Christmastide but we must meet again on the day of December 27th. God speed until then."

Sir George and Lady Isobel made Stewart and Chris very welcome when they returned to Imber Court the next afternoon. They ushered them into the drawing room where a large log fire was crackling in the grate and the room smelled of wood smoke and pipe tobacco. Amelia rose to meet them with an equally warm smile and dropped a deep curtsey.

"We are happily reacquainted, Colonel Stewart, Captain Lennox."

"Tis Lieutenant-colonel Lennox, now," Stewart said. "Our friend has been rewarded for his excellent service to His Royal Highness."

"We have orders that will take us away from Salisbury and from Imber after Christmas," Chris said. "We've come to enquire after Mr Anthony Dean's health while we can."

"Sit you down," Sir George said, "and take a glass of Madeira. I have sent Mary with news of your arrival so that they may prepare for your visit and then I shall task Matthew with leading you to the Dean's home shortly but rest you first."

"Mr Dean, is quite unwell," Lady Isobel said. "We fear for his wellbeing."

"And how is Catherine?" Chris blurted before he could stop himself. He caught Amelia's knowing look and gave himself a mental kick.

"Mrs Catherine Dean is elsewise in good health," Lady Isobel answered, "But naturally concerned for her husband and quite fatigued with his care."

"Is Doctor Hawking in attendance?"

"Indeed he is, daily," Sir George said, "but he is at a loss as to Anthony's condition. He has regained some use to his legs but remains in his bedchamber and will not venture out for any reason."

"He has been asking for you, Colonel Lennox," Amelia said. "He wishes to speak with you most urgently."

"Yes, I apologise. Colonel Stewart informed me of Mrs Dean's letter but my duties took me elsewhere until now."

"Forever the soldier first," Amelia said. She had a smile on her lips but the words were tinted with a gentle sadness.

It stung.

"Colonel Stewart and I are free of those duties until past Christmas. We'll endeavour to be good friends until then."

"Then you must stay here at Imber Court," Sir George, said. "Winter snows are due and we cannot have you travelling back and forth from Salisbury in such chill winds. The coachman will take a note and drive to collect your baggage on the morrow."

Matthew came in and bowed. "If you please, Sir George. Mrs Dean sends word that she will receive the gentlemen at their convenience."

Chris stood. "Then I'll go right away. Stewart?"

"It seems Lieutenant Dean is most insistent on your presence above all else. You go, Lennox. I shall follow at a more sedate pace."

Chris was grateful for Stewart's perception and followed Matthew on foot for half a mile to a mellow sandstone house under a slate roof surrounded by mature ash trees, their naked branches scratching at the dull winter clouds. Chris shivered, mostly from the cold but also in anticipation of what was to come.

# 46

Catherine was standing in the drawing room as a maid showed Chris in. She looked pale and had her hands clasped in front, the knuckles white from tension. He bowed and she inclined her head in response.

"Colonel. Matthew has told of your advancement. I wish you well of it."

Chris took a deep breath. "Mrs Dean. I came as soon as my duties allowed."

"Of course, Colonel. I meant no censure."

"But it was implied."

She sat, flustered. "Not at all. I am most grateful you could find the time."

"I'm staying at Imber Court until past Christmas. I'm at your service until then. Now that we have the sparring over with, tell me about Anthony."

"You are too forward, sir."

*And I want to give you the biggest hug but I have to stand here like a stuffed shirt.*

"Merely concerned. I need to know about his condition."

"Doctor Hawking is better qualified than I to explain. He will be here shortly for his daily round. He has suggested leeches but Anthony will not abide them and I know not what to think."

"Leeches? For a spinal injury?"

"It is not his physical injuries that cause such concern, as incapacitating as they are. It is his moods that change from one minute to the next as if they are waves raging on a broken shore. Now ebbing and sorrowful, then roaring, smashing all before them."

"I was told he had a fall," Chris said.

She nodded, her mouth a prim rosebud of disapproval. "Against all advice he attempted to mount his horse but fell from the stirrup. With so little strength in his legs he was unable to complete the mount. He had refused help from the groom.

"Now he can barely walk without the aid of two canes. Even so he will not leave his bedchamber. His father, his mother and his brother have all attempted to persuade him to join them here in this room but he has refused. His one constant is that he calls for you and will not settle until he has been assured that you will come with time."

"Then I should go up to him. Before I do, you have to know that I did everything in my power to keep him safe but Anthony has a mind of his own and is as strong willed as any young man. In the end, I'm so sorry to say, I could not protect him from himself."

"I thank you for your concern, sir, even if it was to no avail. Go to him now. I'll await you here for news of what transpires between you. I have heard that you possess a healing touch. I pray god you may use it to good effect."

Chris knew what was ailing Anthony. It was an all too common effect of warfare. Post Traumatic Stress Disorder, PTSD, even in the 21st century it was often overlooked or dismissed by medics. Here in the turn of the 19th century it was unheard of. He may know the cause but was at a loss of how to treat the symptoms. He knocked on Anthony's door and pushed it open. Anthony was in one of his ebb moments, watching the freshly falling flakes of snow passing the rippled glass window.

He spoke without turning. "What is it now, Catherine?"

"Not Catherine, it's George. I hear you've been asking for me."

Anthony turned awkwardly on his two canes. His face broke into a weary smile. "George, you came. I am so relieved to see you." He hobbled to a chair and sat with an effort. "As you see I am not at my best. Please sit with me and tell me of your recent adventures."

Chris forced a smile back but quickly told Anthony of the formation of the Corps of Rifles. "That is enough of me, now, tell me of your happenings. I hear you've taken up acrobatics."

"Tosh, George, you mock me. It went to illustrate my uselessness."

"Your determination, Anthony. It proves you won't let something like this get you down."

"There you are, George, always searching for the sun beyond the clouds."

"The clouds always break, Anthony."

"I am in the depths of winter. I cannot see beyond them and the snow."

"Your body can be healed. You just need to give it more time."

"Look around you, George. What do you see? An empty room; such cold comfort."

Chris had already looked around, seen the bottle of gin and the Dragon pistol on the dresser and assessed Anthony's dire state of mind. "You have a warm fire, a comfortable bed and people who love you. You are better off than many."

"Ah! Platitudes. I hoped for more understanding. The fire burns low, the bed is cold, I share it with no one and the love is mere sentimentality for one who is crippled."

"What do you want to hear? That you are useless, that there is no future for you? That you'd be better off dead?" He pointed to the pistol. "Is that the way you see it?"

"I can bear the pain, George, but not the distress I cause to Catherine. Our marriage is not yet consummated, I cannot ..."

"Anthony, I know what the cause of your distress is. You can beat it by being strong. There is a future for you but you need to believe in yourself and in the people around you. You are worth much more to them alive than rotting in a box."

"I so wish that were true. I do not wish to be a burden."

"That's the last thing you are."

"I cannot walk without canes, I cannot work the farm and I cannot pleasure my wife. Of what use am I, sir?"

"I'm sure you give her pleasure by being here. Until your legs heal, you can manage the farm accounts and be useful at a desk. There are ways."

"I envy you, George, always so full of optimism, every problem becomes a challenge to be solved by hook or by crook. I cannot be like you, I have tried but the temper ill becomes me."

Chris heard a knock at the front door and voices below. Stewart and Doctor Hawking had arrived together and were shown into the drawing room. "Listen, that's Colonel Stewart come to pay his respects and Doctor Hawking to check on you. Let me help you downstairs to greet them."

"*NO, George!* I will not descend like this on someone's arm. Allow Doctor Hawking to come but I am too fatigued to see Colonel Stewart. But, before you leave me, I would ask a favour."

"Of course, anything."

"You must use your good offices to persuade Catherine to return to Imber Court."

"She will not go, she's devoted to you."

"If you have any regard for her, which I believe you do, you *will* persuade her. The servants will care for me."

"How can you ask that?"

"Each time I see her face I see not the love of a wife but the concern of a nurse. I can no longer bear that look of pity. It would be of great service to me for you to persuade her to leave."

"Is this why you wanted to see me?"

"Yes. She will listen to you as she would listen to none other. She holds you in high regard."

"I have no influence with her, Anthony. She is her own woman and not given to being easily swayed. It's more likely that she would be more determined to stay if I was to suggest she moved back to Imber Court. Besides, although she hasn't said as much, I believe she holds me partly responsible for your injury and my judgement suspect."

"You will overcome any objections."

"Why haven't you mentioned this to her yourself?"

"For the very reasons you yourself have listed. Now, please, summon Doctor Hawking. He has a concoction of laudanum that I find much to my taste."

"May I take the pistol, Anthony?"

"No, sir, you may not."

Chris met Hawking on the stairs.

"How fares my patient, sir?"

"Not well, doctor. He's preoccupied with his condition and it's depressed him."

"You have some medical skill, what is your considered diagnosis?"

"I can't claim to be any form of medic. I know about first aid but that's it. I'm pretty sure though that the vertebrae in his spine are out of place and putting pressure on the spinal cord. It's that which is causing the problem with his legs."

"I feared as much. There is little that can be done for such a difficult injury."

"There is something called bone manipulation but it could cause more damage if not done correctly."

"Indeed. I know of bonesetters but such practices are frowned upon as little better than quackery."

"It may be his only chance. Make some enquiries, doctor. Unless we can find a cure for him I'm concerned he might lose the will to fight his disability."

# 47

"The laudanum has taken effect and he is sleeping," Hawking said.

Catherine rose to her feet and met him at the door. "You will return tomorrow?"

"Of course, madam." He looked across at Chris sitting with Stewart by the fireside. "I shall make those enquiries we discussed, sir."

Chris nodded his thanks but did not answer Stewart's unspoken question.

"I shall take my leave also," Stewart said. "Until a later hour, Lennox."

"There is a hard frost, Colonel," Catherine said in passing, "be sure to walk with care."

"I shall, madam. I will return on the morrow and hope that Mr Dean is in better humour."

As soon as he had left Catherine spun to Chris and gripped his wrist. "Tell me what it is you have deduced."

Chris put his free hand on hers and for once she did not pull away. "Please sit, Catherine." He pulled a chair closer to the fire for her as night had fallen and the chill was deepening. It seemed that December was going to herald another hard winter. A mini ice age, Chris recalled the historians termed it.

"Anthony is quite ill and there is little in medicine that can cure him. I've asked Doctor Hawking to enquire after a bonesetter who may be able to manipulate his spine and return the use of his legs."

Sudden hope sparked on her face and he wanted to kiss her for it. "Is this possible?"

"It is but it's a dangerous procedure that might result in even more damage being done. Complete paralysis or a stroke which will affect his speech and other bodily functions; or even cause death. It's a high risk treatment."

Her face had fallen again into its sombre set. "Why would Anthony then agree to it?"

"I haven't mentioned it to him yet. At the moment we don't even have such a person as a bonesetter to call on. The medical profession are opposed to such treatment and Hawking may be risking his reputation by merely enquiring about them."

"You raise my hopes but then dash them so quickly."

"You have to know the truth. Anthony will not recover unless his physical injuries are cured. Only then will we have a chance to help him regain his mental equilibrium. He can see no future for himself in his present state."

"But he is well cared for, surely he can persevere."

"Physically, yes. Mentally, no. Where I'm from the condition is known. There is no permanent cure but sufferers can live a normal life with the help of patience and understanding. He was not fully ready for military service and what he saw, what he experienced, together with his injury, has unbalanced his mind."

"You paint a bleak picture, sir."

"There is another thing."

He waited for her to look at him. "He has asked if you would move back to Imber Court, to give yourself some respite. He is concerned that you look so fatigued and thinks some time away from this house will be beneficial."

"I could not possibly abandon him."

"You won't be abandoning him. It won't do either of you any good if you succumb to some illness because you become too tired to fight one off, especially in this freezing weather. He won't be alone. I'll stay with him and the servants until you return."

"You would do that?"

"For you ... for Anthony, of course."

"No one will think the less of me for putting my wellbeing before that of my husband?"

"If any one merely thinks it I will call them out."

She raised a smile and again put her fingers on his wrist. "Oh, George, at times you are quite the fool."

He smiled back as pins and needles zipped up his arm. "I'd prefer the word comedian but I'll settle for fool."

She dropped her hand away as if she had realised an unconscious reaction but Chris was sure the touch had been intentional. It was going to be a hard few days.

Chris spent his time sketching out a training programme for the Corps of Rifles to talk over with Stewart and Manningham. Based on his experience with the Baker Rifle he also devised a platoon drill to reduce the time it took to reload to a minimum and wrote down the headings for each action. It looked good on paper but would need putting to the test by his training cadre as soon as the decision was made on the weapon the army would purchase. He knew it would be a foregone conclusion as he had primed both the Duke of York and Colonel Manningham to plump for the Baker Rifle. It was the barrel that would make the difference and Baker was the only one to design a barrel with a quarter twist.

He smiled at the recollection and mentally patted himself on the back for boning up on the Rifle Brigade's regimental history before joining his battalion. History credited Coote Manningham with being the father of the brigade, the driving force behind its conception. Chris now knew why he had been thrown back exactly to the months before the Corps of Rifles was formed in order to influence those decisions. The Corps of Rifles was an experiment but he would push to have the Rifle Brigade made a reality in the few months that the duke had given them.

Then again, was it just his avid boning up on regimental history that was driving a coma-induced dream? There was no record of a George Lennox in the history books of his day and he wondered, if he was truly in the past, whether those now forward in time would find a mention of him alongside Manningham and Stewart. An intriguing thought but he was happy to stay in the shadows if that was his fate.

He had finally mastered the use of quill and ink without leaving too many blots on the rough paper and remembered to sand the page to finish the job of drying the wet ink.

He put down the quill and rubbed his chin. Headings were one thing but putting meat on the bones another. It would take some time to work out the precise drill moves and check them in practice. In practice he knew that riflemen were of more use as skirmishers and scouts and that putting them in lines for volley fire would negate their singular advantage.

He went to check the time with his Breitling and pulled a face. He would have to find an opportunity to ride back to Salisbury and hope that the clockmaker hadn't yet sold the watch. He now had the money to return the loan and pay a percentage on top for the man's trouble.

The maid entered and curtsied. "If it please you, sir, Mr Dean is calling for you."

"Thank you, Esther. I'll go up right away."

The girl gave him the same comic look she always did and curtsied to leave.

"One moment, Esther. Why do you always look that way?"

"Beggin' your pardon, sir, I mean no offence."

"None taken, I'm just curious."

The girl blushed. "Tis the way you speak , sir, all funny like with strange words."

"I see." Chris could not help smiling. He thought he'd dropped into the idiom well but he now knew he still had a way to go before he could 'talk local'.

"Very well. Kindly inform Mr Dean that I shall attend him now."

The girl gave him a bright smile and curtsied. "Straightway, sir."

He waited for her to rattle back down the stairs before going up. These were always trying times for him as he never knew in what mood he would find the young man. He tried always to be positive but Anthony was sinking ever more deeply into depression.

This night he was at his lowest ebb with a wild look around his eyes. The Dragon was on the bed beside his hand. Hawking had given him some more laudanum earlier but it hadn't had the required effect of sending him to sleep. Chris guessed he was becoming immune to it.

"George, good of you to come. I wish you to give Catherine a message."

"Of course, Anthony." Chris sidled towards the bed, getting closer to the pistol but Anthony picked it up.

"Step back, George, be a good fellow. You may tell her that I cannot take anymore of this anguish and that she is to forgive me and forget me."

"Anthony, please, don't ..." He moved towards the bed but Anthony cocked the pistol and raised it.

Chris sighed. "Put the pistol down, Anthony, please. It will do you no good, I've blown the powder out of the priming pan."

"Indeed you did, George, whilst you thought I slept, and I thank you for your concern but I have replaced it. Please care for Catherine as best you may." He smiled, a weak sad twist of the lips, put the pistol to his temple and pulled the trigger.

# 48

Afterwards, Chris remembered it as the saddest Christmas he had ever spent. Anthony was well liked in Imber and the whole village turned out for his funeral on December 26th.

A series of hard frosts had frozen the ground solid and it had taken the gravediggers two whole days to dig the grave that they stood around on that icy morning with their breath forming clouds in front of their faces. The Deans were inconsolable but put a brave face on proceedings. The Wadmans more stoic but Catherine held a small handkerchief to her eyes as Amelia comforted her.

Chris and Stewart were in full military uniform, he in the green of the Rifles and Stewart in the red coat of the 62nd. Biggin and Pocock were also there bringing a wreath of holly from the riflemen but staying in the background among the villagers.

Chris caught Biggin's eye after the service and beckoned him over. "It was good of you to come, Serjeant."

"Beggin' your pardon, sir, but what was it you said, sir? In all things we protect our own. The lieutenant was one of our own, sir and the men remembered your instruction not to forget that."

Chris nodded. "I have news. You and Pocock are to be made Serjeant-majors. You should choose who succeeds you as serjeants from amongst the corporals and they too should choose their replacements. I am instituting another rank of lance-corporal and all the private soldiers will become lance corporals. I want a list of all names and ranks by noon tomorrow."

"As you say, sir. Thankee, sir, but beggin' your pardon, sir, why …?"

"We have a new task. We are to train a Corps of Rifles on the orders of His Royal Highness the Duke of York. Return to Salisbury and prepare the men for further orders. We'll be leaving Salisbury within the next few days."

He spotted Henry Wadman walking towards him and nodded Biggin away.

"Now, sir," Wadman said. "I believe we have a quarrel."

"We do, Major Wadman, but this is neither the time nor the place. There is enough grief here without us adding our argument to it."

"But what is your complaint, sir?"

"That you set Lieutenant Anthony Dean, your late brother-in-law to spy on me, which I find intolerably offensive to us both."

"Do you wish satisfaction, sir?"

"I'd prefer an apology."

"I cannot apologise as I was merely following the orders of a superior officer."

"Then, sir I will send my seconds to attend you at a future date."

"I have heard of your prowess with a sabre, Colonel, so I shall choose the pistol and be damned."

"Very well, sir. It can wait until a more convenient time when our duties allow."

Wadman nodded and walked away.

Stewart was at Chris's elbow but he hadn't heard him arrive. "Very civilised, Lennox."

"I wish Henry Wadman no harm but I have learned that insults are not to be tolerated in this society. At home we have other ways of settling disputes."

"Even more civilised ways, no doubt. I fear this news will spread and Sir George will be obliged to stand with his son. It is a double tragedy worthy of the bard. Both Henry Wadman and yourself, sir, are held in high regard at Imber.

"I must pay my respects to Mrs Dean. Excuse me."

Stewart pulled at his sleeve. "She will not yet have knowledge of the duel with her brother. I pray you do not burden Mrs Dean with that intelligence. She has more than enough troubles with which to contend."

Chris pulled his sleeve away. "Thank you for your concern, Stewart. I'll bear it in mind."

"Twas advice given in friendship, sir, but go your own way, as is your habit."

"You think I'm callous and uncaring, Stewart?

"I think you have the mind of a soldier and the heart of a lion but sometimes I do believe the niceties of manners are a little lacking."

"You're right. I'm learning but still have a way to go in that department. I will be circumspect and I will be gentle with Mrs Dean, I can assure you of that."

"Then go pay your respects and say your goodbyes. We shall be riding to Salisbury before this day is out."


Chris followed the family to Imber Court where they gathered in the drawing room with Hawking and the vicar. The vicar buttonholed Chris as he walked in.

"Sad events, Colonel Lennox. I hear tell you were present when the accident occurred to Mr Dean."

Chris nodded. "It was unfortunate carelessness on Mr Dean's part. He dropped the pistol as he was replacing it on the dresser, the hammer snagged and then freed itself as the pistol dropped in his lap and ... well you know the rest of the sorry tale."

"A most terrible occurrence and a great loss to Imber."

"Yes, indeed, Vicar. A most unhappy accident caused the loss of a great friend and fellow officer. If you would excuse me I need to pay my respects to Mrs Dean."

Chris took Catherine to one side. In the crowded room it seemed as if they were the only two people there. "How are you holding up?"

Her eyes glistened with unshed tears. "With little enough fortitude. I find this hard to bear."

"We haven't had much time to talk and I want to apologise for not stopping what occurred. Perhaps I could have done more."

"What more could you have done? Twas a terrible accident as you have explained and the whole of Imber was told."

"Perhaps I could have tried harder to persuade him to give up the pistol."

She gave a sad smile. "He would not. I tried also but he had a pair and ordered the servants to ensure one was always in his bedchamber. He was determined not to be without a pistol by his bedside."

"I still feel responsible."

"And perhaps I could have been a more obedient wife. Perhaps there are things we could both censure ourselves on but, I fear, it would have changed nothing."

"I'm afraid Colonel Stewart and I will have to leave Imber shortly."

"To your duties, I know. You will be in my thoughts … for all your kind services to us."

Amelia came across with fire in her eyes and overheard Catherine's remark. "Not all kind services, sir. I do hear from my brother, Henry, that you have challenged him to fight a duel."

"And you would say nothing of this, sir," Catherine snapped. "Is it not enough that we lose one relative?"

"I had hoped to spare you on this day. Be assured I have no intention of seriously harming Major Wadman but he left me no choice. In all honour I couldn't ignore his conduct."

"Honour, sir," Catherine said. "Is it honourable to belabour a man whose family has given you friendship and succour. How heinous was this crime of which you accuse him?"

"It is a private matter, madam. Perhaps you should ask your brother."

"I hear Henry has chosen pistols," Amelia said. "He has not heard, as I have, the talk from the soldiery that Colonel Lennox is as acquainted with that weapon as he is with the sabre. And that he did kill Foxley with a sabre. Foxley, said to be the finest swordsman in Wiltshire. You are no gambler, sir."

"No, Miss Amelia, I'm not but I would rather see myself dead than injure your brother. However, honour must be satisfied and he has refused to apologise. There is little I could do differently."

Sir George was drawn to the argument. "You are correct, sir," he said. "You must forgive my daughter, she is overwrought on this sad day. Henry has explained the circumstance to me. I am duty bound to ask you to leave my house and not return until this matter has been concluded."

"Some might wish you had never come here," Catherine said.

Chris snapped her a glance but could not read her face. "Colonel Stewart and I are riding to Salisbury today so you will be rid of us both. I can't echo Mrs Dean's feelings as

I've received nothing but kindness from this household. The day becomes even sadder."

He bowed, turned and left fearing he would never see Catherine again.

# 49

In the following weeks, the training cadre marched down to Shorncliffe in Kent, on the cliffs close to the Channel town of Folkstone. It had two of Henry VIII's Martello towers on its southern edge and was a mass of chalet type wooden barrack huts and campaign bell tents. Gradually officers and men from fourteen of the fifteen regiments on the Duke of York's list joined them. The 62nd was excused on the grounds of lack of suitable numbers.

The newcomers were all excellent men and ideal training material. As was his custom, Chris concentrated on physical fitness and soon had them marching to the one-hundred and forty paces to the minute that was to become the Rifle Brigade's standard light infantry marching cadence. New clothing had arrived in the dark green serge with black facings, tight pantaloons and black shakos with green hackles. Very close, Chris noted, to his original design and Catherine's watercolour sketch.

It was a busy time for Chris but somehow he could not get Catherine's face from his mind. He had thought her image would fade in time but it hadn't, it was his companion in every unguarded moment. In his mind's eye she had taken to wearing her hair up in a type of bun held in place with a silver comb which allowed her full beauty to shine. It bothered him that her presence should so haunt him. He was a grown man but with what seemed to him to be a schoolboy crush that he could not get out of his system.

The weather had been cruelly cold throughout January but warmed up in early February in time for the rifle selection process at Woolwich. Chris went with Manningham and Stewart, took no part in the assessment process but test fired two of the American contenders. They were good rifles but with barrels that were too long and unwieldy with nowhere for a bayonet to be fitted beneath the barrels. As it was, Manningham talked Baker into submitting his thirty-inch quarter twist barrel with seventeen inch bayonet fixture which won general approval.

Chris took a moment to seek Baker out. "Congratulations, Mr Baker. A fine rifle."

"Most kind, Colonel."

"The initial order is to be eight-hundred rifles. Do you have the capacity in Whitechapel to produce those in good time? I'll need them quickly if I'm to meet my training requirements."

"In all honesty, sir, no. But there are other gun makers in London and Birmingham who can assist in their manufacture."

"Will you expand your works? I can foresee a greater need for rifles in the coming years."

"As good fortune would have it, I have a noble lord who wishes to invest in my business. I believe we have plans to expand Whitechapel and be manufacturing all rifles there."

Chris smiled. It seemed that His Grace the Duke of Devonshire had taken up the challenge. "Then I'd like to wish you good fortune, Mr Baker. A historic moment here today, I believe, and one which we should all profit by. How much will each rifle cost the Exchequer?"

"I believe the amount is yet to be agreed but perhaps thirty-six shillings each would seem a reasonable price."

Chris smiled again. At one pound, sixteen shillings each it would take Cavendish quite some time to recoup his fifteen-hundred pounds per annum but he would get there in the end.

The rifles began to arrive at the end of March and Chris organised shooting contests with prizes for the soldiers. They took to it like camp dogs to cookhouse bones and it became a popular pastime between the not so popular physical exercise and fieldcraft.

Although he did not agree with him Chris had taken Arthur Wellesley's comments to heart and left the digging and camouflage of slit trenches and sangers out of the training programme. He did however get the men to practise the use of cover and concealment with the mantra, shape, shine, shadow, silhouette, noise and movement, that he had first explained to Biggin and his men on Salisbury Plain all those months before.

There was still some inherent mistrust of his new tactics amongst the officers and senior NCOs who still held to their belief that volley fire was more efficient than taking on individual targets. To appease them he continued with his platoon drills but concentrated on the men working in pairs, and thinking for themselves, as his detachment had done to great effect in Portugal.

It was in early May that the camp had a visit from the Commander-in-Chief himself. The Duke of York arrived with his entourage and viewed the training and shooting with a judgemental eye. Henry Wadman was with him, polite but distant to Chris in the officer's mess afterwards.

The Duke took Manningham and Stewart aside and spoke earnestly to them. Then he called Chris over to join them. "Ah, Lennox. We are much impressed with the training and standards of shooting that we have witnessed this day. We do believe that the corps is ready for an engagement. What say you?"

"Four months is little enough time, Your Royal Highness, but the men are experienced soldiers and of the high quality you requested from their respective regiments. I believe it's possible they can acquit themselves well if put into the field."

"How many companies do you have ready?"

"Three, sir," Manningham said.

"Three? Excellent. There is an expedition we are set on and three companies would be ideal to make up the number."

"Is it Belle Ile?" Chris said.

The duke gave him a sharp look. "By god, sir, how is it that we cannot surprise you on this?"

"It is well-defended, sir."

"That is why we are sending nigh on one-hundred and ten ships and eight-thousand men. It would be an ideal testing ground for this new corps of Rifles. What do you know of this?"

"I know Belle Ile can be a thorn in the navy's side, sir. I overheard remarks made on the voyage down to Portugal. It's the largest island off the Brittany coast and maintains a large garrison with strong fortifications guarding a harbour that shelters elements of the French fleet. It doesn't need a master tactician to see its value to the French and why it would be a golden prize for us."

"You continue to surprise us with your acumen, Lennox. By god, sir, if you were not so valuable here at Shorncliffe we would have you on the General Staff.

"Stewart, you will command the corps. Now, when can you make ready to embark?"

"Whenever Your Royal Highness commands us," Stewart said.

"Excellent. We will have the Admiralty despatch a troop ship, and fifth-rater as escort, to Dover. Orders will follow."

"May I request permission to accompany the corps, sir?" Chris asked.

"What, Lennox? What of your duties here?"

"My training cadre is quite capable of continuing the programme without my presence, sir. And it ill becomes me to espouse tactics that I am not prepared to test myself in the face of the enemy."

The duke grunted. "Is our memory so bad that we cannot recall your expedition to Portugal where, we believe, you did put your theories to the test?"

"That was merely a minor skirmish, sir, compared to this major campaign. Tactics would need to be assessed and improved and what better way could there be to gain first-hand evidence?"

"Very well, Lennox. We see the sense of it. You may embark with the corps."

As the duke stalked off Henry Wadman turned to Chris with an arch look that suggested he surmised more than he was prepared to admit. "My sister, Mrs Catherine Dean, is enquiring after your health, sir, I cannot imagine why that should be so, but she requires me to hand you this note." He took a sealed paper from his sleeve and passed it over. "His Royal Highness resides in Folkstone this eve. Should you wish to communicate to Mrs Dean by return I should be obliged to receive a letter there."

"You are too kind, sir. I'll send a mess servant with it as soon as I'm able."

"This adventure to Belle Ile may yet do me the service of disposing of you, sir."

"Indeed, Major Wadman. I do believe it holds the risk of stealing the pleasure of meeting you on the field of honour."

"Then despite our differences I wish you a safe return. Be sure the letter reaches me before we depart at no later than ten of the morn."

Stewart came across the mess as Wadman left, his face wreathed in smiles. "So I am to be the first to command the corps in battle and we shall be brothers in arms, Lennox."

"Indeed we shall, Stewart, but I have a feeling it won't be the French at Belle Ile that tests our mettle but the Spanish."

Stewart gave him a sideways look. "Sometimes, sir, you are quite fey and I understand you not a jot."

"Never fear, there will be a battle, Stewart, a battle, come what may."

# 50

*My dear Colonel Lennox,*

*I have a great desire to apologise for my untoward behaviour at Christmastide. I beg your forgiveness for my cruel and unwarranted remark, brought about by my concern for all involved. My father, Sir George, did explain to me the circumstance and I can know that you are entirely blameless in the matter.*

*My father is determined to not welcome you to Imber Court whilst this Sword of Damocles hangs above us but you would be welcome in my small house whenever your duties bring you to Salisbury.*

*The house is entailed to Anthony's brother, Charles, but he, as yet, has no need of it and is permitting me to reside here between times, which is most kind of him. I shall needs to remove myself to Imber Court in due course but I shall make the most of my independence whilst I may.*

*Amelia also wishes me to offer her apologies and warmest regards for your health. She spends much time with me in sisterly companionship and in the company of Mr Charles Dean who is most attentive to her.*

*I do not believe I am being too forward if I say that we all miss your company and that of Colonel Stewart and would see you return at your earliest convenience.*

*Yours in friendship,*
*Catherine Dean (Mrs).*


Chris read and re-read the letter several times over. To his eye it was ingeniously written giving out so much information with so little content. He tried to read between the lines too but the messages he imagined were so mixed he gave up the attempt. At face value it was a gracious letter of apology from a friend. Her stating that she would be homeless at some time in the future did not surprise him as a wife had no legal standing and any property would pass to the nearest male relative under the entailment laws if there was no male issue from the marriage. Catherine was luckier than most having a family home close by that would take her in. It seemed that Charles was also beginning to seriously court Amelia and would need the house if the marriage went ahead.

Was it a simple statement of fact or a plea for help? The last two lines also had him in a spin. 'They' missed, not just his but Stewart's company. Was that a camouflaged message? Did it really mean that she missed his company? Damn this age where conversations were so coded you could hardly tell a compliment from an insult. One thing he did miss was plain speaking.

He pulled his small writing case from under his cot. He had to reply but to which level and on what level? Should he take a gamble or play the same game? He recalled his words to William Cavendish that he rarely gambled unless the odds were on his side. Were they? Catherine was a widow and now approachable. He had an income and a career. He could offer her a home and marriage without fear of scandalising polite society. Or was it too soon after Anthony's death? Possibly not in this age.

And then … he was an alien from another world, thrown back in time against his will. Could he seriously expect to live a normal life with that secret? Everything he had done, everything that had happened in this era had a purpose; nothing was chance, his every act was seemingly ordained by some force beyond his understanding and the thought that it might all be inside his head was beginning to frighten him. He saw the establishment of the Rifle

Brigade as his raison d'être in this life and once that had been accomplished his reason for being here was at an end. Would that be the end of him or would fate smile kindly on him? Was that any more of a threat than going into battle with the corps in its first campaign? Hedge your bets, man. What was that SAS motto; Who Dares Wins?

*My Dear Catherine,*

*Please forgive this personal mode of address but I feel we know each other well enough now to dispense with the niceties of polite language.*

*You and your family have become very dear to me and I will, of course, strain every sinew to return to Imber at the earliest opportunity.*

*Sadly, that will not be for some months as my duties with the Corps of Rifles will, once again, take me away from England.*

*On my return, with your permission, I will call on you personally as I have something of great importance to discuss.*

*Please convey my warmest regards to Amelia and thank her for her kind thoughts. I wish her and Charles Dean well.*

*I trust you will remain in good health and I will look forward with affection to our next meeting.*

*Your devoted friend,*

*George Lennox,*

*Lt-Colonel, Corps of Rifles.*

Catherine turned the letter over and over in her hands as Amelia watched her.

"Is it bad news, dearest."

Catherine gave her a half smile. "In truth I know not what to make of it."

"From whom is the note? I do not recognise the seal."

Catherine held the note to the window to study the image indented in wax. "Tis St George slaying the dragon. I do believe dear Colonel Lennox is making merry with his cipher."

"I know who plays St George but who must play the part of the dragon?"

"I do fear it must be I who is cast in that mould."

"Surely not. What news is there?"

"He is to be sent abroad once again with the Corps of Rifles and may not return for some months."

"That is sad news indeed."

"I was hoping that he would call into Imber so that I may offer a fuller apology to add to the altogether inadequate words of the note I did send with Henry. Now it seems it is not to be."

"I see you are flushed, Catherine, what else is contained there?"

"He sends his good wishes to you; I believe for Charles's attentions which I may have mentioned."

Amelia gave a musical laugh. "Did you, indeed. Charles and I are spending more time in comfortable conversation and I view him very warmly but there is yet time for proposals. I am in no hurry to see you removed from your home here."

"I thank you, kind heart, but you should not concern yourself overly. This house holds little charm for me knowing that Anthony died in the bedchamber above. I shall not grieve to move back to Imber Court and father's warm hearth."

"But I see we have not yet reached the nub," Amelia said, an impish smile on her face. "In which scene does the dragon appear?"

"Colonel Lennox has an important subject he wishes to discuss. I wonder what that may be? He expresses his devotion to the family and writes that he will stretch every sinew to return to Imber at the earliest possible time."

Amelia clapped her hands. "Do you think …?"

"I dare not think so. He writes that he wishes to dispense with the niceties of politeness but clouds his own intentions with mystery. I do believe the good colonel wishes to keep me in suspense."

"And the dragon he wishes to slay is perhaps the distance between you?"

"Or to slay any notion that we may be together."

"Would he be so cruel? I have seen how his eyes follow you when you are in the room. He endeavours to hide it but he cannot completely keep from showing his desire."

"He is a soldier, Amelia. His heart is hardened by what he does. He may make a decision based on calculation not on love. I am a widow and my fortune now belongs to Charles Dean. I have little to offer a man such as Colonel George Lennox."

# 51

Two ships were moored in Dover harbour. One was an ugly transport ship, squat and broad of beam, narrower at the top deck than at the waterline. The other was a rakish frigate. Chris peered at them through his telescope. "Good god, I don't believe it."

Stewart lounged beside him on the grass. They were on the cliff top overlooking the harbour. "What is it you do not believe, Lennox?"

"The fifth-rater. It's the Aquilon. I'm sure I'd know that rig anywhere."

"You continue to amaze me. Now you are an expert in naval shipping."

"I spent some weeks aboard her. I know her lines as well as the lines on your face, Stewart. I wonder if Cunningham still commands her."

"We shall surely discover that with time. Come mount your horse, they are bringing the East Indiaman to the quay and we shall soon be embarking the corps."

They rode onto the road that led into the port just as the three companies quick marched down the hill, stepping short to avoid slipping and carrying their rifles at the trail.

"Magnificent sight," Stewart murmured, "are they not."

Chris grinned back at him. Over two-hundred years worth of history was encapsulated in that one moment. He was witnessing the beginnings of a famous regiment on its road to glory. "And they're yours to command, Stewart. It must make you proud."

The captain leading the first company spotted the two colonels and drew his sabre in salute. Stewart saluted in return while Chris backed his horse to give Stewart prime spot. It was his time.

They embarked on the East Indiaman and were received by the ship's captain, a naval first-lieutenant. "The Aquilon has hoist a signal, gentlemen. They beg to know who commands the greenbacks."

Chris laughed. "That would be Commander Cunningham. Would you send back the signal, Colonels Stewart and Lennox."

Signal flags were soon rattling up the hoist and flapping from the halyards. The Lieutenant watched the reply. "The Commander invites you aboard the Aquilon for the voyage. He is sending a jolly boat."

"You go, sir," Stewart said. "I shall stay aboard this fine ship with my officers and men."

"Very good, Stewart. A wise decision if I might say so. It'll give you more time to get their measure and know your men. Don't forget to have them on deck at least once a day for exercise."

"Be off with you, Lennox. You are a hard taskmaster but I see the value of your advice."

"I beg your pardon, gentlemen but the jolly boat is alongside the quay," the lieutenant said.

The two ships met up with the rest of the fleet off Portsmouth and sailed southwest for several days before rounding the tip of Brittany and heading due south. The weather that summer had been warm and continued fair throughout July.

Chris was warmly welcome by the Aquilon's officers. Cunningham was more than pleased to see him and teased him unmercifully about his rapid advancement to lieutenant-colonel.

"Surely you're due a promotion," Chris said one morning as they strolled the deck together.

"Overdue, one might say but I am content to command a frigate. They are much sought-after vessels and have the eye of the senior captains. My time will come, Lennox."

"I'm sure it will, captain. Your seamanship speaks for itself, sir."

Cunningham gave him a tight smile. "If that were all I'd be Vice-Admiral Cunningham of the Red but it is not politic in this man's navy. One must have patronage and I am hoping to catch the eye of Vice-Admiral Nelson. It is dead man's shoes, Lennox but I smell changes coming and battles ahead where reputations can be made or lost."

"Beggin' you pardon, captain."

"What is it, master?"

"Belle Ile off the larboard beam, sir. The fleet is heaving to, Captain."

Cunningham raised his telescope and studied the smudge on the horizon. Then he swung the glass onto the flagship, HMS London, a ninety-six gun first-rater. "They make no signal."

"They are luffing, sir. A signal will surely follow."

"You are right, master. It's on the hoist. What make you of it?"

"An order for the captains of all fifth-raters to come aboard, sir."

"Very well. Have the bosun launch the pinnace. Will you accompany me, Lennox? It may be instructional for you to learn how the navy runs its business."

They were rowed across on a gentle sea together with pinnaces from four other fifth-raters. They gathered in the wardroom where Admiral Sir Edward Pellew briefed them on sizing up the enemy's defences by sailing within cannon range of the fortifications which dominated the harbour. "The Frogs will dare not sail out to meet us," Pellew said, "we outnumber them twenty to one and have five first-raters to their two. The dogs will stay in their kennel."

There were several red coats amongst the blue and gold naval uniforms, one of whom was Lieutenant-General Sir James Poultney. He paid little attention to Pellew but eyed Chris with interest. At the end of the briefing his Aide de Camp called Chris over.

"Sir James's compliments. He wishes a word, Colonel."

The general eyed him with open curiosity. "Which one are you? Stewart or Lennox?"

"Lennox, sir."

"Heard a lot about you, Lennox. Not all good, mind. Not at all sure about this greenery you wear, or about these damned rifles. We will see what show you will make when these damned tars get us ashore. That is all, Lennox but I have my eye on you."

"Thank you, sir. I'm sure you won't be disappointed." He took a pace back and gave a crisp army salute before turning away. He overheard a remark from the AdC to another staff officer. "Damned puffed-up puppy can barely speak the King's English. We'll see what this Corps of Rifles is made of. We will send them in ahead of the line."

The reconnaissance attack by the frigates did not go well. The French guns outranged them and were well positioned to repel a seaborne attack. The Aquilon lost her topsails and another frigate her mainmast before they could get close enough to bombard the lower fortifications in stone emplacements around the harbour.

Cunningham was the senior captain and commanded the flotilla. After several more balls hit the ships he ordered a withdrawal and sailed back to the fleet which was hove-to three miles out.

Once again Cunningham was ferried across to the flag ship but this time Chris did not go with him. When he returned his face was a mask and his mouth a grim line.

He took Chris aside. "Damned lobsters consider I should have sailed in closer. What do they know of wind and tide. I would have lost every damned ship under those Frog guns.

"Sir Edward is reasoning with them. I have given him my report and he sees it with a nautical eye. We will abandon Belle Ile and sail south for easier prey. Sir Edward feels, as I, that the defences are too strong to breach and our losses will be grave indeed should we endeavour to disembark soldiery on those shores."

"Beggin' your pardon, captain."

"What is it, master?"

"The London is making signal. We sail due south for Cadiz on the tide."

Cunningham grunted. "Cadiz? Now there's another goose not yet ripe for plucking. I'll wager we fare no better there than we have done here."

# 52

Cunningham was proved correct. The fleet was forced to turn back north by the strength of the French and Spanish blockade.

"I'll wager I know where we'll end up," Chris said one morning.

Cunningham gave him a jaundiced look. "Where pray, may I enquire?"

"Ferrol."

"Ferrol? Why there?"

"We have been at sea for weeks with holds full of bored soldiers without any success to our names. General Poultney will not want to return to England without claiming a victory for the expedition. Ferrol might appear to be the softer target after Belle Ile and Cadiz."

Cunningham cleared his table with a sweep of his arm and unrolled a chart of the northern Spanish coast. "Ah! Here, next Corunna. Pon my soul, Lennox, you choose another hard nut to crack."

"It's an important Spanish harbour. Well sheltered with narrows leading to a safe anchorage and a dry dock. I heard tell that the Spanish anchor four ships of the line there. I believe it will prove too tempting a target for Admiral Pellew and the general to ignore."

"I will not take your wager, Lennox, for I do believe you may be correct in your deduction."

Chris grinned. "Very wise, captain." As he had hinted to Stewart, he knew they would end up fighting the Spanish at Ferrol, it was the regiment's first battle honour and engrained in every Rifleman's psyche. And he was going to be present at it. He felt the thrill of anticipation at the thought of the fight to come.

The Spanish had not sited their eight 24-pounder cannon as well as the French had at Belle Ile, nor sited their fortifications to best advantage. The five British ships of the line pounded them with a carronade for several hours without much response which allowed the troopships to disembark the soldiers at the base of a hill.

Stewart received orders from General Poultney as he watched the battalions of red coats line up behind sixteen field guns. He pointed to the crown of the hill. "Do you feel much will come of bombarding those rocks, Lennox?"

Chris studied the top of the hill through a glass. "Not much damage will be done. The Spanish are well prepared in good positions."

"Sir James has invited us to lead the advance."

"No surprise there. I can see a convex route up the west side that will hide us from the defenders. We can get close enough to engage with the rifles but stay out of musket range until we've weakened the defences enough to dislodge them."

"Point it out to me."

"I'll do better than that. I'll lead the skirmishers."

"That is the job of a lieutenant. How should I risk a man of your rank?"

"I'm here to test out my theories. What better way than to lead an assault?"

"Lennox, you will worry me to an early grave. Very well, if you must. I shall ensure we have the companies in close support."

"I'll take forty Rifles from the first company as skirmishers with a lieutenant and a serjeant. Let the gunners continue firing until they see us enter that line of trees on the ridge to the right. Past those and we'll be in danger of a blue on blue."

"Pon my soul, Lennox, I do declare that your language becomes ever more outrageous but I do discern your meaning. I shall send a message to the gunnery officer to that effect. Fare you well and safe return, good friend."

A soldier had carried up Chris's Bergen and his Kevlar vest. He eyed it before deciding he could not wear it if his troops weren't similarly equipped, it would seem cowardly not to face the same dangers. He still had his single Dragon and he pushed this into his belt. After another thought he dug the Glock out of the bottom of the pack and changed the magazine for a full one. He strapped on the holster, tying the belt around his waist so that the gun was concealed beneath his short jacket. He removed his shako and replaced it with his green beret. He would go into battle wearing the bugle badge of The Rifles.

The forty skirmishers had formed up and he walked over to inspect them. A familiar voice called them to attention.

"Serjeant-major Biggin? What one earth are you doing here?"

Biggin grinned his tobacco-stained grin. "Beggin' your pardon, Colonel, but I could not be lettin' you off without me there to take care of you."

"Biggin, you're a rascal of the first water. I should have you busted down to corporal but I am pleased to see you. Is Pocock here too?"

"No, sir, beggin' your pardon, sir. He wanted to come but the captain remaining at Shorncliffe could not spare him, sir."

"One less for me to worry about. Who is your officer?"

"Lieutenant Beckwith, beggin' your pardon, sir, as good an officer as any, sir."

"Where is he?"

"Receiving his orders from the colonel, sir. He comes forward now."

Beckwith marched up and saluted. "Lieutenant Sidney Beckwith, sir. With Colonel Stewart's compliments, we may start the advance."

"The colonel has explained what we are about to do?"

"Yes, colonel. I am to obey your orders and instructions implicitly."

"Good. You'll go far, Beckwith. The heights are broad enough to take a single skirmish line but we will keep to the right of that outcrop of rocks until we are through the tree line. From that point on the Spanish will see us but we'll have the advantage of the rifles. I'll hold the centre with the bugler. You take the left flank and Serjeant-major Biggin the right. All clear?"

Both men nodded, saluted and marched to their respective posts. A bugler had stepped up to Chris's side, a young boy of fifteen. He looked pale but determined and reminded Chris of Willoughby.

"Bugler, sound the advance."

The crisp clear notes sounded and the skirmishers moved forward spreading out as they went and into their pairs. The bugler stayed in Chris's shadow but there was no need for further orders as the well-drilled riflemen went about their business.

The field guns were firing solid shot towards the top of the heights but seemingly making little impression on the rocky ground.

The skirmishers reached the line of spindly trees and waited for the barrage to stop. Looking behind him Chris saw that Stewart was as good as his word and the three companies of Rifles were closing up.

One by one the guns fell silent. "Play the advance, bugler," Chris said.

After another ten paces they saw the ramparts and above them the heads of Spanish soldiers. The Spanish had seen them and a volley fired in their direction but no ball came close. The leading riflemen began dropping on one knee and firing back.

A little too soon, Chris thought, another fifty yards and they would be making more hits. The second rank of rifleman now took over the advance as the first rank reloaded. They dropped to their knees in turn. Now hits were being made and he could hear the cries of the wounded. Now they were within a hundred yards and the Spanish fired another volley but with little effect.

The skirmish line was bunching together as they neared the crown of the hill and two men fell as the Spanish got the range. Rifles fired in retaliation and more Spaniards dropped.

"Bugler sound the charge," Chris yelled.

The notes echoed out and the skirmishers rushed forward with bayonets fixed. They scaled the low ramparts easily and got in amongst the defenders. Chris held his sabre in one hand and the Dragon in the other as he led the Rifles through the emplacement.

The Spanish put up a good fight and they found it hard going to push the defenders away from the ramparts. Another two riflemen died. Chris emptied his Dragon into a soldier and felled another with his sabre. They were on the verge of being overrun when men from the leading company poured in behind them putting the Spanish to flight.

The captain commanding it came alongside him. "We have them on the run, sir. They are beaten."

"No they're not, captain. They will be coming back at us. Prepare to man the defences."

# 53

The Spanish defenders were reinforced from the garrison and launched their counter-attack. All three companies of the Rifles had made it to the summit but the red coats, labouring under their heavy kit, were in no position to give support.

Chris relinquished command of the remaining skirmishers to Beckwith and joined Stewart at the centre of the formation. Biggin and the bugler came with him.

"We have a fight on our hands," Stewart said as he watched the ranks of Spanish infantry massing. "They will not wait for the redcoats to reach us, they will attack straightway."

"There's got to be a whole regiment there," Chris said. "It's going to be fun."

"The front is too narrow," Stewart pointed out. "They will not be able to commit a full force to the attack."

"And neither can we to the defence. We should pull the rifles back to the ramparts and use them to our advantage."

"It comes hard to give up ground so fiercely won but I see the sense. Bugler, play the recall and reform."

The young boy licked his dry lips. His uniform was spattered with blood and Chris remembered that he was showered with it when he shot the Spaniard.

"Spit, boy," Stewart ordered. "Time is pressing."

The boy mustered the saliva and played the notes. Men in green swarmed back to the ramparts and took up new defensive positions.

"Here they come," Chris muttered as a wave of Spanish Infantry poured up the slope towards the emplacements. Stewart had been right, they presented such a narrow front that the rifles had too few targets to make a difference to the numbers. Some twenty Spaniards fell but it was not enough as they pressed on to close quarters.

The British had the advantage of the higher ground and the cover of stone ramparts but the sheer numbers of the Spanish were pushing them back. With no time to reload they were using bayonets and rifle butts in an attempt to hold them off. Part of the line collapsed and the enemy rushed through.

Chris yelled a warning and took some men to try to fill the gap. Biggin came with him, sweat running down his face and a bloody sabre in his hand. He shot Chris a weary smile but the light of battle was in his eyes.

"Swift and Bold, Colonel Lennox, sir."

"Swift and Bold, Serjeant-major. Let's see what they're made of."

They met the Spanish head on and fought fiercely hand to hand but more were coming through. In a brief lull he saw that Biggin was under attack from two assailants and jumped to help.

Biggin fell and one of the Spaniards raised his sword to run him through. Without thinking, Chris dropped his sabre, pulled the Glock and shot both Spaniards where they stood. He turned to see another rifleman on the ground and those on their feet being pushed back. He fired again and put down another three Spaniards. It gave his men enough time to gather themselves and close the gap in their ranks.

The Spaniards turned and fled. Chris looked around for the reason and saw lines of redcoats behind them. He pushed the Glock back under his jacket and bent to help Biggin to his feet.

"Beggin' your pardon, sir," Biggin gasped. "How was that possible?"

"An infernal new invention that's not yet trustworthy. It's a government secret, Serjeant-major, entrusted to me. You are to mention this to no one."

Biggin nodded. "Twas you who saved me, sir. I should die before I would tell a soul."

"Good man. Now let's get our wounded tended and our dead buried with honour."

"Aye, sir, I shall attend to it."

Chris found Stewart. He had been hit but was still conscious. Officers had gathered around him and he was propped against a rock, a bloody bandage wound tight around his chest.

"Ah, so you are still alive, sir," Stewart said. He gave a dry cough and screwed his eyes shut for an instant. "I thank god for that. I saw your foray and believed you would die with that number against you."

"I had good men with me. They fought like lions."

Chris dropped to one knee and checked the wound. It did not appear to be as bad as he had feared but he knew that even superficial wounds could quickly turn septic. Stewart struggled to rise but Chris pushed him back with a gentle hand on his shoulder. "The Spanish won't be back, Stewart. They'll withdraw into the garrison at the town behind their defences."

Stewart coughed again. "The first battle of the Corps of Rifles and we acquitted ourselves well, did we not."

"It will go down in history and men will talk about it for centuries to come."

"I do believe you are prone to exaggeration, Lennox, but I should like to believe it so."

A small group of red-coated officers rode up the hill towards them. Stewart turned his head to watch their cautious approach.

"Ah, here comes Sir James with his staff to assess the circumstance. I trust he will be pleased with our endeavours."

"Suitably impressed, I'm sure," Chris said.

The general's pompous AdC came over and bent over his saddle to speak. "Stewart, Lennox, Sir James sends his compliments and wishes to offer his congratulations."

"We thank Sir James," Stewart said, "and enquire as to his further orders."

"He asks that you remove your Rifles to the coast for embarkation."

"We are not to assault the town?"

"No, Stewart. Sir James believes the cost too high for the gain and we will once again set sail for Cadiz."

"Come then, Lennox, let us rally the men."

"No, not you, sir, nor you Lennox. Sir James requires you take Colonel Stewart and despatches back to England on the Aquilon. Make ready to leave on the morning tide."


Chris was sorry to be leaving the corps behind but he knew that the expedition to Cadiz would be as abortive as the first attempt and that the fleet would return home with nothing except the newly earned reputation of the Corps of Rifles which would culminate in the forming of the 95th Regiment.

As sorry as he was he was more pleased to be returning. He had personal matters to attend to and a burning desire to see Catherine. Stewart had been well cared for by the ship's surgeon together with liberal quantities of Chris's antiseptic powder and was recovering well. He had few qualms about leaving him at Portsmouth.

Sir James had handed the despatches to him personally in a leather satchel then sat and stroked his jaw as Chris stood on the other side of the wardroom table wondering what was to come next.

"I watched the skirmish through my glass, Lennox. I did think the Spanish had bested you and that you would retire defeated but I was amazed at the fortitude of the Rifles and the skill at arms they displayed. I have said as much in the despatches to His Royal Highness. You have the honour to see them delivered personally to Horse Guards without delay on your return to Portsmouth."

"Yes, Sir James. With all possible speed."

"I believe I was wrong about you, Lennox. I believe your tactics will come in useful in future cases. Lightness and speed of manoeuvre took the heights whilst the line regiments struggled. It was an education. Now be off with you, I have a further campaign to plan and Sir Edward wearies me with his objections." He waved Chris away, the interview over.

The memory ran through Chris's mind as the ship sailed into Portsmouth on the dawn tide. He said his goodbyes to Stewart, Cunningham and the officers and wished them calm seas for the months ahead. He knew what lay in store for the British navy and its hero, Nelson, but could not say a word about it.

He took the coach to London and went straight to Horse Guards. It was late in the evening but lights burned in the windows and he found Henry Wadman still at his desk.

"I have despatches for His Royal Highness from Lieutenant-general Sir James Poultney."

Wadman put down his quill and stared. "Others ... so soon? Has there been a disaster?"

"No, sir, not a great disaster. In fact something of a minor victory at Ferrol but Sir James considered the risk too great to take the defences. The troops have now embarked and the fleet is sailing on to Cadiz for another attempt at a landing."

Wadman sighed. "That will not be welcome news for the duke. He had hoped the expedition would take and hold Ferrol after the failure at Belle Ile."

"It will be in the despatches, major. If there's nothing else I'll be going."

"I am done here. Would you care for a glass of Madeira at my club."

"Under the circumstances?"

"I do not see why we cannot be friends, sir, although we may soon be killing each other."

Chris grinned. "That's most handsome of you, sir. I would like nothing better."

"I take it you wish to court my sister, Mrs Dean?"

"What makes you think that?"

"Come, sir, I have eyes and a brain and can well add up two and two. An exchange of letters between people who hold each other in high regard leads me to suspect more than just friendship."

"Has Mrs Dean mentioned anything …?"

"Not in so many words, sir, but I do believe she awaits your presence with some expectation."

"Would it … distress you?"

"I had thought you an adventurer but you have proved me wrong. I would be proud to call you brother-in-law."

"Then it makes this duel a total nonsense."

"Indeed, sir but honour must be satisfied. We shall face each other as is the custom and be done with it. What are your plans?"

"I'm going to Salisbury for a personal matter and then on to Imber to visit Mrs Catherine Dean."

"Very well. Shall we make an arrangement to meet on the dawn of the day you proceed to Imber? We shall then have the business concluded and done when you meet with Mrs Dean."

"That's an excellent idea. Where shall we meet?"

"An ideal place is the henge near to the Salisbury turnpike. It is within easy distance of Imber and on my route from London."

Chris had a moment of indecision. He had bad memories of Stonehenge but agreed with good grace. "Very well, the henge it is, two mornings from now."

# 54

Henry Wadman had horses stabled in the cavalry barracks at Knightsbridge and he loaned a mare to Chris for his journey to Salisbury. He kept to the turnpikes and paid a shilling for each stretch of the road. Expensive for the time, the equivalent to a day's wage for a soldier, but it made the journey easier and he was in a hurry.

He rested the horse at coaching inns along the way but begrudged the time. It was growing dark when he rode into the 62nd regiment's barracks outside Salisbury's gates.

The regiment's new colonel had not yet been appointed so Chris made himself at home in Stewart's old quarters and ate with the officers that night. These men were to form the basis of a second battalion but few knew what lay in the future for them and the talk around the mess table verged on despondency as most of the officers were still on half pay.

Chris cheered them up with tales of the expedition and how well the men from the 62nd had acquitted themselves. He did have an ulterior motive as he needed two seconds to join him at Stonehenge to see fair play.

Henry had promised to bring two of his own friends from London and the duelling pistols kept in the Brigade of Guards' officers' mess for the express purpose of settling disputes amongst the officers. He persuaded two captains to stand for him and to meet him at Stonehenge before dawn on the next but one day.

The following morning he hurried through Winchester Gate and made for Silver Street and the clockmaker. The small bell tinkled once again as he entered and Mr Burden rose from his table to greet him. As soon as Burden recognised him his face fell.

"Oh, Captain Lennox, I have sad news. I have been unable to sell your timepiece. None of my clientele found it elegant or dainty enough to be worth the asking."

"That's excellent news for me, Mr Burden, as I've come to reclaim it and repay the loan."

"It is such a pity, sir, for the design is most intriguing. As a clockmaker I am astounded by the ingenuity and workmanship but it has since lost several days although I have shaken it every other day as you have instructed."

Chris smiled. "It's the problem with the months, some being shorter than thirty-one days. The date has to be adjusted at the end of those months by hand using the small knob."

"Ah! My reluctance to affect the water ingress prevented my meddling with it." He turned and opened a small drawer in his table, took out a soft leather pouch and laid it on the table. "I believe you will find it in good order, Captain."

Chris opened the bag and glanced at the watch. "You have taken great care of it, Mr Burden, I thank you. For your trouble, I'll add fifty guineas to the loan as interest."

"That is too kind, CaptainLennox. I am inconsolable that I could not be of more service."

"It's Lieutenant-colonel Lennox now, Mr Burden. Here is your money." He handed over the same leather bag that Burden had given him. "Do you wish to count it?"

"Surely you jest, Colonel. It is on your word as a gentleman and I would not impugn it."

"You are a wise man, Mr Burden. If things go according to plan, I might soon need a long case clock of my own. If I do, I'll purchase it from you."

Although he had agreed with Henry to fight the duel before going to Imber the thought of seeing Catherine again drove him to reconsider. He had his horse readied, strapped his Bergen behind the saddle and set off for Imber. It was a beautiful early autumn morning and he was in good spirits as he rode across Salisbury Plain. In fact he was in better than good spirits, he felt elated and for the first time in a year as if he actually belonged in this era and not just a vagabond from another time.

He knew he would not be fully welcome at Imber Court so rode directly to Catherine's house. The closer he got the more his heart started to beat until it became almost painful with blood pounding in his ears. Facing the enemy in hand-to-hand combat was nowhere near as frightening as the thought of what might happen on the other side of her oak door.

Esther opened the door to him and her mouth dropped open in surprise. She stuttered a welcome and gave him a quick curtsey.

"Is Mrs Dean at home?"

"Indeed, sir, she is, sir. I shall announce you if you would be pleased to wait in the withdrawing room."

The room was empty but there was a fire in the grate even though the day was warm. He felt the heat and ran a finger around inside his tunic collar. He did not sit, he couldn't, his nerves were stretched like piano wire. He put out a hand and was surprised to see a slight tremble. Nerves, schoolboy nerves. How could he let her get to him so much?

There was a rustle at the door and Catherine stepped in with Amelia behind her. She had been working in the kitchen and still had a dab of flour on her cheek. She looked stunning. She dropped a curtsey.

"Colonel Lennox. This is a pleasant surprise. No one apprised us of your coming."

Amelia slipped in behind her, a half smile on her face. "Indeed, Colonel, a fully unexpected surprise. To what do we owe this undoubted honour?"

Catherine passed him and he caught a faint whiff of rosewater. "Won't you sit, sir. Twould be more comfortable."

"I would like a private conversation with Mrs Dean, if that's possible."

Amelia curtsied. "Very well, sir. I shall be outside this door should you need me, Catherine."

"Well sir?" Catherine gave him a quizzical look but with a half-smile on her lips.

Chris had rarely been lost for words but now they failed to come. "I really don't know where to start. I was a stranger with no family to speak of but now I have rank and an income and ..."

"What are you trying to say, sir? All this is very apparent to me. You are indeed a gentleman of wealth and admirable status."

"Do you find me ..." Chris searched for a word that he had heard others use, "... agreeable?"

Catherine's lips twitched. "Indeed I do, sir. Most agreeable."

Damn, Chris thought, this is getting to be like a scene from Pride and Prejudice. "Look, Mrs Dean, Catherine ... will you marry me ... if it's not too soon ...?"

Catherine's face lit up in the most beautiful smile he had ever seen. "I thought you would never find the words?"

"And ...?"

"Of course, my dear George Lennox. I have loved you from the moment we first met. With your green face and your care of Thomas you stole my heart. How could I possibly refuse you?"

Chris reached across and pulled her petite frame into his arms. Now he felt completely at home.

The door opened and Amelia burst in laughing and crying at the same time. "At last we have something to celebrate. Hearty congratulations, dearest ones."

"We'll marry as soon as possible," Chris said. "I'll get a special licence."

"They are so expensive," Catherine said.

"Yes, but you're worth it and I can't wait for much longer. My regiment is barracked at Shorncliffe and my duties will take me back there far too soon. We've got a lot to talk about, a lot of decisions to make, but your happiness comes first, Catherine and I'll do whatever needs doing to make sure that happens.

"Oh, hell, will I have to get your father's permission?"

Catherine laughed and kissed him gently on the lips. "I am a widow, I no longer need a father's permission to marry but I do believe it would be politic should you wish to ask him."

"Will I be welcome at Imber Court?"

"Ah! The duel," Amelia said. "Not until that happening is done with."

"Henry and I have decided on tomorrow morning at dawn in the circle of the henge. We've come to an amicable agreement that won't involve any harm coming to either of us. We'll return here together and I'll ask Sir George for his blessing then."

# 55

The morning was clammily warm. The heat of the day had not dissipated overnight but there was the threat of rain on the westerly wind.

Chris had decided to dress in his waterproof combat suit and strapped on the Kevlar jacket over the top. It wasn't that he didn't trust Henry but with the momentous event of yesterday still fresh in his mind he wasn't prepared to take the risk. He also brought his Bergen with the trauma kit as additional insurance.

His two brother officers stood with him as Henry and his seconds dismounted on the far side of the henge. One of them strode over with a wooden box in his hands. He opened it on two beautifully inlaid Wogdon & Barton duelling pistols with ten-inch smoothbore barrels.

"Choose you weapon, sir, should you be so kind. They are both loaded and primed. Should your seconds need to examine them before you make your choice?"

"That is unnecessary, sir." Chris picked up the nearest pistol and weighed in in his hands. It was much heavier than his Dragon and twice as heavy as his Glock but it wouldn't cause a problem to use. It was .52 calibre and the lead ball would make a dreadful mess should it hit flesh and bone.

The second returned to Henry who took the other pistol and nodded to Chris.

Thunder rumbled in the background and Chris had an awful feeling of deja vu.

They stood back to back in the centre of the henge. Daylight was strengthening and the sun was edging over the horizon to the east. To the west the clouds were thickly black and thunder rumbled again.

"An early storm," Henry whispered over his shoulder. "It will soon pass."

"Not before we're soaked," Chris whispered back as the rain started to fall.

"Then let us be at this before we catch our death," Henry said.

"Are you ready?" The second called. They both nodded.

"Then take ten paces, turn and fire. One, two …"

Thunder rumbled again, or was it horse hooves on the turf, Chris wasn't sure as he concentrated on the paces. The count reached ten and he turned.

Henry raised his pistol. It was pointing straight at his head. The pistols had hair triggers, the slightest pressure at the wrong time and he would be a dead man. He raised his own pistol and centred the sights on Henry's chest.

Henry fired. He felt the ball fan his cheek as it passed. "That was close, sir."

Henry dropped his arm. "I could not let you off entirely without some concern for your life, sir."

Chris grinned. A horse snorted in the background. He kept the pistol level for a moment and then slowly raised it until he pointed to the sky. Lightning arced upwards and then down. The last thing he heard was Catherine's scream. *"George!"*

"Bloody hell, the lieutenant's been hit by lightning. Get on the radio and get the medics down here sharpish. There should be a team up at Imber."

Right, Sarje, I'm on it," the radio operator said.

Norton grabbed two men by the webbing. "Come on you two, with me. Move your arses, let's get over that fence and see what we can do. The rest of you clear off the road and bring some bolt cutters so that the medics can get through the wire."

They scaled the fence and ran to Chris's supine body.

"Shit, look at that helmet, split right in half."

"Get it off him," Norton ordered. He dropped to his knees and put his fingers on Chris's carotid artery. "Pulse, only just there."

"He's stopped breathing, Sarje."

"So would you if you'd had a million volts up your jacksy. Tilt his head back and check his tongue."

"That bloody green smoke grenade is starting to fizz," a soldier said. "Lightning must have set it off."

"Well don't be a dickhead, get it off and toss it away. Just bloody make sure the wind's in the opposite direction or we'll be eatin' it," Norton yelled.

More soldiers were cutting through the chain fence making a hole wide enough for a vehicle. Norton put his finger back on the carotid. "Shit, his heart's stopped. Quick, help me get this body armour off him."

They ripped off the Velcro straps and Norton started on chest compressions, "Nellie ... the ... Elephant ... packed ... her ... trunk ..."

There was a screech of tyres from the road and a Land Rover with a red cross in a white square burst up the bank and through the fence, rocking to a halt on the gravel path. A door swung open, an army medic jumped out and dashed over. She pulled Norton aside. "Out of my way, Serjeant." She dropped to her knees and started her own CPR routine.

Norton was pleased to hand over the job. "Yes ma'am."

"What happened here?" She asked between breaths."

"It was a lightning strike, ma'am, hit Lieutenant Lennox square on."

"Jesus. How long since his heart stopped?"

"Two minutes, maybe a few seconds more."

" Help me get his shirt off. Nobby, where's that defib?"

"Behind you, ma'am."

She reached around and found the box, stripped out the two pads and placed them on Chris's bare chest. "Everyone stand clear."

There was a thud and Chris's body jumped. She put a stethoscope to his chest. "Still, nothing. C'mon, you bugger, live."

The defibrillator fired again. For a second nothing happened and then Chris drew in a ragged breath.

He opened his eyes and looked into the medic's beautiful face with her hair pulled back and secured by a silver comb. "Catherine?"

She smiled the most wonderful smile and pointed at the name tag on her breast. "Doctor Catherine Dean. Most of my friends call me Cat. Welcome back to the land of the living, Mr Lennox."

Chris gave her a weak smile back. "I'll always call you Catherine."

"Always is a long time, Lieutenant."

"We've got the rest of our lives."


So it was all a dream, Chris reflected as he laid back against the pillows on his hospital bed. It had all seemed so vivid and real. Maybe the lightning had jangled his brain. He had lived a whole year in the 18th and 19th centuries and woken up ten minutes after being struck by lightning. It was a story worth telling if anyone was daft enough to listen. Maybe he'd write a book about it … someday.

He was getting bored; he'd been in this ward for nearly two days. Two days of tests and more tests, none of which had picked up the impossibly minute particle of dark energy lodged in his cerebrum. He was due a MRI scan early the next morning but after that he could see no reason to remain in hospital.

The jagged zig-zag marks of his 'Maori tattoo' were beginning to fade and the stubble was growing fast on his chin. The male nurse had offered to shave him but he'd declined. He was getting the use of his right hand back and it wouldn't be many more days before he could do the job himself. It seemed that his body clock had remained in the 21$^{st}$ century which, thankfully, was just as it was before he left it on his mental excursion into the past.

It was close to visiting time and he looked expectantly towards the door. Only one other bed was occupied in the four bed ward by a man in his sixties who spent most of his time sleeping and wasn't much company. The door swung open and Norton came in and flopped into the only chair. Chris couldn't help a surge of disappointment.

"You all right, boss? I've brought you some grapes."

"Yeah, cheers, Serjeant. Anything going on I should know about? "How did the exercise go?"

"Bit of a washout as it happens. We got there too late for the kick off and missed the best part. Company commander's after your hide for taking that detour. He says flogging's too good for you. The colonel's after your balls and the Gurkhas are laughing their heads off as they pissed all over the company, us bein' a platoon short. The National Trust is askin' who's going to pay for the fence repairs but otherwise it's all kosher. Boys send their regards an' all that.

"They're gonna resched the exercise for next month."

"Good, I'll be back by then."

"You're lucky to be alive, boss. If that field ambulance hadn't o' been passin' when it did, if we'd had to wait ten more minutes, that would've been curtains. My Nellie the Elephant routine wasn't slicin' the bacon."

"Born lucky, I guess." He was hit by a sudden sense of great loss. Catherine was just a figment of his imagination, driven by the image of the beautiful army medic looming over him like Florence Nightingale.

"Yeah, you're a lucky sod, all right, boss. That cracking looking medic, the one that saved your arse, is down in reception asking where your ward is. I nipped up quick before she got here."

The door opened and Cat Dean walked in, a bunch of grapes in a brown paper bag in her hand. "Oh, overkill on the grapes I see."

Norton stood. "Not to worry, ma'am. I'm partial to a grape." He grinned at Chris and took the bunch he'd just brought. "I'll find a good home for these."

He reached the door. "Oh, there was one odd thing. Your Glock, boss. Two of the mags were half-empty."

Chris's jaw dropped. Cat put a gentle finger under his chin and closed his mouth. "Catching flies, George?"

It shook him. "What did you call me?"

"It's a little family saying we had as kids … but the name suits you."

"Is that all?"

She gave a delightful shrug. "What else should it be?"

"I wondered."

"I was wondering about something too. What did you mean by saying we've got the rest of our lives?"

A porter wheeled him up to the scanner on the next morning and he was slid into the tube with a set of headphones playing soft music to dull the noise of the equipment. He gave the technician the thumbs up. This was routine and painless.

The scanner started to hum, rising to a dull roar as the magnetic field increased in intensity. He put his hands to his head as a pain started to grow in his temples. His body bucked in agony and there was a blinding flash.

"George, dearest, speak to me."

Chris forced open his eyes just as sunlight seeped through the clouds above Stonehenge and shone on Catherine's beautiful face. She had his head in her lap and he could see tears streaking her cheeks.

He raised his hand to wipe them away. "Don't cry, Catherine … I'm back."

# Author's Notes

Now it's time to sort fact from fiction.

The information on the Large Hadron Collider is correct. I doubt that they run it up to 18 TeVs though, even with recent safety improvements.

It's a recorded fact that a man in America struck by lightning was saved by water that ran down his arm and earthed him. He had a tracery burned into his skin that matched the trails of water and looked like an intricate tattoo.

If Jane Austen's works are anything to go by, polite conversation in 18th century upper-class society was very convoluted. I've simplified it in this book for ease of reading but hope I've still managed to retain a taste of the culture and language of the times.

Imber was a thriving if isolated village at the turn of the 19th century. The Wadman family really did live at Imber Court. The Deans were also a well-known farming family which eventually took over Imber Court from the Wadmans. However, the characters of the Wadman and Dean families included in the story are all fictitious.

Imber was taken over by the War Office in 1943 to provide a training ground for American troops and is still controlled by the Ministry of Defence. The only original buildings remaining are St Giles, The Bell pub and a dilapidated Imber Court.

All the historical facts regarding the forming of the Corps of Rifles are accurate although I have changed the dates around somewhat. The Letter from the Duke of York to the colonels commanding the original fourteen regiments that formed the corps is accurately recorded, except that the 62nd Regiment was not involved in forming the Corps of Rifles and neither was Lieutenant-colonel Stewart its colonel. Its first battalion, however, did suffer extreme losses in the American Revolution, where the use of the Kentucky Long Rifle was instrumental in its defeat and the battalion suffered further losses in Haiti due to disease that caused it to cease functioning as an active formation. A second battalion was formed in 1800 but disbanded in 1802 before being re-formed in 1804.

Between the dates this novel is set, 1799-1800, Arthur Wellesley, later the Duke of Wellington, was in India earning his knighthood. It's purely an act of imagination that he returned to England during this period.

Both Lieutenant-colonel Stewart and Colonel Manningham, an influential equerry to the king, are real people and were instrumental in the forming of the Rifle Brigade. It's a fact that floggings were rare in the regiment. Now simply called The Rifles, the regiment retains its original spelling of serjeant and its motto is 'Swift and Bold'.

The events leading up to the adoption of the Baker Rifle are accurately recorded. However the action taken by Chris Lennox's detachment in Portugal is purely fictional. Bonaparte never invaded southern Portugal in 1799, nor did he build any fortifications or try to create a supply route from Cadiz. The French Grenadiers are accurately described but were never engaged as depicted although two officers, named Fouquet and Perrot, did actually command regiments of foot grenadiers and horse grenadiers respectively in Bonaparte's army.

HMS Aquilon was a real ship, although not commanded by Commander Cunningham, a name picked from the list of naval officers of the time. The *Hercule* was captured from the French and served with the Royal Navy.

The amounts awarded in bounty for the capture of a ship like the *Hercule* are correct.

Brooks's, which still exists, was then a gambling club frequented by gentlemen with a serious gambling problem, often 'wagering' on the oddest things. The Duke of Devonshire was a member during this time but there is no record of him investing in Baker's gun making business, which is my (slightly mischievous) fiction. The physics involved with tossing and spinning coins are correct but depends on the type of coin used.

I stretched history somewhat with the clockmaker Josiah Burden. Burdens did make clocks in Salisbury but not until the middle of the 19th century. Josiah Burden is a fictitious person.

Most of the other main characters are fictitious. Chris Lennox was a name I settled on before discovering that a Colonel Charles Lennox, the 4th Duke of Richmond, had challenged the Duke of York to a duel in 1799. Lennox missed the duke's head by a whisker and the duke refused to return fire saying that honour had been satisfied.

The duke was a colourful character who caused public scandal with his sexual liaisons, some incidents ending up in a court of law. He was though, responsible for modernising the army and ending some of its more antiquated practices.

Duelling was very much a part of upper-class life in the 18th century. Swords and pistols were used and there was a thriving industry in the making of duelling pistols with several gun makers in London alone. The calibre of the pistols was such that they were much more likely to cause serious injury or death than a duel with swords. It's interesting to note that using rifled pistols in England was deemed ungentlemanly and to use unrifled pistols on the continent was considered cowardly as rifled barrels were so much more accurate.

I have added a degree of imagination to the action sequences but the attack on Ferrol did take place in 1800. The British Corps of Rifles advanced up a ridge and was attacked by a Spanish detachment which it drove back with some loss. On the morning of 26th August a considerable body of Spanish attacked the British on the heights of Brion and Balon but they were repulsed. British casualties were 16 killed and 68 wounded, a number which included Lieutenant-colonel Stewart. The Spanish lost 37 dead and 102 wounded.

In 1801, Stewart commanded the regiment which took part in the British victory at the Battle of Copenhagen, acting as marksmen aboard Royal Navy ships led by Vice-Admiral Horatio Nelson. One company was under the command of Captain Sidney Beckwith.

One last thing. The French officers were noted as taking an interest in Lennox's brass cartridge cases and had them returned to Paris for examination. The metallic cartridge was developed by a Frenchman named Louis Flobert in 1845. The Flobert cartridge simply consisted of a small bullet fitted inside a percussion cap. Shortly afterwards, another French gunsmith named Houllier invented an alternative to the rimfire-type Flobert cartridge, known as the pinfire.

I liked the idea of an anachronistic connection.

Ed Lane,
Lincolnshire 2016

# Addendum

In one part of the book Chris Lennox is mentioned as listing headings for a platoon rifle drill for the Baker Rifle. It was a complex operation and for those interested it is copied below from the original drill manual:

PLATOON EXERCISE FOR THE RIFLE

The words of command for firing and loading are as follows:

*Caution – Prime and Load*

At which the flugelman (wingman) steps in front.

*I. Prepare to Load*

1st. Is the same as the first motion in the *present*. [The rifle is to be raised about two inches by the right hand, and brought forward a little from the shoulder, at the same time the left hand is brought briskly across the body, and seizes the rifle with a full grasp even with the shoulder.]

2nd. The soldier half faces to the right, and in the motion brings down the rifle to an horizontal position just above the right hip, the left hand supports it at the swell of the stock, the elbow resting against the side, the right thumb against the hammer, the knuckles upwards, and elbow pressing against the butt, the lock inclining a little to the body to prevent the powder from falling out.

*II. Load*

1st. The pan is pushed open by the right thumb;

2nd. the right hand then seizes the cartridge (which holds the gunpowder) with the three first fingers and draws it from the pouch;

3rd. the cartridge is brought to the mouth, and placed between the two first right double teeth, the end twisted off and brought close to the pan.

*III. Prime.*

1st. The priming is shaken into the pan; in doing which, to see that the powder is properly lodged, the head must be bent; 2nd. the pan is shut by the third and little finger, the right hand then slides behind the cock, and holds the small part of the stock between the third and little finger and ball of the hand.

*IV. (Cast about) for brevity "'Bout."*

1st. The soldier half faces to the left; the rifle is brought to the ground with the barrel outwards, by sliding it with care through the left hand, which then seizes it near the muzzle, the thumb stretched along the stock, the butt is placed between the heels, the barrel between the knees, which must be bent for that purpose; the cartridge is put into the barrel, and the ramrod seized with the fore finger and thumb of the right hand.

*V. Rod.*

The ramrod is drawn quite out by the right hand, the left quits the rifle and grasps the ramrod the breadth of a hand from the bottom, which is sunk one inch into the barrel.

*VI. Home.*

The cartridge will be forced down with both hands, the left then seizes the rifle about six inches from the muzzle, the soldier stands upright again, draws out the ramrod with the right hand, and puts the end into the pipe.

*VII. Return.*

1st. The right hand brings the rifle to the right shoulder; turning the guard outwards;

2nd. The left seizes it above the hammer-spring till the right has its proper hold round the small of the stock;

*3rd.* The left is drawn quickly to the left thigh…..

To fire on the spot with closed ranks, the following words of command will be given:

*Caution – The Company will Fire.*

*I. Company.*

At this word, the right hand file of each platoon takes three quick paces to the front, the rear rank man steps to the right of his file leader.

*II. Ready.*

At this word, the rifle is brought by the right hand before the centre of the body, the left seizes it, so that the little finger rests upon the hammer spring, and the thumb stretched along the stock raising it to the height of the mouth, the right thumb on the cock, and four fingers under the guard; when cocked, which gently done, the right hand grasps the small of the stock.

*III. Present.*

The soldier half faces to the right, the butt is placed in the hollow of the right shoulder, the right foot steps back about eighteen inches behind the left, the left knee is bent, the body brought well forward, the left hand, without having quitted its hold, supports the rifle close before the lock, the right elbow raised even with the shoulder, the fore finger on the trigger, the head bent, and cheek resting on that of the rifle, the left eye shut, the right taking aim through the sight: as soon as the rifleman has fixed upon his object, he fires without waiting for any command. When he has fired, the right hand quits its hold in facing to the right about, the left swings the rifle round into an horizontal position with the barrel downwards; the rifleman resumes his post in the platoon, in fronting to the left about, brings his rifle into the position to prime and load, half cocks, and proceeds to load, going through the motions as above without further words of command."

# About the Author

Whilst studying at the University of London Ed joined the Officers Training Corps and was commissioned into the Royal Regiment of Fusiliers before eventually joining The Parachute Regiment TA.

In civilian life, he founded a graphic design company where he honed his writing skills on marketing campaigns for national and multi-national companies.

Ed has personal experience with many of the weapon systems he writes about. He is the holder of three gold medals gained in national Sport Rifle competitions and has represented Lincolnshire over several seasons as a member of the County Lightweight Sport Rifle Team.

He took early-retirement which enabled him to devote more time to writing and lives in the Lincolnshire Wolds with his wife Barb.

His novels are a personal salute to the courage, dedication and professionalism of Britain's armed forces.